CENTURY

A novel by
Yvonne Hilton

To melinda - thanks for coming -

Yvonne Hilton

First published by Dog Ear Publishing
4010 W. 86th Street, Ste H
Indianapolis, IN 46268
www.dogearpublishing.net

ISBN: 978-1-4575-1520-0

This book is printed on acid-free paper.

This book is a work of fiction. Places, events, and situations in this book are purely fictional and any resemblance to actual persons, living or dead, is coincidental.

Printed in the United States of America

For Louis Reyes Rivera

Teacher, Mentor, Friend

Dear Melinda,

Everybody needs
a good novel in their
life every now and
then. Here's yours!
Given with Much Love,
Alice
7/2013

Prologue

The choppy waters of the Atlantic swelled suddenly. Dipped then rose again. Icy spray splashed, breaking across the bow of a small row boat. Each wave doused the boat, threatened to swallow it completely. Yet, with oars working doggedly, the boat made its way toward a tall ship moored some two miles offshore, her masts proud against a clear, hard blue sky.

Inside the boat, ten souls depended on the seas to keep them afloat – the two White men rowing and their eight Black captives, five men, two young women and a youth about fourteen. The White men were of a dual purpose – to get to that ship and to keep the captives from jumping out of the boat. This was not an idle concern; if they were not watched carefully, any one of these Africans was just liable to pitch headlong overboard, dragging all the others into the sea. Even the boy might. They never seemed to understand anything about the sea, not its depth nor how quickly their chains would pull them under, even as they struggled to stay afloat. And so, the White men took turns, each barely glancing over his shoulder to gauge how close the boat was to the tall ship; their attention remained focused on the captives.

The eight had all been enmeshed in their chains on the boat's waterlogged floor. The men were able to disentangle themselves first. As each man up-righted himself, and realized where he was being taken, he began to moan, his voice low at first, then rising, joining with his fellows until all were groaning quite loudly, including the boy. Their cries were quickly joined by yelps and shrieks from the women. All looked around wildly – at the two White men, at the mysterious ship floating ahead of them, and backward, toward land – toward home!

For the boy, it was especially awful. If the grown men were crying like women, then all must truly be lost. He had always been able to depend on men. It seemed they knew everything. Certainly, they knew how to control their emotions, even in the worst of circumstances. Although he had almost completed his manhood rites when he was captured, there were still secrets that could only be shared among men.

Now that he was in the company of men who were as terrified as he was, he feared he would never learn those secrets! Waves of panic swept over him, threatening to overwhelm him, to set him screaming like the women.

Instead, the boy shouted at the top of his lungs, "No! I am no frightened woman! I am Osei, son of Okera, grandson of Abena, descendent of Owusu – the founder of our village." Somehow, the shouting steadied his heart and steeled him for whatever was to come.

The White men watched him keenly. One, lanky, young and pockmarked, muttered to the other, "D' ye think 'ee'll try t' jump?"

"Dunno," the other older and equally lanky one replied in a whisper. "Jes' got t'warch 'im careful. Yer th' closes' t' 'im." Both men kept their oars moving in unison.

The other Blacks ceased their crying out in order to stare at Osei as well. All of the captives had come from distant areas and spoke different languages. No one understood anything he was saying.

Finally, he fell silent. And his silence gripped all of the captives. For the boat had now reached the tall ship, where white faces peered down on the tiny vessel bobbing alongside. Suddenly heavy ropes dropped, seemingly from the sky, weighted by large iron hooks. The two White men lost no time grabbing at the hanging ropes and fastening the hooks to several metal rings arranged around the sides of the boat. Almost immediately, it and the passengers began to rise into the air. For an eternity, it seemed, they remained suspended as the boat was being hauled up the ship's unending portside wall.

Just as the boat cleared the railing, a bevy of arms reached in and grabbed at the captives, hauled them up by their chains and splayed them out on the deck. Quickly, the women were yanked up, unfastened from the others and dragged away, one sobbing, the other bawling pitifully. A forest of white legs now surrounded the five men and the boy, still yoked together. All were summarily pulled to their feet.

Now that Osei could see where he was, all of his senses were suddenly assaulted. Everywhere was filth and the stench of rotting wood, comingled with body odors so strong they brought tears to his eyes. He and the men were pushed toward a pair of open doors in the floor of the ship. As they descended the creaky splintered stairs, a damp foul heat rose up and engulfed him, sucking out all air. White men moved among the captives, forcing them to climb onto a top row of wooden shelves and lie flat. Each was, then, shackled to the man on either side. When it was his turn, Osei balked. The spot where he was expected to lie was covered with dark stains that stank of feces. One of the White men, apparently inured to the horrible smell, got up on the shelf himself, pulling the lad along with him. He forced Osei into position, then shackled his left wrist and ankle to the right wrist and ankle of the man already in place. Without another moment's hesitation, the White man got off the shelf and proceeded to load another man into the space on Osei's right side. Then came the rattle of a heavy chain being passed along the wall just beyond his feet. A White man crawled over each man, running the chain through metal loops in the ankle shackles, effectively fastening the captives to the hull of the ship.

The bottom shelves were already crowded with shackled Black men, each lying shoulder to shoulder face up, head toward the narrow aisle and feet fastened by one ankle to the wall. The place was dimly lit by two lanterns fastened to the main ceiling beam. In the flickering fitful light, the men on the top shelves could just make out who they were shackled to on either side. Those beneath were in almost complete darkness. The White men finished their work, scampered up the stairs and dropped the twin doors shut behind them. What little fresh air that had made its way into the hold while the doors were open was now swept out with the men.

Osei had promised himself that he would not die. But with the slamming of those doors, the will to live seeped out of his body. In the fetid suffocating heat of this new dungeon, he felt a fear unlike any he had known thus far.

Chapter 1

THE ST.LAWRENCE RIVER, QUEBEC CANADA (1800)

*A*damp mist was just beginning to lift, yielding to the pale sunlight that spread across a low bluff clearing on the riverbank. Seventy-five people were gathered in this space. Behind them, a forest of white birch stood, their upper branches pointing thin fingers at the pale sky. On either side were ancient evergreen woods, so dense their needles carpeted the ground, their scent filling the air.

Small children who had been carried here by their parents were now coming awake, hungry and demanding food. The women had already started fires, setting out pots brought from their own wigwams, arranging in rows ears of corn to roast in the embers once the flames had died down. There was no chatter from the women, only high-pitched whines from their little ones. Older children were put to work, helping their mothers. They too were silent, even the boys.

Men stood apart from the women, talking in groups, watching the river's wide horizon, waiting for the visitors; they spoke in hushed, deep whispers. Today was too important for them to pay any attention to the women and children. Instead, they kept their eyes averted from the lone Black woman seated in their midst, yet apart from them.

"Our guests are coming; what must I tell them so they know we need to stay here?" Anika had been sitting immobilized in a deep trance, eyes closed, face tilted upward slightly as though savoring a breeze. Her words came in English, even though she had finally learned to speak the language of her adopted village. She had never truly mastered it, so she always had to communicate with her spirits in her first tongue. The question had formed itself inside of her head, but the answer came as a Voice, accompanied by puffs of breath speaking clearly into her left ear.

"Let the Chief talk through your son. Speak only if they address you. Otherwise remain silent."

Oddly the Voice spoke a language that was not English; yet she could understand every word. Years ago, it had been her husband Osei's voice that had guided her; but his whispers suddenly grew silent. Then, when this foreign Voice took his place, at first, she would shut her mind, aching only to hear him again. But the Voice persisted, forcing her to listen until the meaning of each instruction became clear and she could finally give direction to the people.

Anika soon came to accept this ability as vital in her role. She was, after all, the village's shaman. Ever since dawn, she had been asking the same simple question, praying repeatedly for guidance in the very delicate matter of her people now occupying lands that did not belong to them. They expected her to provide for their protection. She waited for more, but both the Voice and its breath were gone. This was all the information that she would receive. It had to be sufficient.

Slowly, she came to herself and opened her eyes. Holding one position for too long made her back ache slightly. Although she shifted only enough to ease the stiffness, she could sense a corresponding movement in the man who had been watching her so intently that even his breathing matched hers. Great Bear's gaze brought warmth to her cheeks that spread through her whole body, chasing away the chill of the early autumn morning.

Now in her late fifties, Anika's face was still unlined. And although not really beautiful, she did radiate a peculiar air, almost like a light that encircled her. Perhaps her most striking feature was her hair. It sprouted from her head in masses of wooly tresses, coiled into separate locks that swept from a high forehead down her back to her waist. Streaks of silver and grey mixed in with brown and black.

On this special day, she wore her finest clothing, a skirt of red woolen trade cloth, leather leggings and a hip-length deerskin tunic. She had covered herself from chin to ankles with a multicolored blanket. Shells and beads adorned her ears, and on both arms were several leather beaded bracelets. Her moccasins were embroidered with the same kinds of beads, shells and bits of leather lacings.

Great Bear stood just to the right of the rock on which Anika was seated. He wore the formal cape and headdress of the chief of his village. He was indeed a bear of a man, broad through the shoulders and somewhat thick in the middle as well. Now past sixty, his deeply lined face was still remarkably handsome. Instead of watching the river's horizon, his eyes remained fixed on Anika's profile.

One youth, standing atop the highest point on the bluff, spotted the canoes when they were no more than tiny specks in the distance. "They are coming!" he shouted.

Everyone turned toward the shore. All other activity ceased as Great Bear's entire village moved to gather in family groups, some seated along the low rising hill, others standing atop it, intently watching the water's wide expanse.

The chief's daughter, Gentle Fawn, came with her children to stand beside her father. She whispered anxiously, "Do you think they will let us stay here?"

"I know not. But I trust your husband to make my words sound pleasing to their chief. And I know Anika's spirits will protect us."

Eventually, five enormous birch-bark canoes glided into full view, creating long lines in the water as the rowers powered their oars in unison. Another full hour would pass before they all finally reached the shore. Once in the shallows, a young man in each canoe jumped nimbly overboard and guided it in, close enough so the travelers could alight on dry land.

As all of the visitors disembarked, several of the village's youths scrambled down the embankment to help the rowers secure the canoes.

A Black man of about thirty approached the travelers, his hand raised. Everyone, the youths pulling in the canoes, the visitors, even the crowd on shore stopped and watched him. The people of the village did this out of habit. His appearance and movements never failed to attract attention. He was as tall as Great Bear, but slim and the color of deepest mahogany; his face was a chiseled mask with a straight nose ending in flaring nostrils and a full-lipped mouth. His head was completely shorn of all hair, save for a single wooly forelock carefully braided and decorated with several eagle and heron feathers. He was Anika's son, Gentle Fawn's husband, and Great Bear's interpreter. And for this most important occasion, he was wearing his finest cape of intricate red and black designs. As he moved, he shifted the sweep of the cape, freeing his right hand for the greeting.

"I speak for Great Bear, my chief. I am called River Otter," he began, addressing the visitors. "Great Bear and his people greet you and thank you for accepting his invitation. He wishes you to know that his heart is gladdened by the presence of his ancient brothers." River Otter spoke the language of the visitors flawlessly.

The delegation of twenty-five included their chief, Tekenna, his interpreter, his two wives and four grown children, along with his entire council.

The interpreter stepped forward. "Your words are good," he said. "Conduct us to your chief."

River Otter led the way as the visitors climbed the steep incline. Great Bear hesitated only long enough to catch Anika's wordless nod before hurrying to meet them halfway. Taller than the visiting chief by more than a head, he made sure to position himself on slightly lower ground. In this way, he would not tower over the man as he greeted all of them in his own words, which River Otter quickly translated.

"My heart is indeed glad that you have come. We welcome you and hope you will stay with us for a long time. We have much to share with you."

These northern Munsee had finally come to hear Great Bear's petition that his village be allowed to make this land their new home. The invitation, sent out as soon as they had arrived in the area and delivered by a single brave who paddled his canoe the great distance south and back across the St. Lawrence River, had remained unanswered for more than three years. At first, Anika had feared that the response would be a raiding party sent to wipe out the interlopers. But in her dreams, as she lay in Great Bear's arms, wrapped in their blanket, the Voice had told her to expect a long wait, but no attack.

In midsummer, a young man, traveling alone as part of his dream quest, had come to the village. When such youths passed through Native villages, they were always given food, shelter and safe passage. He had been traveling northeast from his home in Ottowa. And he brought a message from Tekenna, himself. The chief would bring a delegation, including women, to hear the village's petition. The presence of women was a very good sign. All through the autumn harvest, the village prepared for a full month of feasting and celebration. Great Bear ordered that no effort be spared in welcoming these most important guests.

The celebration began as soon as Great Bear and the travelers reached his village. Even before the visitors had come ashore, every one of the village women had doused her fire, gathered up her children and hurried back to finish the preparations. As the day progressed, there were songs, dances and a seemingly unending supply of food.

Late in the evening, after visitors and villagers alike had dined themselves into lethargy, the two chiefs, their families and councils adjourned to the longhouse to begin the rituals that always preceded important negotiations.

First, a pipe of tobacco had to be passed around the entire group of men sitting in a tight circle in the middle of the longhouse floor. Each man would draw on the pipe before any discussion began. And, of course, the man most senior in rank would talk first.

Tekenna spoke through a wreath of bluish smoke, addressing Great Bear directly. "Tell us the story of how you came this way."

The women sat well outside of the immediate circle, behind the men, Anika among them. She thought that the Munsee chief was asking for the complete history of the village. This would be River Otter's first time translating it. Great Bear cleared his throat for a lengthy recitation. Both men were under great pressure to be absolutely eloquent.

The Munsee chief spoke up suddenly before Great Bear could begin his narrative. "Every chief can tell the history of his people from the beginning of their time. What we wish to hear tonight is how you found your way to this land. Who led you here?"

Tekenna may not have been as tall as his host, but he was fully conscious of his power over Great Bear's people. When he had finally made the decision to come, he intended to determine whether this village was the first of yet another wave of converted and weakened Christian Natives. If so, he would deny their petition immediately. He had no patience with such groups. They were as bad as White Christians, with their pious interference in his people's ways. Absolutely intolerable! As soon as he had seen Great Bear, however, he'd decided to at least consider their request. This was a chief who appeared to understand what it meant to be what the Christians called "an Indian." But Tekenna *was* uneasy about the two Blacks in Great Bear's immediate circle. He could sense their influence over the chief was stronger than that of the Native members of his council. Who were they, really? And how had they come to be so important?

River Otter glanced anxiously at Great Bear as he translated Tekenna's question. Great Bear responded without thinking, "Our powaw was guided to this place." River Otter translated the statement into, "Our shaman was guided here." When Tekenna's eyes widened with interest, Great Bear realized his carelessness.

"I did not see your shaman – your powaw – earlier while we were eating. Where is he? He must be quite powerful if he is able to guide your people to a place he has never seen."

Great Bear felt caught. He had not wanted to have to tell this man anything about Anika, at least not before the chief had become familiar with his village and their story. Although it was not forbidden, Great Bear knew that there had never been, in the history of his people, a powaw who was also a woman. He suspected the same might be true for Tekenna and the Munsee. Yet there was no easy way for him to escape the trap he had stepped into.

"Your people have traveled a long way and should rest. Tomorrow you will meet our powaw. The story you want to hear first should come from the one who can tell it best." Great Bear kept his voice deliberately even, hoping Tekenna would not be offended by the rebuff.

The Munsee chief hesitated for a moment, but then agreed, "My people are tired as I am sure you are also. We will hear the story tomorrow."

Great Bear shifted slightly so he could see the women seated behind him. His movement was not lost on Tekenna, who added pointedly, "We also want to know of your adopted family."

The hosts rose, all together, and filed out of the longhouse, while the visitors began unrolling bedding for the night. As she left, Anika carefully avoided looking in their direction. She had resolved to remain completely in the background, yet the Munsee chief seemed determined to notice her. And she could sense his discomfort with River Otter as well, even while her son was doing all he could to put Tekenna at ease.

"Anika, come. It is time for sleeping." Great Bear was already taking her hand and drawing her away from the others.

Suddenly, she recognized the problem. Tekanna was both shrewd and observant; he had sensed Great Bear's unusual closeness to her and it had made him suspicious. What kind of a chief was so dependent on a woman that he would constantly turn to her, seemingly for support?

In the middle of the night, Anika was awakened from a deep sleep to feel Great Bear's hand urgently caressing her thigh. Without speaking, he unceremoniously turned her on her back, mounted her and began making love. He did so simply, honestly, with a need that was akin to the need to breathe. Anika responded to the insistent pumping of his heart, responded in her blood, felt him in her veins and let him inhabit her whole self. Only when they finished together did he murmur, "Anika, Anika, Anika," into the hair at her temples.

She heard the unasked question and answered him. "Be strong; be patient. I cannot yet tell you what to to do."

Great Bear rolled his body off her, but wrapped one arm around her waist, drawing her close. "I am too afraid to let Tekenna know you are our powaw. Your spirits led us here. If you tell him about them, they may be angry. What if they desert us?"

"They have never failed us before!" Anika whispered firmly. "They will surely help us now. Do not worry. "

A moment later, he was asleep. Anika lay awake for some time, listening to his even breathing. Perhaps the Voice would come with more instructions. But weariness finally closed in on her and she slept too.

Chapter 2

"*A*nika! Anika… Annie!*"

Had she been dreaming? No one called her by that name any more! It was Osei's voice – surely, unmistakeably his! Too long silent yet so clearly remembered. Its music had only added to the powerful attraction she'd felt almost from the first moment she'd laid eyes on him. So gentle was that voice, so deep, as though he were speaking out of the depths of himself. And always whenever he talked to her, his voice would drop into the lowest register, even when he was angry. Most of the people around her raised their voices in anger; his would drop a full octave. One would have expected such a voice to come out of a big man, but Osei was slim, and tall – like his son would become, once grown.

"*You must not tell that man your story! Not yet!*"

Anika was suddenly fully awake. And for a moment, she could not remember where she was. Osei's voice had taken her back into the pain from which she had barely been able to escape, would never have escaped without his guidance. Now she was locked in once again, back in that room they had shared – suddenly alone and utterly terrified.

"*Listen, my dearest one! Listen to me! Great Bear must tell his story first.*"

Osei had never called her "dearest one," not in all their time together. At those words, the fear drained out of her, leaving her sharply alert, breathless and ready to focus on his next instructions.

"You will not be able to put the man off with a lie. He can know that you are the priestess – the healer of this village. It will not seem strange to him. Once he knows the truth, he will listen to the whole story."

Anika waited for Osei's voice to continue, the almost-forgotten hunger for him filling her entire body. But there was only silence again. Finally, she realized she had been holding her breath for so long that she was becoming light-headed. She breathed a sigh and turned on her right side, facing Great Bear, who still slept soundly. Perhaps it had only been a dream after all. The chief moved closer, drawing her against his chest and resting his cheek on her forehead. The tightness around her heart eased as she inhaled again, taking in Great Bear's scent, a combination of wood smoke and fresh sweat as familiar to her as her own. Sleep, however, was completely out of the question. Why had it been Osei's voice this time after so many years of complete separation? The question the Munsee chief had asked must mask some hidden danger. Anika realized she could not let herself be overwhelmed by hearing Osei's voice again. What was most important was that now, she had the rest of her answer.

The following evening, just before the council fires were to be lit in the longhouse, Anika drew Great Bear aside. Taking his hand, she halted him just as he was about to enter the longhouse door.

"Not yet. First, walk a ways with me."

Great Bear's face had reflected his deep uneasiness; his brow was furrowed and the corners of his mouth were tight. At the sight of Anika, immediately, his expression softened.

"I will not join you in the longhouse tonight. Last night, my dream told me what you must say to the chief." Anika moved closer to Great Bear and, taking his arm with her free hand, pressed him to bend down so she could whisper into his ear. "Tell him about me. Speak the whole truth – that I am the powaw because spirits come to me in my dreams. And it was those spirits who led us here. Then you must make him listen to the story of our village."

Immediately, she released him, turned and headed in the direction of their wigwam. Great Bear remained where he was, watching her for several moments before finally turning back toward the longhouse.

Inside, Tekenna was already seated with his council. However, this evening, the order of those closest to him had changed; his interpreter, a short wiry man several years older than River Otter, had been relegated to a position several men away from his chief. Since he could not speak Great Bear's language, his services would not be needed during the visit.

Great Bear sat down between River Otter and the Munsee chief. Turning to Tekenna, he began an apology. "Our powaw is not here this evening. Yet, I promised you that the story of our journey here would come from – *her*." He paused to allow River Otter to finish his translation. "Our powaw is a woman, my wife. She is called Anika. She has dreams, sometimes even when she is awake. In those dreams, spirits come and tell her what we must do. My village is alive today because of Anika's spirits; so we always follow their words. She is not here now because her spirits told her not to come – that you must hear the story of my people first. In that story is the reason we have come to this place. The story is long, but we have prepared for you to stay with us for the whole telling."

Tekenna shifted, his movement reflecting irritation at this news. His interest had been greatly piqued by the revelation about this village's shaman. Now, he really wanted to hear from her directly but even as important a sachem as he would not dare overrule spirits. Still, it might be possible to learn more than just the history of this village.

"Very well then, tell us your story. But I would make a request of your interpreter first."

River Otter translated the Munsee chief's words somewhat hesitantly. When Great Bear nodded his assent, River Otter turned to Tekenna. "My chief gives me permission to ask what it is that you wish from me, Great Chief?"

"Tell us the name of your people and the language you speak. It is not one I have heard before. Also, as you give your chief's words, use his names for things before you use ours. In this way, we may learn some of your language. You can do the same for your chief, if he wishes, whenever you speak for me."

River Otter translated the request and again Great Bear nodded. Then the chief made his own request.

"Please, I would know what the language of your people is called."

Tekenna said, "We Munsee speak Lenape."

And then the tale began.

Chapter 3

THE UNKECHAUG (1643 – 1783)

"We are called Unkechaug, as is our language. My people had always lived along a river we call the Puspatuck." Great Bear's voice took on the sing-song quality of a memorized narrative. "But long ago, we also used to make summer camp near the Canarsee. One night, our powaw had a dream. In this dream, a great fire broke out and consumed the corn fields of the nearest Canarsee village. He understood the dream meant that the Unkechaug had to move camp the very next day.

"When the Dutch soldiers came, our people had been warned by Manitou, the Great Spirit, Himself; so we were already gone. This was the first time we were saved. We went back to the Puspatuck and stayed on our own land. Our numbers grew; the people soon were so many that we had several villages. Our lands stretched from the Secatogue to Yannocock. And we thrived, until the missionaries came. These men wore strange black clothes; they were kind. But they called our religion 'heathen' and they said the powaw was evil.

"This was in the time of my grandfather," Great Bear continued. "He was a young man when the missionaries came. They made all the people Christian in every village but his. His village still believed in the Ancient Protection given to us long ago by the powaw who had saved us from the Dutch. They would not give that up, so they left the Puspatuck and moved east. My people lived in many places after that. Always, we tried to avoid our neighbors, both human beings and Whites, for we knew we would be forced to change our ways. It seemed all the people in Nekequewese (eastern Long Island) were being turned into Christians.

"At last, we found a deep forest at Montauk, where the land meets the open water. Here were no other people's villages, no White men's farms. We built our wigwams in the woods and planted our gardens in the fields nearby. There was game in the woods, fish in the streams that ran across the land, and oyster beds in the deep waters.

"For the rest of his life, my grandfather lived in this village. Only once did outsiders come. Some braves from the Meuntaukut found our hunting grounds on their way to fight the Mohawk. Later, some of our braves left the village to fight with the Pequot against the Whites, and a few joined the wars in Massachusetts. Everyone who left swore to keep the village a secret. And none of those for whom we fought ever spoke about us either. The braves who returned to us said people called them 'Unkechaug of the Forest,' and agreed that we were under the protection of Manitou, Himself. In this way our village disappeared from the memories of every other Nation."

Here is the story that was not told in the long house that evening. By 1643, the Director-General of New Netherland, Willem Kieft, had become notorious for dealing harshly with all the Native villages surrounding Fort Amsterdam. When this man ordered his soldiers to strike the unsuspecting Canarsee village under the cover of night, he thought to take care of future problems by attacking and massacring all other villages in the immediate vicinity.

The Ancient Protection that was so central to this Unkechaug village rested wholly in an act of sacrifice performed by the powaw who had had the prophetic dream. This man, whose secret name was Pataquahamoc, refused to leave with the rest of the people. He did promise that a new powaw would be revealed during their journey and that the village would escape the Dutch undetected. They left him behind, trusting the explanation that his sacrifice was necessary.

Pataquahamoc then prepared his own grave in the woods near the abandoned camp grounds. First, he dug a pit about half as deep as his standing height. Next he brewed and drank an infusion of special herbs, which, when taken together, acted as a slow but deadly poison. He then took his thunder stick along with his other sacred artifacts and placed them in their most powerful positions on the floor of the pit. He dressed in the garments he intended to wear when presented before Manitou. Finally, he wrapped himself in a special blanket woven of grasses, bits of bark and long dried vines, then lowered himself down, assumed a seated position and covered his head with the blanket. Thus, he sat until death claimed him. All human traces vanished with his passing; the White men could not even detect that a Native camp had ever been nearby.

Over the ensuing years, each time the Unkechaug had to, they were able to move their village under this protection. By the last migration, the line of powaws had been reestablished. Pataquahamoc's role in the Unkechaugs' salvation became an important piece of the people's history, although his true name was never spoken aloud, nor were the exact details of the story ever discussed. He and his sacrifice were always simply called the Ancient Protection.

On the third evening, as the group gathered in the longhouse, Tekenna appeared dissatisfied and kept watching the doorway. When Great Bear offered him the pipe, he waved it aside. He had been hoping that Anika would finally make an appearance. But she was not present tonight either.

"You say your people were protected for many years, hidden in the deep woods. That cannot be the whole story. I am anxious to know what happened to the protection. And why you had to run away again."

River Otter waited uneasily for Great Bear's response. He too wished his mother would attend the council fire, even if she could not speak. The Munsee chief did seem quite irritated. It was obvious that he wanted to see her.

Great Bear could taste the bile in the back of his throat. Clearly, Tekenna had not been pleased with the previous night's performance. It annoyed him that his people had to grovel before this man just for the right to remain safely on unoccupied Munsee land. Still he had no choice but to continue.

"My father, Neesconconchus (Two Crows) became too sick to continue as chief of our village," Great Bear began, "I was chosen to take his place, even though I was still young and had never been in a war. By this time, all the men, young and old, let their hair grow long, because they had fought in no wars, either…"

Great Bear's Tale

In the middle of a dusty clearing, two young men crouched and circled, each warily eyeing the other. Both sprang at the same time, meeting in a hard tangle of arms and legs. For a few minutes, they remained frozen, neither apparently able to move the other. Suddenly, the taller one got hold of the leather strap of his opponent's breechcloth. Using the leverage of his own weight, he pulled the young man off his footing, threw him to the ground and fell on top of him.

Murmurs of approval came from the crowd watching the match. The older men noted how the current crop of wrestlers was clearly being dominated by the winner of this match.

"He is certainly no longer Peewatsumosquo (The Little Bear)! His father was right to call him Gunchemosquo (Great Bear). Look how much stronger he is than the others!"

Great Bear had been born after the last migration; this was the only village he had ever known. At birth, he had been given the name Woreeco'wequaran (Handsome Eagle). But throughout his childhood he was called The Little Bear, in honor of the clan to which his family belonged. Now, thanks to his size and skill as a wrestler, he had become Great Bear.

A group of young women stood off to one side of the clearing watching. They were all of marriageable age and were choosing their future suitors, based on the strength in a wrestler's arm or the muscular curve of his thigh. Whenever someone won his match, they would titter and cover their mouths, all the while casting glances in his direction. If he was of particular beauty, several girls would stare openly, trying to catch his eye.

Great Bear extended a hand to the young man he had just defeated, helping him up and clapping his shoulder. But his attention was really on the young women. He was searching for one in particular. As soon as he spotted her, he headed in her direction, ignoring the brazen stares of the other girls around her.

"Come," Great Bear urgently took her by the hand. "I would talk with you alone."

She hesitated slightly. "Will you speak to my father?"

"Yes. I promise I will, tonight."

"Then I will come."

As discreetly as they could, they disappeared into the woods.

The girls whispered together for several minutes before turning their attention back to the wrestling matches. Fortunately, there were other available young men to choose from.

She was the only one whom Great Bear had ever considered marrying, the lovely daughter of his father's dearest friend, Aiyeutiionk (War-in-Massachusetts). He had been given that name in honor of his own grandfather, one of the last of the Unkechaug braves to have actually fought in a war.

Her birth name was Soáchpoawa ássas (She-Comes-With-the-Snow), shortened to Snow Bird. Like Great Bear, Snow Bird was also tall, nearly a head taller than the girls her age. At fourteen, she was already striking, with a tight waist, narrow hips and full breasts. Her face was her best feature, dominated by large ink-black eyes and a full mouth whose corners perpetually turned up, as though she were about to burst into laughter. In fact, her disposition was unfailingly warm and kind. Because of this, none of the other girls, not even those of her friends with many fewer physical gifts, expressed the slightest jealousy, though she could and did have first choice of all the young men. The flirtations, however, had been brief and each suitor soon found himself politely cast aside, for Snow Bird intended to marry Great Bear, and no other.

Their affair provided a pleasant amusement for the entire village. The two fathers argued endlessly over the appropriate season for a marriage that had already been consummated and everyone else knew it. Then Snow Bird's mother, Sowhawmensquah (Indian Corn Woman), noticed the ripening in the young girl's figure, and immediately she went to her husband. "Enough talk!" Indian Corn Woman cried angrily. "Have you looked at your daughter? She will drop Great Bear's first child before you two can decide when they should be married. I will not have the people saying Snow Bird opened her legs before the bride price was even settled!"

War-in-Massachusetts did not bother to answer his wife. Instead, he went directly to Two Crows and announced, "I fear Snow Bird and Great Bear have taken matters into their own hands. Let them be married immediately."

The village celebrated the wedding of their young chief with two full days of feasting and games. Then it was time for Great Bear to assume his duties, mostly settling disputes and sitting with the Council of Elders that now included his father. Fortunately, Great Bear did posses natural dignity and reserve, qualities which served him well when presiding over the Council. However, it soon became clear that the new chief took only a passing interest in the problems villagers brought to him. And he rarely spoke at length in the Council.

It seemed Great Bear would have only one true passion in his life, Snow Bird. Marriage did not in any way dampen his ardor. His was the kind of love that, once fixed, could neither be lessened nor changed by time.

Over the next several years, Snow Bird was pregnant more often than not. And with each birth, she grew more beautiful to Great Bear. His male companions found themselves abandoned, for he spent every evening in her company, enjoying his children, which eventually numbered five boys.

Privately, the men decided this woman possessed a charm which could steal a man's spirit, and that Snow Bird had kept her husband's unflagging interest through some unusually strong medicine. In truth, it was as simple and as complex as the linking of two perfectly matched souls. Great Bear felt really happy only when he was with Snow Bird. She had a seemingly endless capacity for expressing sheer joy in being his wife and having his children.

The winter the Whites called 1767 was particularly hard. A series of unusually heavy snowfalls accompanied a severe cold spell. When the village's stores of dried meat and fish were gone and game became scarce, several of the men ventured out of the forest to trade their small store of beaver pelts at the nearest farming hamlet. They returned with blankets, iron pots, some provisions and an unwelcome intruder—smallpox. Within weeks, it was raging throughout the village. The scourge stayed for a month, then left, having taken some twenty men, women and children. Both Two Crows and his wife had succumbed.

Great Bear and Snow Bird lost their youngest son, Weayuhpetapagh (Clever One), a beautiful child just learning to walk. It was an especially difficult loss for Snow Bird. Nothing in her life had prepared her for a death so close. As a woman loved, prized and protected more than others, she had been spared much heartache. Now that it had come, she doubled up as though hit with a body blow. Too stunned to cry, her grief turned inward and poisoned her.

Just as the last victims were being buried and those who would recover were all on the mend, Snow Bird began to show signs of a sickening as devastating as the pox had been, but without the pustules. She spread this new illness to the middle boys, Manamáquas (Fish Hawk), a sturdy youth in his early teens, and the six year-old twins, Contayuxárrax (Brother Gull) and Contayuxápacus (Brother Partridge).

In desperation, the chief turned to the village powaw for help. This man had become the shaman when Great Bear's father was still a young man. When he had first assumed the role, he took the name, Poquetahamansank (Tree Stump), because, as he often said, "I may be cut down, but my roots will hold the soil in place for your gardens."

Tree Stump was the oldest man in the village and he looked the part. His hair had thinned so much that it floated about his head in wispy clouds. And his face, deeply creased with wrinkles, was a weathered nut brown. His eyes, however, were still bright, betraying a keen intelligence, and his sight was remarkably sharp. Most importantly, he was a gifted shaman whose medicines had always been successful.

Nevertheless, the powaw had been nearly helpless during the smallpox epidemic. None of his herbs or prayers seemed to work, once the disease had taken firm hold. When Great Bear appeared at the door to his wigwam, Tree Stump immediately gathered his prayer rattle and bag of herbs. Once he had examined Snow Bird and each of the children, he called the chief aside.

"I will need to stay here. This sickness is new to me and I must try many treatments. Take your son to War-in-Massachusetts and Indian Corn Woman. He is not yet ill and may be able to avoid the sickness. I will need your help during the day, but you must not sleep here either."

Great Bear's eldest son, Squayopamayau (Red Cloud), was only a year older than Fish Hawk. Now fourteen, he was just beginning to sense his approaching manhood. When his father told him the powaw's plan, he resisted.

"I am too old to go to Grandfather and Grandmother. Let me stay and help you!"

Great Bear was too preoccupied to waste time arguing. "Your mother and brothers are very sick," he said. "Thus far, you have been spared. When Snow Bird gets well, she will thank you for obeying Tree Stump's orders." Great Bear knew invoking his mother's name would get Red Cloud to cooperate immediately. All the boys adored their mother and would do whatever she wished without complaint.

Tree Stump was able to determine that, in Snow Bird's case, the fever had affected her heart. By listening to her chest, he could hear a disturbance in its rhythm. The children were more of a puzzle. None of them could turn his head on his own, and any attempt by Tree Stump to manipulate a child's neck resulted in cries of pain.

The powaw set up smudge pots of smoking herbs on the floor near each one's head. Then he began a marathon of prayers, asking Manitou's intervention. Tree Stump now feared his efforts were going to fail completely. Yet, on the third day, Snow Bird's fever broke. While the mother would survive, all of the children died – silently – one after the other, on that same day.

Great Bear was so stunned by the deaths of his sons that he could not move. Unable to help with the burial preparations, he sat on the floor by the fire pit, staring at their bodies, each one laid on his sleeping mat. Snow Bird did not yet know the boys were dead; she was still too sick even to raise her head. Anxiously, she called out repeatedly for her children while her neighbors continued tending to the washing and wrapping of each boy. It was only when the last one was carried out of the wigwam and Tree Stump had helped Great Bear to his feet that the awful reality finally sank in. He and Snow Bird now had only Red Cloud left.

Snow Bird was physically changed by her illness and by the loss of her sons. She seemed to have shrunk in stature, as though grief had sucked the life out of her bones. Yet she was determined to resume her duties as Great Bear's wife. She promptly went back to work, tending her garden and working alongside the other women as they did communal chores.

On a clear evening, less than a week after the burial of her sons, she and Great Bear were sitting together outside their wigwam once Red Cloud had gone in to bed.

"Ks-hamps (Husband), why have you not touched me since the illness?" Snow Bird had turned to face her husband, her huge limpid eyes suddenly brimming with tears.

Great Bear had been sharpening his hunting knife on a stone. As soon as she began speaking he put the knife away and gave her his full attention. "What do you mean? You sleep in my arms every night just as you always have."

"Not sleeping! You never come to me as my husband now. Have I grown ugly?"

"You are—beautiful. You will always be beautiful to me." Great Bear still experienced an almost painful surge of desire whenever he looked at Snow Bird. But he had been too frightened by Tree Stump's warnings to risk having relations with her.

"Our wigwam is empty, except for Red Cloud! And he is so lonely for his brothers. I want to hear the voices of my sons! You are my only comfort now. I want you to take me again."

"Kee'us (Wife), you are not yet well. Tree Stump says it will take time for your heart to heal."

"I cannot wait," she told him simply, "I want more children."

Despite his misgivings, he knew he wouldn't be able to deny her this request. And so, from that point on, he made love to her faithfully, night after night. The exertion often made her heart beat erratically. But no matter what, she would not let him stop, or even leave off for the next night.

Within the year, Snow Bird did indeed become pregnant. She spent the nine months terrified at the possibility of losing either their first-born son or the one growing inside her.

On the day she went into labor, Great Bear would not leave the wigwam. At first, he watched anxiously, leaning over the midwife's shoulder as Snow Bird silently fought each pain. But when her water broke, he could no longer stay in the background. Stepping across the blankets, he positioned himself just behind his wife, supporting her in a squatting position for the birth. The baby finally came, slipping out in a rush of blood and water, the sight of which nearly made him ill.

Suddenly, Snow Bird cried out. "Oh Great Bear! We have our first daughter!"

She was *beautiful,* perfectly formed, even to the thick swirl of black hair lying cap-like on her head instead of standing up in spikes as it had with his sons. Great Bear could not catch his breath; his heart was racing so. This was the only one of his children whose actual birth he had witnessed. Overwhelmed, he immediately fell in love with this child. He was certain her coming had saved Snow Bird's life. Her parents named her Sunhatk (Gentle Fawn).

The first hard winter of trouble ended, followed by a sweet spring and an easy summer. The village finally healed and began to thrive again. It was about two years after the birth of Great Bear and Snow Bird's daughter, just when the leaves were beginning to color. On that bright morning, Red Cloud had left the village with four of his friends to check the oyster beds and to fish some distance away from the shore.

Just before sunset, the friends returned without Red Cloud. They told a tale of White men in a schooner anchored about two miles off the Montauk Point, firing muskets at them from the deck of the ship. The good fortune was they were not all shot, only Great Bear's last male child. He had taken a ball squarely in his chest and had fallen overboard. The youths could not catch him; he sank like a stone.

Snow Bird was still nursing Gentle Fawn. She had the little girl in her arms, preparing to take her inside when they came, all together, to tell her what had happened. She neither spoke nor cried; she simply put the baby down and went into the wigwam.

Great Bear had heard the commotion as he was returning to the village with a newly killed turkey. At first, he would not let himself believe what the young men were all insisting, that his son had been shot. When he was able to understand that it was indeed Red Cloud who was dead, he immediately demanded to know where Snow Bird was.

One of the youths pointed silently to the chief's wigwam. When he finally spoke, his voice shook. "Oh Chief, she went in, but she never came back out."

In disbelief, Great Bear stared at the young man. Then a growing horror filled his heart, threatening to burst it completely. Pushing past the youths, he rushed into the wigwam, and then his legs gave way, sending him crashing to the floor in a half-sitting position. Snow Bird lay dead on her side facing the door, her eyes fixed on the mat where Red Cloud had slept since he was a child.

The entire village suffered with their stricken chief. One woman picked up little Gentle Fawn, took her home and tried to comfort her. The poor child had been forgotten in the crush of tragedy. Now she cried continually for her mother's breast, too young to grasp Snow Bird's sudden absence.

Men went out to search the waters and the shoreline for the young man's body. While they did, the women prepared Snow Bird for burial. They screamed and wailed as she was carried to the forest.

Great Bear, however, remained silent as stone; he moved without seeing where he was going. He ate food that had no taste. The fires his neighbors had built before his wigwam could not warm him. Inside, his heart had frozen in mid-beat, and he could no longer feel warmth or chill or any desire to see his only remaining child.

Chapter 4

At first, the little girl lived with her maternal grandparents. War-in-Massachusetts and Indian Corn Woman raised Gentle Fawn, essentially, without any real attention from her father.

When she was about ten years of age, her seventeen year-old uncle, Peewatsusquirintes (Little Fox), and two of his friends decided to try their luck in the world away from the village.

They left in late summer, and were away for only a few weeks when Little Fox returned, without either of his friends. He appeared to be quite ill; in fact, he and his friends had contracted influenza shortly after reaching the nearest settlement. Without ever having a chance to locate work, the two young friends had succumbed to the illness, dying in the make-shift camp they had created. He alone was able to make it back to the village. But he too died, on the same day of his return.

Influenza was not unknown, even in this secluded village, and it was most often fatal. Both War-in-Massachusetts and Indian Corn Woman, not having even the protection of youth, quickly became ill as well and died within a week of each other. Their granddaughter then came back to Great Bear's wigwam.

Fortunately for her, Gentle Fawn did so closely resemble her father and so little her mother, that Great Bear was eventually able to tolerate her presence for short periods. Now that she was old enough to do household work, the chief would bring her game and fish, which she would cook with the corn she had harvested from the family's fields. They ate together, but always in silence. Over the next four years, father and daughter settled into a routine of quiet mutual solitude.

Hatk'copumusah (Deer-Runs-Swiftly), one of the best wrestlers in the village and an excellent hunter, was only one of the youths to appear at Great Bear's fire, bearing gifts of game or freshly caught fish. It was obvious, the young men now wanted to court Gentle Fawn, but the chief took no notice.

Of all her suitors, Gentle Fawn really favored Deer-Runs-Swiftly the most. However, she kept her preference to herself as she carefully considered each young man. Just as Deer-Runs-Swiftly was about to lose hope, she gave him her answer. Almost immediately, the whole village knew as well. Gentle Fawn had finally chosen her husband!

The women had noticed the chief's complete lack of interest in his daughter's courtship. Now they clucked and whispered about the unseemliness of having no older woman attend to Gentle Fawn's wedding preparations. Who would fix her hair? Who would make sure that she could wear her mother's bridal clothes?

Gentle Fawn already had her own plans. Once she had made her choice, she went to her father as he sat outside their wigwam after his evening meal. "Father, I have chosen Deer-Runs-Swiftly for my husband. May I have your blessing?"

Great Bear momentarily weighed his daughter's question, and then turned away. How could a mere child be contemplating marriage? "You are too young," he muttered, without looking at her directly.

"I am the same age Mother was when you and she married."

Great Bear now looked more keenly at the fourteen year-old, standing before him. She was the same height as her mother. For a brief moment, he thought he could feel the ghost of a pain. But it passed, along with his desire to argue.

"I see. Very well then." He had nothing more to say.

Of course several of the older women stepped forward to help Gentle Fawn prepare for her marriage to Deer-Runs-Swiftly. The wedding of a sachem's daughter was the sort of affair that, once, would have drawn visitors from every neighboring village! However, those days were part of a dimly remembered past. The village now numbered fewer than 80 people. They would be the only celebrants at this festival.

In spite of himself, Great Bear began to take a faint interest in this young man whom Gentle Fawn had chosen, without seeking his advice. Even before his family tragedies, the chief had stopped paying attention to the games that once engaged him. Nonetheless, the young men still used them to show off before the girls.

As had been true in his youth, wrestling matches often took place in the evening, after the day's work was finished. Over the next few evenings Great Bear made it his business to watch Deer-Runs-Swiftly's matches, all of which the young man won handily. After the last one, he approached the youth.

"You wrestle well. When I was your age, I too won all of my matches."

As soon as he heard his chief's voice, Deer-Runs-Swiftly flushed nearly crimson. He knew he had violated every custom of courtship by failing to formally request Great Bear's permission before speaking to Gentle Fawn. Yet everyone said the chief did not like being bothered. And Great Bear had always pointedly ignored him before. Still he forced himself to meet the chief's eyes before answering.

"Thank you. But I am nowhere near as good as you were, my Chief."

"You are unnecessarily modest. I have heard your eye is sharp enough to bring down a deer in full flight. Since you will be providing for my daughter, I would like to test your skill. Tomorrow we will hunt together. Bring your bow and your best arrows."

On the following day, the two men met at dawn and headed into the forest. Great Bear took the lead, but only for a short distance. He halted suddenly, turned and faced Deer-Runs-Swiftly. "You will track our prey today," he said, evenly. "Whether we make a kill or not will depend on you."

The young man heard the challenge and raised his chin defiantly. He was sure of his abilities, both in tracking any game, large or small, and in bringing it down.

Moving silently, the two men continued deeper into the woods. Finally, Deer-Runs-Swiftly picked up the trail of deer, possibly two or three, that had recently moved through the area. He stepped off confidently, now moving silently, then freezing as they came upon their quarry.

Two mature bucks were facing off among the trees, both with lowered heads, pawing the ground; each was intent on driving his rival out of his territory.

Both men took positions behind nearby tree trunks and carefully took aim. The bucks, in full heat, did not detect their scent in time. Great Bear's arrow found the heart of the nearest one while Deer-Runs-Swiftly shot the other just as the buck tried to bolt for the deep woods.

"Not one, but two deer! You are a very good tracker and quick with your bow as well!" Great Bear exclaimed, actually smiling at the young man. "My daughter chose well!"

Two weeks later, the village celebrated the wedding of Gentle Fawn and Deer-Runs-Swiftly with nearly giddy enthusiasm. For the first time in years, Great Bear had put himself in the midst of the crowd, eating, speaking with everyone, and generally behaving as though he was enjoying himself. Gentle Fawn, standing beside her new husband, watched her father hopefully. Perhaps now he could forgive her for being alive.

Deer-Runs-Swiftly was equally quick at getting Gentle Fawn pregnant. When she delivered their first child just nine months later, Great Bear experienced a second pleasure.

This baby girl looked exactly as her mother had, and he remembered how Snow Bird would hang their daughter's swaddling board at eye level and nuzzle her fat red cheeks. Now, Gentle Fawn was proving to be just as gentle and loving, endlessly crooning to this baby the way her mother had done with her. How could she remember all of those songs? Great Bear never could catch the words to any of the ones Snow Bird had sung to each of their babies; they seemed like secrets between mother and children.

During the next winter, Gentle Fawn was pregnant again. A series of gorgeous, icy snowfalls had buried the fields and the forest floor, covering all vegetation and creating a beautiful but deadly desert for the wildlife. Game had all but disappeared from the entire area. The villagers turned to their stores of dried venison, fish and corn, but these too were soon depleted.

In Deer-Runs-Swiftly's home, the young father sat, dejectedly watching Gentle Fawn cheerfully spoon corn gruel into their daughter's eagerly opened mouth. "You must eat some too," he told her, adding, "You are eating for two now."

Gentle Fawn smiled at her husband's hackneyed phrase, recognizing the concern behind his words. Actually, she was both hungry and worried for the unborn child. "I ate earlier, while you were out," she lied.

Deer-Runs-Swiftly wasn't fooled and grew angry. "How did you eat? What is there here for you to eat? I myself saw you put the last of the corn in that pot! There is no more food! Do not lie!"

His outburst, nearly a scream, so startled her that Gentle Fawn dropped the wooden spoon. The baby began crying, frightened by her father's loud voice. Now everyone felt the fear. Deer-Runs-Swiftly wanted desperately to take back his words, but they were out now, swirling around the walls of his wigwam. Unable to stand the look of hurt and terror in Gentle Fawn's eyes, the young man leapt to his feet. "There will be food for my family! You and our children will not starve!" Immediately, he made for the doorway.

"Where are you going?"

Gentle Fawn was truly alarmed now; she could see how desperate her husband had become. In this state, he was liable to do something foolish, even dangerous. He paused, as though to answer her, but he had no more words, only this awful need to act. Snatching aside the blanket and skin coverings, Deer-Runs-Swiftly plunged into the whirling blizzard; he was wearing only a shirt, leggings and moccasins.

Gentle Fawn followed him out into the snow, calling after him, but he stubbornly refused to hear her. He quickly disappeared into the tree line. Frantic now, she bundled up the baby and herself and ran to her father's wigwam.

"Father, please! You must go after Deer-Runs-Swiftly!"

Great Bear heard his daughter's voice before he could make out her figure stumbling toward his wigwam. Standing just outside the doorway, he strained to see her through the thickly blowing flakes. Not until she was within arm's length could he see that she had brought the child.

"What is this about going after?" the chief demanded. "Where has he gone?"

"He means to find us food." Gentle Fawn was crying now, almost uncontrollably.

Great Bear took four youths with him to search the woods around the village. There was no possibility Deer-Runs-Swiftly had actually hoped to find game in the dark during a snowstorm. What Great Bear feared was that the young man would simply stay outdoors until nearly frozen to death in hopes that, in a weakened state, his spirit would guide him to a sure source of food. It was a risky gamble; death could as easily run down a man's spirit and capture it before the spirit could grant the request for guidance.

After two days, they found the missing husband and father. He had eluded detection by climbing the tallest tree he could manage. Once up, the wind and elements had full access to his unprotected body. Although he might have clung to his branch throughout the night and perhaps into the following day, the cold inevitably brought sleep. He dropped like a stone and, if the fall did not kill him outright, the deepening cold of the following night must have certainly finished the job.

When Great Bear saw the crumpled body, he turned away, gesturing to the young men to see to his son-in-law. Without a word, he strode out of the forest and back to the village, leaving them to carry Deer-Runs-Swiftly back to his wife and child.

Gentle Fawn was inconsolable. She cried so much at first that the women feared for her unborn child. It took all of her strength to recover enough to see to her husband's preparation for burial. It was Gentle Fawn, herself, who washed and dressed him. She showed the body to their daughter, instructing the little girl to bid her father goodbye. They buried him near his wife's mother and brothers.

A break in the weather resulted in just enough of a warming trend to allow the snows to melt somewhat. Game, hitherto absent, finally returned to the forest surrounding the village. And men went out on successful hunts, bringing back enough meat to stave off impending starvation.

But, Great Bear remained certain that evil had come to live with him. He withdrew completely from close contact with anyone. For a time, he refused to eat and could not sleep. Each night, he roamed the perimeter of the village, circling and re-circling the cluster of homes and fields. The winter melted into a cold, wet spring, and still he grieved, private and apart from his daughter.

Nor could he bear even the sight of his grandchildren. When the second baby was born, another girl exactly like her sister, Great Bear took his bow and arrows and went on an extended hunt, lasting several days.

Chapter 5

QUEBEC (1800)

For the first week, the Munsee delegation feasted and rested from their long journey. On one particular evening, while everyone was still gathered outside around the huge communal fire, Tekenna approached River Otter out of Great Bear's earshot.

"I understand that Great Bear's wife – your mother – has been forbidden to speak at the council fire." the Munsee chief began, mildly enough, "Why has he not spoken of her in his story?"

"Oh Great Chief, Great Bear has been telling you the story of his village. My mother was not there yet."

"But she is here now. And you are here also. You are both part of the Unkechaugs' story. Tonight I will hear about her and you. Tell your chief." With that, Tekenna turned on his heel, and left.

River Otter went to find Anika first. She was sitting with Gentle Fawn and three other women; together they were making a large bark basket. He caught his mother's eye, gesturing to her to slip away and join him. She left the group and met him behind a stand of trees.

"Mother, I've just been told that Great Bear must tell our story, tonight," River Otter said in English. "He doesn't know it! In truth, neither do I, not all of it! What will we do?"

"Tekenna said this?" Anika spoke very slowly.

"Yes." River Otter paused for a moment, then continued, "Mother, you've never told me anything about our family. I only know of you and Father and the time before you sent me away."

"Son, I don't know much about my family either. I do remember my mother and father, and my brothers." Anika's voice trailed off; her gaze suddenly shifted to a spot just beyond his right shoulder. She began walking in that direction, passing him. He turned to follow her, but she stopped him.

"No, don't follow me," she said, with her back to him. "Just give me some time alone. Go find Great Bear and tell him Tekenna's words. Tell him not to worry. Together we will give the chief what he wants."

River Otter did not move. "Mother," he said very deliberately, "you must understand that the Munsee, like all the other Lenape people can trace their ancestry back for hundreds of years. They don't really respect us because we were slaves. Slaves, to them, are defeated people who have no lineage to relate. Our family story will carry no weight with Tekenna."

Anika stood silent for several minutes; then she faced her son. When she spoke again, her voice was soft, but just as firm and final as River Otter's had been. "Whatever Tekenna and his people may think of us, the Whites have defeated them too. They have had to run, just like us. And they are surely no better off than we are! Now go and speak to Great Bear."

She left him standing there, chastened and silent.

That evening, just after everyone had gathered in the longhouse, Anika suddenly appeared in the doorway. Instead of sitting with the other women, she joined the circle of men at the council fire. She carried her prayer rattle and a bag of herbs, which she placed on the floor in front of her. Then, head cocked to one side as though prepared to listen, she waited, and everyone held his breath expectantly. Suddenly, she began to speak English, quickly, in a crisp almost unnatural voice. And River Otter had to rush the translation in order to keep up.

"I will take you back to the time of my grandmother, a White woman from across the sea who came to these shores as a servant. My mother named me after her."

Chapter 6

Annie's Tale

*I*n the spring of 1709, Annie MacAlister disembarked a schooner out of Newcastle, England, in Charlestown harbour. She had come all the way from Scotland to seek her fortune in the Colonies as the indentured servant of John Howard Marshall, who owned about 1000 acres on one of the Carolina islands.

Annie was a pretty wisp of a girl, barely thirteen, with reddish-gold curls, clear hazel eyes and skin like porcelain. She and her widowed mother had been living as tenants on a farm, some 10 leagues west of Dundee, which had once been owned by her father's family, but was lost due to heavy debts.

Sean MacAlister had been a good man but a poor provider, owing to his abiding love of strong drink and an inability to hold on to money. When he died of a diseased liver, in 1707, he owed large sums to nearly every landowner in the county. To settle his estate, his farm and all his worldly goods were sold at auction.

The good fortune, if it could be considered as such, was that the man who bought the farm graciously allowed his widow and daughter to remain in their nearly empty house, provided they could pay the rent. Cate MacAlister, a more prudent manager than her husband, took up raising laying hens and sold the eggs at market. In this way, she was at least able to keep the roof over their heads.

But for Annie, her future prospects were not bright. In Angus, where they lived, there was little money to be made at home. The only recourse for young folk hoping to make any kind of a fortune was to sell themselves into indentured servitude in America.

In Annie's case, she heard about this opportunity by way of a traveling troupe of actors who stopped one night on the farm. They were headed south-east, to Glasgow, where, according to one of the mummers in the troupe, you could sign on with any of the several companies in service to the English colonies.

Annie immediately packed her meager belongings and bid Cate farewell.

"I'm guessin' I'll not be seein' ye agin 'n this life, Daughter," the mother cried bitterly. "Them as leaves fer that wild place niver come home!"

"Ah, but 'tis m' only hope of a better life! Dunna deny me that wit' yer tears!"

Cate could not bring herself to stand in the way of Annie's "better life." On the next morning, the girl joined the troupe for the trip to Glasgow.

Although this was the first time she had ever been in so large a town, thanks to the helpful mummer, Annie had no trouble locating the offices of an agent for the Crown. She made her mark on documents she could not read, but that specified her term of servitude in the Carolina Colony as seven years. And she swore that she was "of age," and not otherwise bound in service. The agent gave her papers of passage and bundled her, along with her things, into a wagon filled with young men, all bound for Newcastle. Here they would board a ship for America.

John Marshall had high hopes and good resources—forty people, slave and indentured, had been able to clear his lands, put up a house and quarters, and plant a good rice crop. His success made him an ideal master, one able to honour his obligations; Annie considered herself fortunate to have been pur-chased by such a wealthy young man.

There was, however, one difficulty that Annie had to overcome – the Gul-lah language, so freely spoken by all the Black slaves. Although she badly wanted to fit in, at first, Annie could comprehend almost nothing that was said. She felt rude constantly saying, "Please, I dunna understand ye." Yet, absolute necessity made her a quick learner. The men and women were so kind and patient as they helped her learn the meanings of the oh-so-colourful phrases. At the same time, they all seemed quite charmed by her thick Scot-tish brogue.

In short order, she was established in the laundry house where her duties included washing, soap-making and mending. The work was hard but it suited her. She was indoors for most of the day, away from the blistering sun that would have quickly ruined her complexion.

Cato was the strongest man in the Quarters. Tall, muscular and black as ebony, he could work waist deep in the rice fields for hours longer than any of the others and still play banjo in the evenings when the rest of the hands were too tired to join him in song.

After her duties were finished for the day, Annie would often wander over to the fire the workers made each night near the cabins to listen to the music and watch Cato's fingers fly over the strings. The unfamiliar rhythms and melodies unlocked a strange sadness inside her, somehow reminding her of her mother and the windswept moors she had left behind in Scotland.

Annie soon found herself drawn to the music-maker. And Cato came to appreciate her attention. On many an evening, after the others had gone to bed, the two of them would remain by the fire long into the night.

Over the next seven years the friendship that grew between the two blossomed into an unexpressed love. Almost from the time he first laid eyes on her, Cato began dreaming of Annie. She seemed otherworldly, like those *angels* the preachers shouted about during the outdoor Sunday services Master Marshall sometimes provided for his slaves. But Cato was certain he had no hope of ever possessing such a being, and so, he was always careful not to appear romantically interested.

Now, just as her servitude was ending, it seemed Annie was taking every opportunity to seek him out, even during the daytime, offering to wash his clothing "special" and smiling shyly whenever she looked at him. The truth was, she had been falling in love with Cato for just as long as he had been thinking about her. But she, completely oblivious to any restrictions between the races, had simply been waiting for him to approach her.

When they finally did make love for the first time, it was on the eve of her freedom. And it happened outside, under the stars, where they had always met. On this night, beside the dying fire, Annie could not bring herself to go back to the cabin she shared with the other single women. If Cato could not recognize her hints, then she would simply have to be more direct. When his banjo finally fell silent, she leaned against his shoulder and, taking one of his large, rough hands in her two small ones, pressed the calloused palm against her breast.

When he felt the flutter of her heart, Cato hesitated for one painful moment, then pulled up her skirts and dropped his breeches. But when he tried to penetrate her, he found to his horror, that her virginity was intact.

"Law' seaks ge'l!" he moaned, almost in agony. "Yenna ayin' nebber been wit' no man? Tain' roight f'me be duh fus! (Lord sakes girl! You've never been with a man? It's not right for me to be the first.)"

Annie was much too close to gaining her deepest desire to be denied now. "Yes!" she breathlessly insisted, "Yes! I want it t' be ye!"

So Cato tried to be gentle with her, taking his time and explaining each step, before taking it. She was just thrilled by the whole experience, and told him so, repeatedly.

On the following afternoon, Annie found herself painfully anxious to see him again. Not wanting to wait until dark, when the workers would return to the Quarters, she headed out to the rice fields.

On the way, she passed a copse of low myrtle, from which came a thrashing sound followed by a series of loud moans and then a woman's scream. A second scream dissolved into joyous giggles, and she realized that this was not an assault but rather two lovers coupling.

Reaching the fields, she quickly spotted Cato swinging his scythe, beheading huge swaths of rice stalks. He was working with such a vengeance that he did not notice her approach. He almost cut her down.

"Law, Annie! Wuh fuh hunnuh cum 'eer? Tayin' safe. Eye 'mos cut yuh! (Why'd you come here? It isn't safe. I almost cut you!)"

Just looking at him was almost too much. Annie had to catch her breath before she could say, "I must see ye t'night, away from th' others!"

That evening, just as the sky went from deep blue to black, the two met some distance from the Quarters in a clearing very close to the rice fields. Cato spread his only blanket on the ground, and they used their clothing as partial covering for their naked bodies. Annie begged him to love her like a real woman. "I dunna want ye t'treat me different than yer other women. I know I'm not yer first. Love me like ye loved them!"

"Hunnuh uh too liddle ge'l. Eye 'fraid uh hu't yuh! (You're too small. I'm afraid I'll hurt you.)"

Instead of answering him, she straddled his body, covering his face with hot kisses, then gently sucking on his lower lip.

Cato gave in at that point and rolled her on her back. By this time the moon had risen, bathing the clearing in an unnaturally bright light. He could see its silvery reflection in the paleness of her eyes, now opened wide and fixed on his face. A blue vein stood out against her white throat, beating rapidly. He ran his tongue along its length and began to stroke her with unfettered passion.

Annie inhaled sharply, then let out a scream that sent a frightened flock of starlings circling skyward. Scream followed scream until she reached a shattering climax and they both collapsed. As he tried not to let her take his full weight, she wrapped both arms around him, holding him as tightly as she could.

"Oh, Cato," she gasped, "I thought my heart would burst!"

Cato was too spent to talk. He shushed her with a kiss and fell asleep. Just before daybreak, he woke her with the reminder that they both had to return to the Quarters. Annie caught his hand just before they parted.

"T'night? Come be with me!"

This day passed more slowly than any in her whole life. The other women doing laundry passed looks and sly smiles as they watched her absentmindedly scrubbing the same shirt over and over. Finally, as the afternoon sun was sending its gold through the open doors, one of the women took the shirt out of her hands.

"Chile, g'won!" she laughed. "Yenna ayin'done nuh wu'k t'ddey! G'won, nuh! Fyeen' yuh man!" (You ain't done no work today! Go on! Find your man!)

Gratefully, Annie hugged her and flew out of the laundry house.

Cato was already waiting in the clearing when she reached the surrounding trees. At the sight of him, she felt her heart kick hard, momentarily taking her breath away. He had such an easy inherently regal stance, arms loose at his side, head tilted back slightly. She ran to meet him and literally fell into his arms, her heart pounding now so violently that she nearly fainted.

Cato drew her close but then held her away, his face filled with concern. "F'gawd seak, Annie," he cried, genuinely alarmed. "Yuh haw't beat'n fit t'bus'! Hunnuh aw'roight?" (Your heart's beating hard enough to burst! Are you alright?)

"O'course I am! It's just, I love ye so! An' I need fer ye t'love me! Now!"

Cato, though consumed with desire, could not shake the small worry now seeded in his mind. This time, when he kissed her throat, his lips pressed against a vein already swollen and throbbing. He ignored her pleas of "harder, harder" and held back, moving as gently as he could. Even so, as she reached the moment of climax, she sent a loud shriek heavenward, followed by a series of shuddering gasps as she slowly came back to earth.

But their real problems were just beginning. Annie was now free to leave the plantation while Cato was enslaved for life. During their nightly trysts, he very seriously cautioned her against losing her chance for freedom.

"Annie, de Blak peebles wah lib 'roung yeh, dey gib dey lifes t'be free, lak hunnuh be. Massa Ma'shal, e ghee yorn, hunnuh tek it!" (Annie, the Black people here would give their lives to be free like you. If Master Marshal gives you yours, you have to take it!)

His plea was so earnest that she felt compelled to seriously consider his arguments. Still, whenever she tried to imagine leaving him, she found herself bursting into tears.

"Cato, yer my darlin' an' my heart's true love! I know I canna be without ye!"

"Den, if'n hunnuh gwine stay, us gotta git maah'ied. 'N I whan it wroit doung hunnuh be m'wife!" (Then, if you're going to stay, we have to get married. And I want it written down that you're my wife!)

Cato insisted there be a recognized marriage, in hopes that this might, at least, keep the two of them together permanently.

There was no difficulty getting Marshall's permission to be married, since he was certain he could keep Annie working on the plantation for her board, and no other pay. Moreover, he reasoned, any children born of the union, although legally free because of their mother's status, would be coloured, and therefore easier to enslave through various other means.

With her former master's blessings, the only remaining problem was for Annie to convince her lover, once and for all, that everything would come out right. She argued she should marry for love since there were not many other prospects for a lone White woman who was freed but had nothing else of her own. However, Cato continued to advise her, and others in the Quarters said it too, how she ought not to throw away her chance to leave for "better."

The dilemma was solved when Annie discovered herself with child in late autumn. She and Cato were married in the Quarters, with much celebration, ring-dancing and feasting. It was like Christmas! Marshall provided a keg of rum, extra flour, a fresh-killed hog, and a length of muslin for her wedding dress.

After the festivities, Cato installed his bride in a newly built split-log cabin with a carefully leveled dirt floor.

For Annie, the joy of each day was her husband's return from the fields. After her work in the laundry ended, she would hurry back to the cabin to prepare his supper. Always, she found some treat to include, sorghum to pour over his corn pone, or even a bit of pork rind. She was aided in her culinary endeavors by the women who worked beside her day after day. These women, all older by several years, took her in hand, offering advice on everything a young bride should know about cooking and often slipping her something special to add to Cato's evening meal.

Since the women had each borne several children, they also freely advised her on how to navigate the shoals of pregnancy. When she was out of earshot, however, the women would voice great worry to each other. Two, Beena and Clara were especially concerned; both had befriended Annie when she, a frightened thirteen-year old, had first appeared in the wash house.

"Dis ya Buckra ge'l too liddle an' Cato be a big Niggra. Dey pick'ney lak' gwine be too big fuh tuh buth! (This White girl's too small and Cato's a big Negro. Their baby will probably be too big for her to birth.)" Beena contributed as she stood just outside the wash house door, taking her usual short break. As she spoke, she carefully aimed a stream of tobacco juice at a patch of weeds growing beside her left foot. She grew her own strain of tobacco on an acre just behind the Quarters for Master Marshall's personal use, and, of course kept a little for herself.

"Oh yeah!" Clara agreed helping herself to a piece from Beena's dried tobacco plug. "Her gwine hab one ha'ad tyem, fuh sho! (She's going to have one hard time, for sure!)"

And, as if to confirm their dire predictions, Annie did begin to have problems. One day, when she was about four months along and beginning to show, she was trying to transfer a load of wet wash from the big iron cauldron to a wooden wash tub for rinsing. As she reached into the hot water, up to her elbows, a wave of dizziness swept over her. Fortunately, Clara had been stretching bed linen on a frame nearby. She looked up just in time and was able to catch Annie before she pitched head-first into the wash water. Beena and several others ran to her aid as well; they laid her on one of the wooden benches, insisting she be still until the spell passed. As soon as she could sit up unaided, all the women, in a chorus, ordered her to go home.

All went well for the next few months. Annie remained in the Quarters, excused from the heavy work of washing and ironing. She now lavished all of her attention on Cato, barely able to wait for his return each evening. When he'd finally reach home after sunset, exhausted and hungry, he'd find his meal hot and ready, but also a wife anxious for lovemaking.

Cato adored Annie and was unfailingly aroused by her advances. But the nagging worry about her raging passion taxing her heart persisted. Often, he would be roused from a deep sleep to feel it violently thumping against his chest as she'd lay atop him, plying his face with kisses.

One night, as she hugged him tightly after a particularly vigorous session ended with her ecstatic screams, the baby suddenly announced itself with several good kicks.

"Oh, Cato," Annie gasped, "I woke our babe! Here, feel!" For the first time, it became real to her. She guided his hand across her belly until he could feel the tiny movements. After that night, he insisted they exercise restraint when making love.

Annie finally agreed without further argument. Besides, she was beginning to have these dreams.

The crunch of a boot on gravel had awakened her. Now that she was heavy with child, any slight sound could disrupt sleep. But this was different; there was a scattering, as though several people were scurrying around their cabin.

Suddenly the room was filled with strange men, White and Black!

"Cato! Get up now!" one White man ordered, directing the others toward the bed. "Ya been sold, 'n we come t' take ya!"

Annie threw out both arms, as though she could shield her husband. But Cato caught her across the shoulders, attempting to put her behind him.

"T'ayin' true, wha hunnuh say! Massa Ma'shal, e ayin' sell me 'way fum eer!" Cato's shouting clashed against the White man's.

"Ye canna take him," Annie screamed. "We're married, legal! We're married! We Got Papers What Say So!"

The White man laughed and the other Whites joined him.

"What sort 'a foolishness ya talkin', Missy. Ain' no such 'a thing as a 'legal' marriage t' a nigger! 'Specially seein' how yer a White woman!"

Only the Black men in the group hung back; one even made a move toward the cabin door. The man in charge turned on them.

"Where th' hell ya think yer goin'? Git yer arses over there an' tie that nigger up! We ain' got all night!"

They obeyed, taking hold of Cato and trying to pull him out of bed. Annie, still screaming, threw both arms around her husband's neck and refused to release him. One of the White men grabbed her by the hair while two others forced her arms apart.

Fearing she would get hurt, Cato shouted at her to calm herself; that this was all a mistake and everything would be alright, somehow.

But she could not stop screaming, shrieking louder, louder, until she could feel her heart wrenching itself free of her breast and the vessels bursting in her throat. And she was choking on her own blood!

The dream came in several variations, each one ending with a separation and her hysterical shrieks. Awakening, Annie would tell herself she was just overwrought, that she loved Cato, perhaps too much. Moreover, she realized how excited and more than a little fearful she was at the impending birth of their child. Cato, sensing her movement, would curve his body against her back, pull her close and gently stroke her belly. The sensation of his breath against her cheek always calmed her and she would be able to drift off. Yet, even as sleep closed in, she could still hear her own screams and, in the back of her throat, taste blood.

As she entered her eighth month, it became clear that, while the baby was growing well Annie's health was suffering. She began to experience brief spells during which her heart would suddenly beat rapidly, causing nausea and faintness. Anticipating the sick feeling, she began to avoid eating unless Cato was present.

At first, she was able to hide her illness and lack of appetite from him. But he soon noticed her pallor, now so pronounced that her skin had become translucent, a network of blue veins visible. So he made it a practice of returning to his cabin at mid-morning to make sure she took at least a bowlful of mush. Often, this meant sitting with her on his knee and feeding her with his own spoon. He also appealed to the women who had worked with her in the laundry house, especially Beena and Clara, to watch out for her. They all agreed that she did look "roight peak'd" and that they would make her eat.

The efforts of the women were somewhat successful. Because she wanted so desperately for the baby to thrive, Annie forced herself to eat the meals they brought. None of these good women had much to share, so their dishes were Spartan, frequently consisting of little more than fried okra pods, dandelion greens or more mush, with a little fatback for flavour.

The young wife did begin to gain some weight and colour. But the disturbing sensations in her heart, far from easing, grew more frequent. Whenever she was with Cato, she tried to make light of the spells, blaming her racing heartbeat on her passionate love. He, by now helpless with worry, could only hold her tightly and try to offer soothing comfort.

One especially hot July morning, Cato left the cabin early, as was his habit, without waking his wife. Later, when the sun was high, he would return for some mush and a cool drink of well water. Annie awakened about an hour later. As she rose from their pallet to draw water for that morning meal, she felt her insides painlessly pour out from between her legs. Suddenly terrified, she ran out of the cabin, clutching her belly with both arms and screaming at the top of her lungs for her husband.

"Cato! Cato! Help me! Come!" Her screams carried through the Quarters, collecting excited children and elders.

He heard them faintly as he was bringing in wood for the fire. Drawing one deep breath, he tore across the clearing, up the road and through the Quarters. People pulled back at his approach and closed ranks in his wake. He reached the cabin door followed by a wave of folk, with Beena at the head.

"Whea Annie at?" he demanded of her.

"Out back! Mind hunnuh, don' scare she!"

Cato pushed roughly past the woman's arms, outstretched in warning. There was a sticky patch of blood joined by a long trail leading around the cabin to the clearing in the rear, where Annie always made her fire. A clutch of women surrounded Clara, who was cradling and fanning a form on the ground. Cato could feel his stomach catch as he looked down at his wife, for Annie had turned into a ghost, white faced and icy to his touch. He snatched her up anyway then looked around wildly. There seemed to be no way to stop the lifeblood from running out of her.

"Git Mawm Chu'ch! Gwine, ya!" Beena now dispatched the oldest child to the last cabin in the Quarters.

No one was sure how Mawm Church had come by her special skill of birthing, but she was known to deliver more children alive than the White doctor in Beaufort Village. She was a frightening figure of a woman. Of indeterminate age, she stood over six feet and weighed as much as a man of the same height. As she strode through the Quarters behind the terrified messenger, people parted for her as readily as they had for Cato. Reaching the yard, she wordlessly surveyed the pandemonium.

"Hunnuh bring de ge'l in yah, (You bring the girl in here)" she told Cato.

Gesturing impassively, Mawm Church directed the now subdued husband to lay his wife on their bed. She then waved him away and began an expert, thorough examination of Annie, palpitating her swollen belly and listening for the baby's heartbeat.

With her ear pressed to the abdomen, Mawm Church began to hum softly. Finally, she sat up and faced Cato. Her voice was uncharacteristically gentle. "Yuh pick'ney alive. Soon nah. (Your baby's alive. It'll be born soon.)"

For the next five hours, Annie screamed, almost without stopping for breath. Each shriek made Cato want to jump out of his skin. He paced the dusty yard, tearing the leaves off the lowest branch of a spindly tree growing nearby as he continually kicked savagely at any vegetation in his path.

"Wish't Eye ayin' nebber tetch de ge'l!" he sobbed loudly, "T'ayin' roight fuh she suff'rin' so! (I wish I'd never touched the girl. It ain't right for her to suffer so.)"

No one dared even to try offering him words of comfort.

Finally, unable to contain himself, Cato strode into the cabin. Mawm Church was massaging the sweating girl's stomach. Annie's eyes were glazed and unfocused; her shrieks now a continuous wall of noise. But even in her agony, she wanted only Cato. Catching sight of her husband, she screamed out to him. "Cato! Darlin', I'm dyin'! Take our babe! Oh Sweet Jesus, free me o' this pain 'n take me home!"

As if in answer to her entreaties, the baby was born at that moment. And, as Mawm Church pulled the milk-coloured infant free from her mother and deftly cut the cord, Annie suddenly fell silent, her eyes now fixed on the small form being held up for inspection.

Cato moved to his wife's side, and then stopped. Something was terribly wrong with her face; it had suddenly gone slack. Mawm Church saw it too. Handing the baby to Clara, who was standing nearest in the doorway, she began vigorously pressing and squeezing the now empty womb in a vain attempt to staunch the red tide that spread across the pallet and began to fall, drop by precious drop, into the dust. But it was too late, Annie's heart had already stopped; she was gone.

When he realized what had happened, Cato let out a horrible shriek that could be heard throughout the entire Quarters. Then he threw himself across Annie's body and would let no one touch her, not even to close her eyes.

"Cato," Mawm Church said softly after a bit, "Son, hunnuh got t' tu'n she loose nah'. De ge'l gone." (You've got to let go now. The girl's gone.)

She took a firm grip and pulled on Annie's arm with one huge hand, while steadying Cato with the other. Finally, she was able to pry the dead girl out of her distraught husband's arms.

Calling out to the several frightened men who had come running when they heard his cry, she ordered them to restrain him while she made the poor girl presentable.

"Y'all cya' 'ee oat deh 'an hol''ee," she ordered. (All of you take him outside and hold him)

Seven of the strongest men took firm hold of Cato and pulled him out of the cabin. At first, he struggled against them, crying wildly. Then Beena and several of the other women, each one moving carefully past him, now entered the cabin to help Mawm Church close the eyes and mouth, then bathe and dress the body.

When he next saw his wife, she looked so peaceful. Cato, though still devastated, was somewhat comforted. He kissed her and whispered a farewell. "Eye jus' know'd hunnuh on'y be mynes a liddle whi'el. Hunnuh up in hebben now, wi'duh res' a dem aeng'ls. (I just knew you'd only be mine for a little while. You're in heaven now, with the rest of those angels.)"

They buried Annie in the slaves' graveyard. The people who had become her family now gathered to pray over her and to mourn. No one bothered to ask Master Marshall if he wouldn't have preferred that she be buried with White folks. In truth, the idea never crossed his mind either. For love, she had given up her freedom to marry a slave and had born him a Black daughter. As far as Marshall was concerned, with the mother gone, there was now no question about the baby's slave status.

Chapter 7

*A*lice was one of the women who helped Mawm Church lay Annie out.

A handsome, strapping dark-skinned girl, Alice was a young widow. The year before, she had married her lover, Sampson, tall, good-looking and absolutely careless. Only a month after their wedding, the unfortunate bridegroom stepped into the arc of another worker's scythe. The blade caught him full in the groin, slicing through a major artery. He bled to death before his companions could get him out of the rice fields.

Unbeknownst to either of them, Sampson had already gotten Alice pregnant. Two months before Annie would go into labour, Alice had her baby, a girl. And less than a week before Annie's death, the new mother put an apparently healthy infant to bed, only to find a corpse in the morning.

Cato knew about Alice's tragic circumstances, but his newborn daughter needed to be fed. Death was a familiar presence in the Quarters, and time spent alone grieving was too often a luxury for people in bondage. When he approached her with the request that she be the wet nurse, she promptly took Annie's baby, giving this infant the milk her own could no longer use.

Cato left the baby with Alice and tried to return to his cabin. But he could not stay inside, and he was afraid to sleep in the bed that he and Annie had shared. So, he spent each night sitting on a stump near his door.

Eventually, after more than a week, the weariness got the better of him. That evening, instead of taking his seat, Cato walked over to the cabin that Alice shared with another family. When he reached the open door, he could see her sitting by the fireplace, nursing his baby. Without even thinking about it, he just walked in, mumbling to himself that he was just checking on his daughter.

When she saw him standing there, Alice quickly covered her bare breast with a piece of cloth, as Cato shifted from one foot to the other. For several minutes they avoided looking at one another. Finally, wordlessly, he sat down beside her and within minutes fell asleep with his back resting against the fireplace wall. Alice continued nursing and when she finished, placed his baby in the rough wooden cradle that had been her daughter's. She draped her only blanket over Cato, gently so as not to wake him, then lay down, fully clothed, on her pallet.

From that night on, Cato came every evening, usually after the family had gone to sleep. He would take the baby from Alice and sit holding her until he grew too drowsy. Alice would then take the baby and cover him where he sat.

To Cato, studying his daughter's tiny cream-coloured face was cause for endless amazement. Bringing this small being into the world had cost his beloved Annie her life. And yet, he could feel no bitterness toward the child. On the contrary, he was discovering that the only time he was free of pain was when he was with her, and Alice.

As for Alice, nursing Annie's daughter had relieved more than her full breasts. She began loving this child, even from the first moment she'd held her. At the same time, her maddening grief had begun to ease. Cato's evening visits, silent though they were, now seemed to soothe her as well.

One such quiet evening, Cato broke the silence. "Alice, Eye got t'ast hunnuh sompin'," he began hesitantly. "Yenna ayin' got no mo' fambly. 'N dis 'eer pick'ney 'a mynes bin needn' she mudda'. Ifn' hunnuh maah'y me, us kin be yuh fambly. (Alice, I need to ask you something. You don't have any more family. And my baby needs her mother. If you marry me, we can be your family.)"

Her answer was immediate. "Yeh. Eye'l maah'y hunnuh. (Yes. I'll marry you.)" After all, Sampson and her daughter would wait for her in heaven; Cato and this baby needed her now.

Once that decision was made, Alice immediately set about reclaiming Cato's cabin. She moved the sparse furnishings around, placing the bed against the opposite wall. Then she swept out the entire room with handfuls of salt, to keep away evil spirits who were always drawn to places where people had died in pain. Cato would later declare that he could feel the difference in the place, like it was brand new.

Next there was the problem of naming the baby. Alice suggested Annie, but he flatly refused. Understanding that he could not bear to hear his love's name repeatedly, she proposed another one.

"If'n hunnuh don' myne", she ventured, "Eye wanna call she, Em, fuh m'own mudda'. (If you don't mind, I want to name her Em, after my own mother.)"

Cato agreed his daughter could carry Alice's mother's name, especially since mother and daughter had been separated in the sale that brought her to this plantation.

Their easy relationship eventually matured into a deep, companionable love. Neither would tread on the other's private pain, but they shared their daily lives completely. And Cato found in Alice a lover who could meet his every need. He and she would eventually have five more children, all sons.

Because she knew how much he and Annie had loved each other, Alice made sure that Em knew her birth mother's name had been Annie. The little girl grew to resemble her mother, with curly strawberry blond hair and hazel eyes. Em, however, was several shades darker, with a remarkable golden cast to her skin. The older folk would comment endlessly on her unique colouring.

"Cyaan pass, she! (She can't pass for White!)" Beena would note as she'd take ever longer breaks from her washing duties.

And Clara, who always joined her, would observe, "But she plenny lik she mudda' nah! (But she does look a lot like her mother now!)"

It was agreed that this golden child was too dark to be mistaken for a White woman but too light-skinned for the fields.

Alice would never permit it anyway, using the excuse that a fever Em had caught when she was still a toddler had made the girl too frail for fieldwork. During the long, sultry months when the Whites were away, no one would force any of the children into the fields anyway, so Em was never put to work outdoors at all. Alice did, however, train the child well in all the domestic arts; she could cook, clean and serve with the best.

Chapter 8

QUEBEC (1800)

*A*ncient African spirits now joined Great Bear, Tekenna and their councils in the longhouse this evening. Only Anika could see them, but everyone could sense a presence. Some of these ancestral ones crowded into the circle where both chiefs and councils were sitting. Others hovered above the fire, secreting themselves in its smoke. Several came and sat with the women, causing a general shifting and movement; women are often quite sensitive to spirits. One of Tekenna's wives became so uncomfortable that she quietly left the longhouse.

Anika knew she had to salute these sages. Their coming was unusual, a special gift. But to do so aloud might frighten the visitors. Instead, she stood and raised both arms to the ceiling, so everyone would understand that she was praying silently.

"Old Ones, you only come when I am most in need! What is it that I must do?"

"Surrender your body to us. When we speak through you tonight, we will tell more of the story that you do not yet know."

Anika could feel herself losing consciousness and sinking to the floor. A moment later, when she sat up, she was in a deep trance. A host of different English-speaking voices came out of her mouth, as her mother's tale unfolded. And, although River Otter was translating, every person in the longhouse was riveted by those voices...

CHARLESTOWN, SOUTH CAROLINA - 1720-1722

The clutch of dusty Black children played with gleeful abandon at the back of the Quarters on the Marshall plantation. Located some five miles outside of Beaufort and expanded by 150 acres, it had now become the largest, most prosperous plantation in this part of the colony. The Marshall family was only in residence during the winter, escaping the malarial marshes of St. Helena Island for their Charlestown houses during the hot summers.

Now it was March, and a June wedding had been planned for the only Marshall daughter, Sophie. She would need to take house servants with her, particularly a personal maid, to her new home in Maryland.

Samuel and Lizzie had come down from the House to the Quarters to select a child who had not yet been put into the fields; only a "fresh" youngster could be properly trained as a house servant. One child, Em, now long legged, with delicate features and a cloud of reddish-gold hair caught Samuel's eye.

"Ayin' dat de Buckra ge'l pick'ney? (Ain't that the White girl's child?)" he said to Lizzie.

"Alice raise she up. Train she gud, whut Eye 'ear" (Alice raised her. I hear she trained her well.)"

They spoke their Gullah most times, except whenever they'd be 'round their master or his family. Lizzie had befriended Alice when they both were motherless children, new to the plantation. Even after becoming one of the house servants, she would visit Alice and Cato's cabin whenever she could. She knew first-hand what Alice had done with Em.

That was good enough for Samuel. Though she was only 10 years of age, Em was chosen as Young Missus' personal maid and was expected to travel with the other servants to Charlestown that spring. She would never see the Beaufort plantation or her parents again.

The wedding was to be the event of the season. Miss Sophie Marshall was marrying Mr. Evan Grant, a physician from London who had been able to secure a position in Charlestown and a small tract of land along the James River. His profession, combined with his holdings made him a "gentleman". John Marshall himself would never have qualified for this distinction had he not been fortunate enough to acquire enough property and slaves to secure his claim to a place in Carolina society.

Sophie Marshall, at sixteen, had reached the perfect marriageable age. An extremely pretty girl with thick chestnut hair and good colouring, she was nonetheless quite shy, especially around men. So when the inevitable suitors would call at whichever house the family was residing in at the time, it was her father who would entertain them. At first, Evan Grant was just one of many.

He had first noticed Sophie the previous summer during church services and had been smitten immediately. For the rest of the season, he haunted the Grant's Charlestown house, watching for her and planning his strategy for gaining an invitation. But the crush of young hopefuls coming by on Sunday afternoons, sometimes in twos and threes made him realize that he would never win her attention by visiting in that crowd.

Evan surmised, correctly, that there would be much less competition out at St. Helena. On a warm Sunday during the following winter, he appeared at the Beaufort house with a bottle of good rum. A servant led him to the veranda where Marshall always rested after services.

"Sir, it's kind of you to allow me to call on your family, and on Mistress Sophie, if she's about." Evan ventured a glance over his shoulder, hoping she was somewhere nearby.

"My daughter is indisposed with a fever and unable to receive visitors." John's eye fell on the bottle. It carried a well-known British seal. "However, I believe that *we* should talk a bit, since I venture to guess your intentions. Sophie will not be choosing her suitors. She has left that task to me, as any dutiful daughter should."

Evan understood the situation completely. Sophie's "fever" lasted for the rest of the winter. Whenever he called, it was always John who played host and eventually the two men struck up quite a friendship. The marriage was, for all practical purposes, arranged over rum and tobacco on Marshall's veranda.

Evan Grant had made good use of his natural assets all of his life. As an orphan in the back streets of Belfast, he had used every bit of charm that a cherubic face and considerable native intellect could muster to win himself an apprenticeship with one of the most successful physicians in town.

When Evan was about 16, the worthy doctor had taken up residence in London. By this time, the young man was accompanying his benefactor on all of his rounds, including forays into the operating rooms of the local hospitals. Medicine was little more than a craft involving knowledge of herbs, leeching and how to set bones, along with a recognition that death is, at all times, inevitable. Once he'd understood this, Evan was soon able to perform as well as his master.

However, money, or more properly, securing his fortune was always foremost in his mind. And a fortune was not to be had in England, without title or a good marriage. So, instead of applying to Oxford and hoping to take over the old doctor's practice, Evan took his skills and some one hundred pounds and secured passage on a ship bound for America.

He landed in Charlestown harbour in the fall of 1732. Within five years, he had established a practice and set about to begin the purchases of property and slaves that would win him a place in society. Evan's goal was to make a successful marriage, wind up his affairs in the Carolinas and move further north to Maryland where the climate was healthier.

Sophie was introduced to her husband-to-be only a month before the wedding. Her father summoned her during one of Evan's visits.

"Sophie, I believe I've found you a good man. He's a doctor, established, with a practice in town and a decent-sized parcel of property not far from here." John smiled expansively, warming to his own words. "Evan Grant! He'll make you a fine husband!"

The young woman could barely bring herself to meet his eyes. When she did finally look up, a rosy flush coloured both cheeks and she managed a faint smile. Evan decided that she was even prettier than he'd remembered.

Once they were married, Sophie continued to live with her parents while Evan made plans to move his new wife and household to Maryland. Establishing connections would require several extended trips to Baltimore to purchase a house and set up his new practice. He also wanted to lay hold of several hundred acres outside of town to grow tobacco. The sale of his Charlestown practice and the St. Helena property would not be sufficient to fund everything. He would need a generous line of credit in order to purchase both the land and slaves.

Marshall was the key to securing the initial loans, and Evan did not wait long to broach the subject with his new father-in-law. The discussions were difficult at first; John found the idea of borrowing faintly repellant.

"In my day, you were given a grant of land based on service to the Crown! I used my capital to purchase my first gang of men. That was all I needed. The sale of my crops has always covered my expenditures, then and now! It's just not good business to use borrowed funds to stake yourself in the first place!"

"Sir, you are quite right. And if land grants were still being given, I would be in service right now. But, as you know, the Company that holds the Maryland Colony respects only cash. You've seen what I am capable of. When I came here, I had naught but my wits. And I did prosper. With your help, I know that I can do so again!"

Marshall could not argue the point further. This was his daughter's husband and, most importantly, his choice for her. In the end, he helped Evan secure several loans, and he himself made a substantial outlay of cash and slaves.

Evan was able to buy both a town house in Baltimore and a tobacco farm some ten miles west of town. In January of 1739, he and Sophie left Charlestown with their personal servants, just after Christmas. By this time, Sophie was pregnant with their first child.

Chapter 9

QUEBEC (1800)

*A*nika's voice rose and fell, taking on the intonations of both narrator and each character. Tekenna watched her as much as he listened; noting the ease with which she slipped from one role into the next – so naturally, as though possession by spirits was an everyday occurrence. As Anika continued the story, the Munsee chief found himself hanging on her every word, his eyes fixed on her face…

MARYLAND (1729-1758)

Em did make a superb house servant. Within a year, she became essential to the Grants' social position in Baltimore. As a new physician, Evan would have needed to court a clientele already serviced by several older, more established doctors. He found that he could arrange to entertain potential patients, literally at a moment's notice, because Em always had the parlour set for visitors and a full meal ready in the kitchen. She was able to accomplish this by organizing the entire household staff, using both the methods her mother had taught her and those she had devised herself. Sophie could always entertain most successfully, with no thought to details, since Em was so able. She would even remember which flowers would be in bloom season by season, with bouquets tastefully placed in each of the sitting rooms.

Because she did prove to be so efficient, Evan and Sophie soon gave her complete control of the household, along with the freedom to come and go as she pleased.

"Ma'am, can I carry your bundles to your wagon? You do seem powerfully laden."

Em turned slowly in the direction of the voice. The man who had so courteously addressed her stood directly behind her, with his back to the sun, so that she could not really see him properly. He had removed his hat, revealing long wooly hair roughly parted in the center. His general shape was exceptionally broad across the shoulders and, although he seemed tall, he was only a head taller than Em.

"If you will so direct me," he continued, "I will endeavor to follow."

"Well, sir. My wagon sits yonder under the oak, and I do appreciate the offer."

Demurely, Em relinquished the three parcels she had been struggling to balance, along with a basket of fresh loaves and a rather large goose. The man took everything in one fell swoop, leaving her hands free to lift her skirts out of the mud. She followed him, taking the opportunity to study those of his feature that she could now see. The man moved with the open stride of one whose time was his own. Em guessed at his status.

"Sir, you are free?"

The stranger stopped and turned to face her. His smile mocked her hesitance. "That I am, Ma'am. Purchased myself five years ago from a local smith. A cooper I am by trade, one of the best, entirely self-taught. My shop sits at the corner of Charles Road." He continued standing there, obviously waiting.

"Oh, do forgive me! I'm Mr. Grant's Em. He's the doctor on Lombard Street." Em felt her face growing warm with embarrassment as she spoke, though, for the life of her, she could not figure out why.

"I know who you are." The man, still smiling, gazed at her steadily for a moment before moving off again. When they got to the wagon, he loaded the parcels, loaves and goose in back, and then helped her up onto the seat. To her surprise, he climbed up beside her and took up the reins. "Please allow me to drive you home."

"Oh. Well, yes. Of course you may."

Once they reached the Grants' house, Em led the way to the kitchen. At the door, she thanked the stranger. "Can I know your name, kind sir?"

"Certainly, ma'am. It's Rufus," he paused deliberately, "Liberty." Then he set the parcels on the kitchen table and left quickly.

Rufus Liberty had often watched for Em over the ten years that she had been doing the shopping in Baltimore Market. He had never taken the opportunity of speaking to her before today. Always, she seemed to move with such crisp, deliberate steps, as though a clock was ticking somewhere in her head that she kept ahead of. If he had to turn away for even a moment, she would be gone. It did not matter much, however; as long as he needed to save every cent he could hold on to, he had nothing to offer any woman.

When Old Langly, the blacksmith had purchased him in '29, he told Rufus he did not plan to continue the business for many more years.

"I can sell you and this shop for £200," he said, quite earnestly, at the time. "If you wish to buy yourself, I can let you go for £100."

The sum had been as hard for Rufus to raise as if he were Sisyphus. The hours that he could hire himself out were so few, in spite of the fact that Langly did very little work, an occasional bridle or set of shoes here and there. On too many days, he was forced to wait alone in the shop while Langly squandered whole afternoons in the corner pub. But when the old man did return, he would demand a full accounting and collect every penny, returning nothing to Rufus.

It might have taken a lifetime to acquire £100, but Rufus benefited from a stroke of absolute luck—bad luck for Langly, as it turned out.

One day, while in his cups, the old man had stumbled in the rutted road outside his shop. There had been a hard rain; the mud was both slippery and deep. When the smith went down, he fell on his face and was too drunk even to turn his head. He suffocated where he had fallen and his tavern-mates found him thus, hours later.

Having left no heirs and few debts, the local governor declared that all of Langly's goods would be sold at auction with the proceeds going into the Colony's coffers. Rufus appealed to the Colonial officials to accept what monies he had saved as payment for his freedom. Because there were no relatives to contest, the good men accepted the £45 and granted papers of manumission. Now a free man, Rufus chose as his last name, the most important word in life to him and the only one that he could read.

"My name is Liberty, Rufus Liberty, sir. If you will hire me, I will work for you diligently. I am honest and trustworthy. You will never have reason to doubt my word, for I speak for myself."

This became his standard speech, each time he sought work, and it usually worked. Often, Rufus would hire himself out over the next two years to men who held a basic distrust for free Blacks. Maryland planters would complain endlessly about the powerfully negative influence such un-chattled men had on their servants.

It required all of Rufus' powers of persuasion to get Ansel Smith, the town cooper to take him into his shop. After a fifteen-year apprenticeship, Ansel had finally taken ownership when the only remaining cooper in Baltimore retired. And he had no intention of allowing any Black would-be apprentice to learn his barrel-making skills. Of course, Rufus watched covertly whenever he could, and, being resourceful, was able to pick up Ansel's techniques almost as quickly as if he had received proper lessons. In no time, he was his employer's equal. Now, he could save all of his meager wages, and in less than a year had amassed enough to begin, secretly, to purchase his own more modern tools.

Once again luck intervened to shorten what surely would have been years of working for the now very successful young cooper. One night in early winter, a fire had broken out in the wooden shed behind the shop. Ansel's house was adjacent to the shop and just behind the shed. Nevertheless, the fire had gotten some headway before the flames were visible to passersby.

Because the hour was late, there would be no one on the street until the Night Watch came by sometime after midnight. Ansel was awakened by a strange reddish glow outside of his window. By the time he realized what the unusual light meant, the fire had spread to the shop itself. The man literally leapt from his bed and, clad only in his shirt, ran outdoors to try and save his livelihood.

The front of the building was not yet in flames, giving Ansel false hopes that he could fill buckets from his well and damp the fire in the back. What the hapless man did not realize was that he was improperly dressed for the work at hand. He filled his large wooden bucket and ran to the back of his shop to throw its contents when the tail of his shirt caught fire. Rufus had taken up residence in rooms above the kitchen of a nearby inn. It was he who heard Ansel's screams. Although he came out running, reaching the shop well ahead of the now aroused neighbours, there was nothing to be done for Ansel. Many hands were able to accomplish what the unfortunate man could not do alone; the fire was extinguished before more than superficial damage had been done to the shop. The now badly burned cooper, however, could not be moved. He died on the floor of his shop.

Of course, a community needs a cooper, and Rufus, as it turns out, was the only trained cooper immediately available. With a little work, he was able to renovate the shop and get back to business. It soon became clear that he was an excellent craftsman; his barrels were practically water-tight. In spite of his colour and status, both the local merchants and farmers from outside of town became reluctant, then loyal clients.

As his prospects grew, Rufus began to think of marriage and a family. For a freedman, however, this was a prospect with complications. There were very few free women of colour in Baltimore and none on any of the outlying plantations. Rufus would have had to seek a wife in Philadelphia or even New York. On the day that he worked up the courage to speak to Em, he had already decided on her for his wife. No other woman would do.

Rufus decided to make his request directly, first to Em, then to the doctor. Getting her alone to speak to her about courtship was the first difficulty he encountered. As it happened, she seldom allowed herself to be off duty in the Grant household, so he had to use a creative ruse in order to visit. One evening, just after dinner, he appeared at the Grant kitchen door with a new barrel and several smaller crates.

"Please let your master know," he explained to the cook who answered the knock, "that these are part payment for my customer's treatment."

The man immediately went to fetch Em, since she was the one who accepted all coloured visitors having business with the doctor.

Em had begun to prepare for bed. She came from the house bareheaded, adjusting her neckerchief and apron. When she saw that it was Rufus, she stopped in confusion. He repeated his request for the cook's benefit, while gesturing surreptitiously for her to step outside. Once they were out of earshot, he took both of her hands in his own. "I hope you will not think me too forward, but I have so wanted to speak with you."

Rufus could hear his heart beating. The sound interfered with his thinking, but he plunged on. "I have watched you over the years while I purchased my freedom and established myself. Now that I have a trade and some means, I feel that I have something to offer…ah—ah—a woman."

The last words nearly died in his mouth. It was impossible to go on. Em was watching him so intently; it seemed her eyes had grown larger, her face receding around them. Rufus lost himself in their near golden depths and he could not catch his breath.

"Have you come a-courtin', Sir?" Em barely breathed the words, with a coquettish air she did not know she had even possessed.

"Yes, Ma'am."

"And you wish me to accept your visits?"

Rufus nodded mutely, having lost the power of speech.

"Very well then." Here, she smiled. "I shall be able to receive you on Thursday evenings after supper. You can meet me in the carriage house."

Em had never realized how the presence of a man who so obviously adored her could awaken in her such a sheer and all-consuming lust. During their first Thursday tryst, Rufus almost reverently took her hand.

"Mistress Em," he began, and she responded by kissing him, quite suddenly, full on the mouth.

"Oh, I didn't mean to be so forward," she cried, drawing back aghast. He had called her "mistress" as though she were someone important. She was his from that moment.

"You care for me, as well? Ah, Mistress Em, you cannot know how happy this makes me!"

Thereafter, their courtship quickly advanced to lovemaking. Once they had begun to spend whole nights together, they met in Rufus' small house behind his shop.

By now, Rufus was so much in love with this woman that, for the first time in his life, he could not plan even a day ahead. How had he hoped to marry her? He had no recollection that he'd planned to formally approach Grant with an offer to buy her freedom.

In short order, Em was with child, and the situation now became critical. One did not impregnate a slave without the master's consent. Nevertheless, Rufus was nothing if not courageous. He decided to make the appeal immediately; Em, however, had deep reservations. This was Maryland, after all, and Rufus had committed an offense that could get him hung. She proposed a completely different plan.

"I will secretly be your wife." Em had taken this opportunity to tell Rufus how she thought they *had* to proceed. "This child will also be a secret; when it is born, you will keep it and I will visit to nurse it."

They were now facing each other on his narrow bed. Rufus gently laid both hands on Em's bare stomach. Freedom for his family had become his overriding goal. How could she ask him to hide the fact that now he had both wife and child?

"Have you taken leave of your senses? How can you keep your condition secret? Will you not-?" Although he spoke softly, his face revealed deep distress.

"Rufus, please." Em had but to say his name and Rufus could refuse her nothing.

She also felt concerned, but not for freedom for herself or even for the unborn child. Her lover had to be protected. Over time, Evan Grant could be dealt with. The important thing was to keep their relationship a secret until the best possible moment. When that might be she did not know, but she knew it was certainly not now.

Meanwhile, Em decided that she could hide her condition with a simple change of wardrobe and the realization that, to her master and mistress, she was, for the most part, more of a reliable presence than a real person. Sophie might notice that she was gaining weight but would think little of it. Grant would notice nothing.

Once, only a few years after the move to Baltimore, when she was about thirteen, Em was in the back parlour arranging a bouquet of lilacs in one of Sophie's crystal vases. Evan had been secretly watching the girl ever since she'd become Sophie's personal maid. On this particular afternoon, after checking that the hall was empty, he decided to finally take his pleasure. He slipped into the room and surprised Em, summarily pulling up her petticoat while dropping his breeches. The encounter had been cut short by the sound of approaching footsteps in the hall. Even at so young an age, Em was self-possessed. Moving smoothly out of range of his groping hands, she opened the door and glided out, closing it discreetly behind her so he could arrange himself in private. Nothing was ever said about the incident. Evan never again even looked directly at her.

Because she could not trust any of the household servants with her secret, Em had to convince Evan and Sophie that the plantation house needed her touch, even though Evan spent only an occasional weekend on his farm. Since there were no social obligations pending, her daily presence was not really needed, and she set off accompanied only by Ben, the coachman. Once she had established herself in the rather ramshackle house, she sent Ben back to town with the admonition not to return for two months.

One of the Black folk on the farm who had been part of Marshall's wedding present was the adult daughter of Mawm Church. This woman was, like her mother, a skilled midwife. Both mother and daughter had survived capture in Africa and had been sold together in the Charlestown market. Daughter was the name that Mawm Church had called the woman, and she never went by any other. People on the Beaufort plantation used to whisper that Daughter must have had another name, but neither woman ever used it and no one ever dared ask. Daughter was as tall as her mother and nearly as broad. Yet somehow, her face possessed a dark beauty that was missing in the nearly masculine features of Mawm Church.

It was to Daughter that Em confided her secret. The woman immediately came up to the house, bringing a small cloth roll. She took over the kitchen as her living quarters. Here she made meals for Em, bringing them into the main building, even though Em would have preferred eating in the kitchen with her. As the time grew close, Daughter brought thatch and bedding into the kitchen and made a pallet near the fireplace.

On a warm September evening, Em began her labour. When the pains became regular, Daughter led the sweating young woman to the pallet.

"Us gwine wait ober yah (We're going to wait right here)." Daughter was as laconic as her mother.

Unfortunately, labour proved to be long and difficult. Em had never experienced anything close to the pains of her contractions. Though thoroughly ashamed, she could not stifle her screams. Daughter watched impassively, occasionally turning the poor woman on her side and massaging her back. As night dragged on, it seemed the baby was resisting being born. By now Em was nearly beside herself. Daughter brought in a bucket and began placing cool wet cloths on her forehead.

At last, the baby presented itself in the breech position. Daughter placed one hand on Em's abdomen; with the other, she reached into her vagina. Ignoring Em's imploring shrieks of agony, the woman expertly turned the child so that the head appeared. The little girl was born full term but tiny. Daughter took the little thing and held her up for Em to see.

Almost is if by magic, the awfulness of the night evaporated. Reaching for her daughter, Em joyously took the child into her arms.

"Wha hunnuh gwine call yuh pick'ney (What are you going to name your baby)?" Daughter sat back on her heels, a satisfied near-smile tugging at the corners of her elegantly sculpted mouth.

"Annie." It came out unexpectedly.

Em had not really thought about names, nor was she remembering her mother's stories about the woman who had died giving her life. Yet, once she'd spoken the name, she knew its rightness.

But there were problems. The baby, at first, was unable to nurse. She could not seem to find the energy to suckle, even when Em guided her little mouth to the breast. Daughter installed mother and child in one of the bedrooms and vanished for several hours. When she returned, she took the baby from Em.

"Where are you taking her?" Em asked in alarm.

"Ef'n de pick'ney don' nu'se fum hunnuh, hunnuh gwine lose she (If the baby won't nurse, you'll lose her)."

Daughter and the baby were gone for about an hour more. When, at last, the woman returned, she wordlessly handed the infant to the mother. Miraculously, the little thing began to suckle, slowly, with great pauses, but successfully. The first hurdle to her survival had been cleared.

All too soon, the two-month period was drawing to a close. It was late fall, but Em could not yet safely take Annie outdoors. Now she would have to come up with another plan to hide her child's existence.

The holiday season, with all of its attendant balls, was beginning in town, and Ben would soon be returning with the wagon to take her back to Baltimore. In the few remaining weeks before his arrival, she assembled a small crew of men from the fields to clear the land around the house and do several major repairs. Each day, she would take on a household task herself, sewing a set of curtains for the front parlour using fabric she found in a forgotten trunk, and cleaning all of the rooms from floors to ceilings. When they left the house, she knew Grant would not doubt that she had accomplished what she'd promised.

Em decided to take Annie back without explanation. As she mounted the wagon, Ben glanced at the bundled-up infant but said nothing. He spent the first part of the trip chatting genially about events that had happened while she was away.

"Barley died a week after you left." Barley was Grant's favourite horse.

"Was Master Evan very upset?"

"Didn't come out his study all th' next day, 'cept to refill his flask."

Ben coughed phlegmatically and spat several times for emphasis. After a pause of several minutes, he continued on a different topic. "Missus expectin' agin'."

Em shifted uncomfortably, taken aback by this turn in the conversation. "How do you know this?"

"Mr. Ashcroft's maid tol' Cook."

Ashcroft was one the older physicians in town and had the best reputation for delivering live babies. His maid was married to Grant's cook.

Ben said no more, only occasionally coughing and spitting for the rest of the trip. Em was grateful for the silence. Plausible explanations for the infant were going to be difficult to come by. When the baby became fussy, she moved to the back of the wagon to nurse. Ben seemed not to see, nor did he change his pattern of cough-spit-spit.

Rufus had become nearly frantic with worry during Em's absence. Although she'd warned him not to, he found himself haunting the streets near the Grants' large red corner house. At her insistence, Rufus had promised not to ask any of the servants about her. It was all he could do to keep from knocking on the kitchen door and making up some excuse to speak to her. He knew only that she had left Baltimore, not where she was or when she might return. Perhaps, if he worded his request cleverly, whoever answered the door would let on as to her whereabouts.

It was early evening by the time Ben pulled the wagon into the driveway in back of the house. Rufus had been standing in the shadows created by a large old mulberry tree in the yard. He nearly cried out when he saw Em alight with the bundle that was his child. She turned in his direction, stood still for a moment, as though she'd seen him, then turned back to the wagon. She spoke softly to Ben, who grunted once, then moved away. Taking his courage in hand, Rufus stepped out of the shadows.

"Em! Oh, my God! I…" He literally swept both her and the baby into a crushing embrace. When she touched his face with her free hand, she found his cheek wet with tears.

Annie stayed with her mother, becoming part of the Grant household. Em, in those first few hours after her return, decided on a plausible story to explain the baby's presence. She chose to confront Sophie and Evan together, after they had finished their supper. While the maid was clearing the table, she entered the dining room silently, as was her custom.

Sophie was discreetly wiping her mouth. It seemed that pregnancy made her hungry for foods soaked in gravies and sauces. Invariably, some would wind up on her chin. That made Evan furious, and he never hesitated to reprimand her on her poor table manners. His were no better; he chewed loudly with much smacking of his lips, but Sophie, ever the lady, never defended herself by bringing this up. On this occasion, Evan had caught her in the act and was about to launch into his usual tirade when Em cleared her throat, the signal that she was present.

"The house is ready for your next visit, Master Evan."

Of all the servants, Em alone was permitted to address her master and mistress without first asking their leave. Evan looked up with some irritation. She always seemed to decide to speak just as he was about to correct his wife, but what she said was always timely information. So he had no ammunition with which to attack the practice. The fact that he secretly found her efficiency, indeed her whole *person,* somewhat intimidating also served to silence any protest he might want to make.

Em continued smoothly. "I have brought back an infant that was abandoned on the front porch. I could not find out who she belonged to, but I am sure you will not mind. She will be no trouble. And Mistress Sophie, I shall personally train her to take care of this next baby."

Sophie looked grateful, both for the offer and for the reprieve. Turning to Evan, she spoke sweetly. "Is not Em a perfect jewel? How kind of her to take pity on an unfortunate Black foundling! Of course, you may keep her, Em! Master Evan and I insist!"

The matter was effectively closed. Whereas Evan might have voiced his concerns about whose baby this could be and whether one of his Maryland neighbours was now out one baby slave, the women had successfully ganged up on him.

Chapter 10

Sophie's next baby was born six months later, and was a girl. From the first, she was a handful, colicky and given to screaming at an irritatingly shrill pitch. Evan and Sophie baptized her Evelyn Mae, after Sophie's mother. The child quickly became Em's responsibility, thereby creating the first real difficulties between her and Rufus.

In those early months, Em secretly wet-nursed Evie Mae, as everyone called the baby, along with Annie. It was the only thing that would quiet the infant for more than a few hours. The effort so taxed Em's strength that she lost her appetite and nearly became ill.

Rufus, seeing his wife becoming unaccustomedly thin, now grew furious at the whole arrangement. He again insisted on speaking to Grant about buying his family.

Em, desperate to keep their marriage a secret, arranged a short visit to the plantation, seeking Daughter's help. This time, the woman gave her a brew and a supply of its ingredients. The tonic worked like magic. Em was able to regain the ability to eat and soon was as plump as before.

Rufus would find that freedom was much more elusive for his wife and child than it had been for him. At first, he argued endlessly with Em about approaching Grant with an offer to purchase both her and their daughter. Em would always respond that she was fearful for his safety. Secretly, she also feared the unknown thing, freedom, itself. Rufus had his work, in which he took great pride. Em knew she was an excellent servant; she could not envision herself without her occupation either. However, she also understood that for

Rufus the situation of having a slave for a wife was nearly intolerable. There was no possibility for a real home life. She still could only stay with him for one full night a week. Her solution was to spend almost all of those nights in lovemaking. This kept Rufus satisfied while they were together. It did not, however, change his desires nor alter his ultimate goal.

Over the ensuing years, their weekly couplings eventually produced more children, four sons. All of Em's later deliveries were so much easier than her first that she was able to have each baby in her own room, by herself. The boys were sturdier than their sister had been and, as each was born, she was able to leave him with Rufus, slipping away to nurse him several times every day.

The boys eventually grew into helpers for their father. Rufus, however, feared constantly for their freedom. He kept his youngest sons with him but hidden from public view by restricting them to the workrooms in the rear of the shop. As each reached the age when he could begin training, Rufus would let the boy spend part of the day out front. The next youngest child would then become responsible for his baby brothers while the shop was open for business.

The years passed in the Grant household with few remarkable events. Sophie had two more sons, their births conveniently coinciding with the births of two of Em's sons. Em continued the secret wet-nursing for Sophie's babies as she had for Evie Mae.

As for Evie Mae, she was growing into an exquisitely beautiful, headstrong and spoiled little girl. The problem was that she was much too smart for a girl; in fact, she had an insatiable thirst for information and a hardy constitution. Running, climbing, throwing things and challenging her brothers occupied much of her interest. What she loathed were baths, being clean and keeping quiet. Both Sophie and Em struggled with her, and soon despaired of ever turning her into a presentable young lady.

When she was 10 years old, Annie was given to Evie Mae as a companion and personal maid. Em had tried to teach Annie household skills and, while Annie tried obediently to follow her mother's example, she never mastered her mother's flair for creating wonderful illusions with flowers and fabric. Nor could Annie duplicate her mother's powerful organizational abilities. Annie did, however, manage to exert influence over her young mistress in areas where both mothers had failed utterly. Evie Mae had by this time developed a for-midable temper and had not outgrown the tendency to throw tantrums. She could scream herself purple in the face, frightening all the adults with the threat that she might burst a blood vessel. Annie, however, was unmoved by this ploy, particularly when it followed the news that a much-needed bath was ready and steaming in the kitchen. If young mistress was not willing to take a bath, then Annie would not spend that night in young mistress's bed, pro-tecting her from bad dreams. For Evie Mae was from babyhood beset with night terrors of one sort or another. Annie had been put to bed with her in an effort to calm the child, and it had worked wonderfully. Evie Mae could not go to sleep without her. Once in bed, she treated Annie like a "lovey," hugging and cuddling the girl, usually for the whole night.

Now Annie used Evie Mae's need for her nighttime presence whenever she had to force her mistress to do something distasteful, like bathe and put on clean clothes, or sit still in the parlour, on those few occasions when she was to be presented to guests.

When they were both 14, Annie was presented with the challenge of having her mistress "come out" in Baltimore society, a signal that suitors could call on Evie, who by now had dropped the Mae. For her part, Evie knew all of the eligible young men; she had beaten most of them in races or other games. Because she was so determined, Evan had given in to Evie's demands for an education and had allowed her to be tutored along with her brothers, both the older one and the two younger. She had a remarkable head for figures, and a powerful memory; she could recite whole Bible passages and do sums in her head more quickly, even than her father. By now, she was also stunningly pretty, small, with a complexion like a Dresden doll. Every young man in Baltimore did, in fact come to call. Sunday afternoons were always taken up with male visitors, sometimes two at a time. And Evie was ruthless in her humiliation of these would-be suitors. If she could not, as she secretly wished, possess the social freedom of a man, she would make every man who came pay for the privilege of courting her.

Annie watched her mistress' behavior with a mixture of curiosity and loathing. She didn't particularly care if she was rude to suitors. But she could not fathom Evie's continued hatred of baths. And she deeply despised sleeping with Evie, particularly during her "monthlies." In fact, whenever that time of the month came round, Annie would make up a pallet outside Evie's bedroom door if her mistress balked at taking a bath before bed. The threat of the pallet usually worked, but on those rare occasions when Evie was obdurate, Annie would take the bath herself and sleep outside the door. It did not matter how much the girl called to her, cried even, Annie held fast. On one such evening, after bawling loudly for half an hour, Evie threw open the door and delivered a resounding slap across Annie's face, causing her nose to bleed.

"You awful snippet!" Evie screamed at her, "Come in here at once!"

Annie neither answered nor moved. The blood spurted from one nostril and ran between her tightened lips.

Evie was instantly contrite. Throwing her arms around Annie's neck, she tried to pull her into the bedroom, but the girl would not budge. Annie was almost a head taller and weighed more than Evie. And she physically recoiled at the dead fish smell emanating from her unwashed mistress. Perhaps, for the first time, Evie smelled it too because she never again refused Annie's insistence on a bath.

It was just about this time that Rufus made the decision. By now, he had grown weary of Em's excuses. If he never approached Grant, he would never be able to claim his wife and reveal his family. During one of her regular visits, he confronted her. "I have saved about £100. On Sunday, I intend to visit Mr. Grant and make him the offer."

Em was horrified at his proposal. She knew well enough how Grant would react to Rufus' revelation of his relationship with her, much less his offer. Grant would have him whipped—or worse! Then Grant would demand *his property*, their sons. Casting about desperately for something that she could say to Rufus to counter his decision, she took both of his hands, forcing him to face her.

"Rufus, please! If you suddenly appear at the door, Master Grant will surely have you arrested before you can make any offers. What will become of your business, and the boys? Why not let me continue to handle this. You cannot simply demand that he sell me and Annie. We are worth much more to those people than £100."

"How do you know what you are worth to *those people*? I think *they* are worth more to *you* than I am—or our sons!"

The words hung in the air between them. Rufus stood with both feet planted apart. An almost unbearable rage had come over him and was now making the blood pound in his head. At the same time that he so desperately loved this woman, he knew that, if he could not have her free, he would have to let her go. Em was thunderstruck at his outburst. Her beautiful eyes widened, and then brimmed with tears.

"How can you say such a thing?" she cried. "Have I not done all I could to protect you and our children? Do not our sons know their mother? Who nursed them, each and every one until he weaned? Am I not here to nurse the baby as well? Who brings food, clothing, money even, whenever I can?"

Rufus knew every word she spoke was the truth, and that pained him even more. Em had done all this and more; she had given him sons to carry on his name and the business. Oh why could she not lust for freedom for herself and Annie as much as he did?

Now they were at an impasse, for Em and their daughter were probably so far out of his reach that he could never save enough money to buy them. Moreover, in Maryland as in the other southern Colonies, White owners frowned on the practice of allowing freedmen to buy their families and remain in the community. Even if he were not jailed for touching Em without her master's permission; even if he were somehow to acquire a sum that Grant would accept, they would all have to leave Baltimore, and perhaps the Maryland colony. His business would be ruined, for no White man would give him a fair price for it. And he could not hope to reestablish himself in another area as profitably and with no competition.

Hopelessness planted itself deep in Rufus' heart. Its bitterness poisoned everything he had loved in Em. One Thursday afternoon, he came in from the shop for dinner. The boys were seated around the table already eating.

"Where's your mother?" he demanded of his eldest, Rufus Junior.

"Mama's upstairs, gettin' ready t' leave," the boy replied, without even looking up from his plate.

Rufus exploded. "Why are you at the table without your Mama watching you? What kind of manners have we taught you? You don't eat without your parents!"

He turned on his heel and took the stairs two at a time. Em was in the front bedroom. She had just finished nursing their youngest, and he was already toddling out of the door. He grabbed at Rufus' leg as his father passed, missed and sat heavily. Almost immediately, the baby picked himself up, backed himself downstairs and ran to join his brothers.

Rufus was beyond rage. He stood staring at Em; she already had on her bonnet and cape. "Where are you going?" he shouted. "It's only midday!"

"Mistress Grant is entertaining this afternoon. I must get back early." She realized, even as she spoke, that it was the wrong answer.

Rufus's hand found one of his heavy shoes while she was still speaking. Had she not moved quickly, it would have struck her squarely in the head. Em stood stock still for one eternal moment. Then she calmly walked past him, down the stairs and out the front door. Aching, he watched her go, unable to follow her or stop her or bring her back.

Em could not return even though it meant cutting her ties with the boys and abruptly weaning the baby. The following week, she called Annie to her and instructed the girl to take two bundles to the cooper's shop. Annie had never visited her father or her brothers, although Em did tell her about them once she was old enough to understand the need for secrecy. Her mother expressly forbade her ever mentioning their existence to *anyone*.

Annie became the mid-week visitor, bringing provisions and little-used cast-off clothing belonging to Grant's sons. She used her new duties as an opportunity to get to know her father and brothers, young Rufus, Frederic, Samuel and Marcus, not yet a year old.

In 1757, a free woman did take up residence in Baltimore, and Rufus promptly made her acquaintance; her name was Ruth Sampson. A widow, she came as a traveling milliner, offering to make fine hats for the wives of the gentlemen. In less than two months he proposed and she accepted.

It was a marriage without passion on Rufus' part, but Ruth didn't mind. She was seeking security, not romance. He was kind to her, solicitous even, and he made few amorous demands. A barren woman, she took to Em's boys as though they were her own. She also welcomed Annie's continued visits. And she never questioned the whereabouts of the children's mother or why she never came to see them. Ruth knew, without needing to be told, that the freedom of Rufus's boys rested on *her*, and not a slave, who was their mother.

One afternoon that summer, a quiet tapping came at the Grants' kitchen door. Annie was preparing a bath for Evie and heard the knock. When she opened the door, she was thoroughly surprised to see her father standing there, hat in hand.

"Please fetch your mother," he said quietly.

He seemed strangely formal. Annie took to her heels, running, which she knew was forbidden in the house. Something in Rufus's face had made her feel that she needed to find Em quickly. She almost ran into her mother in the rear parlour.

"Annie! You know better!" Em's soft voice had an edge.

"Mama! Poppa's here!"

Annie was so breathless that she forgot to whisper. Wordlessly, Em swept past her daughter and out to the kitchen with Annie following as closely as she dared.

At the sight of Em, for a moment, Rufus despaired of his mission. He had not laid eyes on her since that day in his house, and he had put out of his mind how beautiful he found her. But the moment passed almost as immediately, driven out by his grief.

"It's Frederic. He has died."

Em fainted dead away.

Frederic, the second son, was his mother's favourite. And he adored her. He had been a dimpled fat baby who nursed lustily and seemed always to have a smile for everyone. Even as a little boy, he relished the role of big brother to the younger ones, and he could make up delightful games that kept them entertained for hours.

The illness that took him at the age of eight had begun with a slight fever that rose quickly, followed by swellings behind both ears. Ruth had nursed him diligently, sitting up with him through the worst nights, when both the fever and the pain in his neck made rest impossible. Rufus had been beside himself, for there was nowhere for him to turn for help. Together, they watched as the child grew worse. On the evening that he died, Frederic called out for his mother just once before slipping into a deep sleep from which he would never awaken.

Annie found her mother's reaction to Frederic's death more than puzzling. Once Em had been revived, she coolly thanked Rufus for bringing the news and sent him away. Then she returned to her duties without so much as a glance in her daughter's direction.

For her part, Annie was devastated; she began crying, quietly, because she knew better than to do otherwise. She would continue to cry silently for weeks after. Em shed not one tear that anyone ever saw. But privately, her heart, broken over Rufus's betrayal, died with her son.

Chapter 11

QUEBEC (1800)

*A*nika's ease of possession completely overwhelmed the Munsee chief. He had seen a few powerful shamen in his day, but none so intimate with spirits that they could call on them at will. No wonder Great Bear depended so on her guidance. Tekenna realized that he had become quite intrigued by this woman, and he wanted very much to speak with her, alone.

But custom demanded that he, at the very least, seek Great Bear's permission, and he would need her son present to interpret his request. Then, should it be granted, River Otter would have to be there to translate while he and Anika conversed. Both requirements presented problems. Tekenna did not want to signal his interest in Anika by making any kind of special request that would put the Unkechaug chief or his son-in-law on alert.

So, during the communal evening meal, taken outdoors around a huge fire, the Munsee chief began a casual conversation with Anika, all the while directing his questions to River Otter.

"Your father was a free man?" Tekenna wanted to know. "How is it that he did not simply claim his family as is his right?"

River Otter translated the Munsee chief's question directly into English, his voice flat and hard. As he had expected, the man had no understanding of this kind of slavery. He wished he could answer for himself, but the chief was obviously waiting for Anika's response.

She and River Otter exchanged a long glance. At length, Anika answered, also in English.

"Son, explain to the chief that White men believe they have more rights than anyone else. My mother's master would never have allowed my father to have her, or me. And he would have taken my brothers as well. He had the law on his side in this matter. My father could lay no claim to either his wife or children."

River Otter's Lenape translation completely silenced the Munsee chief. Yes, it was true that, in his own experience, whenever he had encountered them, White men always seemed able to claim that the "law" was with them, especially when it came to the concepts they called "property" or "religion." So this woman, Great Bear's wife and the powaw of this village, had been a slave. And not even her free father could save her.

Later, during the storytelling in the longhouse, Tekenna asked Anika to take up her narrative.

"Tell us more about your masters."

Everyone waited expectantly for this part of the tale.

COURTSHIP AND MARRIAGE - 1758 Phillip and Evie

Phillip Hamilton was, perhaps, the most interesting of Evie's suitors. To begin with, he was not a Marylander; his home was New York. As the only living heir of a successful tea and provisions merchant, Phillip had recently inherited his father's business. And, as his mother had been dead some ten years, he was now without any family encumbrances.

In the autumn of 1757, he found himself in Baltimore harbour, having sailed down the coast on one of the ships that regularly put in at various Colonial ports. It was actually happenstance that had brought him south rather than north to Boston. The actions of a group of Boston merchants, levying a protectionist tax that favoured their local products over British imports coming in from the other Colonies, threatened the very products that his father imported. The town's actions had created a rather volatile situation with the merchants in the other Colonies who were all up in arms, particularly when their ships docked at the port of Boston and their goods were taxed.

The ruffians who worked the docks seemed to have caught the madness as well, even though Phillip was certain none of them understood the economics of the situation. He thought it prudent to investigate other calmer ports, and so he began by docking in Maryland. Here he found a ready market for the good English teas, spices and cloth that were the staples of his family's trade.

On the overcast afternoon of his first day in Baltimore, he happened to be crossing Calvert Street when he noticed a carriage. More accurately, he noticed one of the occupants, an absolutely exquisite young lady who was behaving in a decidedly unladylike manner. It was Evie, having a near fit at being kept waiting while Sophie stopped to greet a friend. Both Evie and Annie were left in the carriage. While Annie composed herself and prepared to enjoy a rare opportunity to watch the sights outdoors, Evie immediately began to fidget. Looking around at her mother, who had alighted to stand at the door of her friend's carriage as they conversed, Evie complained in a voice loud enough for both women to hear.

"I really do not see why we cannot go straight home. I am tired of being outside. Besides, it looks like rain and I will not abide getting wet. I want to leave! Now!"

Evie was screaming by the time she had finished. Annie cast a sidelong glance at her mistress, wishing she had permission to soundly box the girl's ears. Thoroughly embarrassed, Sophie made a hasty excuse and hurried back to her carriage.

Phillip watched as the carriage started up quickly and moved smartly down the street in the opposite direction. He was amused, intrigued even by this high-spirited girl whose face and neck had flushed quite fetchingly during her tirade. She was obviously still rather young and he wondered if she was receiving company yet. Looking around, he noticed that their carriage had been stopped near a dry goods merchant's shop. He stepped inside.

"Help you, good Sir?" the proprietor asked, approaching from the rear of the shop.

"Why yes, in a manner of speaking." Phillip's mind worked feverishly making up a plausible reason to ask the shopkeeper's assistance.

"I am new to this county and anxious to look up a cousin on my mother's side. I believe I saw her drive off just now. Was she in your establishment? A lady, in the company of a younger lady and a servant?" Phillip hoped the man would not ask for a name.

"You must mean Mistress Grant and her daughter. Why, you did just miss them. But no matter, they live just at the end of this street. A short mile's walk in that direction."

The man had been moving toward the front of the shop as he spoke. Now he pointed in the direction the carriage had taken. Remembering that he had come to Baltimore to trade, Phillip spent about half an hour longer with the shopkeeper. When, at last, he took his leave, he had negotiated a rather profitable deal for some Chinese silk.

Now armed with a name, Phillip made it his business to find out as much as possible about the parents so as to arrange a suitable means of gaining an introduction to the daughter. This proved less of a problem than he had feared. One of his business contacts in town was a patient of the doctor's and offered to introduce Phillip after the next Sunday services.

Evan liked Phillip immediately. The young man had spunk and ambition, much like himself when he was starting to make his fortune. More importantly, Phillip had inherited his father's profitable business. The fact that he came from a town known for its rudeness and wild ways did not trouble Grant at all.

Sophie, however, was greatly troubled. Evie was her only daughter and Sophie wanted her to marry a local young man. That the girl had shown absolutely no inclination toward any of them, and Sophie knew this, did not keep the worried mother from objecting to Phillip. She, herself, had never been anywhere but the Carolina coast and Maryland. For her, New York might as well have been on the moon.

When he first came to call, Evie sized up this potential suitor, deciding that he was good-looking and fairly clever, though Evie was sure he was less so than she. Moreover, he had a business, which also, piqued her interest. There was much she was sure that she could do with a business, even if it was not hers directly. Secretly, she had begun to worry that her father might try to marry her off against her will, possibly to one of the older men who had lost a first wife. Knowing Evan, Evie was certain whomever he chose for her would prove to be an idiot. She decided, quite coolly, that, if she had to marry someone, Phillip was a better choice than most. And moving to New York would get her away from the social restrictions of Baltimore. So, when the inevitable proposal came, Evie was ready with her answer.

Phillip could not believe his luck. Here was easily the most beautiful young lady in Baltimore agreeing to be his. The courtship, however, had to be brief; he was needed back in New York within the fortnight. Sophie became so distraught at this news, coming as it did on the heels of her daughter's announcement of the engagement, that she took to her chambers for a week. This effectively left Evie free to decide on an early wedding that would allow her to join Phillip as soon as he could purchase an appropriate residence.

Planning Evie's wedding would become, primarily, Em's responsibility. Outwardly, she seemed unchanged, as efficient as ever in her duties. Neither Evan nor Sophie had noticed the strangely vacant look that came into her eyes whenever she was not actively engaged in a task.

Annie, however, knew something was wrong with her mother. Em was no longer the warm, concerned woman to whom she could turn whenever she needed to. Now, when Annie approached her mother, she found the shell of a woman, one who mechanically provided *things*, a mended frock, the evening meal, a bundle to take to Rufus' shop. Em seldom spoke to her daughter other than to give instructions. To the rest of the household staff, she had even less to say. By now, all of them knew what Ben had suspected about Annie, and, of course, they all kept silent, especially around Em. Now, they surmised that she had learned of some tragedy involving Annie's unknown father, and everyone sympathized with her unspoken grief.

Still, the wedding of Mr. Grant's only daughter had to be the social event of the season. And under the circumstances, Em was faced with the burden of coaxing Sophie into thinking about what she wanted for this most important occasion. Sophie was spending her days either in bed or on a chaise on the bedroom balcony. Em would bring in her meals and use the time to present her plans.

"Mistress, I thought we might have the church service in the morning and entertain the guests afterward in our garden."

"Do whatever you think best," Sophie sighed. "Of what importance are my wishes? Evie has decided to marry that *person* and go live in that dreadful place!"

Sophie could not move her thoughts past her daughter's defiance. Em treated her indifference as permission and began laying plans for Saturday morning nuptials followed by an elaborate garden party.

It was a glorious morning in June, when Evie and Phillip were married in the Calvert Street Anglican Church. On that same night, the wedding night, Phillip made his first visit to Annie's room.

The reasons had naught to do with Evie's personal hygiene. Annie had made sure her mistress was clean and sweet, even though she had no idea about what happened in a marriage bed. Neither was Phillip disappointed with the appearance of his wife's body. Naked, she was even more beautiful than he had imagined.

In fact, it was Evie's passion that, at first surprised, then frightened him more than he cared to admit. Whereas he had anticipated taking his time and teaching a bashful bride about lovemaking, Evie literally pounced on him as soon as they were in bed. Crawling on top of him, she covered his face with kisses; then abruptly bit him, first on the neck, then on his tongue, drawing blood. As they began, she wrapped her legs around his waist the way a common trollop would. When she reached her first climax, she screamed so loudly that he expected the entire household to come crashing through their bedroom door. Finally, she allowed him to remain in her only long enough to satisfy herself again. Afterwards, she ordered him to his side of the bed and warned him not to crowd her. Almost instantly, she was sound asleep.

Phillip was left feeling strangely unsatisfied until he remembered that Annie was in the small room just next door. Slipping soundlessly out of the bed, he eased open the door between Evie's bedroom and the adjoining hallway and let himself into Annie's sleeping quarters.

The click of the door latch awakened her. A small voice in her head warned, "Someone's in my room!"

Annie had barely digested the thought before she suddenly found herself flat on her back, pinned to the bed and being pressed under a man's weight. Terrified, she had squeezed her eyes tightly shut as the assault began. Now she opened them and found herself face to face with Evie's brand new husband! Phillip quickly covered her mouth, cutting off the scream.

"Hush now," he hissed. "I won't hurt you!" Even as he spoke, he was trying to force his fully engorged penis into her.

Instinctively, Annie clamped her legs together as she struggled futilely to get out from under him. But she was no match against his determined efforts. By the time Phillip realized that she was not going to submit easily, he was much too far gone to stop. In his passion he nearly ripped her apart.

"Why did you not stop your thrashing?" he whispered harshly, trying to catch his breath. "Now you are all bloody!"

Phillip stood up, suddenly ashamed at the sight of the trembling, disheveled girl. He let himself out, tossing back the admonishment, "Clean yourself up and say nothing about tonight."

For a long time, Annie lay on the soiled bed unable to move. When she did finally try to sit up, she was struck by a wave of nausea so intense that she barely made it to the slop jar in the corner. It felt as though she were disgorging her whole insides. Finally, she went into a spell of dry heaves followed by hard coughing. When that ended, she could finally breathe and move. And, for that moment, she felt clear, as though she had vomited up the worst of the horror. She stripped her bed of the bloody sheet and spent the rest of the night on the bare straw-filled mattress ticking, hiding under her worn coverlet. Sleep, however, was out of the question; she was much too frightened that he might return.

Her fears were well founded. After that first night, whenever Phillip and Evie made love, Annie would receive a midnight visit as well.

The second time was the very next night. Although Phillip warned her to lie still and not fight him, she was still so tender that his movements caused nearly excruciating pain. She struggled almost involuntarily, whimpering the whole time.

"Please, Master," Annie moaned at one point, "It hurts so!"

"You are being quite tedious!" Phillip told her angrily. "You make things worse for yourself!"

She so desperately wanted to ask someone for help, but there was no one. And she feared Evie's wrath should the girl find out. Just when she was most in despair, help came from an unexpected quarter.

Em approached her daughter late one afternoon. Taking her hand, she drew Annie out into the back yard. "Master Hamilton has been to your room, has he not?"

Em still had hold of Annie's hand. The poor girl hung her head; large tears gathered in her eyes and began to drop, forming small wet depressions in the dust at her feet.

"Yes, Ma'am," she answered in a small voice.

The mother's lips tightened. "Well! We shall just have to see to it that he cannot give you anything."

Annie began crying wildly, now completely terrified. "Mama, what can he give me?" She imagined her body covered with hideous pox-like eruptions.

"Just hush now. I mean, a baby. We do not want that."

Em drew her daughter into her arms, something she had not done since Frederic's death.

Annie was not much comforted by the idea of a baby either. Em, however, assured her that there was someone who could prevent her becoming pregnant.

Within the week, Em had prevailed upon Evan to send both her and Annie out to the farm to complete a project in the house. Once there, she went to find Daughter. This time the woman brought with her a leather pouch filled with what appeared to be black dirt.

"Roung onc't month, befo' hunnuh staht bleedn', tek'n mix-up dis yeah wi' watah 'n drink it." (About once a month, before you start bleeding, mix this with water and drink it.)

Annie had never seen or heard anyone like Daughter before, and she was too dumbfounded to remember her manners. It was Em who took the pouch and thanked the woman. Daughter fixed her eyes on the young girl for several minutes, looking her up and down. With an approving grunt, the woman nodded once, then walked away.

At fifteen, Annie had grown into a young woman who, although she had some of her mother's features, clearly looked most like herself. Like Em, she was long-legged, with a full bosom. But Annie had narrow hips that made her appear slim. She was sloe-eyed, with skin the colour of rubbed walnut and a head full of fine, kinky hair.

Annie's hair had, for years, given Em the most difficulty. It broke easily if combed too vigorously; so she learned early on to treat Annie's hair gently. Still, her daughter had to be presentable, so she took the time to train the hair into first three, and then as the girl grew older, four plaits. The process involved a thorough washing, followed by carefully greasing Annie's scalp with rendered fat. Em would use some of Sophie's flower-scented water in the oils that she combed through her daughter's hair to soften it before sectioning and deftly creating underhand plaits.

By the time Evie married Phillip, Annie could oil and plait her own hair just as well. And to Phillip, the warm sweet smell of her hair was completely intoxicating. This served only to increase his desire and the frequency of his visits to her bed.

Fortunately, Phillip did indeed leave for New York shortly after the wedding with the promise to return before the end of the summer to take Evie and Annie back with him. Once he was gone, Annie made sure to take the first dose of Daughter's potion under Em's watchful eye.

But by the end of the second month, Phillip had returned to Baltimore to fetch his wife and servants. He immediately arranged for them to move into a town house on Crown Street, then the location of some of the "better" families of New York. Within two more months, Evie was pregnant. Annie continued taking her monthly dose and now kept an even more careful watch for her own menses. And Phillip's nocturnal visits continued.

Evie did not suffer pregnancy with any amount of good graces. As she grew larger, her temper grew more foul, especially at the prospects of being confined to the house, as ladies in her condition were expected to be. Evie would have none of it; she regularly ordered the carriage and went out, scandalizing the ladies in her social circle by appearing at teas and musicales.

During a short outing to do some shopping, when Evie was nearly due to give birth, she got into a heated argument with a merchant over the price of his crockery. She returned home only to immediately go into labour. Two hours later, half the town knew about Evie Hamilton. As soon as the contractions became painful, she started screaming, and not with anything approaching the normal cries of women in their first pregnancies. Evie emitted horrible yells that rose to shattering shrieks as each contraction began and intensified.

Outside, neighbours and strangers gathered in knots, wondering at the terrible caterwauling coming from the tenth house on Crown Street. Phillip, scared nearly out of his wits, sent immediately for the doctor, then made his escape. When the poor man came on horseback because the summons had been so urgent, he found an hysterical young woman, no where near ready to deliver and no master to give directions to any of the servants. All of the household staff had taken refuge in the kitchen in a vain attempt to get away from the noise. And Phillip had made his way to the Queen's Head Tavern on Pearl Street and sequestered himself in one of the back rooms.

Annie, left in charge, had rushed her mistress into bed at the first hint of labour. Now she tried vainly to calm Evie, believing, rightly, that so much screaming was not going to benefit either mother or child. Evie, in her rage and terror, had completely lost all ability to be rational. When Annie let her squeeze one of her hands whenever the pain became intense, Evie applied so much pressure that the hand became bruised and swollen.

"Try to get her to breathe normally and stop that damned yelling!" The doctor, now having shed his coat and waistcoat, rolled the sleeves of his shirt and tried to examine Evie, who roughly kicked his hands away.

"You must get her quiet! She retards the child's birth by refusing to breathe properly!"

Annie grabbed Evie by both shoulders and shook hard. "Mistress Evie! Listen to me! It's Annie! You have to stop this! At once!"

Evie by now was near apoplexy. Hideously swollen veins stood in her forehead and swelled her neck to almost twice its normal size. She seemed not to hear Annie; she drew breath only to bellow and screech.

"Shall I strike her, Sir?" Annie hoped he would say "yes."

For an instant, the doctor considered it. "No. You may leave a mark. If you can cause her to bear down, while yelling, I may be able to deliver the child."

Annie climbed up onto the bed. Pulling her mistress into a sitting position, she positioned herself with her back against the headboard and propped the young woman in front of her, resting on her knees. With each scream Annie forced Evie forward. At first, she balked, fighting to lay prone again, but Annie held her fast.

At length, the movement of the contractions forced Evie to bear down, to push with all her strength. On the second such push, during which Annie was sure that this had to be the last, that Evie could not survive another, the baby came forth, followed immediately by the afterbirth. Evie promptly fainted. The doctor glanced up briefly, in obvious disgust, and proceeded to examine her thoroughly. When he was satisfied that she was not about to die, he turned to Annie, who had leapt from the bed and caught the baby as it slipped out.

"You have saved your mistress's life and that of the babe as well. Tell your master that I will be sending the bill."

With that, the doctor rolled down his sleeves, donned his waistcoat and coat and took his leave.

Annie, left with this unfamiliar being, tried to remember what her mother had done after each of her brothers was born. Em had always kept her out of her room during the actual births, but Annie would stay by the closed door, stealing peeks through the keyhole. Now she remembered that the newborn needed to be cleaned and wrapped up. One of the maids had left a pitcher of warm water and a basin on the window table. Annie carried the slippery thing to the basin, plopped it in and poured water over it. Once cleaned, she wrapped it in a large towel and laid the baby on the bed next to Evie. Realizing that she had no idea of the sex, Annie briefly unwrapped it and determined that it was a boy.

Eventually, Evie awakened and sat up, looking around for her child. Annie solemnly placed the infant in his mother's arms, carefully watching her reaction. For a moment, Annie feared that she would violently reject the baby that had caused her so much pain. She stood ready to snatch the child away if Evie made a move to harm him.

"Oh you sweet thing! How beautiful you are!" Evie practically gushed with joy and obvious pride. "Oh look, Annie! See how marvelous he is!"

She had opened the towel and was freely examining every part of her son.

Annie released the breath that she had been holding. Evie announced that she was hungry, ravenous really.

"Let me go fetch you something to eat. Then I shall send Master Phillip up to see his son."

Annie had no intention of going anywhere near Phillip herself. Instead, she sent a boy over to the Queens Head to let him know that it was now safe to come home.

When she discovered that most of New York was whispering about her "shameful performance," Evie, at first, feigned haughty disdain. Privately, however, she realized that she had lowered herself in the eyes of people whose respect she would need, including Phillip's. Apparently, most ladies were actually able to give birth without screaming the house down. She decided to make it her business to pay attention to any woman she thought might be expecting.

The Ladies' Presbyterian Guild gave an afternoon tea once a month, on Thursdays, in their meeting house on Wall Street. Although she wasn't a member, Evie had always liked to attend, just to keep up on the society gossip. Now, however, she planned to watch for Mildred Stewart, an acquaintance, she'd noticed at the last tea. Mildred had appeared wearing obviously loosened stays, a sure sign that she was expecting.

As soon as Evie espied the now-obviously pregnant woman, sitting very close to a table laden with sweet cakes, she hurried over. "Oh, Mildred, how are you doing? You look so well, though I can see that you're almost due!"

"I do feel quite well, thank you." Mildred reached for a cake as she spoke. "This isn't my first, you know. But then, all my confinements have been remarkably easy. My husband brags that I could drop a baby while he slept, and never even waken him." She gave Evie a supercilious smirk and helped herself to another sweet.

Evie was sure Mildred was making fun of her, to her face! It was going to take all of her composure just to listen to the woman without slapping her! Nevertheless, she just had to find out how to heroically bear the agony of childbirth.

"It never hurts you?" she said, after pausing to collect herself, "That is amazing! I do wish I knew your secret."

Mildred must have recognized Evie's desperation. Her expression suddenly softened. "Of course it hurts, my dear!" Now, she leaned in close and whispered conspiratorially, "The key is to breathe *with* the pain, not fight it. You'll find that the breathing will make the whole affair much easier."

Evie's eyes widened in astonishment. But this was so simple! She knew how to breathe, and if that was all she needed to do to bear that awful pain, well, she could certainly do it. Evie reassured herself that, by the time she was ready to have her second baby, her courage would put even Mildred to shame.

Chapter 12

QUEBEC (1800)

A spell of mild weather settled in, creating almost liquid evenings. In the longhouse, the young women who set up for each night's council fire left embers banked in the fire pit; there was no need for the added warmth of a full blaze.

Seated beside Tekenna, Great Bear had said very little since recounting the Unkechaug history and that of his own family. But he had become acutely aware of Anika's growing effect on the Munsee chief. And why not? Even now, after all their years together, she owned his heart completely by her mere presence. Suddenly he spoke up. "Tonight, Anika will tell you the story of her first husband, River Otter's father."

Surprised, Anika looked questioningly at Great Bear. He had never asked her about this part of her life. She thought he understood how painful the memories were, how dear. But Great Bear's eyes pleaded with her not to refuse him. Clearly, *something* must have told him to make this request. And so she began....

Osei's Tale

The sloop *Mary B* stood at anchor in the deep harbour of New York for the fourth day. Captain James Drake was growing weary of the annoyance of having to wrangle with the locals about unloading his goods. Today, on deck, he was about to descend the gangplank for yet another irritating meeting with the Colonial customs officials. This time, he could be gone for hours.

"You! Will! Come here," he shouted.

A tall young man with almost blue-black skin stepped out of the captain's cabin. He was striking, not just because of how the white shirt he wore appeared almost snowy against the ebony, but because he was so remarkably handsome. His were the kind of perfectly proportioned features that village artists in Africa carved into magnificent masks.

He had been kidnapped as a teen, fresh from circumcision, but not yet finished with his manhood rites. Now he was about 25 years of age. Although he had no official title, belonging as he did to Captain Drake, he functioned as first mate whenever the vessel was docked and the captain had to leave for any length of time. This was because, among the many talents he had acquired since his enslavement, the most useful under these circumstances, was an ability to count, cipher and keep books. Should anyone come looking to do business with the captain, Will could take care of him.

Will was the name that his first master had chosen to give him when he was sold in Barbados. His name at birth was Kwesi, because he was born on a Sunday. At his Adinto, Mpuei ceremony, his father, Okera, had named him Osei, which means "maker of the great." After his capture, this became his secret name, one that he never spoke aloud.

On that bright awful afternoon, he and his age group friends, Sekou and Kumao, had been sent just to the edge of the forest to bring wood for the evening fire. It was a dangerous time for everyone, what with people disappearing every day. Mothers could no longer leave their younger children in the care of an older child when they accompanied their husbands out to their distant fields. All too often, parents would return to find the older child gone, kidnapped by strange Black men. Young men and women sent on errands by their parents would disappear, never to be seen again, leaving broken water pots or dropped baskets with spilled contents alongside the road.

The elders who were shepherding this age group through their rites were faced with the problem of protecting the youth, both males and females, in a decidedly unprotected environment. Custom required of both sexes that certain rites be performed in specific parts of the forest. In the past, these youths would have been sent out alone to accomplish the rites of endurance, but that was now out of the question. Still, there were important lessons that the elders taught the young initiates each day after sunset. A quantity of saplings would have to be cut for that evening's fire. It was on such an evening that Osei and his two friends were given this task and sent out together to protect one another. It proved to be a costly mistake.

The kidnappers had become efficient at setting their traps. Kumao was caught first, when the men threw a large net over him. Osei, seeing his friend drop to the ground, struggling and screaming for help, ran toward the net, intending to cut it, and anyone who tried to interfere, with his machete. He never heard Sekou's warning shout, as another man felled him with a rock to the back of his head. Sekou took to his heels, but there were men hiding behind trees in front of him. Two tackled him as he ran past.

When he awoke, Osei discovered that he was chained, neck and right ankle, with his hands tied in front, as were his friends. Six of the strange men each took a length of chain, both in front of and behind the three youths. One of the men motioned for them to get up. Without waiting for compliance, others, in turn, yanked the hapless boys to their feet and marched them deeper into the forest.

Osei and his friends had never been this way before; indeed, no one in the village used the forest as a thoroughfare. Every sensible person knew that the forest was the home of evil, angry and vengeful spirits. Osei, already terrified, became more so as he saw the forest close around and above them. Perhaps these men were somehow in the service of bad forest-dwelling spirits and were taking people away to appease them.

At length, they reached a place where the trees thinned and light could penetrate. By now, the sun had set and the sky above them was violet, a deeper blue near the horizon. Here there was a fairly wide road filled with over one hundred chained men and women. Apparently, many kidnappers had been working the region, for Osei saw several people from neighboring villages whom he had met at market festivals and other celebrations. Kumao was chained right behind him, but Sekou was dragged away toward the front of the crowd. It would be the last time Osei would ever see his friend.

This group was sufficient in number to be marched straight to the coast, a trip of about ten days. The kidnappers spoke no language that any of the captives understood, so naturally they used sticks and fists to move the frightened men, women and children. Osei counted at least a dozen children, both boys and girls, under the age of ten.

One mother had a child, just learning to walk, on her back. The poor thing kept crying and trying to get down. One of the kidnappers, apparently believing the child would slow them down, snatched it out of the woman's shawl and hurled it into the brush beside the road. The mother screamed and fought to get loose from the ankle chain that connected her to the person just in front. Of course, she could not, but the commotion brought the entire line to a halt.

The kidnappers now argued among themselves, apparently disagreeing as to the wisdom of their companion's decision. Finally, they seemed to settle on some course of action. One of the men went back to the woman, who was howling and refusing to move. He released her leg chain and pulled her out of the line. Holding her by the neck chain, he marched her into the brush. Osei craned his neck, trying to watch where they were going, but the collar prevented him from turning his head far enough to see. As the line moved off, there was a loud crack, a sound he had never heard before. The man who had taken the woman away now trotted quickly past him, alone. Osei suddenly felt a sickening lurch, as though his insides were about to come up. For the next two days he was unable to stop himself from shaking. As he walked, he could feel the trembling, either in one leg or both hands. Sometimes it was his head that would quiver up and down.

Each night, the kidnappers would stop to rest the group, since the captives had been forced to walk all day. This was also the only time that they were given any food. At first, Osei found it impossible to eat the cassava paste, just a handful smeared on each person's palm. He would wait until whoever was doling out the food had moved off; then he would rub the sticky mess into the ground.

It was not until he began to feel lightheaded that he realized he was starving himself. At this point, he made the important decision to stay alive. Once thus resolved, he found he could swallow the foul-tasting handful if he just held his breath until it went down.

Kumao, also had been unable to eat, and Osei realized he would have to convince his friend to do likewise.

"Why? Why should I try to live? I don't want to be a slave in some foreign village!"

"For me!" Osei pleaded, "Do it for me! Don't leave me alone!"

At last, Kumao relented, but at his first attempt to get the mess down, he nearly choked. Thereafter, he avoided the food as often as he swallowed it.

The line of captives eventually reached the coast. Here, as at many other points along the Atlantic, was a huge fortress, a stone castle with turrets and dungeons. Osei's group was led down a series of steep stone steps into a wide hallway with several heavy wooden doors spaced along each wall.

By now, the Black captors had disappeared to be replaced by what Osei was certain had to be *lepers* in strange clothing. Like lepers, these men had sickly white skin; some of their faces were pock-marked. And all of them stank horribly. Osei, at first, became dizzy at the stench whenever one came anywhere near him.

One of the white-skinned lepers produced a massive iron ring of keys and opened one of the doors. Beyond was a single large, window-less room into which all one hundred or so captives, still chained and bound, were herded. There was no source of light other than the torch carried by the leper with the keys. When he slammed the heavy door and left, the room was plunged into pitch blackness. Osei thought that he had suddenly gone blind. Someone screamed in terror and immediately the whole group was shrieking.

Several of the lepers returned to investigate the noise. One opened the door and threw a flaming torch into the room, barely missing the nearest captives. A man worked his way close enough to the flame to expose his rope-bound wrists to the fire. Once his hands were free, he snatched up the precious light before it went out on the floor. By moving the whole line of captives around the perimeter of the room, he was able to locate a crevice into which he could wedge the torch, thereby creating enough light to calm the others and reveal the details of the room.

The scattering of straw on the stone floor seemed to be moving. As the group became aware of this, someone investigated by kicking at the moving straw with a free leg. A gigantic rat scampered across the floor, followed by five or six more. Osei had never seen such creatures, but others of the captives seemed to recognize what they were. A woman cried out. Suddenly, everyone was leaping about, trying vainly to escape the dozen or so rats that ran across people's feet and leapt against their legs. By now the rats had become agitated, and for hours the captives were kept in a state of consternation by their efforts to avoid being bitten.

For Osei, this was a completely new terror. A rat bit Kumao, who screamed and grabbed hold of him. Vainly, he searched around with his bound hands for some sort of weapon to protect them both. But, of course, the captors had made sure to clear the holding rooms of heavy pieces of wood or loose stones.

After an interminable length of time, the lepers returned, swinging open the heavy door and creating enough light to scatter the miserable rats. They now herded everyone out into the wide hallway. Two especially foul-smelling lepers moved among the captives, examining those who had been bitten. These, they unchained and separated from the rest of the group. When they reached Kumao, Osei tried to clutch at him as the two unchained the youth. By now, Osei had some idea of the fate that awaited those who had been separated out. He felt the familiar lurching in his gut, along with a growing sense of panic, as he watched his friend being led off with the others. Once they had turned a corner and were out of sight, the remaining captives were marched in the opposite direction.

The hallways seemed endless, now opening into wide galleries with high, vaulted ceilings, then narrowing into tunnels that closed in on the captives, forcing them to walk the passages sideways. Suddenly, there came a breeze and the scent of salt air. Osei, having never been near the ocean, could not identify the smell other than to realize it was fresh and came from the outside.

A cry of fear went up from those at the front of the line as they approached an open door and the source of the breeze. For here was no land, only open sea, and far off, a large strange boat unlike any seen before. The first eight captives were released from the others and taken out through the door. Once they were gone, another eight were taken, then another. When it became Osei's turn, he was the eighth in line. One of the white-skinned men roughly pushed the first person out into a waiting boat; everyone else followed, tumbling from behind. Two more Whites were waiting in the boat, oars in hand. Without pausing, they began to row. Osei righted himself and looked around in horror. The castle, the land, everything was moving away! They were taking him to the giant ship! For the first time, the enormity of his plight struck him full force. If they took him away on a ship, how could he ever find his way home? He would never see his village nor anything else familiar again!

The experience of the ship and the Atlantic crossing became the subject of Osei's nightmares for years after. The captain apparently did not believe in "tight pack"—the practice of having them lie spoon-like, belly to back—that allowed twice as many captives to be transported at once. It had proven "wasteful of crew and cargo"; too many of both died. And so his ship was "loose packed." This meant that the men and boys were allowed just the width of their prone bodies, but manacled to those on either side.

How easy it was to stop living chained in the bowels of that ship! The two men to whom Osei was chained both died on the same night. Somehow, each man turned to face Osei just before death claimed him. The first vomited violently for several hours. Then, when he had nothing left to disgorge, he gagged on his own bile and died, staring at Osei, as though, somehow, he should have done something to help. Once he realized that the man was no longer breathing, all of his courage deserted him and Osei started screaming hysterically. Of course, no one came, either to investigate his cries or to move the body. He screamed wildly until he was hoarse and spent, then turned his head away from the twisted face and now-clouding eyes. On the other side of him was a similarly contorted face with eyes nearly bulging; a thin line of yellow spittle ran out of the fellow's open mouth, forming a sour-smelling pool on the boards beneath the dead man's head.

When Osei screamed again, a voice, speaking Akan, come out of the darkness. "Young one, have courage! We are all here with you. Do not give in to fear. You are not alone."

The strong, comforting maleness of the voice calmed him immediately. His heart had been pounding almost sickeningly; he now felt it slow to nearly a normal cadence.

Osei was never able to identify the man who had spoken to him on that horrible night. Daily, the crew would bring the captives up on deck to wash off their soiled bodies and force them to dance for exercise. He used the opportunity to whisper in his language to each man as they shuffled past each other, but no one seemed to understand him. Finally, he decided that the man did not want to alert the crew to any communication that might go on among the captives.

Once he had figured this out, Osei ceased his attempts. But he held fast to the message, vowing never to give way to such terror again. This was his next important decision. He would do all that he could to stay alive, keep silent in front of the Whites, and crush fear within his heart. He made one more decision. "I will get free one day and find my way back home."

The Atlantic passage took six to ten weeks, barring bad weather or some other misfortune, such as an outbreak of disease among the crew or an epidemic or insurrection among the captives. Osei's ship suffered neither, reaching the West Indies in eight weeks and docking at Bridgetown on the southwestern coast of Barbados. Only twenty percent of the cargo had been lost to illnesses, madness and suicide, manageable numbers by the captain's reckoning.

They were marched off the ship and herded under a huge thatched roof supported on wooden poles. Here White men stripped everyone, men, women and the few surviving children, naked and threw buckets of fresh water over them. Next, the Whites took each one and greased him or her with an unguent that smelled sharp and unfamiliar. Finally, they were led to an open pen. Here the captives were sold in lots. Fifty went to one man who owned three sugar cane plantations well away from the coast in St. Thomas Parish. Osei was part of this group.

By the mid-1700s, Barbados had become one of the most successful of the colonies in the production of sugar cane; as a result, the island had a population of slaves that greatly dwarfed that of the Whites. To keep this dangerous, restive number under control, the Colony had enacted a series of slave codes that restricted the movement of unaccompanied Blacks and prevented the use of drums or musical instruments by slaves. These codes were successfully enforced by the presence of garrisoned British militia all over the island.

Osei got his first glimpse of soldiers as he stood on the block, awaiting sale. He especially paid attention to their firearms. The White men on the ship had also been armed, but with rusty guns that he never saw fired. These soldiers were marching in formation just outside the slave pens. Suddenly, for no reason Osei could fathom, one man shouted something; the entire line shouldered their weapons and fired into the air in unison. The resulting noise and smoke were impressive. He continued to watch this group in hopes that they would repeat the performance. It took his mind off his own circumstances; he did not want to think about what might happen next.

Each new experience thus far had held unique terrors and Osei expected more of the same. The trip upcountry to the sugar plantations was a forced march of several days very reminiscent of his capture. Even the landscape seemed familiar, though reversed. This time a wide clear road came first, then dense forest as they moved north. At each new day, Osei awoke fearfully, braced for an assault. However, the trip itself was uneventful, if difficult.

The man, who had bought him, Josiah Farth, lived on the first plantation, the one established by his father early in the 1700s, when sugar production had begun to be quite profitable. The elder Farth had bequeathed his entire fortune and holdings to his eldest son, in the British tradition, effectively cutting out Josiah's two younger brothers. One, Anthony, soon left Barbados for Jamaica, but the youngest, a somewhat slow-witted but loyal soul named Thomas, remained on the plantation in Josiah's employ as overseer.

Josiah himself always made the trips to Bridgetown to purchase the slave gangs; Thomas could not be trusted with money. However, when it came to keeping slaves in line and getting the most work done, there was no one better. Thomas had sole responsibility for the slaves on the second and third plantations. These were simply vast fields of sugar cane that soaked up the lifeblood of every man forced to work them. Under Thomas's steady cruelty, the gangs worked almost non-stop, year-round. When men became ill or fainted, or even died in the fields, he would force the line to work around them and leave them behind. Many men rotted where they had died because no one could go back to claim the bodies. Not even nightfall stopped the work. Thomas would have massive bonfires built alongside the fields and the gangs would work by the lurid orange glare. With regularity, Thomas employed the whip, thumb screws, the cage and, in the case of an attempted runaway, partial amputation. His lack of imagination rendered him incapable of any nuanced response to a slave's infraction. If the offender was already injured or sick, Thomas's punishment usually killed him.

It was into this hell that Osei fell when his gang reached St. Thomas. Upon arrival at the southern plantation, Josiah turned the fifty men over to Thomas, just as night was falling. Without allowing the exhausted group to rest even briefly, he marched them ten more miles to the second plantation. The only salvation for them on this first night was that he had not been able to order the bonfires before leaving the fields to meet his brother at the main house. And, in his absence, nothing was ever done. Slaves took full advantage of such infrequent opportunities to sleep and eat. It never occurred to Thomas that, were he more humane, there would be less of a need to constantly purchase more slaves.

Interestingly, Josiah rarely visited the second or third plantations. He did realize how destructive and expensive his brother's methods were, and he felt ashamed, privately. But his sugar cane crop consistently earned him a handsome profit. Perhaps, he reasoned, it was better not to interfere with something that worked so well.

It took more than a month for Osei to acclimate himself to the almost twenty-four hour, seven-days-a-week schedule. Thomas allowed work to stop only when he, himself, could no longer remain awake on his horse. He kept his pistol loaded and ready. Sometimes, when he dozed in the saddle, he would awaken with a start and fire the gun in a reflex action. On a few occasions, a hapless worker had been killed in this way.

Shortly after Osei's arrival, Josiah finally learned about one of these accidents and decided to intervene. Summoning his brother to a meeting, he closeted them both in his rear study.

"It has come to my attention that this is not the first worker thus killed. My God, man! Do you know what it will cost me to replace him?"

Thomas was genuinely surprised. He had no idea how much each worker cost and he barely understood his brother's anger.

"This is of no importance. I did not mean to kill the slave. I-I fell asleep on my horse and something startled me awake. I just shot without looking."

"Exactly! You fell asleep because you tried to keep working through the night." Josiah's voice gentled. "You need sleep. Let the work stop after darkness falls."

The idea seemed completely novel. Thomas had been taught to believe that one did not ever allow the work to stop. "If I am not in the saddle, they will not work."

Josiah realized he had to repeat his order. "Exactly. You will stop work at night. Both you and the slaves are to sleep."

This exchange may have saved the lives of Osei and the other fifty men purchased with him. By allowing the men the night for rest, however, Josiah had unwittingly also permitted time for planning. Osei, ever on the alert, soon realized how poorly protected the plantations were. He did not know how widespread the local militia were deployed, but he was certain he wanted to try an escape.

One night, shortly after the night planting stopped, he rose from his blanket on the plank floor of the slave barracks that housed all of them and slipped outside. The sky was starry, with a full moon illuminating trees and buildings. Just as he was about to bolt for the woods that circled the clearing, a figure stepped into his path.

"Young one, do not be hasty; there are dangers here you do not know of."

The man spoke Akan. Osei's heart fairly leaped in his chest. Was this the one who had spoken to him on the ship?

"Come. Follow me."

The man moved off in the direction of the forest, the exact direction that Osei had thought to take. It seemed the man knew where he was going. They walked for some distance, arriving at last at a clearing. Here, the man turned and faced the youth. Steadying Osei's face with one hand, he looked closely at the small scars on each cheek.

"You have the markings of a priestess' son. Had you completed your rites?"

"No, sir, only my circumcision."

The man said nothing for several minutes. He seemed to be pondering a course of action. "It is important that you finish," he said, finally. "Even in your absence, the people of your village need for you to complete the rites. We will do them here, as much as we can. Do you know the plants, their names and what each is used for?"

Osei thought hard for several minutes, trying to remember what he had learned at his mother's side. He wanted to answer truthfully. "Yes." He spoke confidently, "I know them all."

…When Osei was four years old, his mother, Yaa Akua, explained what his position would be, once he reached manhood. As a priestess' son he had been destined for the role of village healer. From that time forward, she took him with her to gather the herbs needed for the various healing rituals. Each plant had its own properties; some were beneficial when used to treat certain illnesses, but dangerous in others.

Akua made up games and used songs, proverbs and stories to help Osei learn the plants' names. His favorite tale was the one about how the turtle, Akykyigie, tricked Nyame, the god of the sky, into revealing the mysteries of the tobacco plant. Then there was a song that he learned with the names of four powerful herbs, along with the parts of the body that each could treat.

Osha is a root. Use it for the throat.
Quassia is bitter. It will make the stomach better.
If you take the oat seed, your mind and heart will be at ease.
Wild yam root is best of all. It heals the whole body.

They remained in the clearing for most of that first night. The man had Osei repeat the names and properties of every herb that he knew. Just before dawn, the man led the way back to the barracks.

"Go in and lie down. The horn will soon blow for the day to begin. I will meet you tonight outside."

Over the ensuing weeks, Osei and his nameless, faceless elder met each night. First, the man instructed the youth in how to recognize plants with similar properties to the ones he had learned back home. Once the pharmacology had been mastered, the elder then questioned him about treatments.

On this particular night, as they sat facing each other in the clearing, he had Osei describe what he had witnessed.

"My mother began taking me to healings when I was eight. I watched her deliver babies too; some came feet first. And once, she stopped the bleeding in a woman who had just had a child. She saved that woman's life."

The elder got to his feet. "It is not enough that you were there! What did you see her do? Tell me about the healing first."

Osei could see himself back in the sacred grove just beyond his village. This clearing, located in the center of a thicket of low brush and tall palm trees, was where all ceremonies of healing took place. Here, he learned specific drum rhythms, sitting beside his father and the other men who played while Akua danced. For it was through the dance that healing took place. Most times, his mother would have the patient dance as well, if the illness was not in the limbs. If this was not possible, the patient's more able family members would dance instead.

In the most extreme cases, where the illness would not yield to any other treatment, Akua would dance alone, powerful dances that drew on all of her energy. She would give herself over to the Goddess completely, becoming Her vessel and summoning all the ancestors of the village to this place. In these special cases, pregnant women and small children were not permitted to be present, lest an errant spirit take possession of the baby in the womb or the unprotected soul of a young child. Osei, however, was expected to watch and learn. He even had his own small version of the *eguankoba*, a barrel drum played with sticks, which had been made by Okera.

Yaa Akua had not been born into a family of village healers. She was chosen as a young girl when she became possessed during a religious festival for the Goddess of Rivers and Streams. Once she became an *akomfo*, a chosen one, the priestess who served the Goddess trained Akua as her successor; as such, the girl was expected to also function as a healer. Her spiritual role did not, however, interfere with her secular one. She married Okera, son of the most prominent family in their village. He was also, by then, a prosperous young farmer who already had several fields under cultivation and only his widowed mother to support. Akua bore him three children, Osei, the eldest, and his two sisters, Binta and Afi.

At Osei's birth, when he received his *Akeradini*, his birth name, Akua was suddenly given a vision, that whoever became his first wife would have to succeed her as priestess. And so, she kept close watch on him as he approached manhood and began to notice the village girls in his age group.

"You must be able to do the dances from memory, and without the help of the drum. Watch me."

The elder spoke up so suddenly that Osei was momentarily startled. He had forgotten he was actually talking to someone; the memories had simply poured out. The man stood up and began an undulating movement. His feet stomped out a complex rhythm that Osei recognized as *Tigale*, a healing dance. Suddenly, the clouds parted and the man was in moonlight so bright that for the first time Osei could make out his contours, medium in height and slightly stocky in build. The man bent and twisted, all the while keeping the beat with his feet.

Osei could feel himself being drawn into the dance's rhythm. He rose and began to follow, first the steps only. But then he felt the drums beating somewhere in the center of his chest, and his whole body became involved in the movement.

At some point, the elder stopped dancing and stood still, watching him as he whirled, first in one direction, then in the other. Osei could hear an entire orchestra of drums, whistles and gongs now. He began a series of high leaps, his arms shooting out before him with each jump that carried him completely around the circumference of the clearing. When he reached the elder, the man stopped him with one outstretched hand. Osei collapsed at his feet.

"You have danced enough. I can see that you understand how to invoke the drums. Tomorrow night we will give you your final marks."

Osei was much too tired to ask the man what he meant. He was happy to get back to the barracks and to sleep for the few hours remaining before first light.

Each morning, when they would assemble in the cane fields, Osei would try to determine which of the men was his unknown elder and benefactor. But the work was too difficult, allowing for no breaks. Thomas had been prevented from working them through the night; now he felt he had to make up for the lost hours during the day. Osei had almost despaired of identifying the man. But on that next night he finally saw his elder's face.

In their customary spot the man built a small fire, which he surrounded with wet leaves so it would not spread. He ordered Osei to sit close beside it. Then he took from his waistband a small piece broken from a machete blade. First, he sharpened it on a stone lying nearby; then, holding one edge with some of the wet leaves, he heated the blade until it glowed. He squatted in front of Osei and ordered him to open his mouth.

"You cannot cry out. Bite hard on this!"

The elder placed a stick of wood between his teeth. Osei could feel his heart beating heavily as the man brought the white-hot blade close to his face. Even with his jaws immobilized, he let out a loud squeal of pain at the first cut. When he felt the blade slicing his other cheek, he nearly fainted. The man looked closely at his handiwork, and Osei could see him clearly, even through the tears. His was the classical Akan face, broad through the cheeks, with a wide mouth and slightly prominent red eyes.

"Now your scarification is completed. You will be recognized as a healer by all who understand such things. Most important, your village is protected."

At the end of the month, on a moonless night, the man handed Osei a small leather pouch attached to two long leather straps.

"Inside this bag are your totems. They represent the ancestors' spirits who must carry you through this life. When the time comes, you must pass them on to your successor. Until then, you must wear them against your body and never remove them."

The man instructed Osei to strip naked and fasten the straps around his waist so they could not be taken off. Then he left the youth alone in the clearing with a large needle and heavy thread. Osei struggled with the sewing until he had succeeded in overlapping the ends of the straps and attaching the stitched belt around his waist, just above his hips. The bag seemed to settle into his body, almost as though it were another appendage. By the time he had pulled on his breeches, he could no longer feel it. The initiation ended with his receiving his totems.

Chapter 13

*J*ames Drake hated Barbados. Or more accurately, he hated the planters who ran the Colony. His dream now was to sell his ship and purchase a plantation on the island. To that end, he had traversed its length and breadth looking for a suitable place far enough from the sea that he could no longer smell its salt. On one of his frequent stops in Bridgetown, he had begun to inquire about land but had met with very little success. By this time, about 100 planters controlled almost all of the most profitable sugar cane operations, and they also held power in the Colonial government. Because Captain Drake could command little in the way of hard cash, since his fortunes were tied to his ship and cargoes, he needed a substantial loan, even to begin discussions toward a purchase. As it turned out, the established planters were not interested in competition, especially from an insubstantial upstart who knew nothing about the sugar cane industry. He found his efforts blocked at every turn.

Drake had been at sea almost continuously ever since he'd first signed on as cabin boy to the captain of a merchant ship sailing out of Bristol, England. He was only twelve at the time, his father just dead of consumption and his mother saddled with seven more children, all younger. When he'd left home, it was with the understanding that, if he returned, it would be with sufficient resources to support his mother and siblings. In any event, his leaving had meant one less mouth to feed.

Within seven years, he had worked his way up from ordinary seaman to first mate on a ship called, prophetically enough, the *Mary B.* By this time, although he was still quite young, he had acquired both considerable seamanship and the confidence of the sailors with whom he had served.

However, the real money lay in human cargo. As an outcome of the War of the Spanish Succession, called the Queen Anne's War by the British, England now held a thirty-year monopoly on the African slave trade in all of the New World's Spanish colonies, thanks to the Treaty of Utrecht, signed in 1713, which transferred the *Asiento*, the special agreement between Spain and Portugal that had allowed Portugal those exclusive rights since 1517. The British colonies of Jamaica and Barbados both needed an almost endless supply of laborers for their huge plantations. And, once independent merchants in London, Bristol and Liverpool were granted permission to run private slave trading companies, there was, now more than ever, a need for ships working the African coast. Literally hundreds were being turned out in the ship-building centers of Liverpool and Bristol.

This meant real opportunity for Drake. On his twenty-third birthday, he was given his first command, the *Amadee*, a cargo ship outfitted with two between-decks large enough to transport up to 400 slaves. With a crew of fifty, drawn mainly from men who had served with him on the *Mary B*, Drake set sail on his maiden voyage, bound for the coast of West Africa, the first leg of a three-part journey that would eventually bring them back to England.

Within two weeks, the *Amadee* had reached Angola. Here, for almost two hundred years, a lively trade in slaves had been going on between *factors*, traders working for local African rulers, themselves originally recruited by the Portugese, and the European ships moored off the coast. By the time Drake and his first mate, an older fellow named Andrew Blellens, came ashore, there was already a full ship-load of captives awaiting a sale. Some 350 men, women and children had been penned in *baracoons*, open-air stockades completely enclosed by high walls made of strong fixed wooden posts.

The factor, a brown-skinned weasel of a man named Madou, grinned continuously as he led Drake and Blellens through the baracoons, cheerfully pointing out the excellent condition of his captives. They had all been bathed, their bodies so greased with shea butter that they literally gleamed in the bright morning sunlight. The women and children were weeping openly, some crying out quite loudly. Each man stared sullenly at Madou whenever the factor came anywhere near him.

Drake began feeling nauseous and inexplicably angry almost immediately. He fought both the nausea and the rage, reminding himself that while ugly, it was a lucrative business and that this nasty mulatto was just doing his job. Drake's iron control paid off, as he was able to purchase the whole lot for fifty bolts of silk, twenty cases of rum and several crates of arms, including muskets and ammunition.

Everything went well during the loading of the captives onboard the *Amadee*. Blellens had previously served on several slavers, as such ships were called. He saw to the securing of the men on the lower of the two decks, with the women and children stowed above. Fortunately, there were many fewer of them than men, so they could be chained loosely enough to be able to sit up. The men, however, were forced to lay back-to-belly on the hard platforms built around the walls, down the center of the hold and enclosing all three of the ship's masts.

About two weeks out to sea, a terrible storm came up. This was the worst possible fate for a ship fully loaded. The *Amadee*, with her added weight, already rode low in the water. The waves, lashed to a towering frenzy, swept over her decks and poured down into the holds. Drake shouted to Blellens to unchain the cargo and bring everyone up on deck. The man screamed back that to attempt it was to risk drowning himself.

With the captives doomed, Drake now decided to save his men and the ship, if he could. But the storm threw up yet another horror. A waterspout formed just off the bow, creating a whirling vortex that swung the *Amadee* around to her portside, and threatened to sweep her completely out of the ocean. Blellens was able to reach one of the lifeboats and release it into the water just before the ship became air born. Those of the crew who were thrown free would have had to fight the waves, now taller than any ship, to reach that boat. Most did not; they were crushed as the whirling water suddenly released the *Amadee*, smashing the vessel into the sea.

Although he had not expected to be alive, Drake broke the surface right alongside the lifeboat and was able to pull himself onboard. He spent the next frantic minutes hauling in those few men who had survived and were able to reach the boat. He looked for Blellens but could not find him. The loss grieved Drake greatly; the man's quick thinking had saved his captain and five of his mates.

Eventually, the survivors were rescued by a passing cargo ship bound for England. Once the ship docked in Liverpool, Drake reported his experience to the trading company that had owned the *Amadee*. The merchants, surprisingly, understood the situation. After all, the company did have insurance against just such misfortunes. They even offered Drake a second vessel. However, the experience had turned him against ever again directly participating in the trade.

Years later, he would say that, while adrift with the five that did survive, he had made a heartfelt and solemn pledge to God never to deal in human cargo on the high seas again.

Drake's subsequent voyages were to ship goods, cane and rum between the West Indies and North America. He was never, by any stretch of imagination, in favour of abolishing the African trade; slave labour was too much needed. Nevertheless, he discovered that he was made increasingly uneasy by the horrible conditions he constantly witnessed in his travels across Barbados and on his visits to the other islands. He knew he could own and manage a plantation in a more humane manner and still command a profit.

By now, he had fallen in love with the island. It had happened the first time the *Mary B* had put in at the Bridgetown harbour. Every one of her sailors had crowded on deck, anxiously waiting to get ashore where prostitutes of every hue were shamelessly parading their lush wares up and down the docks.

Drake, watching the show from his position on the bow, had noticed a lone woman in an open-top sedan chair. She was wearing a pale lime-green gown with sleeves slit to the shoulders and an extremely low-cut bodice, revealing skin the colour of coffee, liberally laced with cream. Her face, at first, was almost completely hidden by a wide-brimmed hat trimmed with ribbons that matched her gown. Two Black chairmen, bared to the waist, had suddenly appeared and taken up the chair's support poles. Just before they'd started off, the woman had abruptly turned in Drake's direction, and his heart had skipped several beats. Even from so great a distance, he could see that her face, framed by masses of black curls, was exquisite. Her coming down to the docks, essentially unescorted, had advertised her availability as a lady of the evening. Drake was now determined to have her, at least for this first night.

The captain had searched for the woman in every parlour in central Bridgetown, giving her description to each Madam, and receiving barely civil negative replies for his pains. Drake had been about to give up when he'd come upon a rather ornate but dilapidated house on the corner of an alley just off Swan Street. Nothing about the place indicated that it might be a house of prostitution, but Drake knocked at the door, nonetheless. He was shocked when the lady, herself, answered.

"Bonjour, Monsier. Que désirez-vous? (May I help you?)" she asked, her voice, a contralto so rich and heavy that he felt drenched in its honey.

For a full minute, Drake could not even answer her. Now face-to-face, she was even lovelier. The flickering lamp, hung just inside the entryway, cast shadows under her softly curved cheekbones and full lips, while its flame was reflected twice in wide golden-green eyes. Her thick black hair sprouted wild from a high rounded forehead and cascaded over her shoulders.

"Monsier?" she repeated.

"Forgive me," he stammered, "I don't know your language. Do you speak English?"

"But, of course. How can I help you?" Her English was so thickly accented that it sounded almost exactly like her French.

"I-I-...wondered whether you—were accepting visitors. I am a man of some means—and—I-... would like—would love to avail myself of your company this evening." Drake delivered this last part in a rush.

"Vous êtes seul? Sorry, are you alone?" She glanced behind him quickly as she spoke.

"I am."

She waved him in, standing aside. He noted that she had yet to smile or even answer his request. Wordlessly, she led the way up a long winding staircase and opened a pair of French doors, the paint peeling on both. Even in the dim light, Drake could make out the contours of a room dominated by a tall four-poster bed draped in yards of sheer fabric. The woman faced him squarely, lifting her chin almost defiantly.

"I cost 50 francs, sorry £50. You will pay? Yes? I cost as much as a White whore because I sleep only with White men."

Drake was momentarily taken aback. She sounded so very hostile; perhaps she meant him harm. But his urgent desires, coupled with her heart-stopping beauty, trumped all caution.

"Yes! Of course! Only, please, tell me your name."

She answered, "Lizette." Then she opened the front of the morning gown she'd been wearing, letting it fall to her feet. Naked, she approached him, gently took his face in both hands and kissed him.

The next morning, before returning to his ship, Drake promised to provide enough money for her to give up her profession if she would agree to be his mistress.

Lizette had laughed, "Do you know how many White men have made me the same promise? If you return, then I will consider your request!"

For James Drake, that night had driven out all thoughts of any other woman. He did not care who or what Lizette was; she had to become his and his alone. And if that meant finding the means of completely supporting her, he would, by acquiring his own plantation.

The name, Josiah Farth, was well enough known around Bridgetown to come to Drake's attention. Everyone knew Farth came to town whenever he got word that a ship had docked and was to unload a cargo of captives. At the time that Osei was bought, the captain had been among the White men watching, but not taking part in the auction. Drake took note when Josiah completed the sale and then ambled over to the planter as he was signing papers. Removing his hat, Drake addressed him. "Good afternoon, Mr. Farth," he said pleasantly.

Josiah turned to face the man. He did not like being interrupted in the midst of business dealings, and his response was brusque. "Sir, I believe you have me at a disadvantage. You seem to know my name; yet we have never been introduced."

"Oh please forgive my familiarity, sir. I intended no disrespect. Your name is well-known across Barbados, as is your face. Please allow me to introduce myself. I am James Drake, Captain of the *Mary B*, docked a little south of here."

Drake nodded in the direction of his ship, a trim, well-outfitted sloop. Josiah was somewhat mollified by the man's tone and by the fact that he did seem to posses some means. He knew something about ships, spending as much time around the docks of Bridgetown as he did. Many of the vessels that survived the Atlantic crossing arrived in terrible condition even with the cargo intact. Looking more keenly at the *Mary B*, he was impressed by what he saw. He now desired to attend to the man standing before him.

"Forgive my ill temper," he smiled. "This business does require a strong stomach at times. As I have concluded here, perhaps you will join me in an ale."

He gestured toward a nearby tavern and Drake immediately took him up on the invitation. The two men spent about an hour chatting amiably over several ales. Drake displayed a sympathetic, yet unobtrusive interest in the difficulties of managing several sugar cane plantations. And Josiah soon found himself describing how his brother's treatment of the slaves forced him to replace them more often than he would have liked. By the time he was ready to leave, Josiah felt comfortable enough with James Drake to invite the captain to visit his plantations whenever the man happened to be travelling in the vicinity.

Three months later, Drake made a trip to St. Thomas Parish. He had made it his business to find out about Josiah's holdings in more detail and from several sources. He knew, for example, that the man had needed to replace almost 100 slaves over the past six months, due almost entirely to maltreatment by the brother, who, word had it, was a half-wit and a brute. If Josiah Farth allowed this kind of waste, perhaps his finances were such that an offer to relieve him of some land would not be entirely unwelcome.

The road that led to the main plantation was nearly choked with underbrush. As the horse he had rented for this part of the journey picked its way gingerly over twisted vines and rotted stumps, Drake wondered how on earth Farth was able to make so many trips to the coast, let alone get his harvest out. He reached the main house around noon time, hot and thoroughly drenched in sweat.

Josiah was delighted at the visit. He lived alone in the large, somewhat dilapidated house that his father had ordered built. The original design was supposed to be fashioned after the grand manor houses in England, but on a much smaller scale. However, this proved impossible to translate in a tropical climate, so the designer had resorted to something employing columns and verandas surrounding a two-story structure with many rooms and hallways. Since his father's death, Josiah had paid little attention to its upkeep; his efforts were all directed at keeping the plantations profitable.

Drake showed no interest in the house but immediately asked if he could see the plantations. Together, he and Josiah rode out to the cane fields where Thomas was directing the day's labours.

As Drake sat in his saddle watching the rows of men, his eye fell on one. For the life of him, he could not later remember what it was about this one worker that caught his attention, but he found himself watching this particular slave. Suddenly, a cry went up; one of the workers had swung his machete too close and laid open his own leg. Almost immediately, the young man Drake had been watching leapt over several rows of the ripe cane and reached the injured man. They both disappeared. Thomas shouted to the line to keep working as he spurred his horse into a gallop, heading toward the rows of cane that now hid both men. Drake immediately followed, with Josiah bringing up the rear.

Osei saw the accident happen and reacted immediately. He remembered how he'd been taught to stop bleeding in a gushing wound. When he reached the downed man, it was clear that an artery had been cut; already he was losing consciousness. Osei grabbed a handful of leaves and, applying pressure with both hands, crushed the leaves against the open gash. He was still at it when Thomas reached them.

Had Thomas been alone, he would have ordered Osei to leave the man and get back to the line. Moreover, the mere presence of his brother and a guest was not what stopped him, but rather the fact that Drake interrupted him as he was about to speak.

"My word! What's that slave's name, the one treating the injured one?"

Thomas was completely baffled at the question. None of the workers had names; the idea of naming them had never occurred to him. It was Josiah who answered, trying to smooth over what he realized could be perceived as an un-Christian practice.

"That one is called William—after William the Conqueror." The name amused him, once he'd said it. "We call him Will, for short."

"Please call to him. I want to ask him where he learned to treat wounds."

Josiah turned to Thomas, who had been trying to follow the dialogue but had become confused when his brother said the name.

"Thomas, call to Will. Tell him we wish to speak with him."

Of course, Thomas did no such thing. There was nobody in the field by that name.

"What is it you wish me to do?"

"Just call out, Will. Goddamn it!"

The direct order helped clear up some of Thomas's confusion. Whoever Will was, Josiah wanted him to call him. He did so promptly.

Osei looked up in the direction of the shout. He recognized the man who had purchased him and who was now gesturing him to come. The third man he had never seen before. By now, he had been joined by two of the injured man's companions, one of whom he showed how to continue the pressure on the wound as they carried the man out of the cane field. Osei then got to his feet and made his way to where the White men were.

"That was very quick thinking, Will. Where did you learn to minister to wounds?"

Osei looked respectfully at the strange man. He had picked up only a few words of English: *come, go* and, of course, *get to work*. He had no idea what the man was saying, so he watched his face and tried to read the tone of his voice.

"Can you speak any English?"

Osei, unable to understand any of these words either, was completely at a loss. But he knew that somehow this man could be his salvation. He struggled to remember any English that could help him now. Suddenly one word came to him; he tried it, hoping it would make sense.

"Little." He watched for a reaction.

Drake laughed heartily. "Well, if you only speak a little, you can learn more. I am very much in need of a man who knows some medicine. Josiah! I want to make you an offer for this man!"

"I could not let him go for less than £250."

"If you can see your way clear to come down a bit, I have £150 hard cash with me right now."

The offer of cash was irresistible. Since the last harvest, Josiah had been chronically cash poor, as were most of the planters, once they had invested their profits in land and equipment upkeep. He agreed to the sale, adding that Drake should have supper and stay the night. He then ordered that Osei be secured in the kitchen.

Osei spent the best night of his life since his capture. Josiah had only one house servant, an old cook. This man made Osei a pallet of rags in the corner next to the back door. The length of chain that Josiah had Thomas use with a leg iron was enough to allow Osei to relieve himself outside and bury his waste away from the kitchen door. Cook gave him some of the same fare that was being served to the White men in the dining room. Osei was even able to wash his hands in the pail by the door before eating.

The following morning, Drake set off for the coast with his new acquisition. He felt he had made a successful contact in Josiah, particularly now that he had seen the man's holdings. The visit had also gained him some important information about the Farth brothers that he was sure would serve him in the future. It was clear, for instance, that Josiah drank entirely too much for his continued health. His swollen face was perpetually red and all the veins in his nose were broken. Thomas, though not yet out of his twenties, was entirely incapable of caring for the property and almost certainly stood to lose everything once his brother died.

Drake made up his mind to visit St. Thomas each time he docked in Barbados. He was certain that, in a few years, if he timed his visits carefully, he would be in a position to pick up some of Farth's property at a much better price than he could ever get now while the man was alive.

And so, Osei went back to sea, this time as a sailor. In his first year, he learned English well enough to communicate. More importantly, he learned his new master so well that he could anticipate what Drake needed almost before the man could voice it. And he set about to learn how to decipher the marks the White men made on paper and in their books. These magical marks seemed as important to Whites as his totems were to him. Osei decided that anything the White men valued, he would master and use to his advantage.

Chapter 14

NEW YORK (1761)

*O*n this particular day, Phillip had decided to take a walk down to the harbour. Several ships were anchored at the various wharves; his eye fell on one rather trim sloop with a Black man on deck. Something about him caught Phillip's attention, so he stopped to study the man.

Osei noticed the well-dressed White man standing on the dock near the gangplank who had been looking in his direction for some time. Somehow, the gentleman made him uneasy and he decided to move out of the man's view. As he did so, Phillip mounted the gangplank, stopping midway, and called to him.

"You! Where is the captain of this vessel?"

Osei turned to face the man and immediately dropped his eyes. "That would be Captain Drake, Master. He is away presently doing some business."

"Can you tell me the nature of the cargo?"

"We carry molasses, aged rum and some goods from various places. If you wish, Master, I can fetch a manifest."

Osei went below and returned with several sheets of foolscap covered with lists of items and their prices. These he handed to Phillip, who scanned the pages, then broke into loud laughter.

"My God! Your captain is a thief! These prices are ridiculously high!"

"Oh no, Master! Those are the selling prices. The wholesale prices Captain Drake negotiates with whoever comes to buy from him. If you are interested, I can help you until he returns."

Phillip studied the lists again. They were written in a neat close hand. Suddenly, he looked up, fixing Osei with a piercing glare.

"If I wanted 30 kegs of molasses, how much would your captain charge me?"

Osei quickly calculated the price at exactly half of what was written on the list.

"So the captain suggests that I set the price of the goods that I buy from him at 50% more than I paid?"

"No, Master. You may set your prices as high as your customers will pay. Captain Drake will charge you half of the written price."

"Can you read?"

Phillip's tone was challenging; the question startled Osei. His sense of discomfort grew into an edge of fear. "I can cipher a bit and copy out sums."

"Did you write this list? Is this your hand?"

Osei felt trapped. It was illegal for slaves to be taught to read in so many places. Actually, he could read all of Drake's business correspondence and was the one who regularly copied the manifests. He was about to elaborate on the lie, when a shout from one of the crew indicated that the captain had returned and was, at that moment, mounting the gangplank.

Relieved, Osei turned to his master. "Master James, this gentleman has come to see you. I gave him your manifest."

Having thus explained Phillip's presence, Osei quickly took his leave and went below. Everything about the encounter unsettled him. And each time he had felt thus, his situation had changed, either for better or worse.

On deck, Phillip found himself face to face with the captain. Realizing he had come on board uninvited, he introduced himself and extended a hand. Drake had been eying him closely. Very rarely did a gentleman board his vessel; usually it was a servant or underling who would make the overtures. Drake suspected the man had ulterior motives.

"Sir, I am Captain Drake. How can I be of service to you?"

Phillip decided to be direct. He too realized how untoward his behavior appeared. Had he intended to purchase goods, he would have dispatched one of the lads from his warehouses with a list.

"Actually, I was just getting a bit of air, my offices are not far, when I spied your man on deck. He cuts a mighty fine figure. Have you had him long?"

"Ah! So t'was Will caught your attention. Yes, he does dress up well. I've had him now for about eleven years. He is my good right hand. Figures and does sums as well as any Englishmen, he does! Knows a bit of medicine too!"

Impressed, Phillip pursed his lips. After a short pause, he asked the question that had been sitting in the back of his mind all along. "I have long needed a man with those abilities. Would you take £1000 for him?"

"Why, Sir! He is easily worth twice that amount!"

Phillip bit his lip and then quickly composed himself. He was on familiar ground here. "I offer you £1500."

"The man's not for sale."

Phillip sighed. He knew Drake would not come down on the price. But the fact that he had named one gave Phillip some hope. This man *was* worth £2000, at least.

"£2000 it is, Sir! In cash. You drive a very hard bargain."

Now it was Drake's turn to sigh. In truth, he had made plans for this to be his final year of sailing. A year earlier, Lizette had presented him with a son. Although Lizette and the baby were presently living in her house in Bridgetown, now he desperately wanted to settle down on his own estate with her and their child.

Fortunately, Drake's suspicions about Josiah Farth had borne fruit just a month before, and he was already about to wind up his affairs in New York. In another month, he expected to be back in St. Thomas, where, he was certain he could afford to purchase Farth's main plantation, at least.

Once he had his land, Will would not be as necessary. Moreover, Drake felt more than a bit uneasy about taking him back. Lizette had seemed *very* taken by Will on the one occasion that he'd come to her house looking for the captain to settle a dispute between several crewmen and the Colonial authorities. She had gone down to answer the knock. When Drake had come out onto the second floor landing several minutes later, she was still standing in the open doorway just staring! By now, Will had retreated into the street where he'd waited, eyes carefully averted. As Drake reached her, Lizette had suddenly come to her senses. She had remembered to kiss him when he took her into his arms. And she'd closed the door behind him.

Although Drake never mentioned the incident, it had remained with him as a nagging, disquieting memory. Nor was he reassured when Lizette began coming down to the docks, ostensibly to surprise him aboard the *Mary B*. Perhaps it would be better for him just to sell Will to a wealthy merchant here in New York. The man would be very well cared for.

"I shall accept your offer—particularly since it is in cash. John!" Drake called out to a mate nearby. "Fetch Will from below."

John returned with Osei. The young man looked decidedly crestfallen.

"Will, this gentleman has made a very generous offer for you that I have accepted. I want you to gather your things and go with him."

At the words, Osei raised his head and looked first at his new master, then at Drake. He said nothing, but his eyes filled with treacherous tears. Drake took his shoulder and turned him away from Phillip.

"We've been together for so long; I daresay he's a bit shaken. Give us a moment."

He took Osei below deck. "Buck up, man! You're going to retire to a comfortable life on land, even before I do!"

Osei nodded dumbly, unable to trust his voice. Of course, Drake had no idea of the real reason for his tears. He swallowed hard and nodded again, indicating agreement.

"Good! Now hurry with your things. Let's not keep the gentleman waiting!"

After Drake had hurried back on deck to finish the financial arrangements, Osei went into his quarters. Here, he cried in earnest, hard, wracking sobs that left him dry and in pain. When he mounted the stairs, carrying two small bundles, he appeared composed; only his reddened eyes threatened to give him away.

Chapter 15

OTTOWA (1800)

K *s-hamps* (Husband)! Why did you force me to tell this tale tonight? You knew I could not refuse. What were you thinking?"

"Anika. We both have been watching Tekenna. He did not like any of my stories. Yet with yours, he becomes more fascinated each evening. He... if he enjoys your voice, it is a good thing for you to do the talking."

"That is not an answer! I could have told any other stories; how we escaped from our village, how I came to be the powaw even—many others! Not this one!"

"Why not! Why do you object to this one? You know my pain. Why can I not know yours? Why can I *never* know what is in your heart? It–it's as though you shield me still! Do you think me too unwell, too *weak*?"

"Great Bear, I never thought you weak! I honor you always. And I 'love' you more than my life."

"There it is. So small an English word, this 'love'. It means nothing real to me! I don't 'love' you, Anika! You are my heart! My blood! My life! This is what I will always feel for you."

"Oh Great Bear! How I wish I had the words to match yours! Do you doubt my heart? Truly, it belongs to you now! But you must remember what I was like when I first came to the village. So sick it took all of Tree Stump's efforts trying to get me well. I don't know if I can tell this story and not get sick again."

"Anika, I think you must try. River Otter has never heard it, and I-I-I just have to hear it too. Ask your spirits to protect you. They will listen..."

NEW YORK (1761)   Osei and Annie

When Osei, new to the household, first saw Annie, his heart fell. She was coming down the hall toward him from the rear of the house and looked distracted. A small frown creased her forehead and she had her head bowed. When she looked up and saw him, she suddenly smiled. Something stirred in him at that smile, a memory of a girl from his village whom he had liked in the innocence of his youth.

Before, when he was still on the plantation, there had been no women, a source of real hardship for the other men. Osei, however, always had running on his mind; he knew that could not include such entanglements.

Once he belonged to Captain Drake, he had tried not to become involved with any of the women he'd meet in their many ports of call. However, whenever the *Mary B* docked in Barbados, Lizette would keep after him, even though she'd become Drake's mistress. And it was she who finally gave Osei his first sexual experience, a hurried, terrifying encounter in her bedroom closet. Osei had expected they would be discovered any moment. Afterward, he resolved never to be alone with her again. He needed to keep Captain Drake's complete confidence so that he could execute his plans for escape. Quietly, he had begun to learn as much as he could about navigation, not to further enrich his master, but to secretly raise a crew of former captives eager to return home, steal a ship and sail it back to Africa.

Phillip's surprise offer to purchase him and Drake's acceptance effectively killed those plans. Now he was faced with the final blow, a young woman whom he found attractive.

"No!" he told himself furiously as soon as he saw Annie.

Osei began to rationalize his refusal to acknowledge any interest in this girl. Being landlocked and restricted to whatever businesses Phillip had purchased him for could not keep him from his dream of escape. Now he would just have to figure out a plan to run away. It would take time, but he had as much of that as he needed. However, he could not take anyone with him.

Phillip's dalliances with Annie put the idea of marriage into Osei's mind. Her room was next door to his in the garret. On his very first night, he heard the footsteps followed by the sound of a door latch being lifted. Shortly thereafter, he could hear Phillip's grunts accompanied by the sound of her sobs. It was the weeping that Osei found unbearable.

In the days that followed, he decided to first approach his new *mistress*. He had learned to read the faces and behavior of most Whites, and he suspected that Mistress Hamilton would gladly agree to his marrying Annie, if that would stop Phillip's nocturnal wandering.

Several days later, in the early evening, Osei tapped politely at the door to Phillip's study. Evie always spent about an hour at his desk after supper, going through his books. When they were first married, she had used the period right after they'd made love to make any requests she suspected Phillip might resist. Her timing was inspired, for he, anxious to have her asleep, and to make his escape, never failed to agree to anything she asked. Evie thus secured her place as unofficial bookkeeper, both of the business and of the household accounts.

"Come!" She was so deeply engrossed that she barely noticed the knock and her answer was perfunctory.

She looked up with some surprise when Osei carefully opened the door. He remained by the open door with his head lowered respectfully.

"Ah! It's the new servant. Well, what do you want?"

Evie's voice was gentler than her words. She had been more than a little interested by Phillip's new acquisition. At first, she had found his black skin repellent, but then she noticed his other features and how generally attractive he was, especially when dressed for service. Now she found herself stealing glances at him when she thought no one else was watching.

"If Mistress Hamilton will forgive me, I have a boon to request."

"A... boon?"

Suddenly at full attention, Evie turned in her chair so as to face him. He was still standing just inside the doorframe, apparently looking at the floor in front of her feet.

"Make your request, please. And for goodness sake, I'm Mistress Evie. You are part of the household now."

Carefully shifting his feet so that he now stood inside the room, Osei paused, took a breath and continued. "I would most humbly request your permission to ask Annie to marry me. She is of an age to bear children, and I would like for her first child to be mine."

The room became still. Although he kept his eyes lowered, he could see all of Evie; he watched her reaction closely. As he had suspected, she was aware that Phillip made trips to Annie's room at the top of the stairs in the middle of the night. But what to do about it had eluded her. Probably her father had done the same with the female servants; perhaps all of the men she knew did it. Now her face started to colour, twin crimson circles blazed on both cheeks.

"Of course, you have permission! Ask her right away! She will not refuse you, I should think!"

Evie's rage was beginning to make her heart pound. She needed to end this interview before her temper exploded. Swinging round in the chair, she waved Osei away. He turned to leave and then turned back.

"Shall I also speak to Master Phillip?"

"Whatever for? I have given the permission. Annie is *my* servant, not his!"

Now he did leave. Smiling ruefully, he made for the garret stairs. He knew this decision to marry Annie had forever dashed his plans. *Running*—the word had ruled his thoughts every day of his life since his capture. Now he pushed it, and the searing pain that attended it, aside.

It was still light, but the china clock on the mantle in the sitting room was striking eight o'clock. Out in the kitchen, Annie was giving Evie her bath. Evie had, in fact, suggested it, which, frankly surprised Annie, who said nothing. She had made the water especially warm since Evie always complained about being cold toward the end. Now both young women, mistress and servant, were silently engaged in the rhythm of the bath. As she lathered her mistress' shoulders, Annie noticed that Evie seemed more pink than usual, particularly her face and throat. Reaching across to wash her back, Annie also noticed the tell-tale vein pumping visibly in her neck.

Now what has her so upset? Inwardly, Annie braced herself for the inevitable outburst.

But Evie remained uncharacteristically silent through the drying off and the trip upstairs to her bedroom. Once at her dressing table, Evie allowed Annie to loosen and brush her hair. It was, perhaps, the best of her features, thick, wavy and the colour of ripe wheat. Instead of sitting on the low stool, she chose the small braided rug, motioning Annie to take the stool. This was the way they had always sat when they were children and Annie was learning to brush and braid Evie's hair.

Evie pushed her knees apart and wedged herself between so that her head nearly rested on Annie's lap.

"I think that you should lock your door from the inside before retiring." Evie delivered this opinion, actually an order, in a neutral voice.

"Mistress knows I do not have the key to the garret door. Master Phillip keeps all of the keys and he says..."

Evie was on her feet before Annie could recite Phillip's speech about how the master of a house should hold all the keys, if he planned on remaining the master. Practically spitting and hissing, she grabbed Annie by both ears and dug her fingernails into the lobes.

"You do *not* belong to Master Phillip! You are *mine*! Do you hear me? And if I say your door is to be locked at night, then that is what shall happen! I will give you the key myself!"

The pain and unexpected ferocity of the attack brought tears to Annie's eyes. She remained, however, perfectly still, so as not to cause herself more damage. Evie would recover momentarily and release her ears, but Annie was certain her mistress had drawn blood. And sure enough, as soon as she saw the bright red drops form on both earlobes, Evie released them and grabbed Annie around the neck, hugging her close, covering her face with kisses.

"Oh my dearest Annie! Why do you so provoke me? You know how I do love you and so hate to hurt you!"

Annie remained as still as before. These were the moments that she had found so very distasteful, especially when they used to happen in Evie's bed. It seemed like she could still smell the dead fish odor, even though she had carefully washed her mistress' most private areas. Evie's strangely passionate embraces never failed to make her stomach catch and her breath stop. She almost preferred the slaps and pinches. Fortunately for them both, Evie always seemed so taken by her own emotions that she never noticed Annie's coolness.

"I know something, a secret!" Evie breathed the words into Annie's ear and then looked at her face. Smiling, she continued. "Will has something to ask you. When he does, I want you to tell him yes."

Annie felt herself growing warm. Of course, she had been completely smitten with Osei. Who would not be? He was the first handsome young Black man she had ever seen up close. She had even gone so far as to hide behind the parlour curtains sometimes, just so she could watch him without his knowledge. Then she would daydream endlessly as she went about her chores, picturing the proud tilt of his head, how his hands seemed so strong and capable, even when they were still. He never took any notice of her. And this seemed right, since she had no sense of herself as someone anyone would find attractive. Instinctively, she knew that Phillip's midnight visits had nothing to do with her appearance, only with her availability and her youth.

Suddenly, Evie seized Annie's face with both hands and held her fast. "After tonight, he will never come to your bed again! I swear it!" This she delivered between clenched teeth, her face inches away from Annie's. Then she kissed her full on the mouth and released her.

Annie had remained seated on the low stool, so that, when Evie stood, she towered over her. Now Annie rose to her feet, reestablishing her height over Evie. That act of standing seemed to break the spell and Evie turned away, once again the pampered mistress.

"I'm tired and will lie down now. Tell Master Phillip I wish to see him before I retire."

Once Annie had helped Evie into the tall four-poster and closed the bedroom door, she found Phillip in the rear parlour taking a brandy.

"Mistress asks that you come see her before she retires." She spoke from the doorway, remaining out in the hall.

Phillip appeared not to have heard her. He was seated with his back to the door and did not turn around. Annie was about to leave, anxious to get upstairs, in case Evie had not simply been teasing her about Will.

"Oh Annie, Annie. When will you learn that Mistress Evie only wants me for one thing?"

He had been sitting in one of two small rockers that could also swivel on their bases. They were the latest furniture fashion in Europe, and he had been able to import a pair. He'd presented them as a gift to Evie after bringing her to the house. Now he swung the chair around to face the doorway and Annie could see that he was quite drunk, the decanter on the sideboard nearly empty.

"Please, Sir. She will not abide being kept waiting."

It had been a risky thing to say and she immediately regretted her choice of words. Usually, Master Phillip was not visibly intoxicated, no matter how much after-supper brandy he drank. In his present state, however, she did not know how he would react to the suggestion that she, a servant, suspected he too feared Mistress' temper.

Phillip rose somewhat unsteadily. Once on his feet, he gave Annie a silent look that promised a long, difficult night ahead; then he passed her. She heard him mount the stairs with heavy footsteps and waited until she heard the bedroom door close before hurrying to the back staircase.

When Phillip climbed the front stairs to the master bedroom, he was seething. "Cheeky wench!" he muttered through alcohol-stiffened lips.

When he was finished servicing Evie, he'd give the girl something to think about! He knew how much Annie disliked his visits. But the realization only reinforced his need to rationalize his behavior. He was not raping her, he told himself. Nevertheless, he had to force himself on her each and every time. And she did cry so pitifully. She rarely made much noise during the act itself, but, whenever he could bring himself to actually look at her, silent tears poured, unchecked, down her cheeks, running under her nose and commingling with the mucus. She never wiped them away, just let them run.

For the life of him, Phillip could not understand why Annie would not simply get used to his visits the way other men said their servants did. It made him both desperate and angry, whenever he saw the tears. In his deepest heart, he wanted her to understand his hunger for her and to desire him as well.

Evie had apparently fallen asleep by the time he reached the room, so he quietly took off his shoes and breeches. He slipped into the bed, facing his wife, watching for signs that she might actually be awake. Evie sometimes feigned sleep until he was just getting comfortable; then she would pounce on him with a demand for immediate, quick lovemaking. This time, however, she seemed to have actually drifted off.

For several moments, Phillip watched her face, so smooth and creamy in the half-light. If only she were as sweet-tempered as she appeared in sleep!

He lost no time hurrying into his pants and shoes. As soon as the bedroom door closed behind him, she opened her eyes and turned on her back, her face as calm as when her husband had been watching her. "We'll just see who goes skulking about this house after tonight!" Her plans were well laid.

Earlier, Evie had found Osei in a rear hallway just as he was about to retire to the garret.

"Call Annie into your room as soon as she comes upstairs. It is important that you follow my directions on this matter. You must ask her to marry you tonight, without fail!"

"Yes, Mistress Evie."

Osei, as always, kept his head lowered as he spoke. She would not be able to see the rueful smile that tugged at the corners of his mouth. So, she had engineered some plot to free her servant from the amorous demands of her husband, Osei thought. For the first time, he allowed himself a grudging admiration for this woman, the first White woman he had encountered, and one with a real mind. He found himself remembering his mother in her role as priestess. Neither her husband nor her children dared question her authority whenever she was serving the Goddess. This woman had that kind of potential, but no societal authority whatsoever. For that single moment, he felt actual sympathy for his mistress.

Osei was waiting for Annie when she got to the top of the garret stairs. He motioned for her to follow him into his room, which was even smaller than hers, little more than a closet. When he closed the door they were face to face. There was hardly space even to turn around; they both had to sit on his narrow bed. He began by introducing himself.

"Please forgive my small quarters. They call me Will, and I know you are Mistress Evie's Annie. I wanted to speak with you."

Annie was completely flustered. She had never carried on a conversation with anyone in her life. And now, here *he* was, waiting expectantly for her reply. For several minutes, she sat there dumbly, her hands trembling in her lap, unable even to look him in the face. Then she remembered Evie's teasing remarks.

"Do you have a question to ask me?" her voice barely above a whisper. "Mistress said you did." The words sounded painfully foolish to her ears, but she could think of nothing better to say.

"Oh, well, yes, I suppose I do." Something she said must have made him smile. "But before I ask my question, would it please you to palaver with me a short while?"

Annie lost enough of her shyness to stare at him. His accent was so strange, and she did not understand the word, palaver.

The sound of heavy footsteps on the stairs startled them both. She immediately recognized it and began to shake. Osei motioned for her to be still. Moving silently to the door, he leaned against it and listened. Phillip lifted the latch to Annie's door. They heard him enter the room and utter a muffled oath when he found it empty. There was a long silence. Then the sound of his footsteps descending. They remained still for several minutes more, waiting for his possible return.

At length, Annie whispered, "Do you think he will come here?"

Osei could see that she was still trembling. Awkwardly, he took her hand. "If he comes, he comes. I have your mistress' permission to speak to you. And, as she has made plain to me, you are *her* servant, not *his*."

When it became clear that Phillip was not going to return, Annie's obvious fear subsided. But she was still in the presence of this much-too handsome man who wanted her to talk with him! A wave of shame suddenly washed over her. Osei was still holding her hand; now she wished that he would let go.

"You know Master comes to my room sometimes?"

"I have heard you crying. It is not right that you should have to endure his visits, if they cause you such pain."

"He will just come tomorrow night. And make me sorry for being out of my bed tonight!"

"I have a plan that will keep him away from now on. But you will have to trust me."

The conversation had now come down to the all-important question. Annie heard his voice saying the words, but she could barely believe them.

"If you will marry me, Mistress Evie has promised that she can keep Master Phillip from bothering you ever again."

Annie's heart forgot to beat for a full second. He was obviously waiting for an answer. She stole a glance at his face; the expression was unreadable. Perhaps she was supposed to make a witty remark, but she was incapable of saying anything smart. Did he truly expect an answer?

"Please, Sir," she began, now completely miserable, "I cannot expect you to… marry me just to keep Master from my bed."

"I know it seems as though that is the only reason I ask. But—but there are others, good ones." Osei fell silent. Gently, he stroked the hand he still held.

Finally, he said, "I know we do not know each other. But back in my homeland young people sometimes meet for the first time on their wedding day. You are the right age and… very good-looking. My only question is, am I agreeable to you?"

It was almost too much! Annie could only nod yes; her voice had completely deserted her.

Finding Annie's room empty was an unpleasant shock. Phillip, for a moment, could not think where she might be at this hour. In his drunken state, he did not even remember that Osei also had a room in the garret. Next, he realized he had better get back downstairs. Evie was not above playing some trick on him, even without knowing where he had been spending part of his nights.

Once back in the bedroom, he again removed shoes and breeches. Easing himself under the feather-stuffed comforter, he unwittingly placed himself in just the right position to receive the full force of her suddenly raised knee directly to his crotch! Unable even to scream, the pain was so intense, he fell out of the bed on his back. Looking up through tears of agony, the first thing he saw was his wife's face leaning over the edge of the bed.

"Phillip! What happened? Why are you on the floor?"

She was staring at him in apparent amazement. Suddenly, he was no longer drunk. His mind worked feverishly to explain why he was just getting into bed. Obviously, he had startled her and she had moved reflexively.

"Phillip, are you *just now* coming to bed?"

"No! Yes! I-I went to relieve myself! Sorry if I startled you!"

Evie's eyes fairly glowed malevolently, even in the filtered moonlight. Could it be that she knew all and was simply getting even? For a moment, Phillip could have sworn that none of this was accidental. But he knew he dared not confront her, else he might find himself explaining other absences.

"Love! Come! Are you hurt? Let me see!"

He climbed into the bed, grateful that, whatever the cause of her anger, it had not been any worse. Evie had taken her painful revenge and would now, he hoped, be mollified. He prayed she would understand his inability to perform sexually. She did examine the damage minutely—so much so that he was nearly most painfully aroused. However, she soon lost interest and broke off touching him.

Exhausted, he fell asleep almost immediately. She, however, lay awake watching her husband. Tomorrow, she would complete her solution to Annie's problem.

At breakfast, next morning, as Osei served warm porridge and cream, Evie suddenly addressed him directly.

"I understand you would like to marry Annie. Of course, if she is ever to marry, it should be now. She is almost twenty. Have you asked her?"

Osei paused, taking in her entire statement before responding. Without raising his eyes, he moved to a corner of the table where he could watch both her and Phillip's reactions. Phillip was obviously surprised, unpleasantly so. His face had reddened noticeably, and the muscles in both jaws twitched vigorously. However, he said nothing. Osei realized he would have to frame his answer carefully. Annie may have belonged to Mistress, but he was Phillip's property.

"As you gave me permission to, I did speak with her this evening past. And she did say, 'yes.'"

Here, he shifted slightly and addressed his master. "I do beg, Master Phillip, that you give me leave to take her as my wife."

"Oh I do, indeed, I do!" Phillip's reply was hearty and jovial. Only the continued tightness in his jaw line revealed how false the heartiness was.

At Evie's insistence, Osei and Annie were formally married two weeks later, on a Saturday afternoon in the Quaker Meeting House, just off Crown

Street. Evie chose the Friends because they were the most liberal in allowing marriages of slaves in their meeting houses.

Annie wore her mistress' wedding gown; it was almost two inches too short, a bit loose in the bodice and tight across the shoulders. But to her, both the gown and the entire day were perfect. Evie and Phillip, their two children, Phillip, Jr., and Sophie, as well as Circe, the Hamilton's cook, all witnessed Osei's statement of vows and Annie's timid agreement to "love, honour and obey" her husband.

Once the party returned home, Evie had arranged for there to be a special meal laid in the kitchen, attended by Master, Mistress and the entire household. Circe had several meat pies and a side of mutton that she served with roasted corn and boiled pudding. There was even a keg of grog.

After the family had withdrawn to the front of the house, the servants of the surrounding families came by to greet the newlyweds and to get some of the food. Osei and Annie entertained until nearly midnight. When the last guests had left and Circe had retired to her quarters above the kitchen, Osei took Annie's hand.

"I have a surprise for you." He led her out into the back yard to the carriage house. "This is our new home, a gift from Mistress. We have the room above."

This room occupied the entire second floor. Below, the family coach and a stable for two horses were housed in two sections of the ground floor. Here, there was also a huge fireplace that could warm both floors, since the chimney extended up into their new living quarters. That room contained a rough wooden double bed, two chairs, an old dining table and a washstand. To Annie it was heaven; Master Phillip would no longer be able to get at her!

Once he had decided to marry Annie, Osei finally allowed himself to be attracted to her. There was about her an unconsciously seductive quality, a naturally graceful way of moving that made a man turn and watch her, and then think about her long after. He found himself anxiously anticipating the pleasures of her body and the joy of denying Phillip any further access to *his wife*! Those thoughts almost made him forget his private pain.

As it turned out, their wedding night was to be, for Osei, an exercise in restraint. Annie was not a virgin, but she had never experienced real lovemaking either. He was more experienced, thanks to Lizette and his few subsequent encounters whenever the *Mary B* had docked in a Caribbean port. However, this was the first time he would be with someone whose affections he wanted to win. Now that they were alone, she glanced once at the bed, then nervously at him. She was so obviously uneasy that Osei reluctantly decided not to satisfy his own desires tonight but to give her time to adjust. So he quickly undressed, only to his shirt, drawers and hose, and got into bed. Turning to his new wife, who was still in the wedding gown and showing no inclination to remove it, he gently invited her to lie down.

"Annie, do not fear; I'll not touch you. It is very late and we must both be up and about early. Come to bed."

Annie released a long-held breath. Osei promptly turned to the wall so she could remove the gown, stays, petticoat and skirt. Once in her shift, she gingerly climbed into the bed alongside him. But it did seem to her that she had a duty to at least offer herself to her husband. The thought made her feel a little ill and excited at the same time.

"Please, take your pleasure. I don't mind."

"Not tonight," he said, his back still to her. "Tomorrow, when we are not so tired."

He knew there would be no nights when they would not both be exhausted, but, for Annie, tonight was just too soon. He also realized that, beyond his physical attraction to her, there was so much he did not yet know about this woman—including whether he could afford to let himself love her.

By the next day, everything was back to normal, but with an important difference for Annie. The idea that Osei had actually married her, married *her*, sang in her head as she went about her duties. Of course, he was just being gallant, saving her from Master Phillip's odious visits. And she was the only servant of marriageable age in the household. But there were so many other women servants in New York; with his looks, he need not have limited himself to her at all.

By that evening, she had decided to make sure he would never regret choosing her. When the Hamilton household was finally in bed, she found him in Phillip's study, filing his master's papers. Quietly slipping into the room, she came up behind him and wrapped her arms around his waist.

"Before we are both too tired," she whispered, almost breathlessly, "I want you to come to the carriage house with me."

Osei had been struggling with his thoughts about Annie all day. Tonight, he knew he absolutely could not refrain from making love to her. And he hoped, almost desperately, that she would not simply endure his touch. If she did, he was not certain that he would ever want to try again.

When he felt her arms encircle him, his heartbeat quickened. Turning around, he embraced her tightly. Then he took her hand and led her out of the room, leaving half the papers still scattered all over Phillip's desk.

In their room, Osei tried to keep his passion controlled as they undressed by candlelight, removing what seemed to be endless layers of clothing, since both he and Annie were dressed for service. Phillip and Evie had entertained a business acquaintance for dinner, which required that the servants wear the Hamilton livery. For the women, this meant a maroon round gown with white lawn petticoat, kerchief and mobcap. Osei, the only male servant, wore maroon breeches, waistcoat and coat over his white lawn shirt, with linen stock. Tonight, his costume had also included a matching maroon turban, since Evie felt that it played up his "exotic African features."

When Annie was finally down to her shift and he to his shirt, he sat on the side of their bed and drew her between his knees. Very slowly, he raised the shift until it was above her waist. She pulled the garment off, letting it fall on the chair next to the bed. She let him kiss and explore her naked body to his heart's content. Then she took hold of the tail of his shirt, intending that he remove his garment as well. Before doing so, he snuffed out the candle. When he took her into his arms, she thought she could feel something around his body, just above his hips, that contained small, moveable parts. But it became impossible to concentrate on whatever the thing was over the sound of his heart beating against hers.

The rowboat rises and falls with the swell of each wave that rushes in and spreads itself across the wide expanse of sandy beach. Osei's blood knows this place, though his eyes have never beheld it. This is the coastline of his country. Unable to wait until they reach the shallows, he leaps over the side, landing waist-deep in the ocean. The water is like molasses, holding him back, and his legs cannot move fast enough. But at last he feels the graininess beneath his feet. Running, falling and getting up, he gains the dry land. His joy is too much for words; he must dance! Only in the dance can he be truly welcomed! His arms flailing, the tattered rags of his shirt flying loose about him, he leaps and whirls. At last, he screams with all his strength.

"Annie! Annie! We Are Finally Home!"

Osei awakened with such a start that he actually found himself sitting up. He looked around confused, then realized he was in bed. It had been only a dream, but one so real that he could still feel the sand beneath his feet.

Beside him, Annie stirred, and awakened. She touched his bare arm gently. "What is it?" she asked.

Instead of answering, he pulled her, almost roughly, into an embrace and made love to her fiercely, his body moving to the rhythm of the homecoming dance. He kept at it until he was completely spent and the pain in his heart was gone.

Annie moaned, very softly and just once, but it was enough to bring Osei to his senses. He pushed himself away from her in horror, certain that, in his frenzy, he had torn her apart inside.

"Oh please, do forgive me! I must have lost my reason! Have I injured you?"

"No, of course not. It is your right to take me as you will."

"Annie. I have no right to hurt you. Nor will I ever again. Please, tell me truly, are you in any way injured? I have some healing knowledge and can help you."

The room was in complete darkness and he could not see her expression. Silently he cursed himself for losing control, fearful now that he had squandered his chances at winning her trust.

There was a full minute of silence during which Osei held his breath. When she finally spoke, it was in a voice so soft that she almost seemed to be talking to herself.

"Your heart was beating so loudly, and I feared for you. What has happened to you so bad that you dream it and awaken this way? Hopefully, you will tell me one day. Tonight, I am only glad I was here to give you comfort. I truly was not hurt, but I do promise to tell you if ever I am."

She had understood completely! Osei was so moved that he could not trust his voice. Instead, he kissed her very gently, lay down and drew her close. She turned against his chest, her lips softly brushing the hollow of his throat. Overwhelmed by desire and gratitude, he almost took her again, but by now was too worn out to continue. They were both soon asleep.

The dream returned often, becoming, for Osei, a glorious torment. For whenever he would moan or thrash about in the midst of his homecoming ecstasy, Annie would waken, ready to comfort him. Although that comfort was sweet indeed, he quickly realized their passion would soon be noticed by their masters, Phillip in particular.

The first morning that Annie appeared with slightly swollen lips and dark purple bruises on her neck, ready to get the children up, she encountered Phillip in the upstairs hall. He almost let her pass, catching her forearm just before she got out of reach. Then he pulled her against his chest, and hissed at her through clenched teeth.

"So! You give your *husband*, my servant, the pleasures you denied to me! Was I so foul a lover—and is he so *fair*? He has put his marks all over you! And I'll wager you never sobbed nor wept with him!"

Annie suddenly cocked her head, apparently listening intently. "Master Phillip, I hear someone coming."

"No, no! You'll not fool me with that threat. I know you would lie just to get away from me!"

At that moment, Osei emerged from one of the children's rooms. He stopped, not two feet away from them. Without looking in Annie's direction at all, he spoke to Phillip as though she were not present.

"Ah, Master. Mistress Evie is waiting for Annie in Mistress Sophie's room. Mistress was wondering what was keeping her, as little Mistress is quite hungry."

Phillip released Annie's arm immediately. She ran past Osei, her head bowed, and slipped into Sophie's room. He stood his ground, hands folded before him and eyes respectfully lowered, waiting for Phillip to make the first move. For a long awkward moment both men held their positions.

Phillip, his face deeply flushed, was struggling with an almost over-whelming sense of loss—and jealousy! Now that she was truly out of his reach, he found himself wanting Annie more than ever, with absolutely no hope of ever sharing her bed again. How could she dare prefer this Black man to him? With these thoughts crowding his mind, he now realized he had been cuck-olded by everyone, especially his wife! Evie was definitely at the bottom of this! He had no ammunition, moral or otherwise with which to fight. He had been effectively checkmated! Drawing himself up to his full height, he turned on his heel and descended the staircase, with Osei following two steps behind.

"Will, I have not forgotten that you went behind my back when you spoke to Mistress Evie about Annie. Why did you not come to me first?"

The question caught Osei off guard. He had hoped Phillip was more interested in concealing his trysts with Annie than in pursuing the matter of the marriage. From the hallway encounter, it was clear that, far from relin-quishing her, he had been growing resentful about it all.

"Of course, you are right, Master Phillip. Had I not been so careless as to let word slip out about my interest in Annie, Mistress Evie would not have suggested that we wed. It was her idea, and Mistress does have a great fondness for Annie. I think she just wanted to do something special for her."

By now, both men were at the carriage house door. Osei was about to hitch up the horses when Phillip continued, taking a different tack. "You real-ize, don't you, that I really should forbid you both living here. It's not that clean a place, and it puts Annie too far away from her duties."

Outwardly, Osei's expression remained perfectly calm. Inwardly he could feel a sense of panic rising. He knew that Phillip could very well force Annie back to the garret. Her only protection lay in her mistress' resolute unwilling-ness to be shamed by an open or even a clandestine affair between her husband and her beloved servant.

"Master, please forgive my saying this. But Mistress Evie also made the decision about where she wanted Annie to live."

"Yes, yes, of course, she did!" Phillip's face had become beet-red by now. He was silent for the rest of the trip to his office.

Osei now realized Annie would have to make Evie aware of Phillip's con-tinued pursuit, immediately and very tactfully. He decided to share his plans with her on that very evening, once they were finally alone.

Their nights together had become, for him, the only pleasure he had expe-rienced since his capture, and he was loath to spend any of those precious hours away from their bed. But this could not wait. Once the whole family had finally retired and he had laid out Phillip's clothing for the next day, he met Annie at the door to the master bedroom. Taking her arm, he hurried her back to the carriage house.

When she saw how anxious Osei was for them to get home, Annie assumed he wanted to make love, as they did every night. Once they got back to their room, however, instead of taking her in his arms, Osei drew their two chairs close together. Taking one, he indicated she should sit in the other.

"Annie, Master Phillip still covets you."

Before he could continue, she interrupted him. "He has made that much clear to me, and I'll not let him near me! I'll find a way to stop him from touching me again! I will!"

She was clutching her apron in her lap with either hand as she spoke. Suddenly, the fabric gave way and the garment tore in two. For a moment, they both stared at the ripped cloth.

"If he asks you to go anywhere with him, or to meet him in any room, say that Mistress Evie has instructed you to ask her first. Do speak politely and tell him you will find her *right away* and get her permission."

After he said this, Osei actually laughed aloud at the picture. But he could see that she was much too upset to appreciate the humour in the situation.

"Annie, just imagine Master Phillip's face as he watches you running to tell Mistress about his attempted tryst! Truly, it is quite funny! And, what is more important," he added gently, "I believe she will find a way to stop him."

It was already so late that the first watch had come through Crown Street, calling out the hour. Osei stood, drew Annie close and removed her cap. He began to undo the kerchief knotted at her bosom. "Come. I've missed you all day."

The following Sunday morning, the whole family gathered for breakfast, even the children. Evie announced that it would be nice for Phillip to attend services, since he had not been for the past few Sundays. Just then, little Sophie threw her napkin on the floor and Annie had to pass behind his chair to pick it up. Phillip's head moved, just fractionally in her direction, as though sensing a fragrance in the air. Then his face reddened and an angry vein rose in his right temple.

Osei was standing at attention, just a little behind and to Phillip's right. Immediately, as he noted his master's heightened colour, he positioned himself so Annie would have to go around him, rather than Phillip, when she returned to her station beside the mahogany credenza. Evie, ever the watchful eye, also noticed her husband's discomfort. Shaking out her napkin before refolding it beside her plate, she announced a change of plans.

"I know! The whole family can come to services! We'll take the children to sit in our pew. And Will and Annie will be in the gallery. It's time the children learn how to be still in church."

Usually, Annie was expected to care for the children at home while Evie was in church. However, having everyone there would place Phillip where she could watch him and assure that Annie was with Will.

The services were long and tiring for the children who alternately fidgeted and slept. In the gallery, where the servants were forced to stand the whole time, Osei took the opportunity of slipping an arm around Annie's waist and moving behind her so she could lean on him. With his free hand, he very lightly stroked the inside of her forearm. The time, for the both of them, actually passed rather quickly.

The following day, Phillip, upon returning from his business, decided he needed several hours more away from home. He wanted to spend the evening at the Queen's Head Tavern, but this required a rather lengthy discussion with Evie. By the time she finally agreed to his staying out as late as he wished, she had gotten him to promise he would come straight home, not disturb her getting into bed unless she was already awake, and accompany her whenever she visited her parents in Baltimore.

The negotiations with Evie only served to put Phillip into an even fouler mood. He had been unable to stomach his defeat over Annie. His pride had been severely wounded, but there was no way for him to achieve satisfaction. Not one of his friends would sympathize with the plight of a man denied the sexual favours of a *servant* by his wife's sleight-of-hand maneuvers. If they ever so much as suspected it, they would laugh him right out of New York!

However, he could punish Will just a little. But the punishment would have to be meted out carefully. His man was too talented a servant to trifle with overzealously. Many a master had ruined a good servant by using inappropriate or unduly harsh measures for infractions. No, Phillip decided that tonight Will would drive the carriage and wait with it outside the Queen's Head until his master felt like returning home, however late the hour. Phillip was certain that, if he kept Will out long enough, the man would have no opportunity to enjoy Annie's favours on this night, at least.

Osei recognized that Phillip would be ill-humoured all evening; he had anticipated it, since his master had barely spoken to him the entire week. He took Phillip's curt instructions to "fetch the carriage and be quick about it!" as a clear indication that he would be on service all night.

When they reached Pearl Street, Phillip alighted without so much as a glance in his direction. Osei then made himself as comfortable as possible on the driver's seat. It would have been unwise for him to try to take a nap inside. If a night watch came by and noticed the untended carriage, the cab would be the first place that the man would look. Too many servants got into trouble by falling asleep in their masters' carriages.

It was nearly one in the morning when Phillip finally emerged from the Queen's Head. Osei lost no time driving back to Crown Street; theirs was the only carriage about at this late hour. Once home, he accompanied Phillip upstairs and helped him into his dressing room, just off the master bedroom.

Here Phillip, completely intoxicated, sprawled on a chaise while Osei removed his shoes and hose.

As he was removing the waistcoat, Phillip began to mutter a string of incoherent sounds containing only a few recognizable words. Osei moved to the breeches, deftly unbuttoning the fall and pulling them off. Just as he rose and was gathering up the scattered articles of clothing, Phillip spoke again, only one word this time—very clearly. "Annie."

"Annie?" He repeated it, this time as though calling softly.

Osei froze; a pulse began pounding against the stock knotted at his throat. He quickly hung Phillip's soiled clothing behind the wardrobe door and got out clean things for the next day. Then he quit the room, leaving Phillip snoring on the chaise.

Outside, Osei stopped, trying to recover his composure. A fine rage had risen in him when Phillip had spoken Annie's name. But it was anger at being *here*, in this place—at being enslaved! All he wanted in life was to be free, to take Annie home and to make love to her on his own woven mat, in the hut he had built with his own hands! The desire was so strong in him that the tears welled up, spilling freely. He ran into the carriage house, taking the stars two at a time. He stripped off everything, leaving his clothing in heaps across the floor as he made his way to the bed.

Annie was sound asleep, one arm stretched across his side of the bed as though at the last moment, just before dozing off, she had reached for him. She smelled of soap; she had stolen time for a bath. Osei gently lifted her arm and slipped beneath it, trying not to awaken her. Almost immediately, she moved closer to him, pressing her body against his. In his present state of mind, this was too much. He straddled her and began kissing her with such energy that he was sure she would awaken.

Annie responded by stirring and wrapping both arms around him, then by raising her hips so that, when he entered her, he penetrated her more deeply than ever before. In the midst of their love dance, he became aware of an unmistakable undulation within her. It radiated in waves from a spot that he could feel with each thrusting movement. Those waves took him so completely that he reached his climax immediately. For several minutes after, his heart beat so violently that he could feel its movements against his chest wall.

For the first time in her life, Annie had experienced lovemaking fully. Always before, with Osei, she took much more pleasure in his enjoyment than in the act itself. He always approached her gently, asking permission before touching her anywhere. But it was his attention to her *after* making love that had won her heart so absolutely. Instead of finishing his business and rolling off her, he would hold her until she fell asleep. Sometimes, if she awakened, she could feel his fingers lightly stroking her face, as though memorizing each feature. The first time he did this, she took his hand and pressed the palm to her lips.

"Husband, why are you still awake? Do you want me again?"

His answer gave her such pleasure and sweet release. "Annie. No. It is only that you are so very lovely. It pleases me to watch you sleep."

Thanks to Phillip, she had learned to detest everything about intercourse with her mistress's husband, the thrusting maleness of his movements, the sour smell of his body, the alcohol on his breath, his infernal grunting.

But tonight had been *heavenly*! Unable to move, Annie lay on her back trying to catch her breath. When at last she could breathe almost normally, she turned to Osei. "Is this what you feel whenever we are together? I can now understand why you want it all the time!"

Osei propped himself on one elbow. With his free hand, he gently stroked her cheek, then cupped her face.

"Annie. I cannot fully explain how it is when I am with you! But yes, it is always like this. I wanted you to feel as I feel! And tonight, in spite of… everything else, at last you do!"

The women's voices, rich with laughter and secrets, reach Osei as he enters his father's compound. Akua is sitting in front of her hut, plaiting Annie's hair.

"Ako (First Born)! Come and see how beautiful I've made your wife! She is as pretty as your sisters!"

Annie's smile is hesitant and shy; tears have formed in the corners of her eyes. Akua almost always plaits too tightly.

"Mother, you will make my new sister's hair fall out," Binta laughs, tossing the grain in her winnowing basket. "I now have no hair around my ears, thanks to Mother's plaits!"

"Yes, but your hairstyles were better than any of your friends' and you got the best husband!"

Akua, herself, wears an elaborate head wrap covering hair locked into the long threads worn by a priestess. Osei, still standing at the compound gate, takes in the whole scene: his mother's awesome, ageless beauty; the ripe loveliness of his sister, bare-breasted and unselfconscious; and Annie!

"Wake up! Oh please wake up! Don't cry so!"

He could barely hear Annie's voice filtering into his consciousness. Someone was wailing loudly, gasping and howling. With a jolt, Osei realized that it was he!

"Please tell me what you dreamed! If you tell it, perhaps it won't seem so terrible!" Diffidently, she lifted one of his hands, kissed it and pressed it to her cheek.

Ashamed of his tears, Osei wanted to draw back. But Annie was too close to him now. Even in his dreams, she was with him. And that was the worst part! He could never leave her behind, not ever!

He told her all of it, each detail of every dream he had had since their marriage. They sat up together in bed until they grew too weary and had to lie down. Osei spoke into the darkness, almost forgetting Annie's presence beside him, bringing his African home to life. He even revealed his true name.

"The first part, Kwesi, is my *Akeradini*, the name I was born with. No one can give you that name; it is yours, based on the day on which you are born. I was born on Sunday, *Kwasida* in my language. Boys born on that day are all named Kwesi."

Annie turned to face him. He felt the bed shift with her movement.

"The second part of my name was given by my father. Among my people, fathers always name the children. He chose Osei."

"So you have two names? Say them again! They're both so beautiful!"

Osei could not suppress a laugh. Suddenly he realized the worst of his pain had evaporated. Annie was even charmed by the story of his names! Then he became serious.

"Annie, my name has been my secret ever since I was kidnapped. Now that you know it, you must keep it secret as well! Never, ever call me by my real name, not even when we are alone!"

"I'll always call you Will in front of our masters. When we're alone together—well, you won't mind if I continue to call you, Husband, will you? And you must promise to do something else for me."

"Anything. What do you want me to do?"

"Tell me *everything* that happened to you before you were kidnapped, and afterward."

Chapter 16

QUEBEC (1800)

*G*reat Bear had, in effect, forced Anika's hand by insisting she speak about her first husband. Now that she had begun the story, he finally had to face this hitherto unknown rival for her heart. Each evening, he sat in the longhouse, in the circle around the council fire, listening to her speaking English that he understood much less than she did Unkechaug. In spite of her simple efforts over their years together to teach it to him, and even after River Otter's actual lessons, he still could not really learn it; the language just had too many words for anyone to master.

Nonetheless, Anika's voice held him in thrall. Great Bear watched her mouth forming syllables, his lips moving along unconsciously with her words. Meanwhile, part of him tried to ignore River Otter's translation so he could concentrate on getting the gist of each episode....

1762 - 1775

Of course Annie was with child two months after the marriage. However, one morning when she was about three months along, she was coming downstairs carrying little Sophie and missed a step. Unable to recover her balance, she lost her footing and tumbled down the long winding staircase, still holding the child. As she fell, Annie could feel her body striking each step. Instinctively, she twisted so as to keep the girl on top of her. As they both hit the bottom landing, Annie had taken the full brunt of the fall.

Almost immediately she began to bleed. Sophie, uninjured, saw the blood pooling around Annie's legs and began screaming at the top of her lungs.

The entire household came running, including Osei, who had been out in the carriage house hitching up the horses for the trip to Phillip's office. Osei took one look at Annie and felt his composure vanish. Pushing past his master, who had become paralyzed at the sight of the blood, he swept the child off his wife, snatched her up and was about to run with her back to the carriage house. Evie grabbed at his shirt sleeve.

"What do you think you are doing," she shouted angrily. "Where are you going? She needs a doctor! You idiot! Take her upstairs immediately!"

For a full moment he stared at the woman. Annie was now bleeding profusely. He was fairly sure the baby was gone; he was terrified she might soon follow. He knew that he could save her.

"Mistress Evie, I-I do fear she may die before the doctor can come. If you will permit me, I believe I can stop the bleeding before we lose her."

Evie was clearly skeptical, but she was more frightened at the prospect of Annie dying. She agreed, but insisted he treat her upstairs in the extra bedroom. She followed him up to the room and even swept back the bedclothes. Phillip, by this time, had recovered enough to follow his wife upstairs. However, as soon as he saw Osei raise Annie's skirts, he backed out of the room and escaped down the stairs. There he waited, filled with a combination of fear, loathing and an almost painfully overwhelming desire.

Osei had laid Annie on her back; now he instructed her to open her legs. With Evie watching closely over his shoulder, he began a powerful massaging of her abdomen. Contractions soon began. Annie's eyes filled with tears, but she remained silent as Osei pressed their child out of her womb. For her, that loss was far greater than the pain. Once he was sure that everything was out, he bundled up the bloodied bedclothes and turned her on her side with her back to him. Now he massaged her back more gently, and the powerful contractions eased.

"Is she saved?" Evie's voice, so close to his ear, startled him.

"She will not die now. But it would be good if the doctor could see her."

He said this purely for Evie's benefit. He did not think the doctor would actually come today, even if Evie did send for him, particularly if there were White patients who needed him. Perhaps he could stop by at some point. But it did not matter now. Osei knew of a poultice that would draw out the rest of the blood before it became poisonous. He would apply that, once he got Annie back to their quarters.

Unfortunately, it became apparent that Annie was not well-built for breeding. The first miscarriage was followed by a second, less than a year later. It did not help that the children's demands on her always seemed to increase each time she became pregnant. When Sophie was five and Annie was six months along in her third pregnancy, the child developed an earache one night that set her to screaming hard—she did have her mother's lungs!

Annie, completely exhausted, was already in bed, and Osei was about to climb in beside her when Circe's voice floated up from the back yard.

"Mistress wants Annie to come tend to Little Mistress right away!"

Wearily, Annie got up and began dressing. Just as she was about to put on her mobcap, she turned around and caught sight of Osei's face. He wore an expression that she had never seen before; his eyes were narrow slits and his lips drawn into a tight, cold smile.

"I'll come with you. I have something that will ease the child." He spoke in a calm, even voice.

Annie started to say, "Stay here and sleep," but thought better of it. She was certain that Osei was growing furious.

Once they got to the kitchen, he told her to go up to Sophie's room. "It will take me a few minutes to make the poultice. Lie down with the child. That should soothe her somewhat. But be careful she does not strike or kick your stomach."

Sophie was still screaming and pulling on the offending earlobe when Annie slipped into the bedroom. Both Evie and Phillip were trying to calm the child. He saw Annie first.

"Why were you so long in coming?" he demanded loudly. "You see!" he turned on Evie. "I told you she was too far away from the children in the carriage house!"

"I'm sorry. I had fallen asleep." Annie rushed to the bedside. "I'm here now, Master. You and Mistress can go back to bed. Will's here too. He's making something in the kitchen that will ease little Mistress' pain."

Evie completely ignored Phillip's outburst. She swept past him and caught Annie by the wrist. "Just, please make her stop screaming like that! It's enough to drive one mad!"

As soon as she saw Annie, little Sophie reached out to be held by her favourite caregiver. Annie let the child climb into her lap and fasten one chubby arm around her neck. Then a fresh wave of pain made Sophie scream even louder. She struggled in Annie's arms, pushing against her stomach and flailing with both arms.

Almost immediately, Osei was at the bedside. He took up the little girl just as one foot connected solidly with Annie's right side, causing her to double over. For one awful moment, everyone froze. Then Annie caught her breath.

"It's alright; I wasn't hurt," she gasped, hoping it was true. "Will, please give little Mistress the medicine,"

Osei gently laid the child on one side and placed the folded cloth against her ear. Almost immediately, Sophie got quiet, and a few minutes later fell asleep.

"Will. You are just amazing!" Evie murmured. Then, speaking over her shoulder as she took Phillip's arm to lead him out of the room, she said, "Annie, when you think Mistress Sophie is sleeping soundly and won't be waking us up, you and Will can go back to the carriage house." The door closed behind them.

"The child will sleep until morning." Osei's voice was tight with rage. "Come, I want to have a look at you. She may have hurt you."

"I'm not hurt, not badly." Annie did feel more than a little ill.

Back in their room, Osei undressed her and examined the bruised swelling in her right side. He was clearly still simmering, but he said nothing throughout his examination. Finally, when he was finished, he told her to get into bed.

"You need to stay off your feet. Tomorrow, I will tell Mistress Evie you are too ill to tend the children. Let her take care of them for one day!"

Annie carried this baby for one more month, only to have it still-born. A year later, her fourth was also born dead. She and Osei buried each child in the Negro Burial Grounds, a swampy marsh of hills and valleys just north of the Commons and bounded on the east by the Collect Pond. And with each death she became more determined to try again.

When a fifth also died at birth, Osei began to suspect that a wicked spirit had taken residence in Annie's womb. Back home, such spirits were known among many groups of people by different names, but they accomplished their torment of a hapless woman in the same way, by being born over and over. Each time the baby would die, the spirit would leave it, only to re-enter the woman's womb at her next pregnancy. The only way to defeat the cycle was to get the spirit to reveal its source of power, its charm. Unfortunately, only the children thus born knew the charm's form and location, but they always died before reaching an age when they could talk.

The following year was 1770 and Annie was again pregnant. Just before Christmas, Evie, Phillip and the children traveled to Maryland for the first time since their marriage. Phillip had asked that Annie be taken along as well, just to mind the children. But Evie reminded him that she was due to give birth the following summer, just when they had all planned to return.

So Evie left her in New York with Osei, fully expecting to return in June. However, an unfortunate turn of events prolonged the family's stay in Baltimore. That March in Boston, a mob had advanced on a company of British regulars who opened fire on them. Five members of the mob were killed, including a Black man by the name of Attucks. While the shooting was not, in itself of great moment, when taken together with the growing disaffections over the Acts of Parliament, in particular the Stamp Act and the Towshend Acts, the "massacre" became a rallying cry for those who favoured armed resistance.

Evan was horrified at the prospect of loyal British subjects taking up arms against the Crown, and he insisted that, whatever Phillip might choose to do, the others—Evie, little Phillip, Sophie, two year-old Martha and baby Evan—not take to the roads at such a dangerous time, but remain with him. Although he wanted very badly to return to New York, the possibility that the trip might be perilous finally dissuaded Phillip. He stayed in Baltimore with his family.

Annie's sixth child, a boy was born in July—alive. She had entered labour with the usual grim, silent determination. When she heard the infant actually cry, she sat bolt upright.

"It cried out! I heard my baby cry out!"

"Yes." Osei was near tears.

He had delivered their infant by himself just after sunset. Now he immediately took the child outside to be named. First, he whispered the name into his son's ear. Then, holding him aloft, he presented the newborn to the ancestors. "This is Kwesi Owusu!"

Annie, though weak, had crept out of bed and followed her husband into the yard. Silently she mouthed the foreign words. Osei turned to face her. "Our son's name must also remain a secret with us. To the world, he will be known as Will, the same as me."

Phillip was finally able to convince Evan to let the family return to New York in August. When she found that Annie had given birth to a living child at last, Evie was overjoyed. In celebration, she gave her servant three of her dresses and most of Martha's baby clothing. Little Willy, as they called Annie's infant, found himself resplendent in lacy, white chemises over his diapers.

Chapter 17

BALTIMORE (1775)

*A*s far as Evan was concerned, all hell had broken loose. In spite of the fact that it was treasonous to do so, most of his neighbours were supporting armed rebellion against the King, his King. Politics had never interested him; the taxes that everyone was complaining about were not such a problem in Maryland. It was those scoundrels in Massachusetts who were at the bottom of all this upheaval. They deserved to be punished, and King George had done just that!

As a staunch Tory, however, Evan Grant soon found himself isolated, both politically and socially. Many of his patients stopped using his services. Eventually, he began to feel the effects of a reduced income. Sophie was greatly distressed when the ladies in her circle began to exclude her from their social functions.

It seemed that this madness was spreading unchecked, particularly when it infected his own family. His eldest son announced, one evening, while visiting, that he had been selected as a new member of the delegation from Maryland that would travel to Philadelphia to be part of something he called the Second Continental Congress.

Evan had named his first-born after himself, hoping to begin an illustrious line of physicians. His plan was to send young Evan to Edinborough, or even to London, to complete his studies. When the youth was sixteen, his father did send him to England, where the boy remained for the next six years. When he returned, Evan took him into the practice, proudly announcing that between them, he and his son would soon have most of the patients in Baltimore.

But Evan Jr. had a strong interest in the politics of the Colonies. He had resented the Stamp Act, even though it was passed while he was in London. And he had gotten into more than one row with his classmates over King George's treatment of the Colonials. Once back in Maryland, he paid close attention to events in Boston, and when a boycott of British goods was announced among some of the other Colonies, he was one of the first to champion the cause in Maryland. Evan Sr. became increasingly distressed about his son openly embracing these disloyal ideas.

When fighting broke out in Lexington, Evan Jr. regaled both his parents and his brothers with detailed justifications for taking up arms against the *Redcoats*, as the British troops were called. John, the one closest to him in age, sided with the elder Evan, mostly because he realized that his fortunes depended too heavily on his father. However, those revolutionary ideas, so eloquently espoused, found fertile soil in the mind of Albert, the youngest. He was just seventeen, and the idea of fighting for freedom appealed to him. On the evening that his oldest brother made his fateful announcement, Albert decided to join the local militia. He left his father's house shortly thereafter.

In the midst of everything, Em continued to keep the Grant household running. She listened to the parlour talk after dinner between Master and Mistress and she understood the Colonies had rebelled and were effectively at war with Great Britain. What this meant, she could not say and truthfully did not care about.

Her attentions were directed elsewhere. An influenza epidemic had hit parts of the town, particularly areas where Black people lived and Em was worried about her sons. She did not want to go to Rufus' shop since she might encounter his wife. But the uneasiness grew daily; finally, she could bear it no longer. She decided on a course of action and a means of getting information. Once again she turned to Ben.

"We are in need of four barrels to take supplies out to the farm. Please go by the cooper's shop and order them to be ready by next week."

"They's illness over in dat part of town," Ben said, rubbing his jaw nervously. "I heered the cooper's wife taken sick. She down pretty bad."

"Oh my! What will happen to those boys of theirs?"

Em's alarm was genuine. If Rufus' wife was ill, surely one or more of her sons could catch it as well. She could not bear the thought of losing another child.

"I shall go myself. You need not come with me; just get the small carriage ready."

She made a bundle of food and clean, cast-off clothing. Within the hour, she was tethering the carriage horse in front of Rufus' shop. Inside, eighteen year-old Marcus was alone; he looked up as she entered.

"May I help you, Ma'am?"

Em could not answer him for a moment. She had not seen her youngest son since he was a baby; she stood there marveling at how he had grown. The lad was good-looking, with golden brown skin and his father's dark eyes. All of the children had more closely resembled their father in colouring.

"I heard your mother was ill," she said finally. "I brought some provisions for you and your brothers. Is... everyone else still well?"

Now it was Marcus's turn to pause. His father had not risen early this morning, as was his habit. And when the young man had looked into his parents' room, both of them appeared to be sleeping soundly. Rufus Jr. had left at dawn without disturbing his youngest brother, taking Samuel with him to deliver some barrels. Marcus hoped they would return with something for supper.

Ruth had been in bed for a week, and Rufus Sr. had struggled to care for her while his sons kept the business running. In addition to his duties in the shop, Marcus had had to take over the household, including providing meals. Often, he had been reduced to requesting handouts of food in lieu of payment from those servants who frequented his father's shop for their masters.

Today, however, with his father also in bed, Marcus had to open the shop himself. Even now, his attention was divided between customers and what could be keeping his brothers. He was also deeply worried about why his father was still asleep so late in the morning.

"Oh Ma'am, I fear my father may be ill as well!"

Unexpected tears filled the youth's eyes and ran down his face. Em immediately put aside her bundle and took him into her arms, where he began to cry in earnest. Something about her arms felt disarmingly familiar; Marcus allowed his head to rest on her shoulder.

Once she had calmed the lad, she determined to see what she could do for Rufus and Ruth. Even though there was a real danger of contracting the illness, Em left the shop through the back door and let herself into the front door of the house. The place was just as she remembered it, an unpainted two-storied dwelling of only four rooms. Downstairs the sitting room and kitchen were unchanged. Upstairs, in the front bedroom, she found Rufus and his wife. Each appeared to be unconscious, but Ruth's breathing was slow and dangerously laboured.

The room smelled of body soils and vomit; the bedclothes were dirty. Em took off her kerchief and tied it around her face, covering nose and mouth. She stripped off the top coverings, making a bundle of them outside the door. From a small chest, she took out fresh linens. Before changing both the bed and the sleeping occupants, she opened the narrow window to let in some air.

Rufus stirred but did not awaken. Ruth groaned only once. Em hurried to her side of the bed. As she did so, the hapless woman made a low rattling noise that continued for several minutes. Drawing up a low stool, Em sat and took her hand. This woman had ministered to Frederic in his last hours. Sadly, she would now return the favour.

The death rattle did not continue for much longer. Ruth never moved nor opened her eyes; only silence signaled the end of the struggle. Em leaned in close and placed a hand over the now-still breast, feeling for a heartbeat in vain. Then she rose and searched for a mirror. She found a small cracked shard that had been part of a lady's looking glass in a bureau drawer. Placing it just under Ruth's nose, she checked for breath and found none.

Once she was sure that nothing more could be done for Ruth, Em turned her attention to the bed's other occupant. The body had to be taken away quickly. Rufus had begun to moan and move about as though he might regain consciousness. She worried that he could soon join Ruth, if he became aware that she had died right beside him. In any event, he clearly needed care and his sons were not equipped to provide it adequately. She stood still for several minutes, trying to puzzle out how to remove the woman without disturbing him. Finally, she covered Ruth with a clean sheet, leaving her head exposed, and placed a second one over both of them. She hurried out of the house without returning to the shop.

Once outside, Em tried to remember where the coffin-maker's house was located. After searching up and down several streets, she found him at last in his front yard, working on a new pine box. He too was a freedman, who made coffins for both Black and White patrons. The man got his wagon and returned with Em to Rufus' house.

All three sons were now in the shop hard at work; they did not see the pair alight and let themselves in. Once upstairs, the coffin man pulled the sheet over Ruth's head and wrapped the rest around her. By now the body was cold but still supple, so he was able to carry her over his shoulder. He indicated that Em should remain behind and come to his shop once she had finished her business.

"Missus Liberty ain't goin' nowhere. You kin come dress her when ya done heah."

Em knew she had to tell Young Rufus, Samuel and Marcus about Ruth. But first she needed to tend to Rufus. She completely stripped the bed this time and used the last of the clean linens to remake it. Rufus briefly opened his eyes as she was tucking in the sheets.

"Ruth? Why are you up? Are you feeling better?" He spoke thickly and his reddened eyes were filled with mucus.

Em looked at Rufus but did not answer him; she could not trust her voice to remain steady. Instead, she finished the bed and checked the pitcher on a nearby table; it was empty. She glanced at him again, but he had apparently gone back into a deep, if fitful sleep.

Taking the pitcher, she went downstairs and out to the back of the house where she found that the cistern was only a quarter full. She had to reach well in to get at the water, but she was able to fill the pitcher.

Once back in the bedroom, she used a little water and a clean cloth to wipe Rufus' eyes and mouth. Touching him brought back a flood of painful yet ineffably sweet memories; she lingered over the task for many moments. The years had been kind to him; only a few grey hairs mixed in with the black, and his face was essentially unchanged. How she had missed him all this time! Em could feel hot tears forming behind her eyes. But, instead of brimming and falling, they pooled and then gathered into a great solid knot in the back of her throat. She rose abruptly, almost knocking over the basin and the pitcher. Confused thoughts swirled in her head, and for a moment she almost surrendered to a dizzying wave of emotion.

Somewhere in the distance, a clock tolled the hour. The sound anchored Em, reminding her of all that had to be accomplished in the short afternoon remaining before she needed to be back at the Grant's. She gathered up the dirty linen and descended the narrow staircase. This time, she entered the back of the shop and stood still for a moment.

The three young men had their backs to her; they were deep in conversation. Rufus Jr. was showing Samuel how to hold a sun plane so as to better shape the barrel staves. Meanwhile, Marcus was assembling the finished barrels, using lengths of rope which he tightened before fastening on the hickory hoops. It was Marcus who noticed her first.

"Ma'am? Have you seen to our parents? Brothers, this lady come into the shop whilst you was out. She went in to tend to Ma and Pa."

Young Rufus looked up and faced Em squarely. He had recognized her right away. She made a small gesture at her side with one hand, indicating he should say nothing. The young man's eyes registered that he understood. But when he spoke, his voice was flat and hard.

"Ma'am, there wasn't no need for you to tend to anybody. We're all grown an' able to manage on our own. We don't need you *now*."

"Yes, we do!" Marcus' voice rose in alarm. "Rufus Jr.! Why you sayin' such rude an' wicked things to this lady? She brought us food an' clean clothin' too!"

Samuel ignored the exchange. Something about this woman seemed so wonderfully familiar. All he wanted was to get close enough to touch her.

Em drew a breath; then released it slowly. This was going to be extremely difficult. "Your Ma has passed. Your Pa is quite ill."

All three stared at her as though she had begun speaking a foreign tongue. Then Marcus let out a single pain-filled howl as Samuel unsuccessfully faught back tears. Only Rufus Junior seemed unmoved.

Em resisted the overwhelming urge to go to her two sons, both of whom were now crying hard. "I've had the coffin man come and take your Mama," she continued softly. "I'll need one of you to come help me lay her out."

"I'll come." Rufus Jr. spoke up.

They walked to the coffin shop in silence. All the while young Rufus was struggling to contain his anger; just before they reached their destination, he exploded.

"Why? Why did you leave us? You left Frederic to die and you didn't even care! Samuel don't remember, but I do! An' Marcus, he was just a babe! How could you leave… just… leave?"

The young man's tears flowed freely now, as he stood with clenched fists facing her. Em lifted her chin and met his eyes. He was so beautiful in his rage, this, her first born.

"What did your father tell you about me after I was gone?"

Rufus was too overwrought to answer immediately. Em so wanted to take the miserable young man into her arms, but she knew he would not let her so much as touch him. When he could finally speak, his voice still broke repeatedly. "Our Pa never spoke of you at all. He just said he would find us a Mama. And he did."

Of course, Rufus could not confess to a nine-year-old that he lacked the means to reunite his family, and that his own rage had driven his sons' mother away. Em realized she could never explain to young Rufus how his father's anger, so deeply rooted in love, became too unbearable for her witness.

"I left you because I could not stay. I'm a slave; your Pa was…is free. He could not afford to buy me or your older sister. Yes, you do remember…your sister, Annie? She had to stay with me. We belong to one of the richest, greediest doctors in Baltimore, Evan Grant! He sent Annie to New York to be his daughter's maid when she married. But he would just love to find out I have three more children, and all of them by a freedman! I kept you all a secret, even let Ruth be your Mama, just to make sure you stayed free! And what I tell you now, you must never repeat! If you do, Master Grant will come claim his *property*. Then he'll take you and your brothers, and make slaves of you all!"

Em had said all this in a harsh whisper. To Rufus Jr., it was as though he'd been in complete darkness and she'd thrown open a door, letting in too much light. For a few moments, he couldn't seem to see anything properly. He stood stock-still until Em took his arm and guided him into the coffin man's yard.

The following morning, three weeping sons buried Ruth, accompanied by a small group of their Black neighbors and the servants of their father's customers. By early afternoon when Em met the sons back at the house, Rufus had developed a terrible hacking cough that racked his entire body. He burned with fever and was in constant pain. She made him as comfortable as possible, afterward giving instructions to young Rufus and Samuel to cover their faces when they tended to their father.

"Our Pa goin' t' die too?" Marcus asked the question that now weighed heavily on all their minds.

She did not answer immediately. "We have to leave it to the Lord."

The young men looked at each other sadly. "Come again tomorrow, please Ma'am." Marcus's plea sounded so forlorn, as though he were a child again.

Em turned to Rufus Jr. "My master has a fresh-killed hog and a brace of partridges that were brought up from his farm this week. I shall bring you some when I return. Then I shall make you a decent meal."

She left the three young men standing in the shop door.

Later that evening, Em knocked at Evan's study door. He was at his desk, mournfully going over his books.

"Come."

He did not really want any company. When he saw who it was, he was decidedly annoyed. Then he remembered that he had not spoken to Sophie in several days. One day, about a month before, Sophie had announced she would no longer be coming downstairs to meals. This might be about her condition.

"Is it your mistress? How fares she?"

Em had taken Sophie's tray up first. These days, she spent most of her time reclining on her chaise. As she did very little, her appetite had decreased. Often, Sophie refused the entire meal. This time, Em had gotten her to eat the soup and a little meat.

"Mistress Sophie has taken a bit more today than yesterday, Master; I do expect we will do better tomorrow. Ah, Master." Here she paused.

"Well?" Evan was anxious to get back to the accounting.

"I was visiting some sick folk across town these last few days," Em continued. "There is quite a bit of sickness among the servants over there. I wondered if you have a… tonic I might take to ward off an illness like that one."

"Best you just stay away from those people."

"As you wish, Master Evan. There *is* the matter of the shopping, however. Much of the illness is in the market area. Our reduced means has forced me to go there more often to search for goods at lower prices."

Evan, by now, had become quite angry. How dare she remind him of their plight! Yet, even as words of reproach formed in his mouth, he bit them off. She did need to economize and had been doing so most successfully.

"Oh, very well. Here is a tonic. I think it will do little good, but it may bolster the blood a bit."

He opened the glass-front medicine cabinet and took out a small vial of black syrupy liquid. She thanked him and slipped it into one of her pockets. She had no plans to take the medicine herself; it was for her sons.

The following day, after serving the Grants, father and son, breakfast at the table and Sophie in her room, Em left the house with the provisions she had promised. She had also included some flour and molasses in the bundle that she took to the shop. The brothers were all hard at work when she entered. Marcus noticed her first.

"Look, Rufus, Samuel, the lady has returned. An' she's bringin' us some food!"

She smiled at her youngest. "I believe you must be hungry. I'll go in and fix a meal. Then I'll tend to your Pa."

In the rear room, Em started a fire in the grate and laid out the provisions. The pots were all sooty from having been left in the ashes and not cleaned properly. She washed all of them and then set to work on the table. Once that was scrubbed, she stoked the fire and made griddle cakes to go with the ham. She set the partridges, plucked and dressed on a spit above the flames. When she had cleaned and filled the kettle, she boiled several ears of corn that she had found in the Grants' larder. When everything was ready, she called to the three young men. They came in hurriedly from the shop and literally fell upon the food. It was clear this was the first real meal they had eaten since Ruth's illness began.

Em left them at the table and went upstairs. Both the window and the shutters were closed, casting the room into deep shadows. Rufus lay twisted in the bedclothes, the result of his constant tossing and turning. The fever had not broken; it was, instead, higher than ever.

She opened the window and pushed wide the shutters; light poured into the room, throwing the worn furnishings into sharp relief. There was water in the pitcher, so she used it to soak a clean cloth that she had brought with her and place it on the tortured man's forehead. He looked considerably worse today; his cheeks and eyes had become sunken, and his parched lips were cracked. Of course, he needed to drink! Em went downstairs to find a clean cup. Returning with a small pewter tankard that had probably been partial payment for an order, she raised Rufus' head and managed to force a little water down his throat. She had to do this very slowly, lest he choke, but she was successful in getting him to drink almost the entire amount. Immediately, he fell into a sound, peaceful sleep. Now she could straighten the linens and cover him properly.

Once that was accomplished, she sat by the bed watching him. Occasionally, she reached out and stroked his cheek or forehead very lightly, so as not to awaken him. In this quiet moment, in the house that they could never share, he was finally hers again.

As the afternoon sun lengthened the shadows across the room, Rufus shifted and opened his eyes. He had been dreaming; sometimes Ruth would be walking around their room, moving things, shaking out the covers. However, at other times, it seemed to be someone else, someone he dared not hope nor dream was there. The confusion of images swirled and blended in his fevered imagination until he gave up trying to make sense of any of it. Only, some faceless someone was ever so gently touching him with fingers remembered all too well. Now he shifted painfully, turning toward the light, trying to make out the face still partially covered with the kerchief, hovering above his own.

Em felt her heart turn painfully in her chest; he mustn't have to struggle so. As she removed the cloth, his breath caught. Those golden eyes! That cloud of reddish gold hair! Could it be? It was *her*! He tried to speak, to say the words that clotted his heart, but nothing would come.

"Hush now; be still," she whispered. "I'm here."

She took his hand and placed it first against her cheek, then to her lips. It had been so long since she had been alone with him, not since that awful day in this very room.

"No, I must tell you... how... I've missed..."

The struggle to speak took its toll. Each word was accompanied by a storm of coughing that threatened to choke him.

"Em... Beloved, Em." The words came in a hoarse whisper.

Rufus stared hungrily into her face as he breathed out his life and grew still. Hours passed as evening gathered, darkening all the corners of the room, and still she sat, gazing into the eyes of the man she loved.

Rufus Jr. tapped softly on the opened door. Em answered him without turning away from the bed. "Wait just a moment." She slipped one hand over Rufus' face, gently closing his eyelids before rising. "Come, bid your father goodbye."

"No! No-no-no..."

The young man rushed to the bedside, whirled around and, crying bitterly, collapsed into Em's open arms. She held him tightly, even though at first he struggled against her. Finally, he was able to calm down. He straightened himself and released his hold on her; now he was embarrassed that she had seen him cry.

"I know you got to get back to your master's house, so's not to get in trouble. Me an' my brothers can take care here. We'll get our... get Pa buried."

Em had been away from the Grant household for the entire day and needed to return. When she did, she found that a momentous decision had been reached. Evan met her in the front hall. Surprised and momentarily flustered, she was unable to come up with a plausible explanation for her long absence. It turned out she had not been missed. Evan summarily announced that the family was leaving for England, immediately.

Em simply stared at him. Where was England? How could they be leaving Maryland with no plans made and no time to wind up the family's affairs? Of course, she voiced none of these concerns.

"What would you like for me to do, Master Evan?"

Evan found the question impossible even to contemplate. What could she do? Get him a fair price on his farm? Keep the damned *patriots* from looting his property—which he had bought and paid for? He turned on his heel, throwing one instruction over his shoulder.

"Pack up everything we own! We leave first thing in the morning!"

One hour after daybreak, Em had all the family's valises neatly lined up outside of the house. On her last trip, she brought Sophie downstairs, dressed and bonneted, but completely dazed. She took the poor woman's arm. Together, they waited on the front steps for the carriage. Evan had hired a wagon and driver to bring their belongings to the wharf where a schooner was about to set sail for England. Evan, John and Sophie would take the carriage. Em was to ride in the wagon with the household goods.

As soon as she had Sophie settled and they had driven off, she and the hired driver loaded the wagon with the Grants' small furniture and other portable possessions. The man climbed onto the seat, taking up the reins, but she remained where she was.

"Ain't you comin?" he asked her.

"I believe there was something in the office I was supposed to bring. You go on ahead. Ask Master Grant to send Ben and the carriage back for me."

The man grunted, flicked the reins and drove away. Em was sure he would not remember the message accurately. But she hoped Ben would notice her absence and offer to drive back to the house.

The scene at the dock was chaotic, with people shouting to each other and at their servants. A number of Tory sympathizers, as these loyal British subjects were now so disrespectfully called, had decided the Colonies were becoming too dangerous. Once trusted neighbours were now as likely as not the very ones who would set torch to your house or barn while you slept. A large group was leaving on this ship; the scheduled departure was imminent.

By the time the Grants were finally able to board and have their belongings stowed, the ship was moving out of the harbour. No one noticed that neither Em *nor Ben* was onboard. Ben had indeed noted Em's absence and had returned with the carriage to fetch her. When he got back to the house, he found it empty. Dutifully returning to the harbour, he discovered that the ship had sailed, and he was, effectively, a free man! Not sure where to go, he turned the carriage toward the part of Baltimore where he knew some free Blacks lived. He actually drove past Em without seeing her, as she was walking toward Rufus' shop.

Chapter 18

NEW YORK (1775)

*P*hillip got word of his father-in-law's departure about six months later, when a letter finally reached him. In it Evan had detailed his woes, the loss of his practice and property, including two most trusted servants, and the deleterious effect that those losses and the move itself were having on Sophie's health.

Evan's situation got Phillip to thinking about his own. The New York militia had been formed that spring, and all able-bodied men were expected to enlist. Personally, he had absolutely no preference for either side in this debacle. The Colonists were horribly outnumbered by a hugely superior force; there was no possibility of gaining independence from England. Those so foolhardy as to take up arms were simply asking to be shot or, worse yet, hung as traitors. Unfortunately, this did not staunch the enlistment drives. He was certain he would soon be asked why he had not yet joined the fight.

Evie, too, was worried. She had even less interest in this revolution than her husband. It was simply bad for business, this war, and she wanted it to be done with. Then, almost miraculously, the solution presented itself. She laid out her idea over supper one evening, after the children had been dismissed from the table.

"We shall take the children and go to the Continent for six months. By that time, England will have put down this rebellion, hung whoever was responsible and, possibly rescinded some of the taxes, just to mollify people. We can resume life and you will not have to enlist in anything."

Phillip was thoroughly amazed. How could Evie come up with such simple, yet clever ideas! He agreed immediately, but then thought about the business. She dismissed his concerns, airily.

"Oh, Will can carry on for that long without you. He knows the merchandise as well as you do. And he can supervise the workers also."

"Evie, you are brilliant!" Phillip exclaimed. "Now, about the children, they will need their nurse."

Secretly, he prayed Evie would say that Annie should accompany the children. He had never been able to overcome his lust for her, even during her pregnancies, although he never let Evie see him so much as looking in Annie's direction. It was the *scent* of the woman! Whenever she passed him, she left behind a sweet, slightly earthy fragrance; sometimes it got into his dreams.

But Evie knew him too well. She announced that Circe would be the one to go. Circe was now almost thirty-five and somewhat overweight. She would be safe from Phillip's advances.

"Annie is pregnant and nearly ready to give birth. You know how hard this has always been for her! She stays here! The children are old enough to take care of themselves. Anything they need, Circe can provide."

When Osei learned of the planned trip, he was happy, though not surprised. He too had read Evan's letter, since Phillip had conveniently left it out on his office desk. Osei had also been making it his business to keep abreast of events surrounding the rebellion by listening to talk on the docks and surreptitiously reading the pamphlets that littered the streets. He had picked up the name of a General Washington, who was now leading the Colonists in their war against England. And things were not going so well for these patriots, as the pamphlets called them.

For Osei, the important thing was that if the upheaval caused Phillip and Evie to take their children and leave America, even for so short a time as six months, this could be his chance to escape with his family.

The problem was Annie's pregnancy. She had gone four years; then it came unexpectedly. She was overjoyed, sure that the evil spell had been broken with Willy's birth. Osei was not sure at all. He had explained, as simply as he could, the situation with the charm that only the child could identify.

Osei had tried to get his son to tell him where the charm was. But Willy did not seem to understand what his father wanted.

"Pa, how can I bring you it if I don't know what it is?"

"But you *do* know it. You will know it when you find it. The thing will speak to you; it will say 'I'm here, Willy'."

And so, Willy tried and tried to find the thing that his father wanted. Whenever he was outside playing, he would ask errant rocks and twigs the all important question. "Are you the thing my Pa wants?"

Nothing answered him. At last, he found something he hoped would satisfy his father. He made a solemn presentation just before being put to bed, approaching Osei with one small hand behind his back.

"Here, Pa. I found a thing."

Willy produced a large agate marble, dropped, probably, by some child. Osei gazed sadly at his son; the little boy was staring earnestly into his face, silently pleading to be right. Willy saw his father's disappointment and began to cry.

"No, no, you did well. Please, my son, do not cry!"

Osei lifted the weeping child and held him close. Whatever happened, Willy had done his best. These spirits were wily, especially here in this place, so far from Africa. There, at least, Osei would have been able to appeal to his mother for help.

Phillip and Evie announced the trip to the household a few evenings after the decision had been made. Evie wanted the house closed up during their absence. She sent Osei to Wall Street to rent four maids who would clean everything and cover all the furniture. Within another week, the family's clothing was packed, and ready to be transported to the wharf.

On the day of departure, as friends and neighbours gathered to bid farewell to the travelers, a strange sense of foreboding took hold of Evie. Although she had always had an excellent sense of intuition, it had never before extended to her beloved servant. Today, however, every time she looked at Annie, she had the powerful feeling that she would never see her again. In the small front yard, she pulled Annie close; unexpected tears filled her eyes.

Something in Annie responded to her mistress' distress. Indeed, she too felt the separation was going to be permanent. Instead of simply tolerating Evie's embrace, she returned it, and then she laid her palms on both of her mistress' cheeks.

"Never you fear, Mistress Evie. Annie will always be with you."

Her words worked wonders. Evie brightened immediately, completely missing their undercurrent. "Of course! I shall see you in six months."

Osei watched the carriage pull off and round the corner, heading toward the docks. When they were out of sight, he shepherded his family back to the carriage house. Annie seemed more tired than usual that evening. And, in the morning, her water broke.

This labour was very different from before with Willy. There was very little pain. Osei sat and watched his wife through the first two hours; then he assembled the things he feared he might need for the delivery. From the cellar, he brought up a bottle of full proof rum, the strongest rum produced in all of the West Indies. Phillip kept but a few bottles on hand; he served his rum only on Christmas. Next, Osei heated three pokers in the grate downstairs.

After another hour, when he checked Annie, she was fully ready; he could see the crown of the baby's head. He breathed a sigh of relief. At least it had not been in the breech position. The birth itself was not difficult; the baby simply slipped out. It was then that Osei saw why things had been so easy. This baby was as scrawny as a half-filled rag doll. Its legs and arms were matchsticks, its body so thin that the tiny rib cage stood out like a chicken's. Yet the puny thing lived! It uttered a series of mewling cries, thereby filling its lungs with life-giving air. Annie heard and reached for her baby.

"What is it? Oh let me see!"

Osei examined the infant. It was a boy. Wordlessly, he handed Annie her child. If she noticed its condition, she said nothing, only weakly attempted to put it to the breast. But a terrible dizziness came over her like a wave. She fainted, and Osei was just able to catch the child before it fell.

When he looked at the area between her legs, he saw, to his horror, that the bedclothes were soaked with blood; the red was spreading so quickly that it completely covered the lower half of the bed. His worst fears were being realized. He would have to stop the bleeding at its *source*.

This was a procedure he had learned but never actually performed. Silently, he prayed to the ancestors to guide him as he lifted Annie's shoulders, then her head. She was still comatose, but he needed for her to be completely unconscious. He lowered her, face down, so that her head hung over the side of the bed. She stirred and opened her eyes. He righted her, holding her head back.

"Here. Drink this. All of it."

Osei was tipping the bottle of rum to her mouth. She swallowed obediently, then coughed violently, nearly gagging. It took a great effort, but he was able to get nearly the entire contents down her throat. Annie sighed once, belched softly, and then fell into a deep sleep. Now he had to work quickly.

He laid the baby in the cradle that had been Willy's bed, 'til he outgrew it. Then he ran downstairs for the first poker, wrapping the end that he had to hold with a piece of cloth. In their quarters, there was a small iron gate where the chimney passed through the wooden floor. He opened this gate, allowing a draft of heat and flames to rise, and stuck the still white-hot poker in for another minute. Then he carefully spread Annie's legs apart. She was still fully dilated, and he was able to insert it all the way into her womb. Now he used his free hand to locate its contours, as he carefully moved the poker around the inside wall. It was a terrible effort to avoid tearing her insides or burning her too much. When he was certain that the poker was no longer hot enough to be effective, he withdrew it and watched for more oozing. Only a tiny trickle continued, but this was enough for him to go for the second poker and repeat the process. Annie made a small noise in her throat, but otherwise remained still through the second procedure. And this time, the bleeding stopped completely.

Willy had been sent downstairs to play, with the admonition not to come back until called. But it had been just *forever*, and he was lonely. Annie always kept him nearby and now he wanted his mother. He was also deeply suspicious of whatever secret thing his parents were doing that he was not allowed to watch. The Master's children, with whom he had always played, were gone, and he was not accustomed to their absence. So, although he knew he was being disobedient, he slipped back into the carriage house and climbed the stairs. Lifting the latch, he quietly opened the door to their quarters. His father was bending over his mother, doing something. Then Willy saw the bloody bedclothes and screamed.

Osei, so intent on what he was doing, never heard the boy come into the room and sidle up to stand close by his right leg. Willy's cry startled him so he almost jabbed the poker through Annie's abdomen. Without turning in his son's direction, he roared at the child, for the first time ever.

"I told you not to come 'til you were called! Get back downstairs and do not come up again!"

Thoroughly frightened, the boy bolted for the door, leaving it open in his wake. Osei heard the footsteps tumble down the stairs, accompanied by loud wails. He desperately wanted to run after Willy, but he couldn't; he had to finish and hope he had not injured Annie in the process. He removed the now-cool poker and checked her womb by feeling through the abdominal wall. There was no more bleeding, which meant that, for now, at least, she would not die.

He turned his attention to the newborn. It needed naming, but somehow, he could not bring himself to touch it just yet. He could not even acknowledge the poor thing as his second son. He knew this one was born to die and break Annie's heart yet again. Nevertheless, the infant drew breath and emitted more of the mewling cries. He lifted the babe and wrapped it in one of the blankets that Annie had draped over the cradle. Carrying it in one arm, he went to find his eldest.

Willy had taken shelter under the stairs. His sobs had become dry hiccups by the time Osei found him. He turned his face away from his father.

"Ah, my son, do not be angry with your Pa. Come to me."

Willy slid out from his hiding place and allowed himself to be enfolded in his father's free arm. Osei held the boy close for several minutes; he then showed the child his new brother.

"Come, help me name him."

They went outside into the yard. Osei held the wrapped infant closely as he whispered the name into the tiny ear; then he presented his new son to the ancestors. "This is Kofi Antobam. Have mercy upon him while he lives with us, and welcome him when he returns to you."

Thus did Osei begin to come to terms with what had happened. It was Friday, so his son was born with the name Kofi, for his birth day. But his father had named him Antobam, the Sufferer, for such, he expected, would be this little one's fate.

Once Osei had made Annie clean and as comfortable as possible, his next challenge was to find a means of getting milk for the baby. He could not immediately be put to the breast. Osei had expressed a little of Annie's milk and tasted it; it had the unmistakable odour and flavour of rum. He cast about for a possible wet nurse and remembered that Polly had been due at about the same time. Polly was the wife of Cicero, a free Black man who ran the main ferry service between New York and Long Island. And they were both Osei's most regular patients.

Chapter 19

QUEBEC (1800)

*I*nside their wigwam, the fire in the pit had begun to die. Anika and Great Bear lay facing each other on the sleeping mat. She reached for a second blanket; the nights were becoming cooler.

"Soon the leaves will start to turn. I hope Tekenna is planning to leave by then."

"Anika, tell me about the man who took us across the river."

She pulled the blanket up over his shoulders, taking her time smoothing out each fold. He was sure she had heard him; so he turned on his back and caught hold of one hand, forcing her to stop.

"Tell me about that man, Anika. He meant something to you, and to River Otter."

"So. It's come to this! You will make me tell everything, even in our bed?"

Great Bear sat up and pulled Anika to him. Holding her tightly with one arm, he lay down and reached for the blanket.

"This is not a story for the council fire. It is for me alone."

Anika began softly, gradually becoming aware of another more muted Voice whispering into her ear. Her memories became crystal clear, as she told them. And embroidered around their edges were events she did not know had happened and was sure she had never been told about.

"I used to visit Cicero with… with River Otter. His wife, Polly, was my dearest friend. Even today, I still miss her so…."

Cicero and Polly

Cicero's freedom had come at the cost of his appearance. When he was about fifteen, his first master, the owner of several fishing boats and one who believed in severe punishment as a means of keeping his slaves in line, chose a Sunday to whip Cicero for failing to come quickly enough when called. The very sight of the lash had set the lad's heart to pounding in terror. Instead of taking his punishment like a man, Cicero had screamed so loudly that he could be heard for blocks. Someone made a complaint, and the man was fined £10 sterling for disturbing the peace on the Sabbath.

Once he had paid the fine, he returned to the dock and, taking the butt of his whip, struck Cicero in the mouth for causing him so much trouble. The blow knocked out all of the poor boy's front teeth, leaving a gaping bloodied wound of mangled lips and gums. Then his master grabbed him by the scruff of the neck, dragged him over to the ferryman's boat and threw him aboard.

"You can have him for £10! If I have to keep him one day longer, I might just kill him!"

John Smithson, the ferry owner, took one look at the whimpering, bleeding youth and gasped, "T'wasn't enough ya beat him, a mere lad, so unmerciful? Why, ya scurrilous coward! Ya just about killed him a'ready! Here! Take yer £10 and get th' hell off my boat!" Smithson flung the money in the man's general direction.

The fishing boat captain bristled at the insult and, for just a moment, it looked like he might challenge the ferryman. But then he thought better of it; John Smithson was twice his size. A good blow from one of those huge fists could easily do the captain serious harm. He picked up the coins and left.

Smithson then turned to Cicero. "Foller me!" he ordered the youth and headed toward his tiny house. Once inside, the ferryman tended Cicero's wounds as best he could, which involved staunching the flow of blood and then simply hoping for the best.

There was good reason, beyond personal cowardice, why Cicero's now-former master chose not to confront the ferryman. Back in '41, New York had been gripped with fears about a *Negro plot*, a supposed conspiracy involving Black slaves and a few Whites, to burn the whole city and kill all the residents. John Smithson, then a young man in his early twenties, had recently come to town from Pennsylvania where his Irish family had a farm. As accusations began to fly and hundreds of Blacks were arrested, Smithson's name somehow came to the attention of the Colonial authorities as one of the White conspirators. He was taken into custody and brutally questioned over many days. The only thing that had saved him from the gallows was his ability to prove he hadn't arrived in the city until after March 14, the day the first fires had broken out in the Governor's mansion and at a nearby church.

Notwithstanding when he was finally released, a mob of townsmen was waiting for young John outside Fort George. They planned to exact their own punishment by tarring and feathering any conspirator accused, but not tried. However, they had not reckoned with John being as strong as an ox and accustomed to manhandling animals four or more times his weight. He broke the jaw of the first man who accosted him, shattered the second man's right arm and, when a third tried to tackle him from behind, he caught the man over his shoulder and, with a twist, snapped his neck. The others in the crowd were now convinced of his innocence. They picked up their fallen comrades and beat their hasty retreat.

From that time forward, John Smithson had the reputation of a man not to be trifled with, no matter what. And as far as he was concerned, this was just fine. His interrogation had turned him against the Colonial government, and the willingness of the good citizens to attempt his murder did not ingratiate them with him either. He decided to limit his associations to those whom the authorities and the gentry despised, namely freedmen and those poor Whites who, like himself, had no use for titles or rich men. From this perspective, John easily came to dislike all slaveholders and, by extension, slavery itself.

Nonetheless, he had to make a living. At that time, there was only an informal ferry service between the city and Long Island, consisting of independent boatmen who would take folk across the river on no particular schedule for a fee. When one of these men became ill, John offered to take over. The boatman grew worse and eventually died, leaving John in possession of a good-sized barge. He advertised by word of mouth, offering lower prices than his competitors and a regular schedule of five crossings each day. In no time, John Smithson's ferry service had put the other independents out of business.

As his business grew over the years, John hired men, Black and White, to serve as his crew. This meant most of his profits went into salaries and upkeep on the ferry, leaving very little in the way of savings. He was able to purchase an empty unpainted shack adjacent to the Wet Dock, a recessed area of the harbour where the ferry and other small boats could be safely moored. Here he lived alone, as he never married.

When John Smithson rescued Cicero, he had, by then, weathered sixty years on earth and forty running the ferry service. He let the youth live with him. And he took took Cicero on as his unpaid helper, although he would not let the lad act as his servant. One evening, about six months later, just as the ferryman and the lad were finishing their supper of cold potatoes and cabbage, Cicero finally screwed up the courage to ask the question that had begun to nag him.

"Masta John, how come yuh bought me? All yuh lets me do is t'help yuh on th' ferry. Yuh nev'r beats me an' yuh won' let me serve yuh neith'r."

"So, what is it? Ya want t' be treated like a slave? Is that it? Well, yer not gettin' yer wish on that score! I ain' nivver needed no waitin' on!" For a moment, Smithson's eyes had flashed with barely suppressed anger that was, just as quickly replaced with a mysterious twinkle. "B'sides, he continued, "I got other plans fer ya."

For a long time now, the ferryman had ached to give up the ferry service and return to Pennsylvania. He was certain most of his family and neighbors were gone. But that didn't really matter; he just had a hunger to spend his final days on the land where he had grown to manhood. Cicero's coming was finally an opportunity to train someone who could replace him.

Smithson was a hard master when it came to teaching the young man how to navigate the ferry. And Cicero proved a most apt and grateful apprentice. He learned the East River so well that, within a year, Smithson could let him make the runs on his own.

When he was certain Cicero could handle the business of setting and collecting fares, Smithson finally decided the time had come to retire. He made his announcement at the end of the last run on a Saturday evening, right after the crew, two freedmen, had collected their wages and left the ferry.

"Cicero!" he called to the young man, "Come forward when yer finished wit' them fares!" Although the last run back to New York was almost always empty of passengers, Smithson had said nothing to Cicero until now.

"Yessuh Masta John." Cicero replied and hurried to count out the last monies collected from farmers at the Long Island landing.

"If we both live t' be a hundr'd, d'ya think ya'll ever learn not t'call me master? D'ya, Cicero?" Smithson stood glaring, feet planted apart, arms folded across his chest.

"Th' habit sure been hard t' break, Suh."

"Well, here 'tis. Come t'morra, yer a free man. I done had papers wrote out on ya what says yer free. Startin' wit' th' next ferry run, yer in charge. Th' business is yourn now."

"But, Suh, whea yuh gon' be? Ain't yuh gon' run th' ferry no more?"

"Nossir! I ain't! It's up t'you now. I'm goin' back home t' Pennsylvanie!"

For Smithson, it was as though making the statement out loud had suddenly generated action. He strode past a totally startled Cicero. Grabbing hold of the coil of rope, Smithson turned and tossed it to him.

"See, 'tis as easy as that! Aw, now don't make a face! Y'musta known I meant fer ya t' have it! Why else would I'uv put up wit' ya all this time? Giv'n ya all that grief?" By now, the ferry master was laughing uproariously. "Yes indeed! Yer th' new ferry master!" Smithson was nearly convulsed at the notion of his White customers, many who could barely stomach dealing with him, suddenly having to pay this Black freedman to take them across the East River. "Yes, indeed! They'll pay *you*, or they'll have t' row theirselves!"

The ferry master was still laughing as he stepped off the barge and made his way across the Wet Dock. "Oh, an' th' house is yourn as well!" He tossed this over his shoulder just before going inside.

The next day, Cicero was nearly heartbroken to see his benefactor leave. He cried openly as Smithson boarded the ship that would take him down the coast to New Jersey. From there, he would have a difficult overland journey into landlocked Pennsylvania. The farm owned by his family was just a few miles past the border between southern New Jersey and Pennsylvania.

"Be well, son." It was the only time John Smithson had ever used any term of endearment with Cicero. Admitting that he cared for the young man was something just too foreign to his nature. Embarrassed, he quickly turned away. Hoisting his small bundle of belongings, only a few changes of clothing and a pair of lace-up shoes, he went down the three steps leading onto the deck and disappeared among the other passengers.

Over the next fifteen years, Cicero was able to expand the ferry service by acquiring a flat barge that could carry horses and wagons, thereby allowing him to bring farmers and their goods into the city. The added revenue meant that he could hire another unemployed freedman and schedule an additional run. He was also able to save a modest amount of money.

Unfortunately, Cicero's mouth had healed badly, leaving him with large scarred lips that folded into pleats when closed. By the time he had reached his twenties, his remaining back teeth, no longer anchored to the missing ones, had drifted apart, so that, when he opened his mouth they appeared as scattered stones in a red desert. Eating, also, had become a problem since he had to use lips and gums to help his few teeth do the work of a mouthful. This meant Cicero's table habits embarrassed him so much that he tried never to eat in front of others.

Overall, he considered himself much too homely to approach any woman with the intention of beginning a relationship that might lead to marriage. Physically, he was overly lean, all bone, sinew and compact muscle, with thick, prominent veins visible in his neck, forehead and arms. Although of average height, both his hands and feet appeared to be much too large for his body.

However, in spite of his general unattractiveness, Cicero was no hermit. He found his social circle in the gathering of Black Baptists who held services outdoors, sitting on split-wood benches that they'd set up each Sunday on the Commons. The flock was led by a man called, quite simply, Preacher, whose knowledge of the Bible had been gained through memorizing the entire book as it had been read aloud to him by missionaries. Preacher held six services each Sunday, since no more than twelve enslaved persons could assemble at any time, and Cicero attended them all.

Cicero was able to lead the congregation in the hymns, singing loudly in a rough, tuneful voice, somewhere between a high baritone and a tenor. He would set the melody; then, once the song was underway, he would sing harmony a third below. Several other male voices would chime in, taking the bottom third, while some of the women took a third above. The four-part harmony thus created made the hymns so beautiful that White passersby on their way to their own churches would stop to listen.

But Cicero's special value lay in his "getting the Spirit" at every service. Once his heart was filled with the Holy Ghost, he would testify at the top of his lungs, shouting and dancing until all the other worshippers got caught up in his frenzy.

By the time he had reached the age of thirty-five, Cicero believed he had settled into a life of celibacy. However, one Saturday morning, after his early ferry run, he happened to be passing one of the slave markets that sometimes set up on the waterfront. As he stopped to watch several groups being auctioned off, a woman standing at the back of one of the lines caught his eye. He was never able to say exactly what it was, but something about her stirred his heart. He walked over to the Black overseer who was standing nearby and asked about purchasing her. The man eyed him suspiciously before going over to the auctioneer. He returned with a terse response.

"If'n ya wants to buy th' wench, it'll cost ya £50 sterling, paid on takin' possession."

When White men bought slaves, it was an agreement between "gentlemen" that allowed the new owners to take their property with them and pay what was owed later. Cicero knew he was being forced to show money before he could have the woman.

With less than an hour before his next scheduled trip, he ran back to the Wet Dock. Inside his house, he pulled out a leather bag containing his entire life savings, just over £50 in coins. Frightened that he would be too late, he raced back to the market just as the auctioneer was reaching the line in which the woman stood, head bowed, and clad only in a gunny sack. Cicero approached the Black overseer with his bag. The man took it silently and delivered it to the auctioneer. Once the auctioneer had counted out the coins, he gestured to the overseer. The man released the woman, pointed in Cicero's direction and turned his back on them both.

As she slowly approached her new owner, Cicero could now see that she was more than a little apprehensive. Anxious to ease her fears, he spoke up quickly.

"Yuh free now."

Her eyes widened, then filled with tears. She fell to her knees, grabbed both his hands and began kissing them. "Oh! Mista! Oh, thank yuh! Yuh's my savior!"

Her gratitude stunned him. He couldn't think of what else to say to her. But he couldn't leave her kneeling at his feet either. His mind raced. She had nowhere to go and nothing else except the sack she was wearing.

"I knows ya ain't got nowhere t'live now," Cicero ventured hesitantly. "If'n ya want, ya kin stay in my house. It ain't much, jus' one room, but I kin fix ya up a private space. An' I promise yuh, I'm a God-fearin' Christian man! Yuh ain't got nothin' t'worry 'bout from me!"

And so the woman accompanied Cicero to his house. On the way, she told him that her name was Polly. And, as soon as they reached his door, she began to tell him her life story.

While she spoke, she moved purposefully around Cicero's house, almost as though she knew the place, starting a fire in the hearth and pulling out pots. It was clear that she planned to start supper. She seemed to need to keep her hands busy while she talked.

Polly had been her mother's sixth child and the only one not fathered by the White overseer on the Hudson Valley farm where they all lived.

Sally, Polly's mother, had fallen in love with one of the enslaved workers, Lemuel, and they had always planned to marry. Unfortunately for them both, Sally was a beautiful, dark-skinned girl with a flawless face and an unforgettable form. As soon as Martin Tucker, the overseer, laid eyes on her, he marked her as his, and no Black man was to touch her so long as he still wanted her. Tucker forced her to live with him in his cabin and kept her separated from the other slaves. Still, Sally slipped away as often as she could to see her Black lover.

Luckily for her, the first five babies were clearly Tucker's, so he did not suspect any treachery on her part. In any event, he never let himself regard his children as anything other than human property he had contributed to the absentee owner of the farm he ran. Tucker made certain that Sally would not develop an inconvenient attachment to any of these babies either. He allowed her to nurse each infant for eight months, no longer. Then he'd have the child taken out of his house and placed with the older women who took care of the workers' offspring while the parents were in the fields.

Cicero watched Polly, almost breathlessly, as she searched around for something she could cook. The only food he had on hand was several potatoes and a small side of bacon, which she found in a cupboard by the hearth. She peeled the potatoes, sliced them thick, along with the bacon, and fried them together. As she was tending to the food, she continued her story.

"When I wuz born'd, black as I wuz, couldn' nobody miss how much I favor'd Lem'el, my real Pa. They say my Ma'am sent me t' th' slave quart'r's soon's she seen me. But it didn' help none. Masta Tuck'r foun' out, an' he say he gon' git th' nigg'r what touch'd his 'oman.

"Oh they tried t' keep quiet! But they wuz all 'fraid a' Masta Tuck'r. He jus' look at 'em 'n they git so skeerd, they'd a tol' on th' Devil!

"Well, Masta Tuck'r, he had some 'a them scary nigg'rs tie Lem'el t' th' neares' tree an' he beat my Pa. Whipp'd him f' hours, 'til th' skin come off an' th' meat show'd. They say he jus' got so mad an' would'n stop cuz my Pa would'n scream or nothin'. He jus' beat him t' death! An' th' wors' part, he made my Ma'am watch, so's she'd learn not t' do it agin!"

By the time Polly reached this part of her tale, the meal was ready. She filled plates for Cicero and herself. Then she sat across from him at his table. She began eating immediately, talking all the while; obviously she hadn't eaten in days. Cicero, however, eyed his plate uncomfortably, then pushed it aside and leaned forward, transfixed.

Sally was a changed woman after that, silent and eerily watchful. Even Tucker noticed that she no longer bothered pretending to respond to his touch. When he would finally become angry and slap her after having had dry and tedious sexual relations with her, yet again, she would just lay there, watching him until he'd given up and fallen asleep. As soon as she was certain he was sleeping soundly, she'd slip down to the quarters to nurse Polly, not yet a year old.

Sally did become pregnant later that same year. And this time Tucker felt confident the baby was his. He even tried to make her feel better, bringing her baubles whenever he could get them, making sure she had the best food available.

But, as the months went by, instead of gaining, she began to lose weight rapidly. By the time she had reached her sixth month, she had become nearly skeletal. When she went into labour, much too early, there was clearly no hope for the baby's survival. Then Sally developed a fever and died less than a day later. Only the midwife who attended the birth knew that she had deliberately starved herself and Tucker's last child to death.

When her mother died, Polly was nearly two. As soon as Sally had gotten pregnant, she'd stopped visiting her daughter. It was easier to do that than to take an empty teat to the child. And Sally hadn't wanted Polly to remember her or miss her too much.

Polly really didn't remember Sally, other than as a warm presence that she sometimes felt just before falling asleep. She grew up surrounded by the children of the field workers and far away from the man who had made her an orphan. Because she was small for her age, like her mother had been, she would be twelve years old before being put to work helping care for the babies. And she was twenty, before she was sent into the fields for the first time, where she finally came to the attention of the overseer.

"Th' 'omens what rais'd me up, well they kep' me hid from Masta Tuck'r long as they could. He ain' know'd one li'l nigg'r f'um anotha, so I wuz safe— 'til I got grow'd. But he ain' had no 'oman since my Ma'am an' he's on th' look-out f' anoth'r.

"He musta seen me in th' fiels an' decided I wuz gon' be next. But I already made up my own mine 'bout that! Same day he sent word t' th' quarters f' me t' be up t' his cabin come sundown, I tak'n my scythe t' my face, my arms, an' my limbs. I ain' stopp'd cuttin' 'til I's runnin' blood!

"Soon's I's threw, I jus' went back t' work like ain' nothin' happen'd, bleedin' an' all. Th' 'omens start'd hollerin' an' carryin' on somethin' fierce! Somebody run 'n fetch Masta Tuck'r, an' he wanna know, 'Who'all cut yuh up like that?'

"I jus' tol' th' truth. I say, 'Yuh know, Masta Tuck'r, whilst I's workin,' somethin' jus' come over me an' I done it t' myself!'

"Well! That White man thought I's daft! He got so skeer'd he start'd hollerin' 'bout he cain't have no crazy nigg'r 'oman on no farm where he's at. He sent me right off th' place with a gang a' slaves bound f' market in New Yawk. They tol' us we wuz gon' be sold South, where they really knows how t' handle they slaves!"

All the while that Polly was talking Cicero could hardly follow her words for watching her. The facial scar had barely healed, leaving a long curved pink line down her left cheek. He wanted to touch it, to run his fingers along its length. And he ached to caress her scarred arms, from elbows to wrists. It was as though he could feel her inside of himself, filling every bit of him, leaving no room for the food, now growing cold and congealed on his plate.

"Mista Cicero, yuh has surely saved my life. I don' know how, but I'ma repay yuh some day. I swear it!" She hesitated, then gestured toward the still-full plate. "Ain'cha gon' eat?"

"Miz Polly, I ain't hungry jus' now. I'll eat this t'morra."

"But ya ain' et nothin' since mornin' at least. Yuh shore ya wanna wait that long?"

By now night had fallen. Cicero could hear his heart beating much too loudly. Instead of answering her, he rose and began to get the space ready for her to sleep. He used clotheslines and a blanket to create a private area around his bed. Then he folded blankets and placed them on the floor in a corner, for his sleeping space.

Polly begged him to let her take the pallet rather than the bed, but he steadfastly refused. At last, she gave in and went behind the make-shift curtain. He could hear her undressing and getting into his bed. He spent the night awake on his pallet, listening to the sound of her breathing, and his own heart.

On their first Sunday together, Cicero took Polly with him to services. Word had spread among the congregation that he had used his life savings to purchase her freedom. Several women made it their business to visit the ferry-man during the week to find out what Polly might need in the way of clothing. They were able to salvage several lengths of muslin, and they sewed up a simple gown so she would be able to attend church with Cicero. When the two of them arrived at the Commons just before the first service, one of the women leaned over and whispered a promise she'd come by the house that next week with a few more pieces of clothing for Polly.

As soon as Preacher called for a hymn, Cicero rose, threw back his head and sang with his whole heart. Polly knew neither tune nor lyric, so she contented herself with watching him. At first, she found herself simply enjoying the glorious singing and the sight of him pouring out his praise in a voice that carried over everyone else's. When he suddenly cried out loudly and began his trance-like holy dance, she became transfixed. His open, unabashed fervor caught her up and held her fast. Each of the separate homely elements of his body combined before her eyes into a raw-boned beauty that excited some deep, hitherto untouched part of her. By the time the final service was over, she knew in her heart that this was the man she wanted, forever.

Mealtime was a problem Polly solved that same Sunday evening. She could see that Cicero was refusing to eat in front of her, and she made up her mind to confront him directly.

"I mus' be one poor cook, 'cause ya never wants t' eat my food! Is ya plannin' t'starve yerself?"

Cicero literally squirmed, not wanting to explain how unpleasant he was sure she would find his eating. Polly continued, setting their evening meal on the table.

"I ain' gon' b'lieve ya likes my cookin' 'til I sees ya enjoyin' yer food!"

There was nothing Cicero could do but eat. He began very tentatively, nearly choking as he tried to swallow a too large morsel without chewing it. Finally, he gave up.

"Miz Polly, I makes a whole lot a' noise when I eats, 'cause I ain't got many teeth."

Polly fixed him with a dead-on stare. "Jus' eat yer food! Think I care 'bout noise? I jus' wanna see ya eat!" Then she smiled. As she did, a dimple appeared under her right eye, just where the scar ended.

Cicero's heart skipped a beat at the sight of that smile. For the first time, he sensed she might feel something more for him than simple gratitude. But the realization did little to relieve his painful shyness with the woman.

During the following week, Cicero and his crew ran the ferry, meeting passengers, hauling them and their freight back and forth across the East River, collecting the fares. All the while, he could scarcely concentrate on anything but Polly. In his mind, he relived each of her tentative advances and his awkward responses. The truth was he loved her with all of his heart, had from the moment he'd laid eyes on her in the slave market at Lyon's Slip, although he would not let himself acknowledge the fact. After all, how could she possibly return the love of a man as homely as he?

The ferry schedule allowed for two morning runs, one afternoon and two evening runs. At midday, the barge would be berthed while the men took their dinner. Cicero returned home each day to find that Polly had prepared his food and a pail for him to take to Sam, the young man who served as his mate.

By now, he knew he had to eat freely or risk offending her. She would place his meal in front of him and sit across from him, her eyes following every mouthful, smiling at the sight of his opened mouth and the sound of his lips smacking as he ate. Only when he was nearly finished would she begin eating herself. It was almost as if her whole pleasure during mealtimes was watching him.

At first, Cicero found the experience of eating in front of her both horribly embarrassing and painfully exciting. But gradually, his excitement intensified, overtaking the shame, and he began to relish eating with her. Mealtimes became the first physical connection between them.

That Saturday evening, when Cicero returned after his final run for the week, he found Polly already at the supper table. He hurriedly washed up and joined her, the eagerness already rising in him. As he began to eat his biscuits and greens, he noticed that she seemed unusually pensive. Instead of watching him, she was staring into her plate, as though its contents held the answer to some mystery. He put down his bread and leaned forward.

"Miz Polly, is somethin' amiss?"

Suddenly, she raised her eyes; they were filled with tears. Cicero, alarmed, placed both hands on the table, intending to get up and come to her side. But she stopped him, laying her hands over his.

"I been tryin' not t' be too forward, yuh bein' a Christian man 'n'all. But I cain' hol' it in no longer. Cicero, I loves ya. So, I cain' stay here no more, if'n ya don' love me back!"

A powerful roar had begun in Cicero's ears at the word. Had she said she *loved* him? He was nearly certain that she had used the word. Every sensible thought had scattered, leaving him staring, still half-standing, lips hanging agape.

"M-M-Miz Polly," he stuttered helplessly, "p-please don' say nuthin' yuh don' mean! I-ah... my heart cain't take no foolin'!"

She had begun to gently stroke the back of one of his hands with her index finger, lightly tracing the pattern of veins.

"I ain' foolin'. I wants t'stay wit' yuh. Please say ya loves me too! Don' send me away!"

The roar had gotten so loud that Cicero could no longer hear anything clearly. When he answered her, it seemed to him that he was nearly shouting.

"Oh, Miz Polly, I been lovin' ya ever since I seen ya on the sellin' block! I wants t'keep ya wit' me forever! But th' only'st way is f' ya t'marry me. Will ya be m' wife?"

Instead of giving an answer, Polly rose, came around to Cicero's side of the table and sat on his lap. Taking his face in both hands, she kissed his lips very softly. Then she wrapped her arms around his neck and held him tightly. After several moments, she whispered in his ear. "Now I knows ya loves me, 'cause I kin feel yer heart beatin' jus' f'me. Lord be praised! I's one lucky 'oman."

That very evening Cicero took Polly to the alley where Preacher lived with his wife and seven children in a tiny two-room house adjacent to his master's carriage-making shop. Preacher, a wainwright during the week, was as skilled at making carriage bodies as he was at reciting Bible verses. Because his owner was the wheelwright, and therefore depended on his labour in order to deliver a complete vehicle, Preacher lived almost as a freedman. His evenings and Sundays could be given over to his pastoral duties. However, aside from the stingy allowance of food and clothing that his master provided, his only pay was the meager collection taken up at each Sunday service.

The good man invited them in. His wife greeted Cicero and Polly warmly but did not join them; she was busy putting the youngest children down to sleep in the largest of the three beds that crowded the front room. Cicero explained his need, and Preacher immediately got out the worn Bible he always carried. He led the ferryman and Polly out behind the shop. Reciting the ceremony from memory, he heard their vows and pronounced them husband and wife. Then he accepted the two shillings that Cicero pressed into his palm.

"Brother Cicero. You need t' make your vows in front of the whole congregation! I want t' see you and Miss Polly at the services t'morrow, without fail!"

The promise given, Cicero and Polly hurried home. Now, for the first time, they could be together as man and wife. Once back in their house, Polly folded the blankets that had been Cicero's pallet. Then, with a shy glance in his direction, she went behind the curtained area. After several minutes she softly called his name. He tried to answer her and found he could not; his heart was racing too wildly. She called to him again.

"Cicero! Ain'cha comin' t' bed?"

Her voice galvanized him this time. He lifted the curtain. Polly had undressed completely and gotten into bed. She extended one bare arm, scarred from shoulder to wrist, toward him. Cicero dropped to his knees beside the bed, took her arm with trembling hands and began to stroke it reverently. He kissed each raised laceration, then pressed his cheek against her forearm. When, at last, he lifted his head, his face was streaked with tears.

"Miz Polly, I wish't I could give ya all 'a what ya deserve. With all my heart I wish it! Yuh is th' mos' beautiful thing I ever seen, n' I ain' got th' words t' say what's inside 'a me right now! But, Miz Polly, I got t' confess. I ain' never had no woman before. Yuh be th' firs'!"

Polly dissolved into gales of laughter. She reached out, catching Cicero around the neck and pulling him against her body. She repeatedly kissed his face, laughing all the while.

"Oh, Darlin'! We both virgins! We gon' love each other th' way the Lord intended, ain' we? Don' that make us good Christians?"

Cicero had no knowledge of female anatomy, and only a dim idea about his own, owing to his strict adherence to Preacher's warnings against lust and self-pleasuring. His and Polly's eventual coupling would come only after a very lengthy process of discovery. They began their lovemaking by very tentatively exploring each other's bodies. Luckily for Cicero, his already fully aroused passion led him to touch Polly in all the right places. Polly, for her part, seemed to possess an innate adeptness that allowed her to locate each of the most sensitive areas of his body. By the time Cicero finally entered her, they were both at the razor's edge of ecstasy. Polly wept rivers of joyous tears. But Cicero was seized by an even more powerful emotion. Unable to contain it or to control himself, he screamed her name—and Jesus'—over and over. Then, at the top of his lungs, he thanked God for sending her to him.

A loud banging on the door interrupted them. Cicero, completely alarmed, immediately got up. Pulling on his shirt, he hurriedly drew the bolt. It was the night watch. The man lifted his lantern and thrust it into Cicero's face.

"Heard yellin' over this way! What ya' doin' in there?"

"Masta, wasn't no yellin' here. We was 'sleep."

The watchman looked unconvinced. But these were only Negroes, after all. He was not responsible for protecting *them*. With a grunt of disdain, he walked away.

Cicero immediately closed and bolted his door. He had lied to the man as a protective reflex. With White people of the middling sort, one almost always had to. Neither rich enough to own Negroes nor too poor to be allowed any racial privileges whatsoever, these were the folk most likely to hate Blacks and to give a Black man trouble.

Each day with Polly brought Cicero more joy than he could ever have hoped for. Although she busied herself with taking in washing to supplement their income, she made sure that his care came first. And she anxiously awaited his return both at noon and in the evening. There was always a hot meal ready and, as often as they had the time, extra lovemaking.

At first, Cicero was afraid to make love to Polly in daylight. But one day, when he returned home for dinner, she waited until he had finished his meal, then came around to his side of the table. Lifting her skirts, she straddled his lap. When he discovered there were no articles of clothing between her and himself, except his trousers, he quickly opened the fall, and they made love right in his chair! Cicero went back to the ferry that afternoon wearing an expression that caused his crew to smile at one another and the passengers to exchange perplexed looks.

Within three months of their marriage, Polly began to awaken feeling nauseous, almost daily. She feared she had contracted an illness, and her immediate instinct was to hide the fact from her husband. Cicero loved her so desperately, and she knew that, if he suspected she were ill, he would worry himself sick.

Finally, after Sunday services, she confided her symptoms to one of the Baptist sisters. The good woman looked her over closely, pursed her lips, then made her pronouncement.

"You expectin' a baby. My guess, you 'bout two months 'long. You ain't gained no weight 'cause you throwin' up what you eatin'. Go 'head an' tell Cicero, so he can help you out in the mornin'! It'll be at least another month before you be feelin' better!"

When Polly told him about the pregnancy, Cicero became nearly insane with happiness. He insisted she stop the heavy work of clothes washing. When she reminded him they needed the money, he vowed that *he* would wash each load early in the morning, hang the wash before the first ferry run and iron after his last. He actually did as he promised, well enough to keep Polly's clients happy and paying.

Their child was born seven months later, following an uneventful pregnancy and an easy labour. The midwife who attended Polly was also a member of the Baptist congregation. She proudly presented both parents with their daughter. Cicero sat beside Polly and gazed at the amazing little thing, sleeping so peacefully in her mother's arms.

"Polly! She so beautiful! How I manag'd to fath'r somebody that beautiful, ugly as I is?"

Polly struggled to a sitting position. Reaching out with her free hand, she touched his cheek. "Don' yuh never call yer'self ugly! Yuh ain' ugly! I seen ugly up close! 'N I knows it when I sees it! Yuh perfect, jus' as yuh is!"

They named the baby Sally, after the woman who could only slip away to nurse Polly for a few months, and whose face she could not remember.

Sally was a good baby; she slept through the night, almost from birth, and only cried when she needed to be fed. Then, one morning, when she was just three months old, she awakened warm and lethargic. When Polly tried to nurse her, she refused the breast. By noon, when Cicero returned home, she had a raging fever and was crying constantly. Polly had been walking the floor in circles, holding her.

"Cicero! She don' stop cryin' for a minute! I'm a'feared she real sick!"

Absolutely panicked, Cicero could not respond for a minute. As he cast about desperately for a source of help, he could only think of one person, Preacher. This man might be able to plead with the White doctor to see Sally. He turned and bolted, calling back over his shoulder as he left.

"Never yuh fear, Polly! I'm 'a get us some help!"

The carriage shop was busy when Cicero got there, a clear indication that the wheelwright would not tolerate having his servants interrupted. Cicero had to go around to the rear and wait until he could steal a moment of

Preacher's attention. Even after he whispered his plight to the man, there was nothing Preacher could do until the shop closed at six. Cicero begged him to speak to his master about leaving early, but the wheelwright noticed them. He shouted for Cicero to "move off immediately," threatening to have him jailed for interfering with his servant. Just before getting back to work, Preacher made a quick suggestion.

"One of the women in th' congregation once mentioned that a rich merchant's servant knew some medicine. I think she said th' man's name was Will. Go ask Mary if she remembers who it was went t' this man."

Mary, Preacher's wife, was busy washing clothes when Cicero found her out in the yard behind the shop.

"Oh yes," she told him, "that would be Mr. Hamilton's Will. He don't come t' services, but he once gave Martha a brew that cured her fever. I b'lieve the Hamilton family live on Crown Street."

Once Cicero got to Crown Street, he asked everyone he met for directions to the Hamiltons' house. A White peddler pointed out the tenth house. Then he called out as Cicero was about to approach. "Make sure you speak t' one o' th' servants. Fer God sake, you don't want t' have to deal with the mistress o' th' house!"

Cicero thanked him for the advice and went around to the kitchen, where he tapped at the door. By now, he could see by the angle of the sun that it was late afternoon. A terrible anxiety began twisting its way through his gut. What if no one were home? He tapped again, more loudly. And this time someone answered.

Annie, now eighteen, had just entered the kitchen from the house when she heard the knocking. She called out and opened the door to find the ferryman standing there, hat in hand.

"Miss, I'm lookin' f' Mr. Hamilton's Will. Is he t'home?"

"Why no, Sir. He goes to business with his master. The office and warehouses are on Beaver Street. Do you know the place?"

Almost before she had finished speaking, Cicero was off, running. He shouted, "I knows it!" and "thank yuh!," just as he turned the corner.

Hamilton's warehouses took up most of the block between New Street and Bowling Green. Cicero walked the length of the block twice before catching sight of a Black worker. He asked the man whether there was someone named Will about. The man pointed toward a tall Black man whose back was to them both. When he turned in Cicero's direction, Cicero could see that the man was wearing the finest clothes he had ever seen on a Negro. Cicero, however, was much too desperate to be impressed. He blurted out his situation, ending with a plea for help for his baby.

"Please, Mr. Will, please save my Sally! My poor Polly 'bout beside herself worryin'!"

"Give me just a moment. I will meet you outside, on the corner of Beaver and Broad."

The knot in Cicero's heart suddenly loosened slightly. The man left him on the warehouse floor, disappearing inside an office. Cicero hurried to the designated corner. Within five minutes, the man appeared, now wearing his coat and hat. With Cicero leading the way, they hurried to the Wet Dock.

They reached the house in the gathering gloom of late evening. Uncharacteristically, there were no candles burning inside; even the fireplace was dark. Cicero pushed the door opened wide, admitting the waning daylight. Polly sat in his chair beside the dead fire, gently rocking Sally's cradle. Something about her stillness tightened the knot of fear in Cicero's chest. He could hear his heart beating ever louder, even as he tried to sound reassuring.

"I foun' a man what knows medicine. He can help our Sally."

"Sally beyon' help now, Cicero. She in heav'n."

Polly had watched her baby scream, gag and vomit throughout the day. By early evening, Sally grew ever quieter, for longer periods. In the end, she went to sleep, and Polly, exhausted, placed her in her cradle. It was as she was arranging Sally's blanket that she realized the baby's sleep was not sleep, but death. Polly drew the cradle close to the chair so she could watch Sally's face. Occasionally, she stroked her baby's cheek. As long as no one came, she could pretend that Sally was still with her.

But, when Cicero came home, the spell was broken. Cicero's tears were what finally released her grief. As soon as she saw him crying, she began to wail, a heartbreaking howl of sheer pain. Cicero began to howl as well. Holding each other tightly, they sent their combined cries heavenward.

Osei did not come inside. Instead, he went in search of the man who made coffins for Black folk. He paid for the smallest coffin available and asked it be delivered to the ferryman's house. Then he returned to Beaver Street, in time to close up shop and send the workers home.

Because the hour was late, Cicero and Polly had to wait until the next day to bury their child. During the night, women from the congregation came in shifts to sit with the bereaved parents and to help Polly sew up Sally's shroud. In the morning, twelve mourners joined them for the trip to the Negro Burial Ground. Osei was among the twelve, and he helped the men dig the grave.

On the Sunday following Sally's burial, Cicero and Polly went to the second service. Neither of them could find the strength to rise early enough for the first one, just after sunrise. Although they had spoken little during that week, they had touched each other constantly, stopping, even in passing, just to embrace. Cicero was trying to be strong for Polly's sake, assuming her suffering was much greater than his. He could not have been more wrong.

Preacher called for the first hymn, "Guide Me, O Thou Great Jehovah." Force of habit caused everyone to turn toward Cicero and Polly's usual spot on the front bench. Then, quickly one of the women began singing the melody loudly, and the rest of the congregation joined in, relieving Cicero of the need to start the hymn. He sat, taking deep breaths and swaying slightly with the rhythm through the first verse. Just as they were beginning the second, he rose to his feet, took two steps forward, turned to face the congregation, fell to his knees—and screamed, so loudly and for so long that the singing had to stop! Polly half rose, intending to go to him, and froze as though suddenly turned to stone. All at once, complete pandemonium broke out! Women shrieked and began falling out. Two men joined Cicero in the front, seized by the same powerful *pain* that had been let loose amidst every member. Each man began to scream as well.

Preacher and Mary were the only ones not completely overcome. Mary immediately went to Polly's side, catching her just as the paralysis suddenly lifted and before she fell over in a dead faint. Preacher laid both hands on each kneeling man. In a voice loud enough to carry over the general noise, he began a prayer.

"Oh Lord God Jesus! Look down on all Your sufferin' children, today! Heal this father's broken heart! Strength'n this sorrowin' mother's weaken'd spirit! Bind up our wounds, Father! Shed the light of Your Everlastin' Love on these, the least of Your people! We ask it in Your name, Dear Lord Jesus! Amen!"

The prayer spread like a balm over the entire congregation. Folk helped each other up from wherever they had fallen when the Spirit took them. Mary fanned Polly until she regained consciousness. Then she took Cicero by the hand and guided him back to his seat beside his wife. The ferryman appeared dazed, so much so, until Mary decided that both he and Polly needed some sort of medical help. She called out to Martha, who was just beginning to calm herself down.

"Martha! You remember Mr. Hamilton's servant, Will, the one what helped you? Please go by their place an' see can he come t' Cicero's this evenin'. I don' like the way either him or Polly is lookin'!"

As soon as he got the message, delivered *sotto voce* by Circe, Osei went up to his room and got out the bag of dried herbs that he kept hidden. Since it was Sunday, he could slip away for a few hours after supper without undue notice. He was deeply upset about the death of the ferryman's baby because he was almost certain that he would have been unable to save her. His medicines were too powerful for use with infants.

Once Mary and several other members of the congregation got Cicero and Polly back to their home, the women set about making a meal out of whatever they could find at hand. Mary settled Polly on the bed while Cicero slumped in his chair. She and the other women were able to cook only some greens and boiled potatoes, which they placed on the grate to keep warm before taking their leave. Osei arrived just as they were going.

He examined Cicero, noting the ferryman's complexion had a grayish cast and his neck veins pumped visibly. When he felt Cicero's chest, he found that his heart was beating much too fast and a little erratically.

Osei immediately prescribed foxglove. He set the herbs to brewing in a kettle on the fire while he explained how the medicine was to be taken.

"You will need to make a tea of this herb and drink it whenever your heart feels unsteady or painful."

Cicero roused himself enough to thank this kind man who had not hesitated to offer help when asked.

"Sir, I do thank yuh from the bottom of my heart. Would ya please also look t' my Polly?"

Osei went over to the bed where Polly lay, apparently also in a stupor. He kneeled beside it and touched her forehead; it was very warm. She opened her eyes, saw him and then sat up quickly, too quickly, for she immediately fell back. Cicero tried to come to her aid, but he too was forced to sit back down.

"Please, Sir," he gasped, "What's th' matter wit' my Polly?"

Osei very gingerly palpitated both of Polly's breasts, finding them hard and hot. He rose and came to the table. Pulling the rough bench close to Cicero's chair, he leaned forward so he could face the ferryman squarely.

"Your wife has a fever on account of having too much milk. I can give you a herb for a tea that will dry up her milk, eventually. But you will need to take your wife's milk tonight, and every night until she stops making it."

Cicero was suddenly at full attention. Could this man be saying what he thought he heard, that he was to *suckle* Polly?

"Do not worry. A mother's milk cannot harm you." Osei smiled suddenly, revealing brilliant white teeth. "After all, it was the first food for all of us!"

As he rose to leave, he gave Cicero some final instructions. "You must do as I say if you do not want your wife to become very ill, possibly ill enough to die. Make sure that you completely drain both her breasts each time. Then, in the morning, give her a dose of the medicinal tea. And remember to take your medicine as well, but only whenever you feel that you need it, not everyday."

Once Osei had left, Polly tried to sit up. This time, Cicero was able to get to his feet more steadily. He came and sat on their bed. Taking Polly into his arms, he held her tightly. If his heart beat too rapidly, if it sometimes ached, it was only because he loved her so very much! No medicine could cure this kind of love!

He murmured into her thick, kinky hair, "Darlin' did ya hear what he said? I got t' suck out ya milk, else ya might die! Yuh gon' let me do it?"

She nodded yes. Then, suddenly, she kissed the base of his throat. Even in her feverish state, the idea of his suckling at her breast aroused her, and she hurriedly began pulling off her clothing. "C'mon, Cicero! Do it now! Take my milk!"

Cicero immediately undressed, leaving articles of his clothing where they fell beside the bed. He began by very gingerly passing his tongue over one of her breasts. In no time, he was sucking vigorously at each nipple, smacking his lips loudly, overcome by the taste and texture of the blood-hot liquid!

Polly gasped and shivered, physically relieved and painfully excited by the sounds of his feeding and the thumping of his heart against her body. The experience was so intense for them both that they found themselves making love as soon as Cicero had drained her. Polly's milk was sweet and so warm in his stomach that, for the first time since their marriage, instead of lying awake watching her for hours on end, Cicero actually fell asleep after lovemaking.

The combined effects of the medicines, the suckling, which only proved necessary for a week, and their nightly trysts healed them both very quickly. Although they grieved for Sally and visited her grave every Sunday, Polly and Cicero found their greatest solace with each other. In fact, Cicero wanted to be near Polly so much that he let Sam take the second morning run. He would then go home and help her with the washing. They took turns at the huge washtub; together, they hung the wet clothing and bedding on the lines that Polly had put up all over their yard. When it was time for him to return to the ferry in the afternoon, Cicero would leave her in the yard. But once out of her sight, as often as not, he would be so overwrought at having to go that he would break down in tears!

One night, after they had made love and Polly had fallen asleep in his arms, Cicero softly gave words to his overwhelming emotions. "Polly, yuh cain't begin t' know how much I loves yuh! I ain't gon' never stop lovin' yuh. Not in this life nor in th' next!"

She turned over, wrapping one arm around his shoulder and one leg across his hip. Then she murmured that she was pregnant again.

Chapter 20

The following year was 1762. Annie was now 19 and expecting her first child. Polly, now 22, was close to giving birth for the second time. The two women had become friends, shortly after Sally's death. Once they were married, Osei began taking Annie with him on his occasional Sunday evening visits to Cicero and Polly's house. He wanted to continue checking their health, especially after Polly had become pregnant.

For Annie, Polly was her very first friend. Polly, because she did the Hamilton family's laundry, would often come to Crown Street, and the two women would talk by the kitchen door. Then, as often as she could slip away, Annie would help Polly carry the wash back to the Wet Dock, always with the promise to come in and "set a spell."

The first time that Annie came alone to visit the ferryman's wife was during Cicero's noontime dinner hour. Because he and Polly were often intimate just then, they kept their door closed and bolted. Cicero answered the knock and found himself face to face with the young woman. Later, he would decide it was surprise that caused his heart to lurch suddenly. Almost immediately, he stepped aside so she could enter without passing him too closely. Although he had met her a year earlier and again when she'd visited with her husband, he had never really noticed her before. He had never seen her as he saw her now: willowy, graceful, almost exactly his height, and with a smile that lit up everything around her.

Cicero found looking at Annie during her visits a powerful source of pleasure, but pleasure liberally mixed with fearful guilt. The ferryman told himself that he was just happy because she was such a comfort to Polly. But he found himself becoming more than a little excited whenever he thought Annie might be dropping by.

Sinful thoughts had been a near constant preoccupation for Cicero before Polly came into his life. And he had successfully kept all his carnal desires at bay until he married her. Now, inexplicably, here he was actually thinking about someone *other than* his beloved Polly! Why was God tormenting him? What evil had he done? Cicero, now in agony, secretly prayed that this attraction to Annie would vanish. He begged God not to put temptation in his path, especially now that, in Polly, he had all the love he could ever need or want. Eventually, he was able, through sheer dint of will, to force all desirous thoughts of Annie out of his mind. But their residue simply burrowed into the deepest recesses of his heart.

Polly provided much-needed solace to Annie after her friend had miscarried for the first time, reminding her that "God gon' surely spare yuh th' next one."

Shortly thereafter, Polly herself went into labour. The baby, a boy this time, was stillborn, and she immediately developed childbed fever. The midwife had warned Cicero that this kind of sickness could be deadly for the mother. "That baby been dead inside her for two, three days! It poisoned her blood!"

Cicero, doubled over in agony, again stumbled his way to the Beaver Street warehouses in desperate search of Osei's help. Even though he could see through the glass of the office door that Osei was with Mr. Hamilton, he gestured wildly. Osei appeared not to notice, but almost immediately he came to the door, effectively blocking Hamilton's view of Cicero. As soon as his master returned to his desk, Osei came out. Cicero was crying so hard that he couldn't speak, but Osei guessed things had gone badly.

"The babe did not live?"

Cicero nodded dumbly.

"Polly?"

"She sick," Cicero cried out loudly. "Oh God, she so sick! Please, please, come help her! Don' let her die!"

Osei could see that Cicero was about to faint himself. Taking the ferryman's arm, he propelled him in the direction of his house.

Childbed fever was a fairly common illness that was easily cured—with the right treatment. Unfortunately, even the White doctors sometimes did not know what that was! And, of course poor women, especially Black women, poor or not, often died untreated. Osei decided that a combination of herbs, cleavers, red root and Echinacea root, would break the fever and clear Polly's body of extra fluid. He left Cicero with the promise to send Annie with the ingredients and instructions on how to brew them.

Later that same afternoon, Annie came as promised. She set to work brewing the infusions and then helped Cicero administer the first dose to Polly. Polly, barely conscious, moaned and thrashed about, as Cicero held her tightly in his arms. He rocked her, whispering that he was here and that she would soon be well. Standing near the bed, Annie watched him solemnly.

"Cicero, you are such a good husband! No wonder Polly praises you so!"

Cicero was careful not to raise his eyes to her face. Her praise, like a poison-tipped arrow, had penetrated his heart, opening a dangerous wound.

"Miz Annie, my Polly's m' whole life! You an' Mr. Will been like angels from heav'n, savin' her an' helpin' us like yuh done! I cain't thank ya enough!"

By now, Annie's very presence was exacerbating the aching in Cicero's chest. Part of him wanted to look up, to satiate his eyes with her face and form just this once. But the rest of him could not wait for her to leave, so he could be alone with his beloved. She stood, admiring the pair of them for a moment longer before putting on her cape. Just before she left, Cicero, no longer able to restrain himself, turned in her direction and watched her steadily until the door closed behind her. He stared at it miserably rocking Polly in his arms, for a very long time afterward. All his prayers had been for naught! He simply could not root this woman out of his heart! He was the foulest of sinners, one who coveted his neighbour's wife!

Polly recovered, only to discover herself pregnant again almost immediately. Cicero had wanted to wait, but that would have required their abstaining from sexual relations, something neither he nor she could manage. He especially desired his wife almost constantly, even when they were apart. Having experienced the possibility of losing her, he found his love for her seemed to have increased tenfold!

This time, Cicero decided he had to confess his sinfulness to Polly, in hopes that God would not continue to punish them both. For he was certain the reason for his babies' deaths was his loving Annie. It did not matter that he had never considered the possibility of an affair and would not ever engage in one, even in the remote possibility that Annie were willing. The fact that he could not stop himself from *watching* her, from drawing so much pleasure just from the sight of her, was worthy of punishment!

He chose the hour after their evening meal for his confession. After they had washed, dried and put away the dishes, Cicero sat in his chair with Polly on his lap. Somehow, he had thought the words would come to him, but now, each time he opened his lips to speak, something stopped him. Polly, seeing him struggling, took his face in both hands.

"Cicero! What is it?"

"Darlin', I been unfaithful t' ya!" Immediately, he burst into tears, gasps and sobs.

Polly sat up straight, staring closely at his face. "How's that possible? Yuh ain' never away from me 'cept when yuh on th' ferry!"

"Not wit' m' body, but in m' heart! I been watchin' y' frien', Miz Annie, an'-... an' *thinkin'* 'bout her—sometimes!"

Cicero was crying hard now, partly in relief at having gotten the awful truth out and partly from fear of Polly's reaction. She suddenly began to laugh! Then she hugged him tightly, kissing his tear-streaked cheeks. He was completely dumbfounded!

"Oh Polly! This ain' no laughin' matter! You expectin' agin 'n we already los' two babies, on account a' my sinfulness! Somehow, I got t' make this right wit' th' Lord!"

"Cicero! If'n yuh a sinner, so am I! How many times yuh think I look'd at Mr. Will? He dress'd like a gent'lman an' he look real fine! 'N each time he come here, he touch'd me someplace no man 'cept m' husband aught'a! But I know'd it was 'cause he was helpin' me get well! Yuh ain' no sinner f' appreciatin' my frien'! She pretty 'n good as gold too! Yer heart don' lie, not t' me. If'n yuh was t' be unfaithful, fuh real, I'd know it!"

All the knots of terror that had grown so tight around Cicero's heart suddenly loosened. He had not believed it possible, but he could feel his love for Polly growing even stronger, flooding every part of him. Whatever happened with their children, she would never blame him, nor herself! He remembered a story that Preacher had told the congregation about a man named Job, whom God had pronounced good, and then had afflicted with great misfortunes. Job had simply born his hard lot. And this was what Cicero and Polly would have to do as well.

Over the next ten years, Polly became pregnant eight more times and lost each baby. Not one lived more than three months. Eventually, because of her frequent confinements, and in spite of Cicero's trying to help, she had to give up taking in washing, along with the much-needed additional income. During this time, she came to depend on Annie's visits and help. Annie now brought along food and the Hamiltons' cast-off clothing whenever she came to see Polly. Unfortunately, Annie was experiencing the same fate with each of her own pregnancies, until '71, when Willy was born, and lived!

At first, Annie thought it inappropriate for her to bring Willy along on her visits to the ferryman's house, but she knew that Polly wanted to see her. So, she left the baby in Circe's care. However, Polly wanted to know where he was.

"Ain''cha gon' let me at least look at him? Yuh been tryin' t' have this baby f' so long! I jus' got t' see him!"

And so Willy began to accompany his mother whenever Annie visited Polly, at first in a sort of sling that Osei had made so Annie could carry him on her back. As he grew older, he would toddle along happily at her side.

In spite of his almost constant sorrow for Polly, Cicero convinced himself that he enjoyed seeing his wife's face light up at the sight of her friend and that beautiful child. He took great pleasure in the little boy, especially as Willy learned to crawl and walk. He would explore the whole house, getting into mischief by bringing every forbidden object he could find over to the ferryman for his approval.

"See Uncle Cicero!" He would extend one small hand. "See what I found!"

Willy was such an engaging child! In loving him, Cicero found a way to smother any emotions aroused by his mother's presence.

Polly, for her part, never allowed herself to be permanently saddened by her lot. Even as she cried over each lost infant, she was careful not to unduly upset Cicero, mindful that his heart was easily affected by her mood. Only the hunger to mother a child was so terribly strong in her.

One day while in the open market, she happened to notice a tow-headed, impossibly filthy little boy trying to steal a cabbage off a farmer's cart. Without a moment's hesitation, she went over to the child and held out a copper coin, enough to pay for three heads of cabbage. Silently, the boy took it, glanced up briefly, then ran off and disappeared around a corner. Several minutes later, he reappeared, now accompanied by a small mob of dirty urchins, all extending open palms!

"Alms, please!" cried the little tow-head.

Polly's brow knitted as she tried to puzzle out how best to handle the situation. She had only enough money for the few items she and Cicero needed.

"Ain''cha got no folks t'take care a' yuh?"

"No, ma'am," the child responded stoutly, speaking for the whole group. "They all dead."

"C'mon then, I'ma take yuh home wit' me. I cain't give yuh no money, but I kin feed ya!"

And so began a curious relationship between these White street orphans and the Black wife of the Black ferryman. Every day that she was well enough, Polly cooked up extra greens or boiled additional potatoes for the children who came daily into her yard. They never came indoors. Even though they were abysmally poor, it was still unacceptable for White children to eat in a free Black man's house.

When Annie learned that she and Polly were pregnant together in '75, she asked Osei if there was anything more that he could do to help her friend's baby live this time. His answer, while not exactly callous, was also not encouraging. He had tried to counsel Polly not to keep trying; he was worried about her health.

"I cannot help Polly in that respect. My medicines are too potent for newborns. But worse yet, I am certain she harbours a wicked spirit. Since none of her children have survived, there is no way I can address that which torments her. Some things we must leave to God and the ancestors."

Polly went into labour in the early morning, almost at the same time as Annie did. The midwife who had attended each of her deliveries came as soon as Cicero sent for her. The woman had come to dread Polly's deliveries. Six of her babies had been stillborn; they were the worst! Each one came out dark and bloody and limp as a rag doll. She could tell immediately, even without examining the infant that it was dead. Sometimes, the poor thing actually smelled rotten!

This labour went smoothly, with very little pain. Problems developed as soon as the child's body presented, feet first! It appeared the baby and the after-birth had somehow become entangled right at the mouth of Polly's womb. As the contractions forced the birth canal to widen, the afterbirth ruptured, spewing forth a veritable fountain of blood! Although she tried mightily, the mid-wife could not staunch the flow. In a panic, she shouted for help.

Cicero had never been able to wait outside during any of Polly's deliver-ies; he always stood just out of the way, but near enough to see his wife throughout the ordeal. Now he sprang to her side, just in time to see his baby slip out and lie face down in an ever widening pool of blood. Although the midwife quickly turned it over, revealing that it was another girl, the poor thing had already died. Polly silent until this moment looked up at Cicero.

"I'm sorry, Darlin'," she said in a whisper, just before losing consciousness.

"Polly!" Cicero pulled her to him, crying, "Ya' ain' got t' apologize! Polly?"

She was unnaturally still, no breath! No movement!

"NO! No-No-No-Sweet Jesus! Not My Polly! Please Don' Take My Polly! Please-Please-Please!"

Cicero shrieked, seemingly for hours. No one could take Polly out of his arms. No one could bear to even try. An assortment of the White street urchins, orphans she had been feeding now came to stand in the yard, wide-eyed and solemn. The ferryboat crew, Sam and the other young men, came. Gradually a crowd of Black folk gathered. As many of the Baptist congregation as could come stood outside, crying for Polly and praying, praying hard for Cicero!

The day had turned bright and sunny when Osei reached the ferry land-ing. He noticed that the barge was still moored, as though it had not been taken out, although it was now early in the afternoon. There was even a small crowd waiting for the next ferry. A growing sense of uneasiness made him hurry toward Cicero's house. The front door had been draped in black bunting. Just up Broad Street, he could see the procession bearing the wooden coffin. Two men walked on either side of an almost prostrate Cicero, nearly dragging the poor man between them. Cicero periodically threw back his head and shrieked. Even though there were over fifteen people in the group making their way toward the Negro Burial Grounds, more than were allowed by law, Osei joined in at the end of the line. He whispered to the person nearest him. "'Tis Polly?"

"And her young'un. They both in the coffin yonder."

At the grave site, Osei rolled his sleeves and helped the men dig a decent sized pit. When it came time to lower the box containing his wife and child, Cicero had to be restrained from throwing himself on the coffin, and halting the burial.

"No! No! Not My Polly! Yuh Cain't Put My Polly In Tha' Cold Groun'!"

He continued to scream entreaties to his wife not to leave him. His shrieks rent the air and tore at Osei's heart. Cicero struggled until he was able to break free and reach the open grave. All of a sudden, he fainted and pitched headfirst into the pit, smashing his entire face on the coffin lid. Osei was one of the first men to jump in and pull him out. His lips were split and bloodied; his nose had been broken in several places.

Eventually, they brought Cicero back to his house. Several of the women in the congregation had stayed behind to clean up the blood and change the bed. Osei helped them lay Cicero down so he could examine the ferryman. Cicero, now completely drained, lay like a dead man, barely breathing. Osei was fearful that, in his present state, the ferryman would not live much longer.

Osei had been able to save his own wife and he knew that he could have saved Polly too—were it possible to be in two places at the same time. Because Osei could not come, even had he known what was happening to Polly, Cicero was now alone. The poor man stirred and began to whimper. Osei knelt beside the bed so Cicero could hear what he was saying.

"My friend. Please believe what I tell you now. Polly is not under the earth! She is not dead, but here, with you, by your hearth. You have but to call her and she will come to wherever you are! She is strong now, much stronger than she was in life! She has become-… your-… your angel! Yes, think of her in this way! Believe in her! Let her heal your heart!"

It took Cicero more than a month even to get out of bed. During that time, Sam and the rest of the crew did their best to keep the ferry running on schedule and collect the fares. Sam had been with Cicero almost from the beginning, the first freedman he'd hired when he took over the business. And Sam had helped Cicero recruit the others—Tobias, Luke and Tom. Perhaps because each man shared almost equally in the proceeds, they all now felt responsible to Cicero, even though it meant many more hours of work.

At first, it did seem to Cicero that he would never be able to go on; his heart hurt constantly, alternately beating very slowly and then suddenly racing. Daybreak would find him having spent the endless night awake, staring at the ceiling. He'd get out of bed only when Mary, Martha or one of the other members of the congregation would come by to check on him and bring him food, very little of which he would eat. The women would chide him gently, reminding him that he had to start taking meals or risk becoming weak and ill. Cicero would always thank them, promising to eat later. But the truth was that he was waiting, anxiously really, for the night when his heart would simply stop beating.

One night, as Cicero was tossing about in a fitful near-sleep, he thought he could feel the thin mattress give gently under the weight of someone lying down beside him. He sat up immediately. Tentatively, he reached toward the other side of the bed, Polly's side, with one hand, encountering only air. Yet, he could feel the weight, *her weight*, nestled against him.

"Don' be skeer'd, Darlin', it's jus' me."

"Oh, Polly!" the poor man cried out loud, "Oh, my deares' wife! How yuh gon' leave yuh Cicero behind? I'm so lonely wit'ouchya!"

Just as she had when she was alive, she held him close and kissed him repeatedly. Gradually, she grew closer, her body against the sparse hairs on his chest, moving closer still until she entered his flesh, covering his heart with herself until the pains stopped.

"Polly, please don' leave me t'night. Jus' take me 'long when ya go. Lemme be wit' my darlin'. Please, Polly! I cain't be alone again."

"Darlin', it ain' yer time t' go yet. Yuh got t' bide a while here. They's work yuh got t' do yet. But never yuh fear, Darlin', I'm comin' ev'ry night from now on. Yuh ain' never gon' be alone. N' I'ma bring yer childr'n wit' me. We got eleven!"

The very next morning, Cicero got out of bed and went to help himself to a bit of the porridge Martha had left the day before. He was surprised to find the fireplace lit and the kettle boiling. Even more amazing, foxglove leaves were steeping in his cup on the table. He drank the tea, ate the porridge, got dressed and left. He reached the ferry just ahead of Sam and the other men.

That following Sunday, just as the first service was about to start, Cicero quietly slipped into his accustomed seat on the front bench. When Preacher called for the opening hymn, Cicero sang out the first verse in his strongest voice. He stayed the entire afternoon, and by the third service, he had been so filled with the Holy Ghost that he was now shouting his testimony for the whole congregation to hear.

Chapter 21

QUEBEC (1800)

*I*n the Canadian deep woods, autumn blew in on a sharp northern wind, kicking up rough waves on the river. Soon, a long trip in open canoes would become treacherous.

Tekenna and his entourage had been in Great Bear's village for over a month now. Yet, in spite of the changing season, the Munsee chief was showing no signs that he was ready to leave. Every evening, as soon as his people had finished the meal brought by the village women, he would turn to Great Bear with the same request.

"Ask your wife to continue her story...."

CROWN STREET – 1775

Annie awakened while Osei was still at Polly's burial. Willy had taken a nap on the floor next to the bed. She reached down to check on him; as she did, a searing fire tore through her insides, almost taking her breath away. Still, she had to tend to Willy and the baby, in spite of the pain. Moving as carefully as she could, she eased herself to the edge of the bed, swung both legs over the side and stood up. Her knees immediately buckled and she fell, barely missing her son. Willy awoke to see his mother crawling to the cradle.

"Mama, why are you down on the floor?"

"Come, Willy," she gasped, clutching her belly with one hand while steadying herself with the other, "Help Mama pick up your little brother. He must eat."

Willy, proud to be asked to help instead of being shooed away, carefully lifted his swaddled baby brother and handed him to Annie. He watched in amazement as she guided the tiny mouth to a bared breast. The little thing began to suckle weakly.

"Mama, Pa named the baby. His name is Coffee. And something else I don't remember."

"I don't think his name is coffee," Annie smiled at her son. "Your Pa has given your brother a name from his own country. You have one too. It's a secret name."

"Oh tell me it, Mama! What's a secret?"

Annie reached out to encircle Willy with her free arm. The pain moved like a fire in her belly, limiting her movement. For a moment, she could not speak. Then the baby suckled a little more vigourously, and the agony eased somewhat.

"A secret means you cannot tell it to anybody. Your name is like that. We mustn't tell it to another person. I think when you are older your Pa will tell it to you. But then you must keep it a secret."

Osei had come quietly into their room during this exchange. He stood by the door, too spent from Polly's burial to move. The sight of Annie nursing while talking so earnestly to Willy touched a place in him filled with pain, and with an impossible sweetness. For a moment, he wished only that they could remain thus, sheltered, happy, *free*.

Willy saw him first. Immediately, the child ran to his father. "Pa, Mama says my name is a secret! She says you will tell me when I'm older!"

Osei smiled and lifted the child. Safely in his father's arms, Willy immediately forgot about the name. "Pa, I'm hungry."

Annie tried to rise, but the searing pain momentarily doubled her over, forcing her back to the floor. She looked helplessly at Osei. "I hurt so much. This is so different than it was with Willy."

"Do not try to get up. I will feed Willy, and then bring you up something. Let me help you to bed."

Osei put Willy down and gathered up Annie and the baby. For a moment, he held them both and then deposited them on the bed. It seemed impossible to tell Annie about Polly just now. She would learn of it soon enough. But first she needed to heal. He was frightened for her and about what he had done to save her.

Little Antobam struggled through the first month of his life. He cried endlessly, whenever he was not nursing. Only at Annie's breast was he quiet. During those times, she would study the strangely aged little face. She told herself that he would live, even as she watched him fail to gain weight no matter how often she fed him. His little legs and arms remained match thin; his rib cage was so clearly delineated that she could count the bones. And he actually had lines and furrows in his forehead, making him look more like a worried old man than a newborn. Only his eyes were bright, intense even. And when he nursed, he fixed Annie with an unblinking stare as though memorizing her features. He did the same on those rare occasions when he let Osei hold him. Looking into those ancient eyes, Osei sensed that this child held a very powerful spirit, one who had come for a special purpose. The sense, however, did not give him comfort or even hope.

The only good thing was that, with the constant nursing, Annie's womb was healing quickly. Within a week, the pain had subsided to a dull ache. By the end of the month it was gone completely and she was back on her feet.

The baby, though, remained in terrible pain for the next three months. During that time, his suffering was experienced by the whole family. Annie and Osei got no sleep. They moved Antobam into their bed so he could nurse without Annie's having to rise. Then came the problem of her not having enough milk to satisfy his endless hunger. Osei took the baby and attempted to examine him. Feeling the small abdomen, he discovered a series of soft lumps around the baby's navel. Perhaps this was the cause of the difficulty. But it did not matter; Osei had no way either of identifying the condition or of correcting it.

The fourth month was agonizing. Antobam's wails grew insistent and shrill. It seemed that, even in his weakened state, he was still able to summon strength enough to fill the carriage house with his crying. And Annie's nursing provided no relief, since his hunger completely outstripped her supply of milk. All too often, when she put him to the breast, he found it empty. Then his screams grew fiercer.

Even Willy became frightened at the intensity of his brother's cries. He, child that he was, expressed his fear as anger. "Mama, make him be quiet! How I hate him! You should send him back!"

Annie could not summon the strength to punish Willy for his rudeness. She simply pulled him to her with her free arm and held him while futilely rocking Antobam.

One evening, while Annie was nursing him, weary and nearly dozing, she suddenly became aware of the stillness. Antobam's tiny mouth had loosened its vice-like grip on the nipple. He slowly relaxed in her arms, letting his head roll toward her now free breast. It appeared that he had finally fallen asleep; the intense eyes were closed and his face, for the first time, looked like that of an infant. She knew at once that this was not sleep, but she sat, rocking and crooning to him. His death was more peaceful than any of his life had been.

When Osei came home from Phillip's offices, he found her thus and knew immediately what had happened. He tried to take Antobam from her arms, but she held fast.

"Annie, please, you must let me have him."

"No, no, no, no. No!" Willy had finally fallen asleep, so Annie kept her voice low. But her refusal was fierce as if she had shouted.

"Come then, bring him outside. We must thank the ancestors for his life so they are not offended by our grief."

Annie rose, still clutching the infant. His body was becoming cold in her arms, but she could not bring herself to let him go. Once out in the yard, Osei prayed over his wife and dead child. There would be no burial until sunrise, so they sat on the wooden bench by the door for the rest of the night as Annie held onto the now rigid form of her dead son.

In the morning, Osei went out to notify the coffin-maker that he would need a box in the smallest size. Annie took the baby back inside, wrapped him in his blanket and awakened Willy.

"Willy, son. Your brother died during the night."

The child was horrified that his secret wish had come true. He began to cry. "No Mama! Please tell the 'antsters' to send him back to us! I'll be good; I'll take care of him when he cries!"

Annie wearily took Willy into her arms and held him tightly, but she could summon no words to sooth him. He was all she had now, her only child. Even without Osei's having said anything about the birth, she knew there would be no more babies for her. Now, the pain of that realization intensified her grief, throwing her spirit into the deepest hole imaginable.

When Osei returned with the tiny coffin, they placed Antobam carefully inside. It was almost an hour before Annie would let Osei close the lid. She sat on the floor, gazing at her baby's peaceful face in stunned wonder. At last, she lifted her head, fixing empty eyes on her husband.

"I wish you'd've just let me die."

"What about Willy—and me? We needed you. I-need you now, alive."

Osei had gotten down on his knees in order to face her. He took her by both shoulders. Getting to his feet, he brought her up to a standing position.

"Annie! You must trust me. What happens happens. We can change nothing! We must just go on!"

Fourteen of their neighbours, coachmen, cooks and other servants, formed the silent procession out of Crown Street. At the corner of Nassau, they turned north toward the Commons and the Burial Ground just beyond. Annie held up well, the women thought, watching her carefully, commenting on the fact that this last pregnancy had left her thin and drawn, her hips narrower than ever and her breasts flat. Several whispered that it was "nigh time for her to quit tryin' t' have more children."

"Yuh kin see she ain't built right f'bearin'!"

Two weeks after the burial, British warships appeared in the New York harbour and fired on the city. Every available Black man, slave or free, was pressed into service building fortifications against an expected invasion. Osei went every morning to the docks and worked alongside the other men, in part to deflect questions about his status, but mostly to keep abreast of the latest news. He also tried to keep Phillip's businesses running, although the blockade made it difficult to get goods in or out of the harbour.

One cold afternoon in early December, as he was about to close the offices, Osei noticed a well-dressed White man standing in the street, apparently studying the building. The man seemed to be deciding whether he was at the right address. Osei opened the front door and asked the man if he needed help.

"I am looking for Mr. Phillip Hamilton's Import/Export business. I was led to understand that the offices and warehouses are on this street."

Osei hesitated for a moment before answering. Who was this person, and why was he making such an inquiry? The man's accent was decidedly British, clipped and cold. Clearly he had not been in America long.

"This is indeed Master Hamilton's business." Osei found himself echoing the man's icy tone. "He is presently away, in Europe. I am his man; he left me to handle things in his absence." He very deliberately left off calling the stranger "Master."

The man sniffed once, obviously displeased at Osei's uppity manner. But Osei did not back down; he had no idea what this man might be about. For a moment, both stood staring at one another. Finally, the White man spoke.

"Yes. Well, I guess I should explain. I do know who you are, since your master did tell me that he left you in charge. He and his family are currently in France. And it would appear they will not be able to return as planned. He has retained me through his father-in-law to see to his finances here."

The man apparently felt he had given enough information to a servant. Osei could see that whoever he was, the man was finished explaining himself. Now he would be giving orders. And he proceeded to do so.

"You will make the books available to me immediately. Also any funds on hand, I will take. I've been instructed to leave you with an allowance of £100 to take care of the household and yourself. Should this unpleasantness continue for another six months, I shall return to review matters and give you additional funds."

Osei unlocked the offices, set out the ledgers and brought out the cash boxes. The man sat at Phillip's desk, produced a glass and used it to minutely inspect each line of every page in every one of Phillip's books. The process took over two hours, during which Osei had to stand nearby in case the man had a question. After reviewing the books, he turned to the cash boxes, counting out thousand pound notes into bundles. Finished with the audit, he rose, tossed £100 on the desk, and pronounced everything in order. Osei quietly took the money and waited for the man to leave.

"I fully expect to see you here when I return. If not, we have the means to locate you—and your family. Do not attempt to take advantage of this situation. You are being watched."

At the threat, Osei turned to face the man. Somehow, he could not let this stranger speak to him in that manner without a retort.

"Sir. I have been in service since I was taken at the age of-… for most of my life. If Master Phillip had reason to mistrust me, he would not have left me in charge."

The man smiled or, more correctly, curled his upper lip to reveal teeth in what looked more like a sneer.

"Yes. I know all about you 'faithful servants' appearing to be beyond reproach. All of you, just waiting for the opportunity to rob us blind or run off! Do not attempt to fool me! I know you—not one of you is to be trusted!"

Just then, Osei knew that he could kill this man without a moment's hesitation. He even considered it. The man had a weak throat and pale delicate wrists. He was dressed in the latest European fashion, his coat and breeches of blue satin, the waistcoat in silk taffeta embroidered with ribbons—clothes that most people in the Colonies had neither seen nor could have afforded. Osei was taller and stronger; he would need no weapon other than his own bare hands.

The moment passed. The man was inconsequential to his plans. He recognized the bluff, deciding to let it pass. This British visitor had no way to watch him, especially in the turmoil now going on. Without another word, Osei opened the front door and held it until the visitor had passed through. Then he slammed it shut and locked it. He left by going through the warehouse and out into the alleyway.

Chapter 22

(1776–1783)

*B*y the early summer, the fighting had reached Long Island, with both British and American forces battling for control of New York. The city was, by this time, effectively in British hands. Now it was the British army that conscripted slaves as labourers. All of the healthy male servants and free Black men again were working day and night, shoring up fortifications or manning munitions installations. Once the Patriots were forced to flee the lower Hudson, it began to look as if the Revolution might be put down sooner rather than later.

This was what Osei began to fear, that Phillip might be persuaded to return. However, the fighting continued, and men were still being recruited from the Colonies. Only New York City was securely in British hands with most of its young men either away fighting or imprisoned on British ships. So the plans to return were apparently shelved and the Hamiltons stayed in Europe. It seemed that now was the perfect time for Osei and his family to run away. The city was full of runaway slaves from the southern colonies, most of them clustered in the area between the river and Broad Way. He, Annie and Willy could easily hide among them.

Then the dreams began. Osei saw his mother in the first one. The vision deeply troubled him, for Akua had come in the company of his great uncle, who he knew was dead. Nevertheless, he asked her for guidance as he planned the family's escape. She did not answer; instead, she raised one finger in the cautionary gesture that he remembered so well. Yaa Akua had only to raise that finger and he and his sisters would stop whatever they were doing.

"But Mother, if we are not to leave now, then when?"

No answer. Only the raised finger. And so he waited for the next sign, hoping desperately that it would be favourable. When she came again several nights later, she was frowning, still indicating the time was not propitious. But this time she also spoke. *"Why is your wife not ready? How can I leave the earth knowing you did not marry properly?"*

Now he knew that his mother was truly with the ancestors. How could he reconcile his failure to marry her successor? She must have realized what had happened to him, that he had no choice but to do as he had done. He sent up a heartfelt prayer.

"Mother, forgive me. How could I marry your choice of bride? I was taken away before I was of age!" Osei awoke from this dream covered in icy sweat. Then there were no more dreams for many months.

When they began again, he was grateful just to see his mother. She looked as he'd remembered her, regal, dark, with high cheekbones and large slightly protruding eyes. When he asked whether they should run now, she did not respond to the question. Instead she gave him a completely different answer.

"Your wife must become a priestess. You will instruct her."

"Mother, I do not know the rituals."

"You will instruct your wife."

It was obvious to Osei that there was no way to run away under the protection of the ancestors. He realized the job before him now was to transform Annie into the priestess that would please his mother. He did not persist in his questioning, lest he anger her. If this was her instruction, somehow he would be shown the way.

The man who had shown up at Phillip Hamilton's offices was a barrister from London named Richard Pludwell. He was an officious little man who had made Evan's acquaintance at an event attended by the Grants, father and son. It turned out that, although Evan had lost all of his land holdings, the monies he had invested in British stock, located in other parts of the Americas, had grown sufficiently for him to establish a practice in town and acquire a decent home for the family. He lost no time in responding to Phillip's request, posted from Paris, for assistance with the business back in America. Once Evan learned that Pludwell was planning to travel to New York anyway, he wrote a letter informing his son-in-law of the fact.

Phillip was unwilling to risk going to England for a face-to-face meeting, so all communication between himself and Pludwell would be by post. As a result, there was always at least a six-month delay between correspondences. And it was six more months before Pludwell could reach New York and visit the office.

Although he had tried to assert himself over the servant Phillip had left in charge, Pludwell sensed that the man had seen through his bluster. In truth, he did not like Negroes at all. They were absolutely inscrutable; one could never tell what they were thinking! He was used to looking a man in the eyes; these people always looked at the floor when one tried to address them. Phillip's man, Will was his name, *had* met his eyes, and the defiance was there! It was just as he had always suspected; they wanted nothing more than to kill you! He resolved to visit as little as possible, always during the day and in the presence of at least one British soldier for protection.

When Pludwell made his next appearance, at high noon and accompanied by a Redcoat, Osei was in the warehouses supervising the preparation of an order. The presence of the British had initially stalled all shipments out of New York. Pludwell had been able to pull enough strings to allow Phillip's goods to share space on British ships, both entering and leaving the harbour. As before, Osei set out the books and produced the cash boxes. This time, no words passed between the men, and it was after Pludwell had left that Osei found the £100; the money had been placed on top of a barrel by the warehouse door.

In the early spring of 1777, Osei had the first of a series of powerfully unsettling physical sensations. One evening, just after they had put Willy to bed, his heart suddenly began to pound. Not wanting to alarm Annie, he slipped out of their quarters to sit on the steps. He was, for a moment fearful that he was dying, but the sensation in his chest was not accompanied by a sense of dread. Indeed, he felt a strange and overwhelming presence *within* his body. It was as though someone had taken residence in his heart and was announcing the fact.

Then a voice spoke; it was his *mother's! "You will bathe your wife!"*

This was no dream! Osei stood up, testing his legs. He felt well and strong. Only his heartbeat was such that he could actually hear and feel it. So this was a possession! He had heard of them, had, in fact, seen several. All of the people that he had seen were terrified by the experience, and now he could understand why. Sounds seemed altered by the incessant pounding in his ears. The click of the door latch he'd lifted to reenter their room had a hollow pitch as though he were in a great empty space. When he spoke, the voice was unrecognizable as his own.

"Annie, come here."

She had begun folding newly washed clothes but immediately put them aside and came to stand before him. Wordlessly, Osei began to undress her. He slowly, carefully removed each of her garments, letting them drop to the floor at her feet. When she was completely naked, he lifted her into his arms and held her tightly for a moment, before carrying her downstairs.

Osei deposited her before the large fireplace and went to fill the bathtub that Evie had allowed to be stored in the carriage house so Annie could "take her beloved baths." It was a large porcelain tub with high walls. Osei filled it with hot water from the massive kettle that was kept on the fire. He lifted her in and proceeded to wash every part of her, including her hair, which he scrubbed and rinsed several times. Under his gentle but thorough washing, Annie relaxed into a doze. When he lifted her out of the tub, he wrapped her in a large blanket and used a towel to wrap her hair.

Then he settled before the fire and, with Annie between his knees, he began to twist tiny sections of her hair into tight coils until her entire head was covered with a bristly forest of separate locks. The process took several hours. Osei had never done this before; in fact, he was not doing it now. It was his mother's work using his two hands. And the job was impeccable, as though she had done it herself.

Osei had not touched Annie sexually since just before Antobam was born. After he died and six months had passed without any advances, she decided that she must have become too ugly. Indeed she felt ugly – old and *barren*. Only Willy loved her now! This was the perfect time for Osei to make a break for freedom without either her or their son.

She carried this thought around with her as she went about her newly limited duties. Osei now insisted that neither she nor Willy go out into the streets.

"Annie, you simply do not understand how dangerous it is for a woman, any woman, but especially a Black one! There are British soldiers everywhere, ready to snatch a woman and do her harm. And Willy could be kidnapped and murdered just for sport!"

"Husband, I haven't paid my respects to Cicero, nor visited Polly's grave! Can you not at least take me to the ferryman's house and the Burial Grounds so I can be with my friend and our son?"

Her request seemed quite reasonable to Annie, but Osei literally exploded. "I said, no! Can you not understand what I tell you? *It is not safe! I cannot protect you!*"

He had never shouted at her before. So, he meant to keep her locked up in the house while he alone went out each day! Annie was certain that Osei secretly wanted as much time away from his family as possible.

"He's getting used to being without us so he will miss us less when he leaves," she decided.

That night, after Osei had snuffed the candle and lay down beside her, Annie could not hold back any longer. "You now find my body so ugly you cannot bear to touch me, after making me barren! Why did you keep me alive, if you never meant to touch me again?"

She felt him flinch suddenly, as though her words had been blows. Instantly, he was out of bed. "Is that what you think? You know *nothing* about what I feel! Or intend to do!"

He grabbed his clothing from the nearby chair, threw everything on the floor and spent the rest of the night sitting by the window. For the next two weeks, he refused to share the bed with her.

Then came this one evening when Osei suddenly left their room. Willy was sleeping soundly, his lovey rag pressed against his cheek, when Osei returned and ordered her to stand before him as he undressed her. Annie was so ashamed and embarrassed by her body now; her stomach was still blackened and flabby, her breasts empty and sagging. But when she stole a glance at his face, it was an absolute mask; even his eyes were hooded. As he carried her downstairs, she could feel his heart beating against her. Its ferocity ignited a flutter of desire and fear in her own breast. Was this his way of making love to her again – at last?

Being bathed was beautiful! Always before, she had been the one doing all the work. Under Osei's gentle stroking, she first became intensely aroused but then grew drowsy. It did not matter if he made love to her or not; *this* was perfect. She fell asleep while he was doing her hair.

Just as the last lock was finished, the spell lifted. Osei felt his body being returned to his control. Momentarily, he experienced a sadness. It had been sweet to feel his mother's presence, to have her inhabit his heart and use his body. Now he understood how Annie's transformation would be accomplished. Mother had not abandoned them. In death, she had found him and would not leave him without help. In time, the hair would grow into the long, ropey locks worn by a priestess.

Osei wrapped the blanket more securely around Annie, lifted her and carried her back up to their room. As he settled her and himself into their bed, he gently took his wife into his arms. They made love as she wept tears of joyous relief, which he kissed away.

Now it was essential for Annie to understand that she was to serve a goddess, the Goddess of the Rivers and Waters. This meant Osei had to teach her *his* religion. In her early years living in the Hamilton household, Annie had accompanied the family to church, sitting in the family pew with the children, as long as they were babies. The Hamiltons had attended Trinity Church, the most prestigious congregation in New York, and the one where Phillip's parents had been members. However, that was as far as religion went with Phillip. Beyond tithing and making regular appearances at services, neither of his parents had been particularly religious. They certainly had done nothing more to indoctrinate their son.

Evie had learned her Bible well, but only as an excuse to be taught to read. And although Evan was a staunch Anglican, Sophie was Methodist. Since neither was ever willing to set foot in the other's church, there had been very little formal religious instruction in the Grants' household either. As a result, Annie did not have much to overcome in the way of Christian beliefs. Therefore, when Osei began to teach her about his faith, she was as open as a child.

On quiet evenings after their meal, Osei would sit near the fire with Annie at his feet. She had Willy listen as well and together they learned how God, the unapproachable creator, had wisely allowed His spirit to inhabit everything on earth, from the smallest pebbles to the widest ocean. It was through these natural things that humans could beseech Divine intervention. Moreover, those who had died did not leave their loved ones but stayed nearby, ready in their now more powerful state, to offer protection and help. And God had other help in the form of lesser deities whose purpose it was to listen to the prayers of humans and convey to them God's wishes. The Goddess of the Rivers and Waters watched over the people of the region from which Osei had come.

The possessions continued, in fact, grew more powerful, coming sometimes out of the blue and seizing Osei in the midst of some daily activity. There was no way to avoid the realization of what these visits had to mean. Osei now knew that he was being prepared for the unthinkable. The news came quite simply in three visits from his grandfather.

The first time happened in the Exchange. He was collecting the receipts from a recent shipment and doing his own ciphering in his head of the recorded tallies when a shadow fell across the ledger. Looking up, he first noticed bare black feet and was about to give an alarm when he recognized the ankle beads. Here stood the old man whom he had not seen in over thirty years. Impossible that he could be standing where, only a short distance away, men were working but did not see him. The old man looked as Osei remembered; his white hair bespoke his eighty or so years, and he carried the familiar walking staff for support.

With a strange chill at his heart, Osei realized he alone saw this man who stood smiling gently; for when he glanced away and back, the man had vanished. The air was once again filled with the noise of counting, changing and handling money.

The second visit was in the stable area of the carriage house as he was examining a horse's forefoot. This time, the old man appeared in the sunlit door. Osei felt his heart beat hard a single time, before it settled back into its own steady rhythm. The old man smiled benevolently, leaning on the staff, before he turned and vanished, this time before his grandson's very eyes.

That same night, Osei had a dream in which there was only his grandfather's voice repeating, in Akan, *"A man knows when his time has come."* The visions and the dream sent him into deepest despair. Death, in and of itself, did not frighten him. He recognized it as freedom and a way home. The prospect of leaving Annie and Willy still enslaved was what caused him grief.

It was his mother who provided solace. Only a few nights later, she came to Osei as he lay awake listening to the quiet regular breathing of both his wife and son.

"Why are you sad? Nothing will happen to you until everything is ready. You have been a dutiful son and I am pleased with you. For now, just watch and listen."

Her presence calmed him and he slept soundly afterward. Now he knew he would have the time he needed.

A few weeks later Osei found a letter attached to the front door of the house. It was addressed to Phillip and came from a regiment captain somewhere in Virginia. Osei steamed and loosened the seal only to find out the writer was trying to notify a family member that both Evan Junior and Albert Grant were dead. He resealed the letter and delivered it, along with six months of receipts, to Pludwell at his next visit to the warehouse.

Of course, he had made sure to read Annie the letter from Virginia. When he came to the part about the death of Evan Grant's sons, she grew pensive but said nothing. She remained silent for the rest of that day and seemed preoccupied for several weeks more.

Osei was carefully following news about the rebellion by regularly spending time at the docks and frequenting corners where street urchins would hand out pamphlets. These seditious publications were printed and distributed practically under the noses of the British. Osei would pretend that he was taking a copy for his master and was careful not to look at the paper until he was safely back in the carriage house. Here, he would read the entire pamphlet to Annie.

One day, seemingly out of the blue, after listening to a rather long article by someone named John Adams, Annie suddenly asked Osei whether there had been anything in that Virginia letter about her mother.

"I know you said you read it all, but perhaps there was mention of someone named Em."

Osei put the paper aside and gave his wife his full attention. "Annie, was your mother a servant of Mistress Evie's mother? Her maid, perhaps?"

"She was. My Mama had been in Master Grant's family since before I was born."

"Remember back when I told you about that letter to Master Phillip, where your mother's master said he had left two very trusted servants behind in Baltimore? If your mother was the mistress's personal maid then she must be one of the two. And if the two sons are now dead, then your mother is free!"

The word hung between them and there was silence for several minutes. Annie's mind fixed on the cooper's shop where she used to visit her father, his wife and her brothers. Would her mother have gone to live with them? She could not really fathom how much time had passed, even when Osei told her the letter about the Grant sons' deaths was over six months old. She was suddenly struck by the idea that years had gone by during which she had not even thought about her mother or brothers.

"I wish I knew for certain how long I've been here, in New York. Husband, help me figure out how long it was since I last saw my Mama. Can you, please?"

Instead of answering her, Osei took both her hands and sat her down at their table. Drawing up the other chair, he faced her so that he could command her full attention.

"Annie, being free means your time belongs to you. You must learn how to tell time—and not just by the mantle clock, but in years. Both you and our son must learn what it means to read your names, to count and to tell time, even when there is no clock. When you are free, you must be able to do all these things!"

A strange expression crossed Osei's face as he spoke. Annie, watching him closely, caught it and felt a finger of fear touch the back of her neck. He had said *you*, not *we*; he had not included himself. But, of course, he already knew how to read and tell time. This was what she told herself without believing it.

"He still means to separate himself from us." Her heart said the words, even as her mind pushed the hideous thought aside.

Now, for the first time, Annie found herself resisting her husband's teaching. It was a subtle resistance, and while Osei sensed it, he could not identify any change in her behavior. She continued to listen attentively each evening to whatever he told her about this Goddess of the Rivers and Streams. Yet, as soon she was alone with Willy, every bit of the previous night's instruction had evaporated. Whenever Osei asked her to recount any of it, she simply could not remember one word.

Nevertheless, he began to train her in a simple pharmacology of herbs and plants. Each morning, before full first light, while Willy still slept, he and Annie would leave the carriage house silently, taking to the empty streets.

They always went north, usually on Broad Way. Once past the Ropewalk, heading away from town, Osei's pace would quicken. Annie, still only half awake, would struggle to keep up until she could no longer match his speed. Then, keeping him in sight, she would use the time to catch her breath. Sometimes the route he would take carried them almost to the steep foothills that rose above the North River. Osei would stop and wait for her to catch up, sometimes frowning at her slow pace, but saying nothing.

He would point out certain plants, explaining that they were similar in medicinal properties to ones that grew in Barbados. She understood he had learned to use these plants to cure certain conditions, and she tried to remember what each looked like. But she had never paid attention to any growing things before. It seemed impossible now to remember that one small shrub with bluish green leaves arranged in a cluster of three could cure fever when made into a tea, while another, with identically coloured leaves was a deadly poison if brewed and drunk. The only difference between the two was in the number of clustered leaves.

On one particular morning, after Annie had mistaken milk thistle for mistletoe yet again, Osei threw up both hands and shouted at her. "You must listen! Why will you not listen to me? I have to repeat myself three, four times, and still you refuse to learn anything!"

Annie simply sat down on the ground. She felt as though her legs had lost the ability to support her weight. "Oh please do not so torment me!" She was crying hard now. "I cannot remember what they look like! Just leave me here! Run away and leave Willy and me here!"

So this was what she had been thinking about. Osei stared at his wife, stunned into silence.

"I know you want to be free," Annie wailed miserably. "Always you wanted to be free! Without us, you could, you know! I can't be a princess, or whatever it is you want. I am just too stupid!"

Osei's face contorted into a mask of sheer pain. He opened his mouth as though to answer, but did not. Instead, he took hold of both her shoulders and drew her up to her feet. Then, taking firm hold of one hand, he marched her back to town. Once in the carriage house, he released her. When finally he spoke, it was through clenched teeth.

"It's a priestess, Annie, not a princess. And had I wanted to, I would have left long ago. I will *never* leave you behind! Never! And I *will* free you both! You are not stupid, just stubborn! Now *yield*! Do not try to remember anything. Just empty your head of all thoughts and let my words fill the space. Be silent when I'm teaching you. Listen only to me! Do not *think*!"

Annie could feel his words, like a huge rock, drop into the very center of her being. Her legs, now absolutely insubstantial, gave way completely. Osei pulled her almost roughly against his chest and held her fast.

"I know the power of my mother's spirit, Annie!" his voice was nearly jubilant. "You have but to be still, to free your mind of the questions, and all needed answers will come! If only I could convince you of this!"

"Then you don't plan to leave us?"

"No. Not as long as I live. I promise!"

At first, Willy would be either asleep or outside playing while Osei concentrated on Annie's training. However, in 1777 Willy turned six and Osei determined that the boy needed his attention as well. He decided his son was now old enough to learn how to read and write and to be told a small part of his father's plans for the family.

Osei began to take Willy along to the docks and to the business. In that first year, while the boy watched his father direct the workmen, he learned how merchandise was loaded onto the docked ships, and how to count inventory in the warehouse. Meanwhile, Osei took every opportunity to begin teaching him letters and words out of the earshot of others. Willy proved a more adept student than his mother; he fairly ate up the instruction Osei provided. The boy quickly learned to write the entire alphabet and to count into the millions. He was soon able to copy ledger entries and simple documents almost as well as his father.

During their moments alone together, after the men had gone home, Osei would explain the idea of freedom to the boy. He made the lectures as simple as possible, saying that one day soon he would take Willy and Annie away from Crown Street. On these occasions, Willy questioned him endlessly.

"Pa, do we have to leave our home to get to freedom?"

"Yes. If we stay here, when Master Hamilton comes back, we will be his slaves, as before."

"But Pa, won't he bring his children back? We had fun when I played with them."

"You will be too old for play. And you won't be allowed to read or write any more."

"But Pa, *you* can read and write. Why won't Master Hamilton let me read and write also?"

"Because it is a crime to teach a slave to do so, without his master's permission. Master Hamilton knows I can write; that is one of the reasons he bought me. But he does not know I can also read. This has always been one of our family secrets. If Master Hamilton were to find out and that I taught you as well, he would punish us both, maybe sell us. When we are free, I will not have to hide my skill or yours."

The idea of being sold had never occurred to Willy. When Osei finally brought it up, the boy became silent. Suddenly, freedom became infinitely more desirable, even if it did mean leaving home.

Once Osei had begun teaching Willy, he wanted to entrust Annie with more of the responsibility for her own training. Their early morning treks to gather medicinal herbs now became Annie's field tests. Osei would accompany her as far as the foothills north of the city. Then he would send her to forage for specific plants and Annie would return with what she hoped were the right ones. She made as many errors as correct choices. Frustrated, Osei began berating her, thereby reducing her to tears.

On one such morning, as the sun was rising over the city's rooftops far below, Osei waited for Annie at the bottom of a low hill. Although he had sent her to look for rosemary, feverfew, and wild lettuce, all easily recognizable herbs, he fully expected her to come back with at least two worthless weeds. Already, he could feel himself getting angry.

"Why are you abusing your wife so?" Yaa Akua's voice, low and musical, came from somewhere deep inside Osei.

"Oh, mother! She will not learn! I'm trying to teach her and yet, she refuses to learn anything!" Osei answered out loud.

"How many years did I spend teaching you? From childhood! And I never shouted, never called you names! Why do you expect your wife to learn, in so short a time, what took you years to master? Praise her for everything she learns now! And forget about her mistakes!"

Osei could feel tears stinging the corners of his eyes. How could he have been so stupid, so cruel! Of course Annie couldn't be expected to learn a lifetime of pharmacopeia in little more than a year's time. He could see her off in the distance, walking slowly toward him, carefully studying her handfuls of plants.

When she reached him, Annie held them out for inspection, at the same time, obviously steeling herself for the expected storm of rebuke. Osei took the herbs, shook off the dirt clinging to the roots, and put them all in his satchel. Then, almost roughly, he pulled her against his chest, holding her fast.

"Ah, my dearest Annie," he murmured against the head wrap she now always wore, "please forgive me. I've been a most heartless husband, forgetting that I promised you I would never hurt you. Oh, Annie, I'm so very sorry."

That night, long after the night watch had called out the midnight hour, Annie was awakened by Osei's fingers gently stroking her cheek, then lightly touching her lips.

"Husband?" she said, voice thick with sleep.

"I didn't mean to wake you, Annie, I just—I was watching you sleep." Something in Osei's voice alarmed her. Alert now, she sat up and touched his face.

"Why, you're crying! Oh Husband, what's wrong? Have I disappointed you so much? Is it Willy?"

"No—no—no. Please, Annie. I had one of my dreams; that's all. You know I sometimes cry in my sleep."

"Tell me the dream." Annie said. When Osei hesitated, she repeated the request, now as a demand. "You promised to tell me everything, so…"

Osei sighed. There was no way he could reveal what was really troubling him. Suppose he had misunderstood Akua; what would become of them all if he didn't have enough time to accomplish the task she had set for him?

"I was going home, Annie," he finally said very softly. "In this dream I was going home. And you and Willy were with me. That's why I was crying. They were tears of joy."

In 1779, the Patriots in northern New York were finally able to claim a victory, the capture of Stony Point, thanks to the work of a Black spy named Pompey. The man was able to get a secret password that allowed the American militia to overpower the lookout and seize the fort. The story was carried in several pamphlets being distributed in the city.

In that same year, on his eighth birthday, Willy was thrilled to finally be considered grown up enough to know his secret name—Kwesi Owusu. Because he had been born on a Sunday, his name had to be Kwesi, his father said. Owusu, the name that Osei had chosen, meant "clearer of the way."

"You must never tell your true name to *anyone* outside of the family."

Osei spoke gravely. And he added the all-important caveat. "Especially any White person, man, woman or child! You must swear to this!"

The boy answered in what he hoped was his most adult-sounding voice. "I swear, Pa, never to tell my name to anyone but you and Mama. But you both already know it. So I won't ever tell it to anyone at all!"

Ever more amazing stories reached New York, once the fighting had moved to the southern Colonies. Pamphlets contained accounts of Blacks from western Hispaniola (Haiti), called the Fontages Legion, who fought alongside the American militias during the siege of Savanna. Almost miraculously, the war was finally turning in the Patriot's favour.

In 1781, the British army suffered a resounding defeat at a place called Yorktown. The word on the streets of New York was that the Crown had grown weary of these fractious North American colonies and needed to concentrate on England's other interests. When a peace treaty was finally signed in 1783, the British made ready to pull out of New York.

Osei got the news of the imminent withdrawal early, before the actual treaty had been signed in Paris. Pludwell was making one of his usual, unannounced visits, but this time he was much more talkative and less circumspect. He spoke to the air, addressing no one in particular. Osei, however, knew that the remarks were for his benefit.

"Well, it's an ugly piece of business, this surrender. I never thought I would see the day when England would give up a fight. I daresay your foul, treasonous *republic* will fall apart inside of six months! One thing is sure—I'll not be setting foot in these parts again. Phillip Marshall will have to return and take care of his own affairs from now on!"

Pludwell rambled on for over an hour in the same vein, but Osei had heard the most important part. He needed to find out what this withdrawal could mean to his plans. As soon as the barrister left, he closed the warehouse and sent the workers home with their wages. Then he made straight for the docks where he was sure to find some news.

There were Redcoats milling about. Osei approached a man for whom he had done some dock work. "Please Sir," he asked the man, "Is it true that you will be leaving us soon?"

The soldier had been about to light his pipe. He was a man of about forty and a bit more patient with the Negroes than his younger counterparts. "Oh we're leavin' sure enough. What's yer interest in the matter?"

Osei cast about in his mind for something plausible. "Those of my people who helped you, we hope you will not abandon us."

The man laughed uproariously. "Why, hell, man! If y'd been any more help, we'd a been winnin' 'nsteada losin'! Oh, we'll probably take some what's been in some actual fights, but not the lot o' ye!"

Now Osei understood what he had to do. There had to be lists of those Blacks who were conscripted by the British. He had come to understand that these people were quite meticulous about keeping track of things through lists. He ventured another question to the soldier.

"How will you know who served in the army on our side?" He hoped the man would notice the "our."

"Y'know, that is a good question. Let me find out."

The man immediately turned and walked toward a group of soldiers; he saluted an officer. Gesturing toward Osei, he appeared to be asking the man something. In a moment, he returned.

"There'll be a list o' names posted in the mornin'. All them as can read their names, they'll be able t'board a ship fer Halifax, up North."

Now Osei knew he had to see that list. For the many men and boys who had volunteered or had been forced to join the fight on the side of the British, the promise given was of freedom at the end of a successful war. In point of fact, it had had been in one of the papers Osei could remember reading aloud, that General Washington had made the same offer in 1781. But Osei had no desire to risk his life for either side on so flimsy a promise. Now he regretted not having joined the British, even as he knew that he'd had much more pressing concerns.

Word spread throughout New York that the British were taking thousands of former slaves who had served in the fighting with them on their departure. Crowds of Black men descended on the Governor's House to look at the long sheets of foolscap nailed to the doors; the sheets were covered with first and, in some cases, last names, along with ages or other identifying characteristics.

Osei joined the group at the front of the throng, actually trying to decipher the names. As he carefully scanned the lists, he came across one name that fairly leapt out, Stephen—16.

He remembered Stephen, a lonely child who had been purchased away from his family at the age of six. He belonged to a tinsmith whose shop was on Bridge Street. The man had, unfortunately, been one of the unlucky Patriots captured during the Battle of Long Island, who languished and finally perished on a prison ship. Young Stephen, unable to run the business, was reduced to begging in the street until he volunteered for service with the British. Just one month ago, while on leave, he had come down with a fever. The poor boy lay ill for weeks with no care in the backroom of the tinsmith's shop. When he had died, no one knew until someone came to investigate a bad smell. Osei was familiar with the case because he was one of the few who'd helped prepare the body and attended the burial.

Now he saw that Stephen's name and age could provide him with a means to free Willy. He would send his son in this boy's place. The soldiers would not notice the difference. Although Willy was only twelve, he could pass for sixteen, as he was tall for his age.

There was only one impediment to the plan. Willy would certainly go if he were sure that his parents wanted it. But Annie would not easily relinquish her only child without hope of ever seeing him again. There was no time to consider the decision, however. The British were leaving almost immediately and certainly before the end of November. Osei knew he had to break the news to the family tonight in order to have Willy ready to leave as soon as the departure date was published.

When he reached Crown Street, Osei approached through the alley that ran behind the carriage house. Annie was hanging clothes in the yard; Willy was pretending to help but was actually entertaining his mother with one outlandish tale after another. The youth was good with words. Everything he learned from his father, he'd spin into a story, usually filled with facts exaggerated into fiction. Annie was laughingly swatting at him with a pair of wet drawers when Osei appeared near the corner of the house. He silently motioned to her to come closer. She put down the basket and approached, her expression puzzled.

"Why are you over here," she whispered. "Are you hiding from Willy?

For a moment Osei could not answer. Silently, he prayed for the words that would make this bearable for her. In that same instant, Annie could see he was about to say something devastating. Nervously, she wiped her wet hands on her apron and she kept rubbing her hands against the rough linen long after they were dry. When Osei finally spoke, his voice was hoarse and low, but what he was saying was quite clear—and final.

"Willy has a chance to leave New York on the British ship. They will give him his freedom and take him to a place in the North called Halifax. You must help me get him ready by standing with me when I tell him. If he sees this is what we both want for him, he will accept it and go readily. You must do this for your son." *Please,* he prayed silently, *Please let her understand and help me.*

Annie slowly released a long-held breath. For a full minute, it seemed like she had forgotten how to exhale. Now her face became almost magically composed. Only her voice sounded a bit high and strained. "I'll pack right away. Willy, come! Your father and I have something to tell you!"

Willy had noticed his parents deep in conversation and was already on his way over to join them. Now that he was twelve, he expected to be included in the grown-ups' talk. Still, something in his mother's voice brought him up short and put him on the alert.

"Son, you are truly a big boy now." Annie's voice nearly broke, but she continued, "...old enough to be on your own. And this is good, because your father has found a way for you to get your freedom. But it means that you must leave us."

With those final words, Willy's eyes widened and glazed over with tears. "I can't leave you! Who'll take care of me?"

Annie turned to Osei, a stricken look on her face. He placed both hands on Willy's shoulders. The boy was as tall as his mother.

"My son. We've talked about this,... about freedom, ever since you were eight. It was never going to be easy for me to free us all and keep us together. Most servants can never get away from their masters without being caught and severely punished. We have this one chance, right now, to get you completely free and far enough away that Master Phillip can never find you. You have to go with the British when they sail out of New York! You must do it!"

Willy was terrified. But he realized how important this was to his father. "I'm sorry for behaving like a baby, Pa. You are right; I am a big boy now." He tried to make his voice sound grown and hide the quiver in his lower lip.

Osei then explained the situation with Stephen, telling Willy that he would have to learn to answer to this young man's name.

"Stephen was older than you and he'd fought in the war. You will have to be clever enough to deceive both the British soldiers and the others, at least until you reach your destination. You are good with stories, but I think it would be best if you kept quiet and let the others do all the talking."

Willy perked up. This was like an adventure! He would get to pretend to have been a soldier. The idea of making everyone believe it appealed to him. Best of all, he would get to sail on a real warship!

It proved to be a wise move for Osei to break the news that night; the very next morning, the entire British garrison assembled on the docks in preparation for an evening departure. When the news came down, announced by a town crier, from all quarters, Black folks gathered, some to bid farewell to those leaving, others to plead futilely for the opportunity to also board the ships. Osei, Annie and Willy joined the throng early in the afternoon.

Annie had not slept the night before—did not even come to bed after both Osei and Willy had retired. All night long, she packed, slowly going through Willy's things, sorting out clothes that had grown too small. There were no replacements, so she sat with her sewing basket and carefully opened seams, stitching in pieces of fabric to make tight breeches larger, to lengthen the sleeves on a simple woolen shirt. As dawn was breaking, she was down in the root cellar pulling out potatoes to set in the hearth for baking. She had to keep moving in order to stay ahead of the gathering cloud that threatened to overtake and paralyze her.

Osei awakened at first light and discovered he was alone in the bed. He lay there for a moment, trying to adjust to the peculiar sensation in his chest, a combination of excitement and dread. They were sending Willy away to an absolutely unknown future. He had been so proud of Annie, of how she had remained calm, had encouraged Willy right along with him. She had to have been nearly beside herself. No wonder she'd been unable to sleep.

When Osei descended the stairs, he found Willy already dressed for the journey. He even had on a coat, a castoff that had belonged to Phillip. Annie had cut and re-sewn the garment to fit Willy beautifully. Osei frowned as he studied his son.

"You must not be showy with your clothing. There will be men around you who have seen hard battle and have nothing to show for it. If you appear too well-dressed, they will resent you. Put the coat into your bundle and wear your old frock."

Willy's face fell. Up to this point, he had felt only the sense of adventure. Now he realized that there might be more difficulties than he had imagined. Silently, he did as he was told.

By the time the soldiers had finished reading off the names of those who were eligible to board the several British vessels, there was a line of Black men and boys that stretched for several blocks, from the Ten Eyck and Rugar Wharves and all along Smith Street to as far as Maiden Lane. When Stephen's name was read out, Osei whispered to Willy. "That is how you will be called from now on. Go quickly. And remember your name, Stephen!"

The boy took his bundle from his father and stepped into the line, which had begun to move southward, slowly at first, then more quickly.

Annie tried to keep Willy in sight as he became swallowed up in the throng. Almost without realizing it, she began to walk along with the moving crowd, then to run in order to keep up. At first, it was not difficult to spot him. He was bareheaded and had a brand new haircut, his first ever, courtesy of his father. But he was not the tallest and she lost track of his location. As soon as she could no longer see her son, she began to cry—to run, heave and sob in a vain attempt just to *see* him again.

When he saw that she was attempting to follow the line, Osei ran after her. He feared that she would call out to Willy and ruin the boy's chances. But Annie was not crying out; her grief was making her run. She ran with a speed she did not know she possessed. Osei could not catch her.

The throng, now numbered in the thousands, reached the docks and began boarding several ships, Willy along with them. Annie never reached the wharf; her burst of speed only carried her to Hanover Square. Here, her legs gave way and she fell face forward. In agony and unable to rise, she watched the last of the crowds move away. When Osei caught up with her, she was still lying in the dirt. He pulled her to her feet and tried to get her to stand, but she could not. Finally, he lifted her in his arms and carried her back to the carriage house.

Osei did not take Annie up to their quarters. He had her sit by the fireplace while he heated water for a bath. She appeared to be asleep, but he knew she was giving up and yielding to an ever deepening despair. It was now that he needed his mother's help the most. He had to bring Annie around, to get her to willingly continue her training. When the porcelain tub was filled, he undressed her and got her settled in the water. She slumped listlessly and sank back, her head resting against the back rim.

Osei was about to begin the washing when his mother's voice stopped him. *"Get into the bath with your wife. Bathe her carefully, making sure she sees your face. Look her in the eye and she will come back to life."*

He stripped naked, except for his leather belt and got into the tub facing Annie. It was a tight fit, but he drew her up between his knees and began washing her face.

"Annie, listen to me. Sending Willy away was not to cause you pain. There is a greater plan at work here, and we are its instruments. I believe that we are all meant to be free and that you will see Willy again one day. Please try to hold on."

At last, Annie opened her eyes. They were flat and empty, and, when she answered him, her voice was a monotone. "I will. I know you mean the best for us. I am always ready to do whatever you say."

Winter set in, a hard, cold one with snow almost every week. As 1784 approached, Osei began to pray in earnest for a propitious sign. His mother's answer was unchanged. *"Your wife is not yet ready to assume her role! Continue her training!"*

He redoubled his efforts at teaching Annie how to prepare the medicinal plants, now drying next to the hearth on the ground floor of the carriage house. Although she dutifully followed his instructions, he could tell that her mind was always elsewhere, trying to imagine how Willy was doing and whether he was well. No matter how hard she tried to hide the fact, Osei knew Annie's heart was with her son.

Annie now decided that she simply could not remain indoors, even though the streets were even more dangerous than before. Roving mobs moved through those streets nightly, burning unoccupied buildings and looting stores. The citizens who could, packed up and left, some to try their luck on the Western frontier. Those who could not leave shuttered their doors at sunset and did not venture out again until the sun was high. Although he realized how lonely she was, Osei tried mightily to dissuade her from going out without him. When he could not, he begged her to take precautions.

"Annie, you must never go out after dark. Even if the sky is still somewhat light, if you know that evening is nigh, you must come straight home. Let *no one* ever see your head uncovered!"

"Husband, I promise on both accounts. All I intend to do is take short walks just around the neighborhood. I won't even go as far as the docks nor the market, although I do wish I could visit my children's graves, and my friend's."

"No, Annie. Not the Burial Ground. It's much too deserted. I will take you to the market as often as I can."

Osei continued to open Phillip's office each day and tried to fill outstanding orders. Now that the harbor was open again, ships were arriving and leaving daily. The Black men who worked in the warehouses depended on the wages they received, however meager, and Osei tried hard to pay them on time.

With the departure of the British, the new State Legislature of New York had begun to make laws governing property and levying taxes. Late that September, a letter with the official seal of the State arrived at Phillip's office. When Osei found the letter sticking in the front door, he did not even bother to steam the seal loose. He simply tore the thing open and read the contents immediately, heedless as to which of the men might see him.

August 15, 1784
THE STATE OF NEW YORK HEREBY ATTESTS that the properties and businesses belonging to one Mister Phillip Hamilton Shall be Seized and Sold at auction on or after July 1785, owing to the Non-payment of Taxes to the State for the years 1781 to 1783. Such Seizure and Sale Shall take place on the given Date unless Mister Hamilton make full restitution to the State for all Taxes thus owed.

Osei read the letter three times, first, to make sure that he understood the contents, then to try to figure out the implications. Obviously, Pludwell had not paid any taxes to the State of New York in '81, since, in his mind, no such entity existed. And neither bills nor instructions had been issued during the ensuing years. This was obviously an attempt to seize the property of a Tory sympathizer. Phillip's plan to avoid having to serve in the American army while also sidestepping the label of traitor had now backfired. But Phillip did not know this!

Osei knew it was his immediate duty to notify his master. But to do so would reveal how adept he was at reading, and he wanted Phillip to remain in

ignorance of this fact. However, if he did nothing and the State took possession of Phillip's property, he and Annie would be taken as well. It seemed best,
therefore, to find a way to forestall the seizure. The letter had not indicated an
amount; so Osei decided to post a request to the State in Phillip's name. He
would then have to wait for the response while planning how to pay whatever
was owed.

In truth, Osei had feared that, with the end of the war, Phillip would
immediately bring the family back to the city. But, in the absence of a cen-
tralized city government, a general lawlessness had taken over. The news of
New York's dangerous reputation no doubt must have reached Europe, for
there had been no indication that the Hamiltons planned an immediate
return.

Still, Osei began to feel that he could not put off the escape much longer.
Even without his mother's blessing, he would have to leave before Phillip
returned. He expected his master would try to notify him so the house would
be ready, perhaps through a messenger who was coming to America. He frequented the docks each day, checking whether any word had arrived.

It took six months for the State to respond to Osei's request for Phillip's
tax bill. The amount was in British pounds, although the accompanying letter indicated that other kinds of currency would be acceptable as well. Phillip
was instructed to submit the payment to a representative of the State Treasury,
when he came to the city in July.

As soon as he'd read the letter, Osei emptied one of the cash boxes and
counted out the complete sum. He placed the money in an envelope and hid
it in the office. Then he rushed back to Crown Street, let himself into the
house and left a crudely written note in a desk drawer in Phillip's study, indicating the money's location and what it was for.

Now everything is ready, Osei thought, relieved at having reached a decision. He made up his mind to tell Annie that they had to leave almost immediately.

She was setting their supper on the table when he entered the kitchen.
Even indoors, these days, she always wore the length of cloth as a head wrap
covering her nearly shoulder-length twisted locks of hair. The wraps reminded
him of his mother and how perilous it was to undertake this escape without
her protection.

"Annie, listen," he began, taking one of her hands so she would give him
her full attention, "I've secured a small boat that we can take to Long Island.
Once there, we will travel east. I know the Atlantic is to the east. We can get
another boat and sail north to Canada, where Willy is."

"Do you mean we're running away at last?" She was gripping his hand
hard now. "How soon?" Suddenly, the mere possibility of finding Willy filled
her heart with excitement.

"Within a few days. I only want to make sure no one notices our leaving."

He knew that he was giving Annie a very simple picture of a very complicated, dangerous situation. He, himself, had no idea of the distance they would have to travel nor of the impediments to their journey. But he had to tell her something, so she would be ready at a moment's notice.

Chapter 23

QUEBEC (1800)

*T*he smoke from the council fire rose straight toward the longhouse ceiling where it diffused in a faint cloud and descended upon everyone in the gathered group. The two chiefs, their councils, the families, each and every person in the room now leaned forward, riveted. The story was about to reach a climax.

River Otter had tried to keep Anika's narrative steadily flowing; but now he, too, was being swept away. For the very first time, he was learning about the man whom he had not seen since childhood....

FLIGHT – 1785

On a warm June evening about a week after announcing their escape plans, Osei closed up the business close to sunset and made his usual trip to the docks. This time, as he was about to head for home, a strange Black man, quite well-dressed, called to him.

"Eh, you, Sir. Do you belong to a Master Hamilton?"

Osei could feel his heartbeat racing. He turned to face the man who continued.

"My master just came over from France, where he got a message from Master Hamilton. He said to give you this, if your name is Will. Is it?"

Silently, Osei nodded, took the folded paper and opened it; inside was the Hamilton seal. The man then proceeded to recite the message that he had been given. "Master Hamilton says for you to expect him in July."

There it was. Osei felt rooted to the spot where he stood. When he could think again, he realized that he had stayed out too long. It was almost nine o'clock, well after dark. He tried to think of a way home that would keep him clear of the roving bands of thugs who liked nothing better than beating and robbing any who were still about in the streets.

One such gang stood in the shadows beside a tavern door just ahead. Twenty or so rough men, mostly White former soldiers from the Continental Army, with some Black sailors, would regularly meet under the cover of darkness to carry out whatever mischief they could get away with before daybreak. Most often, it was robbing the home or business of some absent Tory sympathizer. Tonight, they had been unable to settle on a victim and so decided to get drunk instead. It had not taken long, and soon the tavern owner had them thrown out with the warning, "Return, the lot of ye, and I'll shoot ye on sight!"

Once out in the street and in an ugly mood, this group lingered awhile, looking for a suitable target for their rage. Osei turned the corner and saw them too late. He was in full moonlight; no chance of escaping their notice. Almost instantly, they gave chase. By running as fast as he could and ducking around the corner of a building, Osei was able to elude them for a good half-a-block. Once in the building's shadows, he took a chance and stopped long enough to check whether he was still being followed. There was no one right behind him. If he could just reach Crown Street!

Three of Osei's younger, faster pursuers had circled around him. Without his realizing it, they had run ahead and were waiting behind the building. As they saw him pause, one grabbed him from behind and tried to drag him back out into the street.

Osei felt the man behind him and drove his right elbow into the man's ribs. As soon as the man let go, Osei, then, whirled and hit him in the face with all the strength he could muster. When the other two saw their comrade go down, each man swung savagely at Osei. He ducked, causing both men to hit at thin air. Then, seeing that there was no other way to get away, he tried to make a run for the street.

By this time, the rest of the gang, which had been following as quickly as their various levels of inebriation would allow, had caught up with their three comrades. Just as Osei emerged from behind the building, they all descended on him in a snarling pack, pouncing, kicking and striking with fists, clubs and stones from the street. Unable to fight them all off, he instinctively crouched into a ball, covering his face and head, while they rained down blows on his unprotected back and shoulders. When they realized that he was trying to protect himself, they grew even more furious. One particularly drunk sailor snatched up a large rock and drove it right into the back of Osei's head.

Just then, someone on the street shouted that a murder was taking place as the other patrons poured out of the tavern. Their cries, far from stopping the attack, only served to incite the pack into a mob. Tossing Osei aside, the mob of ruffians turned on each other and on the other tavern patrons who had watched them being humiliated inside.

Dub, a coachman who belonged to a neighbor on Crown Street, had gone out with his friends for a pint and had witnessed the entire commotion. When he saw a form roll into the middle of the street, he recognized the shoes. Circling around the flanks of the crowd, he reached the downed man. By now, Osei was bloodied and completely unconscious. The coachman motioned to several Black men across the street, and together they lifted the still form and silently melted into the darkness of an alley. Moving through backyards, they reached the kitchen door of the Hamilton house.

Annie had been preparing to lift a pot from the fire when the men burst into the room, bearing Osei's apparently lifeless form. She dropped the pot, spilling the contents, and ran toward her husband. "What has happened," she cried out. "Is he dead!?"

Dub answered, "He lives yet. Where shall we put him?"

"Upstairs! Bring him!"

Annie grabbed the lantern and led the way to the carriage house. The men carried Osei as carefully as the narrow ladder would allow. Even so, several times, his head struck the wall and bounced once on the stair steps. By the time they had gotten him to the room, further injury had been done, unintendedly, to his already damaged body.

Once Osei had been laid on the bed, the men left and Annie tried to determine the extent of his hurt. His face was unmarked, save for a slightly swollen, blackened eye. But when she tried to lift his head, she felt the movement of the broken bones in the back of his skull. Now she was afraid to touch him further; all she could do was to draw up a stool and sit beside their bed. At one point, his nose began to bleed, just a thin trickle that she wiped away, but the bleeding quickly returned, gradually soaking cloth after cloth.

Eventually, it stopped. Annie continued her watch throughout the night. Once, Osei made a soft sound, almost like a sigh. But otherwise he never stirred. His sleep was soundless; only by placing her ear just over his nose could she even sense breath.

By the time a pale dawn had outlined the window, she was nearly beside herself. Why would he not wake up? None of the folk living nearby was in any way skilled in healing. Only he would have known what to do. She cursed her inability to remember which herbs were to be used to pull poison out of wounds and which could awaken someone unconscious. At last, in desperation, she tried to quiet her mind, to listen for instructions as Osei had constantly reminded her to do. But, as the day brightened into a blazing heat, nothing would come. She forgot to eat and was too afraid to leave the room, even to relieve herself. Sally, Dub's wife climbed up the coach house stairs around six o'clock in the evening and found her rocking and moaning by the bed.

"Lawd, chile! Go downstairs and get you some air! Ain't nothing gon' happen to Will whilst you gone. I'll be right here watchin' him." The woman gently pushed her friend out of the room and firmly closed the door.

Annie stood for several minutes on the other side before she remembered her urgent need. She had to literally run downstairs and out to the outhouse. As she emerged and went to wash up, several women met her at the kitchen door. They had covered baskets of food. The smell made her nauseous, but she tried to hide the fact. Taking the baskets into the kitchen, she turned to thank the women.

"Mind you eat somethin' now," one reminded her. "You be no good to your man if you fall sick as well."

Annie assured them that she would eat, later. She was anxious to get back to Osei. Once she had climbed the stairs, she thanked Sally. "Dub will be wanting his evening meal."

Sally had done nothing to prepare for that meal. She hastily bid Annie goodnight and left. Once they were alone again, Annie suddenly found herself seized by an overwhelming fatigue. It was all she could do to remove her head wrap, apron and gown. Carefully climbing onto the bed, she fit herself into the narrow space left beside Osei. Instantly, she fell into the deepest sleep she had ever known.

It was the chill that awakened her. She shivered and rose to shut the window. It was already closed. Yet she still felt the chill. Looking back at the bed, she could see that Osei lay in a peculiar position on his back with his face turned to the wall. Annie touched his shoulder and discovered the source of the cold. The scream that formed in her throat was suddenly frozen by his voice. *"Hush!"*

How was it possible? Osei's voice came, clearly, out of nowhere. She stared at the figure on the bed; no movement. Yet the voice continued. *"Open my waistcoat, my shirt and the fall of my breeches. Take off my leather belt and fasten it round your waist."*

She forced herself back to the bed. His body was cold but still supple. Willing her fingers to work carefully, she unbuttoned both garments and the front flap of his breeches, feeling around the stilled abdomen. The belt, with leather pouch attached, sat low around his waist. She knew that it was sown on so he could never remove it, but he had never told her why. In fact, he had discouraged her from asking any questions about his belt, saying only that she would know all about it "in time."

"See the stitching underneath? Careful now!"

The voice instructed her how to release the first stitch, thereby causing the others to loosen. Annie slipped the worn strap from under the body. Osei's skin carried black marks where the pouch had rested and where the strap had pressed for so many years. Inside the pouch were several smaller leather packets containing what felt like smooth round stones.

"Do not worry. When you need to know what they are for, you will."

Pulling out the basket of mending, she found her largest needle and threaded it with her heaviest cotton, then took off her shift. It was possible to wrap the strap once around her waist.

"Fix it so that it cannot be removed. Make it tighter. Hold your breath and pull it until it will reach no more."

It took almost an hour to sew on the belt. The old holes gave her guidance, but she had to make new ones under the old to make it fit securely. She sweated with the effort and was cold at the same time. The pain in her chest was so excruciatingly real that she had to touch herself to be assured there was no wound. Each time she heard his voice, she could imagine him rising and swinging his feet over the side of the bed. This had to be a dream from which she would soon awaken.

"Annie!" Osei's voice called her sharply. *"You cannot let your mind wander! Listen!"*

Instantly, she felt herself empty out. The rising hysteria, the physical pain, the sense of unreality receded before his voice. A calm detachment took hold of her whole being, mercifully numbing all her senses, save one.

"Now, fetch help. We must catch the daylight."

The voice was gentle but insistent. Annie pulled on her gown and tied on a kerchief, then wrapped her head. Her legs felt heavy and unreliable, but she stumbled down the stairs and across the street. In the alley, she practically ran into Martha, who belonged to the neighbors across the street.

The woman took one look at Annie's distraught face and guessed the worst. Sam, her husband, had been in the crowd that had brought Osei home. He had predicted to his wife that the poor man was not long for this world. Now Martha took charge.

"Sam," she shouted to her husband, "Git th' coffin man. Will's gone. Here, catch her! Can't you see she gon' fall!"

Other neighboring women took care of the body. They undressed and washed him, struggling to straighten out the limbs and properly cross the arms. Then they dressed him in a clean shirt and breeches. Someone located pennies to place on his eyelids. When the coffin was ready, they wrapped the body in a sheet, carried it downstairs and placed it inside.

Everyone around Annie was careful of her. Here and there, one of the women would stop and touch her, or move her without speaking directly to her. Going crazy at the death of a loved one was not uncommon, especially for a woman who had lost so much.

The now-familiar walk to the Burial Ground had a surreal air for Annie. As always, the men carried the coffin on their shoulders; two women walked with her, one on each side. But only her body was present. Osei was talking to her quickly now, telling her where he had hidden the rowboat and how to mark his grave.

"I want to put that small sapling on his grave."

Her voice surprised the mourners. Their eyes followed her outstretched arm that pointed to a new tree growing nearby. Two of the men, Sam and the coffin-maker, promptly dug it up and gently laid it next to the open grave. The prayers were meaningless and mercifully brief. Almost the entire group had to get back to their various jobs. Sam and the coffin-maker filled the grave and planted the sapling directly over the body.

"Let me say goodbye alone," Annie whispered.

The women shook their heads but said nothing. Even though it was early afternoon, with several hours of bright sunlight still ahead, Annie should not be left on this lonely hillside. But no one dared cross her—she was so unlike the woman they knew. And so they did leave her, walking slowly with many furtive concerned glances cast over their shoulders.

When the last of them had gone, she took to her heels in the direction of the Collect Pond. From the other side of the hill on which the pond sat, she could just see the East River through the trees. Alternately sliding and running, she made her way down the hill to the riverbank, following Osei's voice. She found the boat's hiding place and marked the location with a large rock.

Then Annie turned to reclimb the hill, skirted the pond and retraced her steps back to the house. In the kitchen, she made up a small packet from the provisions her neighbors had brought. Entering the house, she took a single ten pound note from a drawer in the study. Next she mounted the stairs in the carriage house, donned a second gown over the first and tied on a second head wrap. By now the room was stifling and she was soon covered in sweat. But she felt nothing; her senses were completely attuned to Osei's voice.

"When you leave the house, go down to the docks. Make sure someone sees you leave, but make sure no one follows you. Take Broad Street to the Wet Dock. Go to Cicero's house and inquire about the ferry."

Once she was out in the street, it was a short walk down to the ferry landing. Annie forced herself to move deliberately but not too quickly, as though on an errand.

Cicero's door was open, an attempt to catch a nonexistent breeze. She hesitated before tapping the doorsill, momentarily embarrassed. She was certain word of Osei's misfortune had reached the ferryman; she was not sure whether

Cicero knew that he had… She stopped herself; she could not even think the word.

Osei's voice had been silent on the way here. Now it came so suddenly that she nearly fell in the street. *"Ask him when the last ferry leaves for Long Island. Tell him you must have the information. Explain nothing further."*

When she appeared in Cicero's doorway, she looked as wild-eyed and disconcerted as she felt. Without even greeting the ferryman, she blurted out the question. "When is the last ferry? Please?"

Annie had not visited him even once since Polly's death; now she prayed he would overlook her lack of manners.

The man had been whittling at his table; he looked up, startled at her presence. Almost immediately, a smile spread across his homely face. She could see that he had heard nothing about Osei, since he was too obviously glad to see her.

In fact, Cicero still thought about Annie occasionally. Whenever he did, he would visualize her as he had last seen her: big with that last child, sweating in the August heat and still holding the hand of that handsome son of hers.

"Well, Miz Annie," he began, "if it's th' ferry yuh be wantin', I goes out for th' last time at 5:00 this evenin'."

He was about to ask her why she needed the information when something in her face stopped him. She was staring at him as though he had suddenly begun speaking Chinese. She had such a near-crazed look about the eyes that he became concerned.

"Why, Miz Annie! Whatever's th' matter?"

"I just have to know when the last ferry will be leaving! Are you not the one to ask?"

She knew that she was not making sense, but she had no idea why she was asking about a ferry schedule. Worse yet, a terrible sense of panic had gripped her and was now threatening to completely overwhelm her. In another moment, she would be in a state of complete screaming hysteria.

"Just thank him and leave. He has seen you and can report as much, should anyone ask."

Osei's voice was gentle yet quite firm. She obeyed immediately, even managing to thank Cicero before leaving. Just as he had often done when she and Willy would leave, he watched her until she turned the corner. Then he stood for several minutes more, staring at the empty street.

Once out of sight of the ferryman, Annie now took great precautions against being seen again. By crawling under the docks, she was able to hide until nightfall. As twilight was gathering, she slipped out and moved to the shadows of an alley.

"Take off the top gown and your head wrap. Smear them with mud and blood."

She wondered briefly where she was supposed to find blood. The alley was just behind a hog pen. Almost as if by magic, she discovered a fresh hog that someone had butchered and hung up. Its carcass was still conveniently dripping into the muddy pen. She gingerly dipped her frock and wrap in the slimy mess, then threw both under the wheels of a wagon.

Now dressed in her traveling clothes, she carefully made her way to the hidden rowboat, avoiding the main streets and staying on the docks. Once she had reached it, she had to drag it out into the water.

By the time she had gotten afloat, it was nearly nine o'clock. Cicero would have finished his last run and moored the ferry. Now she understood the need to know the time of the last trip. From that point on, the East River would be deserted until just before dawn.

She had never rowed a boat before and the palms of her hands were soon raw. At first, she could not even make the boat move in the right direction. Once she found that she had to row with her back toward her destination, she finally got the rhythm, but she was never sure she was truly headed toward Long Island. The river and everything around it was pitch black in the darkness, but as the night wore on she was able to make out many features of New York's shoreline, even from her unfamiliar vantage point.

It was dangerously close to daybreak when she reached the shallows on the other side of the river. As the sky lightened and pink spread across the horizon, she pushed the boat up onto dry land.

"Daylight must not catch you in the open! Find a wooded place to hide and rest."

Annie wondered what she was supposed to do with the boat.

"Keep silent!"

The reproach surprised her until she realized she had been thinking aloud. Of course, she had to leave the boat where it was; it had served its purpose. She headed for the cover of the woods that lined the shore.

Once she was well into the thick of trees, she sank to the ground. Crawling under some low bushes, she fell into an uncomfortable sleep that was interrupted by a frequent need to change positions.

"Do not sleep on the ground."

Osei's voice woke her completely. If she was not to bed down here, where was she to sleep?

"The ground is not safe. You will have to use the trees, but later. For now, you must keep moving."

The sun filtered through the thick branches at an angle that indicated late morning. Annie realized she had not eaten for more than a day. She opened the pack of food and ate a bit of the bread. Even the small amount filled her; she was just too anxious and excited to feel her hunger. She had to find a road heading east.

It was just at sundown and the Sabbath was over. A gang of Black men and women was walking the road, headed east to someone's distant fields, perhaps to clear them for a new planting. The practice was to march the workers out in the evening and have them camp near the next day's worksite. In this way, they could catch first light already in the fields.

Annie watched the silently moving gang from behind a tree near the road-side. She had seen such lines marching on Sunday evenings when she accompanied her mother out to the Maryland farm.

She slipped into the line, just behind the last man. He half turned his head; the movement was so slight that it seemed more like he was flicking away an insect. Two others who had been walking on either side of him now dropped back, closing in behind her. Two more materialized on either side, so that she was now in the center of a tight circle of men. The one immediately behind stepped up, almost on her heels. Annie moved forward, trying to get out of his way. The two on either side simultaneously moved closer together. This forced her further forward. The silent jockeying continued until she found herself walking with a group of women. The women appeared to take no notice of her. Yet they also moved themselves so that she was always in their center.

Several minutes later, everyone's actions became clear to her. Two White men on horseback galloped along the line, headed toward the rear. They appeared to be counting heads, making sure no one slipped away. Had she remained at the end of the line, she would surely have been discovered.

About an hour later, the entire line suddenly stopped and broke up into knots of people. Annie followed the group of women who were cutting firewood. Together, they made a large fire and set about preparing a meal of corn-meal seasoned with bits of bacon rind for the entire group. Each person seemed to have his own wooden trencher on which several of the women ladled out a portion. Once all of the men were served, the women took theirs. Annie, having helped prepare and serve the food, now could hear her own stomach growling, but she had no trencher. As she was about to find a place to sit out of the way, a woman suddenly handed her one loaded with food. Not only was it a double portion, but there was a whole piece of bacon, with the fat sitting on top of the mush. As she looked up to thank her, the woman moved off, disappearing into the crowd.

Annie sat and ate hungrily. She was joined by the man who had been at the end of the line. He sat beside her with his food and ate silently. Looking around, she noticed that everyone was either in pairs or in small groups; no one ate alone. As people finished eating, they got out rolled blankets in preparation for sleep. The man leaned in close and began to whisper.

"Jus 'cross this clearin's the woods. Yuh tek this 'ere blanket 'n step in there; nobody'll see ya go. Got ta do it 'fore day break, though."

He stood up suddenly, pulling her to her feet at the same time. Now he put an arm around her neck so that her face was partially buried against his chest. Together, they walked toward the dark line of trees. One of the White men, still on horseback, ambled over.

"Where ya takin' th' wench?"

"Only be a minnit, Masta."

The White man laughed heartily. "If she was to be with me, it'd take more'n a minnit!"

These Negroes! No matter how hard you worked them, they could still find the energy to have relations with their women!

They stopped just inside the forest. Here the man handed Annie the blanket and, before she could say anything, returned to the group. She remained where she was for several minutes more, vaguely hoping that he might decide to run too. But he disappeared into the huge group of now-sleeping men and women. She realized the man probably had family that he could not leave. A powerful sense of gratitude rose and flooded her whole being. People who had no hope of freedom had silently protected, fed and helped her take her next steps.

Moving off deeper into the forest, her eyes finally accustomed to the inky darkness, Annie located a tree with low forked branches. She climbed it and secured the four corners of the blanket by spreading it across two stout branches and tying the ends to limbs that protruded from each. Once everything was ready, she bedded down in the sling thus created.

After the first few days, she found a rhythm. Mornings were for finding clean water and, if possible, a meal. Occasionally, if she was able to venture into the corner of some farmer's field, she would dig up whatever root vegetables were still in the ground. More often, however, she was forced to satisfy herself with a drink from one of the many springs that crisscrossed the forest floor. Midday, whether she had eaten or not, was for travel. She let herself be guided by Osei's voice and he would choose the day's route as well as the distance she was to cover; sometimes up to ten miles in a single afternoon.

Then the weather changed. Although it was August, there came a cool spell of days and nights followed by a week of hard rain. There was no way for her to shelter herself or to keep warm. The blanket that was her bed became the coat that she wrapped about herself as she walked. Within a few days, she began to feel achy and unwell; soon she was feverish. Then came shaking chills. She could no longer keep to the directions that Osei's voice kept repeating. By the time the cool wet weather ended, she was wandering around in circles, unaware of having covered the same ground before.

One bright beautiful day when the air was like warm water, Annie found herself sitting on the tumbled-down section of a low stone wall. The trees kept floating away before her eyes. For some reason, try as she might, she could not keep the trees anchored; they would first waver, then lift into the air and hover like misty things. There appeared in the distance a dark stick-like figure that gradually grew larger as she tried to focus past the pain in her head. As it grew, it slowly turned over until it was horizontal. Just as gradually, it became eclipsed in bright bursts of light, followed by a gathering darkness.

Chapter 24

A local farmer was checking the stone walls that marked the boundaries of his land. In many places, the largest stones had fallen over. Wherever he saw them down, he would lift them back into place. But it clearly taxed his spine, which was slightly twisted from an old, untreated injury. With the sun at his back, the man came upon one of the fields that he had let go fallow. At the far end, he could just make out the figure of a person sitting on one of the fallen parts of his wall. He stopped, shading his eyes to see better, as the figure began to crumple. He broke into an awkward loping run and reached the woman just as she'd collapsed.

Solomon Breughel was a Dutch Quaker whose great-grandfather had come to Long Island with one of the earliest groups of settlers and had acquired a large tract of land. The great-grandfather would never benefit from it, as he was killed in an Indian raid. The property was entirely wild when his son inherited it. Reluctantly, Solomon's grandfather purchased a gang of men to clear and plant it. The farm became quite profitable and the elder Breughel found ways to salve his conscience. His son was much more devout. Upon his father's death, the man, now a father himself and a widower also attempted to justify continuing the practice of keeping slaves to manage the work. It was an unfortunate accommodation, one so against his Quaker beliefs that he was finally compelled to free the entire group after only two planting seasons. The damage to his conscience, unfortunately, was irreparable. He turned the place over to a then 17-year-old Solomon and moved across the river into New York, where he died of a fever the following year.

Solomon did not make his father's mistake. He hired men to work as much of the land as he could keep in production; the rest he left unplanted. Some he sold off and used the money to invest rather profitably in the rum and barrel trade. When he married Elspeth VanWyck, he was comfortably well-off enough to build her a sturdy new two-story house, the only house with a second story in the area. They had no children.

In expiation for his grandfather's sin, Solomon not only owned no slaves, but also made it his business to help any who came as runaways to his farm. Today, the woman on the ground had obviously been on the road for a long time and was terribly sick. Perhaps it was already too late. If so, Solomon was ready to bury the poor soul. He touched her face; she breathed, coughed and shivered. As he would a sheaf of wheat, Solomon hefted the woman over his shoulder. She was as tall as he, but far lighter in weight than he had expected, thus enabling him to carry her easily.

Elspeth had been watching for him at the front parlour window, as she always did just before dusk. The moment she saw the woman's limp form, she rushed to hold open the door.

"Good Husband, hast thou brought in another one dead?"

"I do believe she lives yet."

"Well, bring her along. We'll place her in the small sleeping-room."

Solomon followed his wife up the narrow back staircase to a small room just at the top. Inside, the roof sloped sharply, as it was built under the eves at the rear of the house. Elspeth gestured for Solomon to lay the woman on the bed.

The poor thing was absolutely filthy! The dress she wore was so tattered and caked with mud that the fabric shredded, even as Elspeth was attempting to remove it. The shift was in no better condition. Elspeth finally despaired of saving any of the clothing and simply tore off everything. She stopped, completely baffled at the sight of a sweat-stained leather pouch attached to straps around the woman's waist. Her attempt to remove the thing proved frustrating as the straps had been sewn together. Leaving the belt alone, she decided to try removing the head wrap. When, at length, she succeeded in unwinding the dirty cloth, she stopped, aghast. The woman's head was covered in wooly *snakes*! Elspeth touched one gingerly, half expecting the thing to wriggle out from under her finger. But it *was* hair, the same kinky, matted hair that she had seen on the other runaways who had come to her over the years. Those who had not survived, she washed, dressed and buried. She knew about the hair; this, however, was quite different.

For several minutes, she stood silently watching the woman on the bed. Annie barely breathed and did not otherwise stir. Elspeth waited for the breathing to cease or become louder, a sure sign of impending death.

After many minutes, when there was no change in the almost impercep-tible rhythm, she set about cleaning Annie as best she could. She lifted her shoulders and turned her on her right side. Suddenly, Annie coughed violently, dislodging a huge plug of green sputum that landed on the bare wood floor. Elspeth moved quickly to the other side of the narrow bed and administered several smart open-handed slaps between Annie's shoulder blades. This brought up more mucus, now flecked with dark rust. With her airways now cleared, Annie, though still unconscious, began to breathe more deeply. Con-fident now that the woman was out of immediate danger, Elspeth covered her with a quilt and left the room, keeping the door ajar.

"Has she passed?" Solomon asked as soon as his wife appeared in the door-way.

He had been sitting and waiting for her in the kitchen, his large rough hands folded almost delicately on the table. He never stayed to see how Elspeth dealt with the runaways. She had always made it clear that his presence was not wanted during her ministrations. At first, he had tried to help, par-ticularly with the men. But he usually managed to stand in just the spot she needed clear, so that she would inevitably either bump into him or step on one of his feet. Once, when he went to fetch the water bucket for her, he stumbled and spilled the contents on both the patient and Elspeth. From that point on, he was banished from the bedside of any sick runaways.

"She will probably survive the night. But I cannot be certain that she will get well. The poor thing has the pleurisy. She will need a strong physick."

"Hast thou the necessary herbs in the larder?"

"Good Husband, dost thou not remember? I put up all that I needed just this spring!"

Elspeth's mild irritation was so familiar. Solomon never noticed anything in the house; he left all such domestic concerns to her.

"I think this one is un-baptized. Her hair is done up in, I fear, a heathen-ish manner. It is neither in braids nor loose. I shall be unable to comb it or oth-erwise make it presentable. And there is some sort of filthy bag of leather sewn 'round her waist that I cannot get off."

"May I see, good Wife?" Solomon's curiosity was thoroughly piqued. He hoped Elspeth would say yes.

"Perhaps tomorrow, if she lives through the night."

Solomon understood this meant that the answer was no and the matter closed.

Elspeth spent the next two nights at Annie's bedside, applying poultices to her chest and back. On the third night, the fever that rose each evening sud-denly broke. Annie had spent the previous days and nights thrashing about, semi-conscious and incoherent. She finally slept, drenched in sweat but breathing normally for the first time. Elspeth at last felt that she could leave the bedside. She spent several minutes ruefully gazing at Annie's thickly matted hair. Perhaps tomorrow she would bring up her sewing scissors and try to cut off that nasty bag—and those ropey locks.

"I do vow this is not hair, but something unnatural," she mused aloud. "Only by cutting it could I hope to make her presentable."

Once daybreak sent shafts of light across the bed, Annie awakened. She sat up slowly, looking around at the unfamiliar room and surroundings. Nothing that had happened over the past four days could she remember, only that she was last in the woods. Yet, right now, it seemed terribly important to get a bath and to wash her hair. Swinging her legs over the side of the bed, she tried standing. Her legs felt entirely unsubstantial and she was lightheaded. But, by moving carefully, she was able to reach the door. Immediately outside was a steep ladder leading to the main floor and the back door. She carefully descended, stopping on each step to get her balance.

"Ah, so this is the patient." Solomon was seated in his accustomed spot at the table when Annie entered the kitchen on still unsteady legs.

Elspeth had been tending something at the fire; she turned briskly, noting that the woman seemed about to topple over.

"Yes, good Husband. Please see to her before she pitches into the grate."

He did as he was told, taking her arm and guiding her to the bench that served as a seat on the other side of the table. Annie sank down gratefully. The dizziness that had overcome her momentarily began to recede. Now she looked curiously at her benefactors. They were indeed the strangest White people she had ever seen, with their homespun brown clothing. What amazed her most was their manner, with each other and toward her, almost as though she were their equal.

"It would be good to eat a bit. We have stew and a fresh loaf. Please join us, if thou feelest able."

Elspeth placed a fully laden bowl before her and cut a thick slice of the warm bread. Annie looked at the food, then at Elspeth, but she made no move toward it.

"I thank you, Mistress. May I have leave to take this outside?"

"Whatever for? Ah, thou art not used to eating with people like us. Here we have no servants; everyone who eats my food sits at my table."

Elspeth continued to talk, interrupted only occasionally by her husband. At length, Annie asked if she could draw herself a bath.

"Dost thou feel able to bathe thyself without assistance?"

Annie was profoundly surprised at Elspeth's question. If she were too weak to bathe alone, was this woman actually offering to help?

Elspeth sensed her confusion and responded. "I have washed many of thy people in my time, those who survived and those who did not. I think thou couldst use my assistance. However, if thou preferest, I will draw the bath and let thou do it alone. I will remain nearby, in case there is a need for my help."

Once the matter of the bath was settled, they completed the meal. Then Elspeth proceeded to fill a large tub with very warm water and bring out clean towels. With everything ready, she left the kitchen, assuring Annie that she was within earshot, should she be needed.

The bath was heavenly. Annie scrubbed herself clean and washed her hair. When she had finished, she wrapped herself in the largest towel and sat before the fire to twist her hair. Both Elspeth and Solomon watched through a crack in the door as she carefully separated and recoiled each lock. Back in their sitting room, they discussed this unusual runaway.

"Clearly the woman's not a Christian."

Elspeth pronounced the observation as a matter of fact. Solomon pursed his lips but remained silent for several minutes. Finally he spoke. "If this be so, good Wife, where doth our responsibilities lie? Are we not bound to bring her to an understanding of the Master?"

Elspeth was, as always, assured in her answer. "'Tis our responsibility, yes. But it must be of her own free will."

"Then, shall we introduce her to the Friends?"

"Yes, though we cannot force her to join us. We must make the invitation nevertheless."

Together they decided to ask Annie to accompany them to next Sunday's meeting.

Annie felt obligated to join Solomon and Elspeth at this thing they called a meeting. Once she and Osei were married, Evie rarely required them to accompany her, Phillip and the children to services other than at Christmas and Easter. Even on those occasions, for Annie, the novelty of being with her husband in the gallery soon wore off and the experience of standing throughout the service simply became long and uncomfortable.

When Sunday came, the Breughels and Annie rode the wagon for the five-mile trip to the meeting house. Annie was amazed to find out it was a simple wood frame building that had been whitewashed, and otherwise unadorned. Inside was a large, bare room with wooden backless benches arranged roughly in a series of concentric squares.

The Friends filed in quietly, taking their seats in family groups. There were only about thirty-five people present when someone closed the door. Annie sat waiting for the services to begin; she waited in vain. For more than an hour there was complete silence. At last, a man with a weathered face and large rough hands rose. He began in a soft monotone; at first Annie could not make out what he was saying, but, the longer he spoke, the more he seemed to warm to his topic and the clearer his words became. It seemed that he had chosen *her* as his subject.

"Are we not Christians who take in the unfortunate bondsman seeking to break his chains? There are those who say, 'Nay!' And decry our actions! But, brethren, be not faint of heart. Today, we witness in our midst yet another who was called 'slave' and who has now fled to freedom, sitting in the company of Friends Solomon and Elspeth. Many are the times these stalwart folk have stood betwixt Right and the laws of men, recognizing that God's law knows no man's interference. And it is His law that we are bound to obey."

He stopped and sat down abruptly. The silence closed in again. After another hour, someone opened the door and everyone rose, signaling that the meeting was at an end.

As they prepared the evening meal together, Annie asked Elspeth why there had been no service.

"Oh my, but there was a service, as thou callest it. The Friends have no need for someone to interpret God's message. He speaks directly to each of us, in our hearts. When the heart is full, only then does it overflow in speech."

This made sense to Annie and the two women worked a while longer in silence. After a bit, she made another inquiry. "The man who spoke, he was speaking of you. Do you, in truth, help runaways?"

"Why, of course, we do!" Elspeth seemed surprised at the question.

Annie wanted to thank this woman but could not find the right words. So she busied herself stirring the contents of the kettle. Finally she spoke hesitantly. "I didn't know there were such people as you... and your husband. You must have surely saved my life, for I was a long time sick on the road and cannot remember how I came to be here."

Elspeth was setting dishes on the table. For a moment, she paused, then briskly continued placing the plates, bowls and spoons.

"My husband did find thee unconscious in one of our fallow fields. It was fortunate that he did; thou wert, in truth, near death. But thy salvation was God's work, not ours."

From that time forward, Annie made ready each Sunday, and accompanied Solomon and Elspeth to meetings. At first she would sit in the back of the wagon. After a few more times, they were able to prevail upon her to join them on the long front seat, where she would sit between them. On many such Sundays in the meeting house, the two hours or so would pass in complete silence. Annie soon found that thoughts, in the form of words and images began to fill her mind. Sometimes, she would relive a late evening, working alongside Willy in the carriage house, hearing his child's voice regaling her with endless chatter. At others, she would recall how he looked whenever she took him with her on an errand, holding her hand and skip-walking at her side as he'd recount some mischief one of the Hamilton children had done. Occasionally, Osei's face would float before her eyes and she would try to hold on to the vision of him. In the meeting house, however, he was always silent.

In fact, Osei was silent everywhere. Annie began to ache for the sound of his voice, but she could not summon him, try as she might. Daily, as the summer turned to autumn, she tried to drive the new thoughts out of her mind, to make room for him, but even in the empty spaces that she was able to create, he would not come.

Winter did come, uncharacteristically mild. On Christmas Day, the Breughels joined the other Friends in the meeting house for three hours and then returned to the farm for a large afternoon meal. The evening was spent with Solomon reading aloud from the large family Bible. For Annie's benefit, since he believed she had never heard it, he read the story of Jesus' birth from St. Luke, Chapter 2, and the marvelous story of the three Wise Men, from the book of St. Matthew. Annie, far from being ignorant of them, clearly remembered both accounts, having listened as Evie had memorized them. Now the words came flooding back, accompanied by a confusion of emotions that surprised and pained her. She lowered her head so Solomon would not see that she was crying.

Elspeth noticed her tears and interrupted the reading. "Good Husband, I do think that Annie has had enough for today. Let us give thanks for the reading of His Holy Word and retire."

Throughout the balance of the winter and into spring, Annie remained on the farm. She became adept both in the house, working with Elspeth, and out in the fields helping Solomon. Well into his sixties, the hard labour required was too much for him, although he could not admit it, even to himself. Although she had never done field work, Annie discovered that she was stronger and more able than she could have imagined.

She also began remembering the lessons in plant pharmacology that Osei had tried to teach her with so little success. As soon as the ground warmed, in late March, she put in an herb garden right outside the kitchen door. Here she cultivated rosemary, thyme, parsley, comfrey, garlic and several other herbs the names of which she did not know, but she remembered their features. Neither Elspeth nor Solomon favored "exotic" flavours, so Annie did not use any of the herbs in her cooking. But whenever Solomon's aching back would not respond to Elspeth's poultices, without telling her, Annie would slip in a bundle of raspberry leaves, the results of which were nearly miraculous. At first, Annie wondered if she should just tell Elspeth how to improve the poultice. But something kept her silent. Increasingly, she began to sense that the *something* was tied to Osei.

On a warm Sunday in early June, just as the meeting was ending, Annie finally heard the voice she had been waiting for.

"It is time to leave. Take everything you will need as it is given. Go today and do not turn back."

It was a little past noon when they returned to the farm. Annie got down from the wagon first and stood aside as Solomon stiffly alighted and turned to offer his arm to Elspeth.

As they were putting the wagon away, Annie broke the news of her planned departure to Solomon. "I thank you with all my heart for everything you and Friend Elspeth have done for me. I shall never forget you."

Solomon looked troubled. This was unexpected and he had come to depend on her help. "But whither wilt thou go? In truth we did hope that thou had decided to stay with us."

Annie had to brace herself against his obvious disappointment. If he and Elspeth were true to their beliefs, and she knew that they were, they would do nothing to hinder her leaving. At the same time, she did owe them her life. But she *had* to go. The need to leave immediately was like a sharp hunger; her feet felt restless standing still. How could she explain in words they would under-stand? Then it came to her—an unadorned truth! God was calling her to move on. He would guide her journey and He would determine her destination. When she told this to Elspeth and Solomon together, they nodded silently in agreement.

While Elspeth made her a bundle with a change of clothing and a gener-ous packet of provisions, Solomon called her into the parlour where there was an old secretary. From one of the desk drawers, he drew out a yellowed enve-lope.

"These are free papers that I found on a woman who died in the west field, about a year ago. Thou may have need of them."

Annie took the envelope and drew out the manumission papers reverently. She could remember the letters of the alphabet that Osei had taught her and silently spelled out the dead woman's name. Then she refolded the paper and put it into one of her pockets. Within the hour she was on her way. Both Elspeth and Solomon accompanied her as far as the main road. They watched until she was out of sight.

The free papers had belonged to a woman named Laura Brooks. Whoever she was, the age and description may or may not have matched Annie's, but the papers served her well as she made her way East on the main highway that linked many of the Long Island farms with the ferry services across the East River.

During the daylight, she walked at as brisk a pace as she could manage, which gave her the appearance of being about someone's business. Whenever she was stopped, usually by a curious or suspicious White farm owner, she would produce the free papers for inspection. Many of these men could no more read what was written than could she. But each one made a show of care-fully examining the document, then just as carefully looking Annie over. Always, the papers were returned with a peremptory grunt and the man would wave her on her way.

She decided that she would not stop again for any reason unless Osei told her to. His voice was once again in her ear; the joy it brought was palpable.

The provisions lasted for almost two weeks, since Elspeth had included dried meats and preserves along with the bread. Annie would still raid an unattended field for whatever vegetables had not been harvested if she needed to. At night, she would continue to retreat into the forest.

At the end of the second week, she changed her clothes. The apron and gown that she took off were hopelessly filthy and ragged at the hemline. First, she checked her pocket to make sure the free papers were safe. Then she put on the clean garments, carried the dirty clothing into the nearest woods and hid them inside the hollow of a dead tree.

On the fifteenth day of her journey, it rained hard, a steady, drenching downpour that lasted all that day and the following night. Annie remembered it was just such a rain that had made her so sick. But this time, she had better information about how to keep from getting wet and chilled. Finding a field in which there were freshly made haystacks, she crawled under the one nearest to the road. Here she was able to stay relatively dry and, most importantly, warm while she waited out the storm.

The weather did not clear until the following afternoon. Almost immediately, a group of about ten workers who had been waiting for an end to the rain returned to the field and resumed the threshing and bundling of hay. Annie remained in her hiding place until night fell again and they had finally left. Reluctantly, she decided to stay put until just before dawn, when she slipped out of the field and regained the road. She had lost two full days travel time that she hoped to make up. But when she felt in her pocket for the free papers, they were not there! They must have fallen out in the haystack, but she dared not try to go back to find them.

"Oh my God! What am I to do now?" Annie actually cried aloud.

"Hush! You do not need them anymore. Look ahead. The road has ended. Now you must take to the woods."

Sure enough, the wide dirt road, which had become narrower and more rutted, was now little more than a footpath. Ahead was a dense forest, the trees of which had never known the axe. Here were old, knotted trunks, wider than the span of a man's outstretched arms, so tall that their top branches blocked the light of the sun. The forest floor was covered with pine needles and lichen. For days it seemed, she traveled through this wood. The only way she knew night was falling was from the gathering gloom that would gradually spread and suddenly plunge her into blackness. The trees were too tall to climb and she was afraid to lie down, so she kept moving, following the direction of Osei's voice.

For the first time, his whispers breathed softly just ahead of her. *"This way, Annie. No, don't turn around! Come this way!"*

Finally, Annie emerged from the cool darkness of the forest to sun soaked daylight. In the center of the clearing was a good-sized lake surrounded by rushes as tall as a man's head. Osei's voice had been silent for a full day now. She did not know what to do next and anyhow, she was bone-tired. The idea of sleep seeped into her, taking her down to a sitting position. From there, it was easy to simply fall over and make herself comfortable.

"Get up!"

Annie was startled awake; she struggled to her feet.

"Not here. Go into the water."

For a moment, she stood where she was, dumbfounded.

"Take off your clothes and go into the water."

Galvanized, Annie unwrapped her head cloth, pulled off her now-filthy dress, torn petticoat and shift. Naked, she pushed through the tall reeds and waded into the lake. The day was hot, making the water's coolness pleasant against her skin. The small waves created by her movements were sweetly seductive against her legs, thighs, hips. She waded toward the center until the water was just under her chin; she then took one more step. The lake closed over her head. Was this the destination that she had been seeking? The urge to stay underwater was so strong. All she needed to do was take a breath-....

Chapter 25

THE VILLAGE (1787)

Very quietly, Great Bear trod the forest floor, stopping ever so often to listen and test the wind. The buck that he had been tracking for over two hours moved into sight, out into the sunlight to drink at the lake's edge. Great Bear remained in the shadows created by a huge tree, trying to stay downwind. Just at that moment, the wind shifted and the buck turned his head sharply to the right. Catching the man's scent, he darted away back into the forest.

Great Bear sprang toward the vanishing deer in a futile movement, when something else caught his attention. As he turned toward the lake, something sprang up out of the water. Instinctively, he shrank back behind the tree. It was a naked, dark-skinned woman! Great Bear had nearly lost his footing as the scene suspended itself before his eyes. The woman gasped and shook her head, as if to clear her eyes, her mouth. Her hair flew out—long woolly locks whipping about, spraying water in every direction, catching the sunlight. But it was her body that riveted him to the spot. In spite of the different color, in height, in shape and with every curve, it was Snow Bird's! In his dreams, Great Bear had caressed every part of her. He knew her body as he knew his own. Now he felt his heart begin to pound in his chest like something alive. And he was suddenly aroused, as he had not been, not even once, since her death.

This had to be a spirit that literally vanished! At the very instant Great Bear had realized what he had seen, the being disappeared in a great splashing and thrashing of the rushes. Had he not been so overwhelmed, he might have noticed that the woman had created the commotion as she ran into the shallows and became hidden by the high reeds. But he was beyond all calm thought. His legs gave way and he nearly fell.

Supporting himself against the tree trunk, he placed one hand against his chest, willing his heart to ease its hammering. When he could breathe almost normally, he retrieved his bow and arrows from the spot where he'd dropped them, and slowly headed back toward the village.

When Annie had taken that breath, she nearly drowned. Within the same moment, she realized she was not supposed to die here. Her eyes flew open. Finding that she was still under water, she struggled toward the shallows. Fortunately, the lake was unusually clear and she could see where the bottom sloped upward toward the surface. When she stood up, she was in water only waist high. Coughing and sputtering, she shook her head violently and began to run toward the reed-choked bank. Once she had made her way through, she found herself in a meadow. Suddenly spent, she sank to the ground and promptly fell into a deep, dreamless sleep.

When she awakened, the sun had moved from its noontime position into late afternoon. Annie shivered as a breeze touched her naked body. Rising, she made her way toward a spot where the open meadow seemed to end abruptly. At the top of a hill, the land ended in a steep drop straight down into the ocean. Here she stopped, waiting for Osei to tell her to jump.

A group of women suddenly appeared, surrounding her. Annie, not knowing who they were, whirled around to face them, only to realize that they were *savages*. She had never seen Indian women before, only the occasional man, usually engaged in selling something on the streets. The women, perhaps sensing her intent, took hold of both her arms and held her fast.

One young woman spoke some words that dispatched two younger ones. The two took off at a smart clip toward the forest. Meanwhile, the others examined her minutely. One rubbed her skin, chattering to her comrades, while two others fingered her hair. Then one pointed to the leather belt sown around her waist and they all began to whisper together. They wanted to touch it, but not one dared. So they went back to exploring the more familiar parts of her body. The one who seemed to be the leader did not engage in the examination at all. She stood a little apart from the others and watched the proceedings. Occasionally, she would offer a comment, at which point the others would fall into a respectful silence.

The young runners soon returned with a blanket that the leader took from them. Approaching Annie cautiously, she spoke soothingly as she carefully draped it over her shoulders. Taking her hand, she led her away from the cliff, followed closely by the rest of the group. Almost immediately, they were in a dense forest.

Annie wondered idly where they were taking her. It did not matter really; her journey was at an end. Sooner or later, she would be told what to do next.

Until then, it was enough. The tiredness came over her again, and it was all she could do just to remain on her feet. One of the women who had been fingering her hair came up behind her as they walked. She reached a tentative hand toward Annie's head.

"We'usk?" The woman gently touched one of the still damp locks. "We'usk?"

"Hair? My hair? Yes, this is my hair."

Annie realized that she had learned her first word of these people's language.

It seemed to Annie that there was no path to follow, yet the women moved through the densely crowded trees and underbrush as confidently as though there were one. Finally, on the other side of this forest, they came to a clearing of sorts. Many tall trees stood over small domed structures made of interwoven thatch and branches, covered in some cases with animal hides. Annie had never seen anything like them. What amazed her even more was that half-naked men, women and children were crawling in and out of these things; apparently they were the houses of these people. In front of each dwelling there was a pit, surrounded with stones, in which a fire blazed. Women tended large iron pots over these fire pits. It seemed like these people did their cooking outdoors.

The young woman who had sent for the blanket now appeared bent on taking charge of her. She gestured to Annie to enter one of the structures. Once inside, Annie found that the interior was larger than it first appeared. She was actually able to stand upright in the center of the single circular room. Around its circumference stretched a low wooden bench which seemed to serve as a storage area for blankets and other items. Underneath this bench were baskets, pots and what looked like tools of some sort. In the center of this room was what looked like an open pit, similar to the one outside, for a fire inside as well.

Two girls, the eldest about eleven, the other apparently her slightly younger sister, sat in a corner, sewing something. They had nearly identical faces and bodies; only the difference in height made it clear that they were not twins. Both turned solemn, ink-black eyes toward Annie. The woman summoned the girls who obediently came to stand by her. She was apparently introducing them, for she pushed each one forward as she spoke.

"Weesa-wayoa ássas (Yellow Bird), yunksquas (eldest daughter). Wampayoaráquasac (Bright Star), squasses (younger daughter)."

Annie tried, without success, to catch the sound of each name so she could repeat it. The woman then gestured to herself, the eldest girl and the younger one.

"Nee, cwca, Sunhatk. Yunksquas, squasses. (I am their mother, Gentle Fawn. This is my oldest; this is my youngest.)"

She pointed to Annie. "Kee?"

Annie could recognize that the woman wanted to know who she was. She opened her mouth, intending to say, Annie. To her surprise, another name came out.

"Anika."

What had happened? She almost looked around to see who had spoken. Osei's voice in her ear came so suddenly that she jumped. *"It is time to assume the name that you must carry in your new life. Your name means Goodness. You must bring healing to the place where you are."*

The woman repeated Anika's name for the benefit of the girls. Then they each said it. The name seemed to please them somehow. The youngest smiled suddenly and came over to stand next to Anika. Shyly, she took her hand. The eldest, although she stayed where she was, also smiled at Anika.

Now the woman began rummaging in one of the baskets under the long bench. At last, she made a triumphant noise and produced a garment. Holding it out at arms' length, she brought it over to Anika. It was a dress made of some sort of hide, soft as butter and the color of milk. It was elaborately decorated with beads, shells and different colored lacings. Obviously the dress had been made for a special occasion. The young woman placed it against Anika, stretching out the shoulders to check the fit. Deciding it would do, she indicated through gestures and signs that Anika was to put it on.

Anika hesitated, not just because the dress was too beautiful to wear, but also because neither the woman nor the girls showed the slightest inclination of giving her any privacy. Pointing to Anika's waist, the woman did whisper something to the girls that caused the smaller one to snicker and cover her mouth. She quickly snatched the girl's hand away, and the older one gave her sister a hard look. They all watched as Anika dropped the blanket and stood naked, trying to figure out how one was supposed to get into the dress. She turned the garment this way and that until, at last, she located the openings in the shoulders which allowed her to pull it over her head. The fit was perfect. The young woman smiled approvingly; then she gestured for Anika to sit. Gently, almost reverently, she moved closer, her eyes on Anika's hair. She was trying to convey the idea that her hair needed to be fixed somehow.

The youngest girl was much less reserved than either her sister or her mother. She came up behind Anika and took two handfuls of the not-quite-dry locks, first trying unsuccessfully to separate them into single strands of hair, then running her fingers through Anika's entire head. Finally, when every lock was disentangled and hanging individually, she sat down triumphantly.

Anika found the entire procedure intensely pleasurable. Not since Osei had anyone else fixed her hair. She gestured for the child to come sit beside her, reaching out a welcoming arm; the girl fairly beamed as she snuggled against Anika's side. Not to be outdone, the older girl promptly took her place on the other side, so Anika could embrace her as well.

When Great Bear got back to the village, he found a great commotion taking place in the center of the circle of wigwams. Whatever was going on he did not want to have to face just now; he had not yet recovered from the apparition at the lake, which had terrified him. Nothing happened without meaning. He needed to find out what this vision meant.

One of the young men spied him standing just beyond the clearing. This youth ran up and nearly fell on Great Bear.

"Oh Chief! A stranger has come to the village! Your daughter has her! It's a woman with black skin and strange hair!"

A peculiar sensation began in Great Bear's chest. He felt the hair at the back of his neck bristle. Pushing past the youth, he strode toward the crowd of villagers. Anika stood in the center of the throng, with Gentle Fawn and her daughters on either side, almost as though for protection. Great Bear stopped just ten feet away. The crowd drew back as though to give him unfettered space. He circled the small group once, then again. He could barely believe what he was seeing. Here she was, the woman from the lake! What was more, now she was wearing Snow Bird's wedding dress! Without speaking, he turned on his heel and left. The crowd parted to let him pass, and he soon disappeared into the woods.

Several older women, contemporaries of the chief, commented among themselves after he had left. One, whose name was Wequaran'skesucsquah (Eagle Eye Woman) spoke first. "Great Bear still acts strangely at times, does he not?"

Her companion replied. "Oh, he has never gotten over Snow Bird and the children."

Eagle Eye Woman was unsympathetic in her response. "What do you expect? He never mourned them properly. So their spirits stay to torment him now."

"It is too much grief for one man to bear," one of the other women offered in defense. "Even his daughter was not spared, losing her husband like that. And now look how Gentle Fawn has given the stranger her mother's wedding dress. Of course, Great Bear was shocked!"

The women all nodded, agreeing with both the criticism of Great Bear and the explanation for his behavior.

Gentle Fawn insisted that Anika stay in her wigwam. She barely remembered Snow Bird. But she felt strongly drawn to this woman who could fit her mother's clothes so perfectly. On that first evening, Anika, utterly exhausted by now, fell asleep while Gentle Fawn and her daughters were still preparing the meal. When she saw Anika lying on the bench, Gentle Fawn simply covered her with a blanket and left her where she was. Later that night, Anika awakened abruptly to find the girls had curled up next to her, one on each side, and both were sound asleep. Their small bodies added a bit too much warmth, but Anika was so grateful for their presence that, for the first time since her ordeal had begun, she shed tears.

For his part, Great Bear spent most of that first night pacing in circles just outside the village. His emotions swung between rage at himself for having behaved badly in public and at his daughter for being so thoughtless. How dare she dress that…that *being* in Snow Bird's dress! Didn't Gentle Fawn recognize how much the woman's body resembled her mother? Great Bear had conveniently forgotten that Gentle Fawn had been only a baby when Snow Bird died.

Eventually, overcome by fatigue, the chief finally returned to his wigwam and got out his bedding. But sleep kept eluding him. As soon as his eyes would close, he would see *her* standing beside his daughter, in *that dress*!

At first, Anika found the arrangement somewhat uncomfortable, since she could not understand her hostess. However, within a week, she was able to help with all of the chores. At the same time, the balance in the family began to shift—subtly at first, but surely. Gentle Fawn had long hungered for a mother; Anika was becoming her substitute. It was a natural development that even the language difference did not affect. First, Anika took over part of the cooking, showing Gentle Fawn how to add herbs to dishes, like succotash, to improve the flavor. Then came the day when "Squassas" as Anika still called Bright Star, became ill with a fever. She was able to brew a tea that broke it overnight. Now Gentle Fawn was completely in her debt.

She asked Anika through gestures to teach her how to use the familiar healing herbs in new ways. Thus began the early morning trips into the woods and along the meadows to locate goldenseal, licorice and other lichens that had healing properties. As they searched, Anika would use the time to teach Gentle Fawn the English names that now, surprisingly, came flooding into her memory. In turn, Gentle Fawn would show Anika how to pronounce the name of each herb in Unkechaug.

It took Great Bear more than a week to recover from his intense anger and the shock of seeing Anika in his village. Although he behaved outwardly as though nothing had happened, he stayed away from Gentle Fawn's wigwam all that time, forcing her to bring his meals to his wigwam every evening.

On the first evening, he surprised her by asking her to sit with him while he ate. When he actually began talking to her, she was truly stunned. He began mildly enough, asking an offhanded question. "Daughter, the woman who stays in your wigwam, how did you come to find her?"

Gentle Fawn was so happy to have her father actually conversing with her that she did not notice the tightness at the corners of his mouth. She spoke animatedly about finding Anika naked at the cliff's edge.

"We feared she was about to jump. I do wonder how she came so far, from wherever. But she is quite calm now, although we cannot understand one another." Then she asked, "Why do you not come and join us tomorrow for the evening meal? You can meet her for yourself. After all, you are the chief and she should meet you."

Suddenly, Great Bear's face closed in anger. Gentle Fawn quickly sensed that she had touched some forbidden nerve—as usual. Her father was as prickly as a porcupine when it came to conversation. He stood abruptly. "I am finished now. You can take the pot away. Your stew is too dry tonight; it will be no good in the morning."

Great Bear saw his daughter's face fall and realized he was being deliberately cruel. She got up immediately, took the pot and vanished among the trees. His heart ached as he watched her go; she was his only living child and her presence always reminded him of this. Once she was gone, the pain intensified until he could not bear it. He spent that night and the next circling the village, unable even to enter his wigwam and lie down.

On the second night, Gentle Fawn did not find her father at home when she went to take him his meal. She returned with the pot and Anika found her crying quietly by the cooking fire. Putting her arm around the woman, Anika tried to find out what had happened. Yellow Bird, the eldest, came to stand beside her mother.

Bright Star explained the situation, angrily. "Numpsoonk! Naacum cwca skesuc sukerun! (It's Grandfather! He's made mother cry again!)"

Anika caught the word, numpsoonk, and suspected that it had something to do with the chief. She tried to get Bright Star to understand a question. "Is numpsoonk Cwca's father?"

The child stamped one foot in frustration and repeated her statement, this time in a shout. "Numpsoonk cwca skesuc sukerun!"

"Come," Anika reached out her free arm, encircling the now-crying child. Silently, she vowed to find a way to ease Gentle Fawn's hurt. The man who had barged into the center of the crowd on the day she was found was somehow at the bottom of this.

For another week, Gentle Fawn took her father's evening meal and left it outside beside his fire, without stopping to see if he was at home. Each afternoon, when she returned for the pot, she would find that he had barely touched the food.

On the seventh day, Anika stopped her as she was about to prepare the meal. "Let me do it tonight."

Gentle Fawn seemed to understand. She watched as Anika put corn kernels, squash, beans and dried meat into the pot, along with water, green pepper and herbs. When everything was done, they gathered the girls and the family ate first. Gentle Fawn tasted her food and then looked up in surprise.

"Ca coquees ascoot mais-cusseet woreecar! (Your pot of beans and squash is very good!)"

Anika smiled. It was tasty. She dipped out a generous portion into a small iron pot and gestured to Yellow Bird to show her the way to Great Bear's wigwam.

On this evening, Great Bear was sitting before the cold ashes of his fire pit. The rage that had kept him moving night after night was spent. Now he simply felt tired, empty and intensely lonely. Were it not for the fact that the strange woman was in his daughter's wigwam, he would have considered going there. The girls could sometimes amuse him with their chatter, especially since they never spoke to him directly. But she *was* there. And he could not face that, not yet.

He sat with his back to the woods; suddenly, he heard the snap of a twig underfoot. Assuming it was Gentle Fawn bringing another meal, he did not immediately move. But there was something different in the sound of the footstep that made his breathing become shallow and his heartbeat suddenly race. He knew without turning around that it was the woman who had brought his meal. Some small part of his mind wondered at her impertinence, coming to his wigwam uninvited.

He struggled to gather his composure, even as he silently chided himself. "You, *woman*! How can you be so frightened of her? Even if she is a spirit, you are the chief! You must be ready to face her, whatever she is!"

He forced himself to turn around. Calmly, he gestured for her to put the pot on the ground next to the dead fire. Now that she was close enough, he could see she was quite real.

He had never seen a Black person, much less a woman before, and he could not stop himself from staring at her. She was wearing another of Snow Bird's dresses, an everyday shift made of deerskin. He studied how the dress moved as she bent over, how the locks of her hair swung with each movement. Suddenly, he did not want her to leave. Gesturing to her to sit, he went into the wigwam to search for bowls and spoons, creating quite a clatter as he rummaged through baskets, tossing things around. At last, he found two clean bowls, a dirty spoon and a clean one.

He handed the clean utensils to Anika, indicating that she was to help herself. She struggled to remember the word for full, settling finally on "Nee (I)" and placing one hand just under her chin. He shook his head, insisting. And so she placed a small amount in her bowl and a much larger helping in his. Without taking his eyes off her he took a spoonful, and then stopped.

"Woreecan! Neechuntz coritch? (It is good! Is this my daughter's cooking?)"

He knew immediately that this woman had made the stew. The taste was so seductive that he went through three helpings without realizing what he was doing.

All this time, Anika sat, pushing the food around with her spoon. Fortunately, the chief had become so involved with the meal that he did not push her to eat as well. In between each spoonful, Great Bear kept studying her, openly and so Anika took the opportunity of staring back. But, looking at him, made her gradually become more and more uncomfortable. He was tall, she could see, and he seemed large. When she came to his face, however, Anika found that she could not focus. The individual features seemed to separate, wavering, like rippling water. Only his eyes remained fixed, intense and black as coal. She could feel the old wound in her chest opening; a searing pain began in its center and spread outward. She put the still-full bowl on the ground and stood up unsteadily. He watched her intently as she arose, backed away, turned and ran off into the darkness.

Anika was still running when she reached Gentle Fawn's wigwam. She knew she could not stop yet. The pain that had begun when she allowed herself to look closely at Great Bear now threatened to completely overtake her if she did not keep going. Instinctively, she veered around the dwellings and raced through the woods.

Although the sun had set, there was still enough light for her to see the clearing that ended with the cliff's sheer drop. She made straight for the edge and would have sailed over it, had she not been physically blocked. Something palpable rose up in front of her and knocked her to the ground. At the same time, she could hear her name being called – *"Annie!" "Anika..."* by several voices at once, Osei's among them. Suddenly, she was exhausted. She stretched out, face down on the ground and spread her arms out, as though trying to embrace the earth. Words formed in her mind, a plea.

"Oh why will you not let me die? I want to be with you; I want my husband!"

"You are doing what you were meant to do. You have been led to this place. There is much for you to do here. When the time is right, I will call for you to come back to me."

Anika turned over and sat up. The searing pain had vanished; she felt alert, and now her mind was filled with ideas that she could not understand. Then came words, in an unfamiliar language. She tried to repeat the phrases aloud, but each time, the exact syllables would slip away as soon as she opened her mouth.

"Only in stillness and silence can you learn. Say nothing, and in time you will know all that you need to."

And so she sat still, arms crossed on her raised knees, with her face turned up to the sky. Eventually, her head dropped onto her arms and she slept.

An hour or so later, after he had wrapped himself in his blanket and gone to sleep, Great Bear had the dream for the first time. Many nights thereafter, it would return to torment him.

He was back in the sun-drenched clearing beside the lake, partially hidden behind a tree. He had the buck in his sights. He was about to release the taught bow string as the arrow aimed at the animal's heart. Suddenly, shockingly, he was waist deep in the waters of the lake. In a slow, almost suspended motion, a woman rose up out of the water, right in front of him. It was Snow Bird, as she had been in her youth! Beautiful! More than beautiful!

As Great Bear reached out with both arms, enfolding her, she drew him underwater; they were locked in each other's arms as the waters closed over them. And then it was no longer Snow Bird, but the one called, Anika! And she was just as beautiful! And as she held him in a drowning embrace, they both sank, endlessly... endlessly....

Great Bear was jolted awake, unable to breathe. He sat bolt upright; his heart hammered sickeningly. Throwing back the blanket, he discovered to his horror that the bed was wet and sticky! Enraged, he snatched up his bedding and threw everything outdoors. Then, pulling on his breechcloth, leggings and moccasins, he left the wigwam.

Without thinking where he was headed, he reached his daughter's door, but it was much too late for a visit.

Next, he felt drawn toward the forest just beyond the village. He knew where these woods led, and the idea occurred to him that the sound and smell of the surf might calm him somewhat.

The sight of a figure seated in the middle of the clearing surprised him. Who would be here in the middle of the night? With a shock, he realized that it was *her*, the woman, and he did not know what to do. She appeared to have fallen asleep. But what had she been doing and why was she sitting in this place? He could not bring himself to approach close enough to touch her, nor could he leave her here alone. So he seated himself a distance away, crossed his legs and watched her until the first light of dawn. When he saw her stir as if to awaken, he rose quietly and left.

After spending a restless morning inside his wigwam avoiding everyone, Great Bear finally decided to consult Tree Stump about the woman. The powaw was fond of sitting in front of his fire every afternoon, smoking his pipe and enjoying either his solitude or the company of the villagers who came seeking his advice. Great Bear would come frequently to sit and smoke in silence, grateful that the medicine man accepted his presence without conversation.

That afternoon, Great Bear visited Tree Stump's wigwam. He had made sure to time his visit so that he could stay long enough not be at home when his evening meal arrived.

The old man had just finished eating his own meal and was about to light his pipe with a twig from his fire when he spotted the chief coming through the trees. He continued the movement, seeming to ignore Great Bear, as the latter seated himself on the opposite side of the fire. This was the position people took when they wished to speak. Great Bear usually sat beside him, close enough so the pipe could be easily passed between them. For several minutes there was silence; Tree Stump continued to draw on the pipe until the tobacco caught and blazed. Finally, after seeming to struggle for an opening, Great Bear spoke. "A woman has come into our village. She now lives in my daughter's wigwam. I... we must know what this means."

Tree Stump blew a perfect wreath of smoke before saying anything. He seemed almost not to have heard Great Bear's words. At length, he reached out a hand to the chief, indicating that he was to come sit beside him. Great Bear obeyed, about to repeat his statement, when Tree Stump finally replied.

"I do not know what it means. You have not tried to find out for yourself; this I know. Why do you not go to your daughter and ask her? She has welcomed this woman, as have your granddaughters. Your women are wise; they would not invite danger into their home."

Great Bear lowered his head, embarrassed that the old man had been so accurate. Tree Stump had warned him, gently and repeatedly about withdrawing from his family and neighbors. But he would always insist this was not the case, that the people were exaggerating. Then he would refuse to discuss the matter further. Of course he knew everyone was right. It was just that he simply could not muster the desire to change. Today, however, he had to agree to investigate this woman for himself. The very thought sickened and excited him at the same time.

"Anika must be a special woman," Tree Stump continued. "Her coming has to be part of a message from the Great Spirit. Our survival has always depended on our ability to heed messages when they are given. You are the chief. Your responsibility is to do what you must to protect the people. Find out all you can; then return to me."

Abruptly, the old man got up and went inside, a signal that the visit was over. Great Bear also rose. He studied the sky, noting that the sun was still high. He had time to reach Gentle Fawn before meal preparation began in earnest.

Great Bear began the visit by calling Gentle Fawn aside. "I will try to talk to this woman, but you must help me. She seems used to you and the girls. But she does not like me; she ran away when I tried to be friendly."

Anika was busy at the cooking fire; both Yellow Bird and Bright Star were competing to help by pushing each other. Anika stopped them with a look. Handing a long handled spoon to Yellow Bird, she gestured to Bright Star to go fetch the bowls. This was the first time she had seen Great Bear come to visit with his family. And she realized that running away from his presence had been rude; she needed to make amends. She motioned to Yellow Bird to fill a bowl from the pot. Then she took it and stood a short distance from the chief, wishing she knew enough of his language to apologize. When he turned toward her, she extended the food with what she hoped was a sincere smile.

"See, Father," Gentle Fawn exclaimed, "Anika does like you! Perhaps you did not realize you had done something to offend her. She is different than us. I am sure I too have offended her sometimes. But she does not seem to mind for long."

Great Bear spent an intensely uncomfortable evening with Anika, his daughter and granddaughters. As far as Gentle Fawn and her daughters were concerned, however, the visit went very well. They chattered among themselves and, occasionally tried to include Great Bear. For her part, Anika was grateful that Gentle Fawn seemed so happy. However, she could not overcome the sense that something terrible had happened to the chief and that her coming had awakened memories he could not face. And every time she looked at him, his pain connected with her own.

Although he wanted to leave, Great Bear forced himself to stay at his daughter's fire until the meal was over. He even remained while Gentle Fawn went in to tell her daughters good night. Thinking Anika might have been offended by his staring, Great Bear was careful not to look in her direction. They sat in awkward silence until Gentle Fawn returned. He remembered that he was to ask her about Anika, but it was difficult with the woman sitting right there. Nevertheless, he began with an observation.

"My granddaughters seem to like this woman."

Gentle Fawn turned and smiled at Anika so she would know that they were talking about her.

"Yes! Anika treats them like her own. Almost as though they were her grandchildren. And she knows medicine—different medicines than Tree Stump."

She went on animatedly, telling about how Anika had cured Bright Star's fever and was now teaching her about herbs that she had never used, and new uses for familiar ones. After another hour or so, Great Bear rose.

Finally turning his eyes on Anika, he raised his right hand in greeting. "Nee, Gunchemosquoh (I am Great Bear). Hahcami (Welcome), Anika."

Anika silently returned the gesture, being careful to raise the same hand.

Over time, it became clear to Anika that she could best help the people of the village with her knowledge of herbal medicine. Everything that Osei had so patiently taught her, and that she had despaired of ever learning successfully now came flooding back. Ever since Gentle Fawn had let the entire village know about her curing Bright Star's fever, mothers had begun bringing their babies and children to Anika for treatment. Many of these visits were for illnesses that women were expected to care for themselves by using herbal remedies learned from their mothers. However, over a century of isolation had limited their pool of knowledge. Anika's medicines worked differently than the traditional cures; in some cases faster, in others without producing a second illness. Even older women began to come to Gentle Fawn's wigwam to watch and comment on the preparation process.

Early one afternoon, the air was pierced by loud screaming. A girl in her early teens was giving birth for the first time and was hysterical with fear and pain. Anika had been out in Gentle Fawn's area of the communal garden gathering corn, beans and squash. Dropping the basket, she ran in the direction of the cries; the cadence she recognized immediately—a howling that grew in intensity into piercing shrieks coinciding with each contraction.

As she reached the center of the village, Anika saw a growing crowd of women and children around one wigwam.

"Mattateayuh yunksquas (Wicked girl)!" one of the women whispered to Anika as she joined the crowd.

Inside a thirteen-year-old newlywed named Peewatsumoccas (Little Squirrel) was fighting her mother's efforts to get her to squat for the birthing process. The women closest to the entrance were shaking their heads in sympathy with the girl's mother, since Little Squirrel had always been a hardheaded child. They were not surprised that she was unprepared to give birth because she never listened to any of her mother's instructions. Now she was getting just what she deserved, a painful lesson!

Anika made her way to the front and entered. By this time, Little Squirrel was writhing and screaming on the floor, her mother standing by helplessly. For a moment, Anika stood just inside the door, listening to the quiet voice at her ear.

"This one is in no danger. Just place one hand on her forehead, and use the other to massage her belly. She will calm in a moment."

It worked. Almost as soon as she touched the girl, Little Squirrel became quiet and sat up. The baby slipped out effortlessly, followed by the afterbirth. The sudden silence stunned the group outside the wigwam. People asked each other what had happened—had the girl suddenly died? Moments later, Little Squirrel's mother came outside and announced the birth of her first grandchild, a girl.

Tree Stump had also heard the commotion. He came to within a short distance of the throng of women and took up his post, leaning on a long stick that he now used for support. This was women's work and he would not intervene unless absolutely necessary. When the screams suddenly stopped, he became more attentive but made no movement. If the girl had died, her mother would cry out in a moment and he would be needed. But the joyous noise that followed told him of the good outcome. He was about to turn back toward his own wigwam when something told him to wait. The women were chanting a name, "Anika! Anika!" So the Black woman had helped bring about the birth!

Tree Stump knew that if anyone were going to have trouble at this time it would be Little Squirrel. The girl was incorrigible! He had been amazed when she got a husband; although Sheckayomanamaquas (Black Hawk) was no catch. The young man certainly did not live up to his name, having been cursed with very bad eyesight. Were it not for the kindness of his friends who supplemented his poor hunting and fishing skills in addition to the industry of Little Squirrel's family, the young couple would be in dire straits indeed.

Turning these notions around in his head occupied the old man as he made his way home. He decided that Anika required more of his direct attention. It seemed the women were able to communicate with her somehow. He understood this as a gift that women shared—the ability to speak without words. Still, if she could be persuaded to learn the language, she could be of great use to him. Great Bear was not going to be any help in this regard. Tree Stump had recognized the chief's problem immediately; the woman had cast a spell over him. Now Tree Stump decided to see if he could discern the source of that spell.

Because of his status as powaw and his advanced age, each of the households in the village took turns supplying Tree Stump's meals. These he accepted graciously, praising the food, whether tasty or not, and complementing the women on their culinary skills. This assured him of a regular supply provided by women who were happy to help.

The very next morning it was Eagle Eye Woman who brought him his first meal of the day; the powaw told her that he wanted Anika to visit him.

Of course, the woman was curious as to the reason, but she knew better than to ask Tree Stump directly. Instead, she tried to get a hint by requesting further information. "Should I ask Gentle Fawn to come too, since Anika does not speak our language?"

Tree Stump smiled gently. "Eagle Eye Woman, do *we* not speak the same language? What I said, I meant. You may give the message to Gentle Fawn if you think Anika cannot understand what you want. The porridge looks tasty and I am hungry. Please let an old man begin his meal."

Eagle Eye Woman accepted the rebuke and left. It was not the first time that Tree Stump had chided her about her nosiness. She went directly to Gentle Fawn's wigwam and left the message with Bright Star.

The girl found her mother and Anika cleaning oysters with the other women. As soon as she had spoken to her daughter, Gentle Fawn gestured to Anika to leave off the shucking and follow her. The two women took a path through the village that Anika had never traveled, to what appeared to be an unbroken stand of trees. She was surprised to see a solitary wigwam nestled almost invisibly among them.

Even before they reached the entrance, an amazingly old man came out. Anika had never seen anyone who looked that old before. And although she tried to, she could not hide her wonder. Gentle Fawn pointed in the direction of the wigwam, indicating that Anika was to approach. Gentle Fawn, however, remained where she was and, at a sign from the powaw, she left immediately.

Tree Stump gestured toward Anika to come closer. Then he entered his wigwam, waving one hand behind as a signal for her to follow him. Once inside, he had her sit beside his fire pit while he remained standing before her. The powaw began by examining her thoroughly. He had her extend both arms. Taking each hand, he examined first the palms, then the backs. He felt along the length of each arm, massaging and rotating each shoulder. Then he had her stand before him, turn to the front, both sides, and to the back. Yellow Bird had arranged Anika's locks into two long, very thick braids. Tree Stump handled each one, running his fingers along the length and feeling the weight of the hair.

Next, he demonstrated how he wanted Anika to open her mouth and stick out her tongue. Holding her face in both hands, he looked closely at the condition of her mouth and teeth. Finally, he sat down facing her and indicated that she was to sit facing him. From this position, the old man studied her silently. He sat so still for so long that it seemed as though he had fallen asleep with his eyes open.

Anika found herself relaxing under his gaze, so much so that she almost began to doze herself. Ever since the night spent on the cliff, her mind had been racing, creating both tension and fatigue. In these silent moments, the knotted place deep within her began to loosen. At length, Tree Stump stirred and rose stiffly. He raised his right hand, laying the left on his breast.

"Nee, Poquetahamansank (I am Tree Stump) Hahcami, Anika." Then the powaw smiled.

Anika returned the gesture and struggled to pronounce his name. After two tries, during which the old man laughed heartily as he corrected her, Anika gave up. Tree Stump indicated that she could go.

From that day on, Anika was summoned regularly to Tree Stump's wigwam. During the first visits, the old man would show her bundled herbs. Those she recognized she would name in English. Then Tree Stump would tell her the Unkechaug names, insisting that she repeat each one until she could approximate his pronunciation. Then he began taking her into the surrounding fields and woods so she could see them growing in their natural surroundings. On these forays, Anika would also show Tree Stump the herbs that she had learned. Together, they spent whole afternoons creating concoctions.

When he had completed the pharmacology that he knew, the powaw realized his next step in Anika's training would have to involve learning prayers and incantations. And for this, he would have to wait until she could understand the language better.

Great Bear continued to visit Tree Stump and to avoid his daughter. The chief knew that Anika had been spending days at the powaw's wigwam. He was powerfully drawn to the woman and repelled at the same time. So he timed his visits for the late evening hours when she would be helping Gentle Fawn with the evening meal.

On one such evening, as they sat smoking, Tree Stump quietly made an unexpected statement. "The woman, Anika, is a natural spirit woman. I have decided on her as the next powaw to succeed me. But she must have a secure place in the village. You should marry her. In that way, she will be part of your family."

Tree Stump had delivered his observation while blowing several concentric smoke circles. In the silence that followed, Great Bear struggled for a response; his heart had begun to pound painfully. "I… the woman… would not have me!"

"How do you know?" The powaw blew another set of circles. "You have yet to speak to her. This is not a matter for you alone to decide. The welfare of the village must come first. If Anika came to us from out of nowhere, she can leave in the same way. In your whole lifetime, no one has come to us from the outside. And there are those whom we do not want to come. You must keep Anika here."

Tree Stump had turned to face Great Bear. He was watching the chief's reaction closely. "She is not displeasing to you. This I can see. And it has been too long since you were with a woman. It is not healthy."

Great Bear could not say anything for several minutes; inside of him, a veritable war had started. Yes, it was true that he wanted this woman, terribly. Yet, he could not bring himself to admit to the fact, even now. It seemed something awful sat in his heart, something that twisted and turned and would not give him peace.

Tree Stump finally broke the silence. "You are not the only one who has lost a family. When I examined Anika, I saw she too has known the death of those she loved. You are alike. But she can heal you and you can heal her. Alone, neither of you can get well."

Tree Stump's words stayed with Great Bear. He carried them as part of the burden that kept his heart filled with pain. But now that he had identified her as the source of his desire, Anika's presence became an almost exquisite torture. She was often the one who brought his evening meal. And he could recognize the sound of her footstep. At first, to his shame, he would hide in his wigwam while she stirred the coals of his fire and set the cooking pot to keep warm. Only after she had left would he emerge to eat. Finally, disgust with himself won out and he would come out to watch her. Beyond smiles and formal greetings, neither spoke, ever.

Anika slowly began to realize that there was something more to Great Bear's paying attention to her than simple recognition. Whenever she looked at him, she found him staring almost fixedly at her. And whenever she met his gaze, she experienced excruciating pain, commingled with a strange pleasure. The emotions often sent her back to the cliff side on too many nights, seeking word from Osei.

Finally, almost in desperation, she turned over the task of delivering Great Bear's meal to Yellow Bird, much to the girl's dismay. For both Yellow Bird and her sister feared their grandfather and never wanted to be in his presence unless another adult was with them.

Osei had remained silent. The voices that spoke in Anika's ear now were hollow and metallic. And the language was completely foreign. Why was he no longer talking to her? Anika feared that Osei had read her heart and knew of her attraction to the chief. She grew angry with herself at the disloyalty, and she silently made anew her vow to obey, without question, any order given. Still, the unknown voices continued; gradually, she began to understand what they were saying even though the language was not English. Strangely, they were telling her to return to Great Bear's wigwam.

"Go back to the man's house and tell him a story."

"How can I do that? What story can I tell? He will not understand a word I say."

The voice came back like a gong, repeating the instruction. Anika asked no more questions.

On the following evening, she finished preparing her part of the meal. As Yellow Bird was about to pick up the pot that her mother had set aside for Great Bear, Anika stopped the girl, struggling with the words.

"Nee compumusah coquees numpsoonk. (I will take the pot to Grandfather.)"

Yellow Bird grinned in relief. She would not have to spend another hour sitting, silent and still, while Great Bear morosely ate whatever was in the pot. He seemed especially unhappy that it was she and not Anika who came, and he had said as much just the evening before.

"Why did not the woman Anika bring the meal? Have I offended her *again*?"

"I don't think so, Grandfather. She didn't look angry."

Each time Yellow Bird had come, he had seemed more depressed, and it made her both furious and glad. After all, he had upset Mother more than enough times; he deserved some of his own medicine. Yellow Bird, child that she was, could not find any sympathy in her heart for this grouchy old man who always frowned and never seemed happy to see his granddaughters.

As she made her way toward Great Bear's wigwam, Anika emptied her mind, forcing out all words. Into that silent space memories flooded, going back to her years in Baltimore with her mother. A warm sense of pleasure spread through her whole body at the recollections, so much so that she forgot about her destination. It was actually a surprise to find herself standing just in front of the chief's door.

When Great Bear came out, he was face to face with her. His eyes widened in pleased but stunned disbelief, and he stood as though rooted, holding the bowl and spoon.

She placed the pot on the fire, took the bowl from his hands and filled it. "Kee kiummatap, (You sit.)" she said, handing him the food.

Anika did not yet know how to say, "I want to talk to you" in Unkechaug, but she could feel the memories welling up. Seating herself on the other side of the fire, she began to tell her life story in English.

First Em, her mother, came back most strongly. Anika described a woman with beautiful hazel eyes and reddish-blond hair, who could do everything perfectly and who never raised her voice. As she spoke, a peculiar joy filled her entire being. It was as though she had conjured the woman who now stood before both of them.

Great Bear ate almost mechanically, completely transfixed. When Anika glanced across at him, he was staring at her as though he had never seen her before. His face transformed before her eyes; the years seemed to drop away and he was suddenly, amazingly handsome… and… desirable. She began a description of Evie as a child, laughing as she recalled the girl's awful tantrums and the tricks she would play on her brothers.

Great Bear laughed whenever Anika did, even though he had no idea what she was talking about. This whole evening was giving him such pleasure. He had not felt so happy since Snow Bird and his sons were alive. Even after the pot was empty and the evening dew had fallen, he remained seated, watching her. She was magical, so much so that he wished she would never stop talking, never leave his fire.

The evening air freshened sharply and a light but steady rain began to fall. Anika rose and reached across the now doused fire toward the pot. For several minutes, it seemed that all motion had been suspended. Great Bear had risen at the same time, hoping somehow to keep her with him, to entice her into his wigwam. He knew he would not be able to find the right words, and to gesture toward his door was sure to offend.

At last, he broke the silence by somewhat lamely complementing her performance. "Cuttoh weayuh. Tabutni. (Your words were clever. Thank you.)"

Anika responded with a smile and a nod. She had understood the silence between them. Now she realized how strong the chief's need for company was—hers in particular. Still, she felt that she had to have Osei's permission, in his own voice, and it was silent tonight. She took the pot and left.

The rain became a steady downpour, forcing Great Bear inside. Here, he stirred the live coals in his fire pit and got out his bedding. A sharp sense of loneliness had settled over him, coupled with a restless desire to be outside. But no one in his right mind would wander about in a soaking rain, inviting illness. Finally, he wrapped himself in his blanket, and surrendered to the inevitable dreams.

On the following evening, when Anika brought the meal, she found the chief already seated at his fire, waiting expectantly. He had set out two bowls in hopes that she would eat with him. The sight of them, side by side, both charmed and pained her. She filled one, handing it to Great Bear, and ladled a small amount for herself into the other.

Tonight, they both sat as close to the fire as was safe, and Anika continued her story. She described her brothers as she remembered them—all four. Even Frederic appeared as clearly before her as did Rufus Jr., Samuel and Marcus. She told the story of her father, a freedman who had married a free woman because he couldn't afford to buy her mother and her, and how that, coupled with Frederic's death, had broken her mother's heart. But those events had allowed her to finally visit her father's shop where she met the stepmother and played with her brothers.

Suddenly, Anika was no longer reminiscing; she could see her brothers, grown into men, working together in the cooper's shop. In this vision, Em joined her sons, her mouth moving in soundless conversation. But where were Rufus Sr. and his wife, Ruth?

It puzzled Annie so much that she broke her narrative to ask, "But where are they?"

The answer came almost immediately and she said it aloud. "They are dead, both of them."

Great Bear realized that Anika was no longer speaking to him. In his very presence she had summoned her spirits! He felt the hairs on the back of his neck rise and his pulse quicken. An almost maddening desire swept over him, threatening to completely overwhelm him. Its wave washed over her as well and she fell silent, watching him intently.

Getting slowly to his feet, he extended his right hand. Anika could feel herself leaving her body taking his hand in one of hers while, with the other, she smoothed the deep furrow between his brows. Then she kissed away the pain that tightened the corners of his mouth.

"Anika! Wait! Not yet. I have something I need for you to do."

It was *his* voice at last! Her eyes widened and she actually clapped for joy. Suddenly, she was crying and laughing at the same time. Osei's voice took on an edge. *"Calm yourself! You will offend your benefactor."*

She did not know what a benefactor was, but she realized that she had been rude and was about to be even more so. Great Bear was staring at her, his face reflecting both concern and a little fear. She struggled to remember the right words to explain why she could not stay with him tonight, even though he had honored her with an invitation.

"Masakeetmund, nee mekwi. (A great god tells me to come quick.) Nee copumusah. (I must go.)"

So she was being summoned away. Great Bear dropped his hand and nodded. Of course, he could not interfere if her spirits required her presence elsewhere.

Anika ran to the cliff side without stopping for breath. Once there, she sat on the ground in the clearing, waiting for instructions. She was so intent on getting the message she was sure would come that she fell asleep without even realizing how very tired she was.

Great Bear followed her at a discreet distance and hid himself behind a tree. When he saw her head drop onto her folded arms, he crept closer and touched her shoulder. So deep was her sleep that she simply fell over. After watching her for a moment, he gathered her up in his arms and headed for Gentle Fawn's wigwam. All the while that he was carrying her, he feared Anika would feel his heart beating and wake up, but, fortunately, she did not. He slipped inside and lay her down next to Bright Star, covering her with part of his granddaughter's blanket. Then he returned to his wigwam and another sleepless night.

After that night, Great Bear forced himself to be content with Anika's evening visits, and without her sharing his bed. When he had taken the problem to Tree Stump, the powaw had warned him against sleeping with her.

"I told you to *marry* her. She is not here for your pleasure alone. She has come for the whole village. You will just have to wait. Besides, before you can take another woman, you must give honor to the family you lost."

At moments like these, Great Bear found the old man most irritating. But he dared not contradict him since he knew that this was the absolute truth. Even after so many years, he could not bear to speak Snow Bird's name, and he had deliberately erased each dead son's face from his memory.

Great Bear did decide to try to learn English, however, and Anika was happy to teach him what she knew. They spent hours together after his evening meal as she patiently sounded out the names of familiar things in English. He would repeat the names in both languages, and this helped her improve her Unkechaug. Gradually, they settled into a friendship that served as an acceptable veneer for the powerful emotions just beneath the surface. Nothing else was possible, as Anika was still waiting for a message that, day after day, did not come.

Chapter 26

QUEBEC (1800)

One morning, now in the second month of the Munsees' stay, the village awakened to glistening newly colored leaves and grasses that crunched underfoot. An early frost had settled in overnight.

In in his family's wigwam, River Otter lay awake beside his sleeping wife listening to the sounds of his children. All night long, he'd been unable to calm his racing thoughts, even after he and Gentle Fawn had made love. Now one of the twins was coughing, a sure sign that he had kicked the blankets off both himself and, probably, his brother as well. The baby, just eight weeks old, made soft snuffling sounds. Very soon, she would begin a gentle mewling that, no matter how soft, always awakened Gentle Fawn. River Otter got up quietly and covered both his sons with a second blanket. Then he gently lifted his daughter, still on her swaddling board, and placed her in his spot next to her mother. He stopped for a moment beside Bright Star's sleeping mat and quickly kissed her forehead, knowing it wouldn't disturb her. The girl could sleep through anything!

He made his way to Great Bear's wigwam just after sunrise. He had been deeply troubled for the past several weeks. Clearly, something about this entire visit was greatly amiss. The Munsee chief should have made a decision by now. Soon it would be too late for him and his party to make the long voyage back to Ottawa. In his heart, River Otter feared that Tekenna had hidden motives.

Great Bear met his son-in-law at the door and led him back to the outdoor fire pit.

"Is my mother still asleep?

"She left before dawn; she needed to be alone. I thought you were her, returning."

"Great Bear, I do not trust Tekenna! He has taken too long to make up his mind about us!"

"You may be right. But there is nothing we can do about it. If I press him to decide before he is ready, he will be insulted. This is his land. He knows the weather and the river far better than we do."

The two men sat in silence, each absorbed in his own thoughts, both waiting for Anika. She emerged from the evergreen forest, her arms filled with fresh-cut branches, her medicine bag bulging with herbs and grasses. Great Bear saw her first, but it was River Otter who sprang to her side, quickly relieving her of everything.

"My son, you're here so early!" Anika beamed lovingly at him as she spoke. "Husband, did you tell him why I left before dawn?"

"I told him what you told me, which was very little." Great Bear spoke evenly, but he was obviously miffed by both her leaving their bed so early and her meager explanation.

He stood as though planted, both arms folded on his chest. Anika came close to her husband and gently laid her hands on his arms. Immediately, Great Bear dropped his guarded pose as she rested her forehead against his breast. He almost took her into his arms, but then he remembered that River Otter was present.

"Mother, I came so early because I'm worried by how long Tekenna is taking to reach a decision about us. Winter will be upon us within the month. And they cannot cross the river in icy weather." River Otter had spoken quickly, hoping to forestall another uncomfortable moment as the chief and his mother forgot they were not alone.

Anika turned to face him. "Don't be worried, son. I went out to ask about this very thing. We must be patient with Tekenna."

"But do you not suspect his motives, Mother?"

"Of course, he has a reason for his delay. There is something he wants from us, something he suspects we will not want to give him. I am trying to find out what it is. But I have no answer yet."

"What must we do in the meantime?" Great Bear spoke up suddenly, "We cannot continue to entertain Tekenna's people much longer. Our stores of grain and meats are getting low."

"Finish the story," Anika said, adding, "Tonight, we will hear from you, my son."

CANADA 1783 - 1791

Two young men were working silently side by side making a dugout canoe. Both wore tanned deerskin breechcloths and leggings with shirts of moose hide. One wore his hair loose and long in the fashion of unmarried Abenaki men; the other wore a wide-brimmed hat that shaded his face and completely covered his head down to his ears. Only by his mahogany colored hands could one tell that he was not also Abenaki.

"Why Wnekikw (River Otter), why must you leave us now? And in a dugout rather than a birch bark canoe?"

River Otter straightened up to gaze at his friend. Wôboz (Elk) had asked this question repeatedly over the last month, and River Otter had answered him the same way each time. "I am going back to fetch my family. When I have freed them, I will return. The dugout will raise fewer suspicions among the Lenape."

Elk frowned at the answer. He was not really seeking information but another opportunity to try to dissuade his friend from making a very dangerous journey down the North (Hudson) River.

When the British reached Halifax, in December of 1783, they issued papers of manumission to the Africans who had fled New York with them. Willy took Stephen's free papers as his own. Freedom, however, soon came to mean privation and near starvation for a twelve-year-old who had never before been on his own. Fortunately, among his many natural gifts was an ear for languages and a growing intellect, nurtured by Osei's early teachings.

One of the British soldiers, an officer, took a fancy to the boy and employed him as a personal servant for the short time that the troops were garrisoned in Halifax. During this time, the young officer decided to teach Willy the letters of the alphabet and the sounds of several words. When he discovered that the boy already knew how to read and write, the soldier decided to offer him employment when the regiment sailed back to England. However, Willy did not want to leave America and lose the chance to be reunited with his parents. The young officer took his refusal with good humor and supplied him with some money and enough provisions so he could travel.

Willy left Halifax and began a journey that would take him into the frontier of the St. Lawrence River Valley. Here he made contact with several different tribes and picked up much from their several languages. Eventually, he settled among the Abenaki in one of their villages. Here he learned the language fluently and received the name Wnekikw. He added River Otter as his last name whenever he had to speak English, keeping Stephen as his first. Inwardly, he never forgot that he was Willy and Kwesi Owusu. Both names reminded him of his father and of what he needed to do as soon as he was able.

The St. Lawrence River narrows at the headwaters of the Hudson. Willy expertly navigated the rocky shoals where the waters met, and soon was paddling down river. On his right, the mountains of the Adirondacks rose forbiddingly. As the Hudson widened, he hugged the eastern shoreline, rather than the Jersey shore, even though the rocky land above Poughkeepsie provided few comforts whenever he had to stop. New York was on this side and he did not want to have to cross the river when he reached the city.

Three days of steady paddling brought him within sight of the Trinity Church steeple. He brought his canoe ashore at the foot of Warren Street, just south of Elias Degrushe's Ropewalk, and hid it behind the now abandoned block house.

It was high noon by the time he reached the center of town. So much had changed! There were new houses where he remembered open space, and the streets seemed narrower. He only hoped that he could remember the way to Crown Street. He need not have worried, for memory served him well. Soon he was standing in front of the house. But just as he was about to lift the front gate latch, he suddenly lost his nerve.

Willy walked the length of the street, gathering his thoughts and his courage before returning to the tenth house. Walking around to the kitchen door gave him an opportunity to study the well-known features. He looked up at the carriage house window that had been his parents' and his quarters. It looked small and grimy now; his mother had always kept it clean. Again he felt an uneasy chill. At the sight of the filthy window, suddenly nothing seemed familiar. It took him several minutes before he could bring himself to knock at the kitchen door. In his mind, he had rehearsed his opening speech.

The woman who opened the door Willy recognized, but only vaguely. It was Circe, the cook who had not seen him since he was almost five years old. He was relieved that she thought she was addressing a stranger; it made his task easier.

"Ma'am," he removed his hat cautiously as he spoke. "My master is a hunter and trapper by trade. He has sent me round to the houses to announce we have fresh game and fish to sell, if your people are of a mind to buy such."

Circe studied the young man carefully; her eyes narrowed suspiciously. Now that New York was the capitol of the new United States, as folk called the former Colonies, all manner of people, Black and White, seemed to be about.

"No, my people do not much care for wild game. How is it that your master sends you out to bother busy folk? Perhaps you are the one selling. You look like a backwoodsman, yourself!"

Her smile and the twinkle in her eyes belied the harsh words. Willy ducked his head sheepishly as though caught in a lie. "You are too clever for me! Yes, it is I who am the seller."

He wondered how to ask Circe about his parents. It was out of the question for him to confess his identity. In this now-independent country with his British-issued free papers bearing another's name he was sure to be re-enslaved. He had to find another way to get the information he needed.

"I once lived in New York, but have been gone some eight years now. There were several Black families I knew of. Are any still here that lived in the city back then?"

Circe pursed her lips in thought and then shook her head. "Oh, I wouldn't know of such. I left with my master when the War started. But some did stay through it. Cicero, the ferryman, stayed. He might know some folk. Might be interested in some of your game as well."

Circe laughed heartily at her last statement. Her laughter continued as she closed the door. Willy remembered Cicero, even though he was only five when last he saw the ferryman. He remembered the visits he and his mother used to make to Cicero's wife during her seemingly endless illnesses. Surprisingly, he even remembered the way perfectly and was standing at the door to the tiny house a few minutes later.

Cicero looked older and uglier than he remembered. Yet Willy felt a strong sense of pleasure at the sight of him. He changed his story slightly, claiming to have his own stores of game and beaver pelts as well.

Cicero refused the offer but invited him in to share his afternoon meal. As they sat across the table of rough-hewn wooden planks eating boiled potatoes, Willy carefully asked about families who had been in town before the war.

Cicero took a second helping before answering. "Which Black folks was yuh lookin' fuh? There's several what have left these parts. An' a few has pass'd on."

Uncomfortable at Cicero's beginning, Willy started with several names that he could remember. He included Will and Annie toward the end of his list. Cicero knew the business of everyone he named. When the ferryman got to his parents, his voice dropped an octave and became a little hoarse.

"Oh yeah, it was a nasty piece a' business, that one. Ev'rybody knowed Mr. Will and his wife was keeping th' house and business f' they master, what didn't want t' fight in th' war. Th' way it happened, one night, after th' British left, a bunch a' ruffians got Mr. Will in th' street. Beat him so bad they say he never woke up. Died th' very next day, he did."

Willy felt something break inside. He fought to maintain calm and keep the treacherous tears at bay. Cicero had a single small mirror fastened to the wall just across from the front door. Willy could see himself in the glass, could see his expression become tight with the effort.

Cicero appeared not to notice the change in the young man's countenance. He continued. "Now Miz Annie, there's a real myst'ry. On that same day they buried Mr. Will, she disappeared. Oh, they foun' huh gown an' head cloth down by th' docks, but nar hide n' hair of th' woman, huhself."

Suddenly the ferryman began to grin; his gaze became unfocused as he spoke about the events of that day and the ones that followed. He seemed to have forgotten that Willy was even there. "Hamilton, that was they master. When he come back t' New Yawk, he went all over town lookin' f'his servants. Didn't believe Mr. Will was dead 'til folks taken' him up t' th' Negro Burial Ground an' showed him th' grave. Now they mistress, she carried on! They say she wuz out screamin' on Crown Street, hollerin' 'bout, 'My Annie! Whea she at?'"

By this time Cicero was laughing almost maniacally. His voice had risen almost to a shout. Suddenly, he leaned close to Willy and whispered. "She come by here on that last day, Miz Annie did, askin' 'bout th' ferry. Right then, I knowed it was somethin'. I never tol' nobody 'bout it, 'cause I b'lieve Miz Annie run. Yes, I do!"

"Why do you think she's run away?" Willy could barely get the words out.

"Why, I think she always meant t' run; her husband too, I reckon. He just got killed b'fore he could git away."

Willy stared openly at Cicero now, completely transfixed.

"They had this one child, a little boy." The ferryman was still smiling crookedly as he spoke, "disappeared same time as th' British left. 'Bout twelve years old, I'd say. Miz Annie an' Mr. Will never said nothin' an' nobody never asked. But, from then on, I expected them t' go too." Cicero sat back in his chair, the peculiar smile still in place. "When Black folk runs, they crosses th' East River and goes t' Long Island. They's plenty a places t' hide there. Some say th' Indians takes 'em in. Anyways, cain't nobody get 'em back. They never gits caught."

It seemed that the walls of the small room were closing in on him. Willy suddenly felt the overpowering need to get outside. He did not want to reveal this growing panic, however, so he forced himself to ask about two more people by name before thanking Cicero for his hospitality and rising to take his leave.

The ferryman reached into a small crock on the table near his elbow. He produced a silver coin and pressed it into Willy's palm. The young man tried to refuse it.

"Yuh may have need t' ride th' ferry one day. I want yuh t' have th' fare, whenever yuh got t' cross the river. No, please take it. It's f' you—an' another."

Both men were standing now. Cicero's eyes pleaded with Willy to accept the token and his heartfelt need to give it. Willy suddenly sensed that the ferryman knew exactly who he was. Silently, he pocketed the coin and left. After a moment, Cicero followed the young man outside and watched him until he was out of sight. As he always used to do, Cicero now stood gazing at the empty street.

The moment he was sure that Cicero could no longer see him, Willy broke into a run. He did not think about a destination, nor did he heed the curious stares of the people he passed. He took a zigzagged path up Dock Street, making a right onto Broad Street. Where Broad became Nassau, he paused, just to get his bearings, and then ran the length of the city without stopping. At the Commons, he realized where he was headed. Slowing to a walk, he climbed the hill by the now fetid Collect Pond, descended the other side and began to search among the graves.

There had never been headstones to mark the plots. Indeed, unless a family member could tend the grave, it was most often overgrown and lost. Willy realized that he had no way of recognizing Osei's grave, but he kept on looking. The Burial Ground appeared to have fallen into disuse. The few wooden markers still standing were so weatherbeaten that the marks on them were indistinguishable.

At last, he sat on the ground next to a young tree. Everything that had held him together all this time had depended on finding his parents. He tried to picture his father's face. The general contours came into focus, but he could not remember the details; he could not recall exactly where the markings had been on Osei's cheeks. Suddenly, he began crying out loud, wailing as he had not done since he was a little boy. He cried hard and long until there were no more tears. Then he sat where he was, watching the sun begin to set. Gradually, something began to nag at him, something Cicero had said. "I believe Miz Annie run." His mother! The ferryman had tried to tell him that his mother might be alive on Long Island! He got to his feet and ran to find his canoe.

As darkness gathered, he was paddling around the tip of Manhattan and into the harbor. He turned the dugout east and crossed the river. It took him only an hour to reach land. Once on shore, he used the dugout as his shelter for the night.

The next morning, Willy left the canoe on the river bank and headed east on foot. He knew enough to avoid the farms spread out across the western section of the island, from the Sound to the Atlantic. His plan was to bypass all of the White settlements and try to locate the nearest Indian villages. These would most likely be Shinnecock. The Shinnecock spoke a language that was different than Lenape, one of the languages he knew well. But their vocabulary was similar to that of the Pequot.

In his travels through Southeastern Canada, he had encountered groups of Indians who knew about the people from Connecticut, the Pequot and the Mohegan. He had spent several years in the company of peoples who spoke both of those Eastern Algonquin languages and he had become fairly fluent. He would have to depend on this knowledge and his ear to communicate with any Long Island Indians that he'd meet.

It took a week of daytime travel for Willy to reach land he recognized as a colonially-established Indian reservation. There were small wooden houses clustered in the center of patches of cultivated fields. He could tell that these Indians had been heavily influenced by the English. Their homes were cabins, of the type he had seen on the frontier. Although there was evidence of farming, it was nowhere near as extensive as in Canada. He strongly doubted that his mother would have taken refuge among these people; still they might have information. And he needed to test his skill with their language.

He approached one of the cabins just as a woman was emerging. She stood in her doorway and studied him. He removed his hat so she could see that he was a Black man before addressing her in what he hoped was understandable Shinnecock.

"Greetings, Sister." He raised his right hand.

The woman had understood him. Her surprise was evident but she returned the gesture. "Greetings, Brother. How do you come to know our language? You are not from this reservation."

Willy felt emboldened enough to immediately make his inquiry. "I have lived with the Abenaki, the Onondaga and the Oneida. And I learned some of the language spoken by the Pequot. I am searching for my mother. She left New York some two or more years ago and may have traveled this way."

He did not mention her status as a runaway. He was not sure whether the Indians of this area were truly hospitable to Blacks.

The woman folded her arms across her chest. She was of an indeterminate age, but strong and square in build. She appeared to be turning his words over in her mind, for she narrowed her eyes, creating tight lines at the corners. Finally, she seemed to come to some sort of decision.

"Go ask Samson. He is the oldest man on the reservation. He may be able to help you."

Willy found Samson easily, since his was the lone traditional house. The man seated outside beside his fire and smoking his pipe appeared to be in his eighties. Although he wore a homespun shirt, rough woolen pants and boots, his grey hair was long and the pipe was a beautifully handmade relic that had probably been in his family for generations. He too appeared surprised to hear Shinnecock coming from a Black man, and one so young. But his pleasure was completely without suspicion.

"At one time, many of your people came here. We took them into our villages and into our families. Two of my sons have such wives. We call them Shickayos (Blacks) and they are much prized."

Heartened by the information, Willy ventured to ask again about a lone female runaway, probably on foot. The old man knew of no such person. But he did know about rumors that there were Indians who had run away from

White people over a century ago and were said to have disappeared into the forests.

"They would not give up their traditional healers and become Christians. So they left the reservations the Whites had set up for their people and went deep into the woods to the East. No one has seen or heard about them for many years, not in my lifetime even. If your mother kept going east, and if she was not afraid of the big forests, she could be with those people."

Willy could feel his excitement rise and his heartbeat quicken. Suddenly, the pain of missing his mother, that he'd lived with for so long, eased slightly. He asked, "What group of people are these who live free in the woods?"

"They are called Unkechaug-of-the-Forest. They are related to the ones whom we call Poospatuck. You would know their language; it is very much like ours."

On that same afternoon, Willy got back on the road, determined to follow it to its end.

Chapter 27

REUNION (1791)

A group of girls came running in from the fields, shouting that they had seen a man in the woods who appeared to be headed this way. Anika and Gentle Fawn were pounding corn, while Yellow Bird, Bright Star and several other girls were busily husking the ears in preparation.

The group from the fields gathered, chattering excitedly. "It was a man in skin clothing. We could not see more because his head was covered."

Gentle Fawn immediately took control of the situation. "We will go and see. But not everyone."

She selected two young women to accompany her. She looked worriedly at Anika then gave the others instructions. "We must be careful of strangers, especially White men. Please keep the young girls and children out of sight. Bright Star, stay with Yellow Bird and listen to Anika!"

Anika took Bright Star's hand, drawing the girl to her side while keeping her eyes fixed on the departing women. A small, icy finger of apprehension touched the back of her neck; somehow, if there were someone coming, it had to be for her. She took both girls inside Gentle Fawn's wigwam, pulling down the deerskin cover over the door.

Bright Star demanded to know why they had to come indoors when there was still work to be done. "Only part of the corn is ready for grinding. How will we have corn cakes for our supper?"

Yellow Bird turned on her sister in total exasperation. "Why do you never listen? Mother said we have to stay inside until she gets back. And Anika wants us to stay with her! That's all you need to know!"

Before they had a chance to continue this familiar argument, sounds from outside indicated that Gentle Fawn and her two companions had returned.

She called to Anika and her daughters. "We searched the woods and found no one. The girls must have mistaken an animal for a man."

None of the women noticed the figure moving just beyond the line of trees. When he stepped out into the clearing, it was Yellow Bird who spotted him first and screamed, "A... man! It *is* a man!"

Suddenly, there was pandemonium. Women began screaming and running to collect their children. Gentle Fawn pushed her daughters back into the wigwam and tried to shield Anika at the same time.

The man stopped in his tracks, removed his wide-brimmed hat and raised his right hand. "Do not be frightened. I mean no harm. Please, I will not hurt you! My name is River Otter... Willy... and I am searching for my mother, Annie."

The man spoke a language they could understand! Those who heard him halted immediately. Anika could not understand what he was saying; he spoke too quickly for her to follow, until she heard his name, and then hers! Pushing past Gentle Fawn, who was momentarily immobilized, she moved, almost dream-like, toward this stranger who was not a stranger... but dearer to her than life itself.

"Willy?" It came out in a whisper. Could this really be her baby, now fully grown?

At first, Willy couldn't recognize the woman who had separated herself from the others and was coming in his direction. She looked almost exactly like any Pequot or Abenaki. Then he saw her face, her hair – and cried out, "Mother!" He threw the hat away and ran toward her, catching her up in his arms and holding on for dear life. "Oh Mother!" he gasped, sobbing openly, "I thought I'd lost you forever!"

At that moment, Anika knew for certain this was her child. "Willy!" she murmered, "My sweet Willy!" She kissed his face repeatedly. By now, they were both in tears.

All the able-bodied men had been away from the village, either hunting or fishing and were just now returning. Great Bear had taken his canoe out to check the oyster beds. He was about to put the dugout away when he heard women screaming. He dropped the nets and ran toward the village, reaching the first wigwams just as the noise suddenly stopped. Whatever had happened, must have been a false alarm, he decided. Then he saw them—Anika completely enfolded in the arms of a stranger! For several minutes he could not catch his breath. Was this a husband or lover who had been searching for her? Was this the end of his hope for release from his own misery?

Realizing he had to acknowledge the stranger, Great Bear approached the pair, still locked in an embrace. Outwardly he appeared calm; only a vein standing in his forehead revealed that his heart was pumping furiously.

Willy's back was to the chief. At that moment, nothing exsisted for him but his mother, so he did not hear the approach, but Annie did. Over his shoulder, she watched Great Bear stop and struggle for composure before moving in their direction. Very reluctantly, she released her son. "Willy! It's the leader of this village. Let him know you are my son!"

Immediately, Willy turned around, his right hand already raised in greeting, the left over his heart. "Greetings, Great Chief. Please forgive my sudden appearance in your village. I am called River Otter. This is my mother who was lost to me and whom I have finally found."

Great Bear released the breath that he had unconsciously been holding. Yes, of course, this man was too young to be Anika's husband. He openly studied him for a moment before replying.

"Not Great Chief, just chief of this village alone. I am called Great Bear. We have tried to make your mother welcome, and she has become greatly loved here. As her son, you too are welcome. All we have we will share with you. I hope it is your plan to stay, now that you have come and found Anika here with us."

Anika watched the exchange in complete wonder. She could not believe how her son had changed. He was able to speak to the chief in a language they both understood. He had grown tall and lean, and he moved with such grace! Moreover, although she had always considered him beautiful, she could see that he was now as stunningly good looking as his father had been.

Word had gotten around the whole village quickly about the very handsome stranger who was Anika's son, River Otter. Every girl anywhere near the age of courtship had come to stand around, gawking and giggling. Having escaped her mother's watchful eye, Yellow Bird was there with her girlfriends, staring open-mouthed at River Otter. And it was not only the girls seeking husbands who formed the growing throng; older women, children, men still carrying fresh game, the whole village had come to see the second stranger to appear in their entire lifetimes.

"We will build a wigwam for you and your mother." Great Bear turned and ordered several young men to begin the work immediately.

But River Otter demurred. "Oh no, Chief. I will build the wigwam for my mother. Please do not trouble your people to do work that I can do myself. This style of house is familiar to me."

Great Bear smiled slightly as he continued to direct the young men with gestures. "Yes, but help is always good to have. And it is our pleasure."

And so, with the combined efforts of River Otter and several villagers, the new wigwam was raised before nightfall. Anika surveyed her new home with joy and some trepidation. She had gotten used to the closeness of Gentle Fawn and the girls. She realized that always being in the company of the women and children had kept the worst of her memories at bay. Now, with Willy, she would have to relive all of it, especially Osei's death. Her son needed to know what had happened to his father.

But Great Bear had other plans for this first night of reunion. He pulled Gentle Fawn aside and asked her to prepare a feast of celebration. She, in turn, gathered all of the women and assigned cooking tasks, urging each one to make an extra effort.

"We want Anika's son to see how much we love his mother and that we want them both to stay with us."

Even without her father's saying so, Gentle Fawn realized that at any point Anika could leave the village; after all, she had appeared out of nowhere. And now that her son had also mysteriously come, she would have a traveling companion, should she decide just as suddenly to leave. Gentle Fawn discovered she was almost as upset as her father at this possibility, and so she bent all of her efforts toward making this night's celebration as close to perfect as possible.

Just before sundown, women began bringing their dishes. There was succotash, fresh corn cakes, oysters, several kinds of fish and even a haunch of roasted venison, as well as baked squash, tomatoes, pole beans and peppers of various hues. The men had made huge fires in the middle of a clearing that served as the central gathering place for all village feasts.

Anika had intended to help Gentle Fawn prepare her part of the feast. After all, this was a celebration of Willy's arrival—or so she had thought. She was completely surprised when Gentle Fawn refused to allow her to do any of the work.

"This feast is for you *and* your son."

"But why?" Anika searched her vocabulary for more words.

Gentle Fawn hugged her tightly. "Because you came to be with us, and you must never leave us."

Suddenly, it dawned on her that she had become more important to this place than she could ever have imagined. Gentle Fawn clearly was afraid her son had come to take her away, and this feast was her way of showing him how much the whole village wanted them both.

Anika was overwhelmed. She returned Gentle Fawn's embrace with equal passion, anxious to ease her fears. "You are my family now. I won't leave you."

But even as she spoke, Anika was not sure this was true. How could she explain the thing that held her in thrall, the voices that compelled her obedience? If they decreed that she had to leave, she could do nothing else. She wanted very much to avoid lying to Gentle Fawn. Even more, she wanted to ease Great Bear's sorrow. Perhaps this was to be her mission, after all. Just as the thought occurred to her, there came an afterthought, a memory really. *"When the time is right, I will call for you to come back..."*

She squeezed the young woman tightly one last time and then released her. "Go; do all the work. Come for me when you want me." She took her son's hand and led him inside their new home. "Willy…" she began, "Why didn't you tell the chief your name is Willy?" Even as she asked the question, she sensed the answer.

"Mother, I have another name now, one given me by the people I settled with after leaving the British. You must call me River Otter when we're with these people. It will be less confusing." He gazed at her for several minutes before continuing, "I so missed you… and Father." His voice trailed off and a heavy silence enveloped them both.

Just before the festivities began, Tree Stump made his appearance, walking very slowly and supported on either side by a youth. The old man directed his helpers to take him to the entrance of Annie's new wigwam. Here, he prayed in a sing-song voice for the health and longevity of the home and its occupants. Anika and River Otter remained inside until he had finished. Then they were ushered to seats of honor, on either side of the chief. Tree Stump sat next to Anika, and Gentle Fawn and her daughters sat beside River Otter.

The feasting lasted for hours, followed by dancing performed by both the young women and the men. In their earlier traditional feasts, many drummers would have accompanied the dancers, but the need to keep the village hidden had silenced the drums. Still, several men played reed flutes and the women sang as they danced.

The festivities lasted almost until dawn, even while the honored guests and most of the other adults had retired long before that. As befits the host, Great Bear remained until the end. Gentle Fawn kept her father company after sending Bright Star and, later, Yellow Bird to bed.

Anika was careful to continue spending her days with Gentle Fawn and the girls. She also kept up her evening visits to Great Bear's wigwam, only now she often asked River Otter to accompany her, since he could speak so much more fluently. He frequently served as interpreter, thereby allowing the chief to finally understand parts of her life story.

River Otter was anxious to spend some of those evenings alone with his mother, once the novelty of his being in the village had worn off. On their first night alone together, he wanted oh so desperately to ask about Osei, but he chose instead to begin with small talk. It still felt strange to speak English with anyone for any length of time, and he found that he had even begun to think in several other languages. The very simple speech of his youth seemed to have slipped away, and when he talked to Anika, he now called her, Mother, rather than Ma.

"Mother, why do these people call you, Anika instead of Annie?"

It was a straightforward enough question, but Anika did not answer immediately. Her son could not possibly understand how she had come by the name. And she was certain the time was not right to try to tell him the truth. So she bent it somewhat.

"Oh Willy." She sighed, "Your father gave me that name and told me to use it when I got to freedom. He said it meant 'sweetness'... no, 'goodness,' and that I was supposed to... to be what the name says to the people I live with."

River Otter smiled a brilliant, white-toothed grin that made his face even more attractive. "So Father named us all, even you too? Then more soberly, "Mother, please tell me what happened? No, don't look away. Please."

He had moved closer to her, close enough to see her eyes become opaque with pain. She seemed to sink into herself for a moment. Then she looked at him directly with eyes that now had become a little red but were absolutely dry, as though the tears had been burned away.

"They brought him home unconscious. Said he had been caught out alone after dark. He was always careful about that with me, once you were gone. 'Never go anywhere alone after dark.' That's what he told me. And the one time he forgot, they caught him."

Anika stopped, realizing that the pain was getting the better of her. River Otter had leaned forward, riveted, his eyes fixed on her face as though he could see the events playing themselves out as she described them.

"We took him upstairs. We took him up... the stairs... and... put him to bed and... I waited for him to wake up. He didn't look so bad. They hadn't hit him in the face, except for one eye. No, what they did was kick him and stomp him and...."

Suddenly, she got up and went outside. River Otter waited for several minutes before going out to see what had happened. He found his mother bending over the pit that served as a latrine, vomiting. He did not ask about his father's death again that night, or any other.

It was not that Anika did not intend to give River Otter a full accounting of Osei's death. To her, Osei was still very much alive, and she was afraid that talking about that awful night and the following day would somehow separate him from her. He was alive! She would still be in New York were it not for his counsel; she had no way of knowing how to escape except through his knowledge! She had to fulfill his requests, whatever they were.

Osei did make a request several nights later. He came in a dream as a shadow and a voice, but it was unmistakably him. *"Come and dig me up from the Burial Ground. Take me to where you now live and put me in the ocean so I can find my way home. Ask our son and your benefactor to help you."*

The dream woke her up. A wonderful clarity came over her, so strong that she could not stay in bed. Quietly, so as not to disturb River Otter, she slipped out of the wigwam and sat by the cold fire pit until dawn.

River Otter awoke at first light, as had become his habit. It was always best to rise earlier than one's host, he had found. Usually, wherever he was, he would try to contribute something to that day's food supply, either with an early morning hunt or by fishing. On this morning, when he emerged from their wigwam, he found his mother already up, stirring the coals in the fire pit. She had made him some cornmeal mush, which she now served. A large helping for him and a much smaller serving for herself. As he ate, he noticed that she put her bowl down by the fire, and seemed to forget about it.

Anika was much too filled with excitement to eat. "We must go to Great Bear's wigwam. I have a request to make that he will find strange, and I need you to help me explain it."

River Otter nodded in assent. As he was eating, he had been watching his mother's face with a combination of adoration, amazement and uneasiness. Something had happened to her, possibly during her flight or earlier, that had changed the woman he thought he remembered. In his mind, as he was becoming a man, Annie had no personality apart from being the mother he loved and missed with his whole heart. This woman was now surrounded by an aura that was palpable. And these Unkechaug behaved as though she were somehow central to their continued survival. Their village had been here for more than a century, apparently untouched by the outside world. Yet the arrival of this lone Black woman seemed to have affected everyone. Most amazing of all was his mother's apparent ability to expand this mysterious power outward, such that everyone in her presence came under its spell. Yet she was as unassuming, as gentle and loving as he remembered. River Otter doubted that she really needed him to convince Great Bear of anything. It was plain, even to him, that no one was more enthralled by his mother than the chief.

In every Indian community where he had spent any amount of time, River Otter had come across the same tradition, a refusal to accept outsiders unless they became integral members of that community. In most cases, this meant adopting the person, usually through marriage. He was sure Great Bear wanted to marry Anika but did not know how his mother felt about this. He was not certain *he* really wanted it either, although he fully understood the tradition.

It was not just that his father and his mother were still husband and wife in his mind. He simply could not come to terms with the manner of his father's death. Osei had been murdered by common thugs in the street! And River Otter was now wrestling with the possibility that, had his father not sent him away, he would have been at his side. Together they could have fought them off.

Anika and River Otter approached Great Bear's wigwam while the dew was still wet. The chief had also risen very early, and was returning now after bathing in the lake. At dawn, the water was quite cold, so, to warm himself, Great Bear would always run back to the village, a distance that took about fifteen minutes to cover.

He had just reached the wigwam and was catching his breath when they arrived. An expression of surprise and sheer joy crossed his face before he caught himself. Anika greeted him quickly, apologizing for the early, unannounced visit. Then she turned to her son.

"Willy, please say the same words to Great Bear that I say. I want him to understand me. If he asks a question, just say it in English and I will answer. Don't you try to answer for me." Anika laid a hand on his arm as she spoke.

He was surprised and disturbed by her authoritative tone. Even Great Bear looked concerned and unnerved. As she began, they both were completely taken aback by what she was saying. River Otter could do naught but to translate word for word, speaking each sentence as his mother finished. Sometimes, Anika forgot to stop long enough, and she would have to repeat herself.

"Great Bear, I have to ask a favor of you that is… is hard but necessary. My husband is buried in New York in a grave marked only by a young tree. I have to dig up his coffin and bring him here. Then, I have to take him to the ocean and set his coffin in the water. River Otter and I have to do this, and I need you to come with us."

Great Bear had been following the translation, listening to River Otter's voice, but watching Anika's mouth form the words. He wished he could understand her directly, for her voice set off a whirlwind of emotions, making it hard for him to grasp the message of what she was saying. When he finally understood that she was asking him to join her on a journey to bring back her husband's body, that she was not going away forever, as had been his deepest fear since the beginning, he was so relieved that he agreed immediately.

"Tell your mother I will come. We must also tell Tree Stump and get his blessing."

Anika said, "Thank you, Great Bear," in English. It was one of the first phrases she had taught him, and it gave her an opportunity to address him directly.

Great Bear was still so overwhelmed that he could not remember the response. He could only stand where he was, looking at her intently. Anika also fell silent, once again under the powerful spell of her own unacknowledged desire.

After several minutes of watching them stare silently at each other, River Otter spoke up a bit hesitantly. "This trip will take some planning. I may need to leave the village for a short time to get the things we will need."

At the sound of his voice, Anika came to her senses. Embarrassed, she excused herself and her son. Taking his hand absentmindedly, she drew him away.

As they were heading back, Anika suddenly stopped, remembering something important. "We will have to go to Gentle Fawn's wigwam and tell them about this trip. I don't want her to worry."

Even as she spoke, Anika knew the young woman would not be comforted much by anything that she could say. Then she had an idea. "Willy, I want you to tell Gentle Fawn about our leaving and coming back in your own words. Tell me what you are saying to her, but you say it first."

Anika had noticed how Gentle Fawn's eyes followed River Otter whenever they were in each other's company. It was clear that he had found a place in her affections. Hearing the news of the trip from him might ease her heart somewhat.

By the time they reached her wigwam, Gentle Fawn had begun her cooking. River Otter greeted her with an apology for the unexpected visit.

"Gentle Fawn, I am embarrassed that we have come to your fire empty-handed. Please forgive my rudeness and my news." He stopped and turned to his mother, translating an approximation of his greeting into English. "My mother has asked me to accompany her on a journey back to our former home to bring my dead father here. We are to place his body in the ocean."

At the word, journey, Gentle Fawn's eyes filled with tears. Anika placed a hand on River Otter's arm, interrupting his explanation. "Copumush nee (Come back I)." She took the young woman in her arms.

River Otter smiled at his mother's broken Unkechaug. Then he spoke up, getting Gentle Fawn's attention. "I promise you we will return. Besides, your father is coming with us."

"My father? How did you get him to agree to join you?"

River Otter shook his head in mock amazement. "My mother just asked him!"

Gentle Fawn suddenly laughed through her tears. "Oh, of course! My father would do *anything* for Anika!"

Early the following day, River Otter woke Anika to tell her that he would have to leave. "We will need a horse and wagon for… the coffin, and clothing for you and the chief. I have no money, so I'll have to hire myself out to make some. I fear that I may be gone for as long as a month, but don't worry; I will return with everything."

Anika smiled at her son. Of course, he would return; he was under his father's protection. She had dreamt this very conversation just a moment before she awakened. Only it was Osei speaking to her. Amazingly, he had placed these exact words into his son's mind as well!

Before leaving, River Otter went alone to Great Bear's wigwam to speak privately to him about Gentle Fawn. The young man had made what he believed was a strategic decision, one that would take some of the pressure off his mother. Gentle Fawn was attractive and, most importantly, intelligent. He had been studying her, noting how all the women in the village, even those much older, looked to her for guidance. She loved and honored his mother. And her daughters seemed to like him. If Great Bear agreed, River Otter intended to ask Gentle Fawn to marry him.

He met the chief on his way to his daughter's wigwam, and fell in step beside him. After explaining his trip, River Otter broached his main topic. "Great Bear, before I leave, I would ask your permission to court Gentle Fawn, if she will have me."

Great Bear stopped and looked sharply at him. "Have you? Of course, she will have you! I will tell her to marry you immediately!"

This was perfect! If River Otter married Gentle Fawn, then Anika would have to stay, and Great Bear would be able to convince her to marry him sooner or later.

"Please, Chief, do not order her to accept me. I want to court her on my own. Besides, I think she likes me, at least a little."

River Otter knew that he was being unnecessarily modest. Ever since he had become a man, wherever he went, women always seemed to find him attractive, but it had never mattered to him before. Now, at least, his looks had gotten him the attention of someone he could consider for a mate. Gentle Fawn was older, by a few years, and no doubt more experienced sexually. These became, as he turned them over in his mind, additional attributes rather than hindrances. He warmed somewhat to the idea of winning her affections.

Exactly thirty-one days after he had left, River Otter returned on horse-back and laden with parcels. He reached the village in the early afternoon when women were still in the fields and men were out hunting or fishing. In the surrounding woods, he had hidden a wagon in which he had left shovels, a load of burlap and several coils of rope.

Anika was not in their wigwam, nor was Gentle Fawn in hers; both women, along with Yellow Bird and Bright Star, were down by the shore, shucking a mound of oysters. This was where River Otter found them.

"It's River Otter! River Otter's back!" Bright Star sang out the announce-ment and dropped the oyster she had been working on.

She ran to greet him, followed closely by her sister. The younger girl danced around him while Yellow Bird watched her sister in annoyance. Finally, she shouted in exasperation, "Stop behaving like a child!"

Before they could get into an argument, River Otter quickly kissed both girls' cheeks, whispering something to each one. Yellow Bird called out. "Mother, River Otter says he has something important to ask you. And he wants to talk to Anika."

Bright Star added, "...And he brought us each a gift!"

What River Otter also brought was clothing for himself and Great Bear, homespun shirts, breeches, boots, rough coats and wide-brimmed straw hats, as well as a woolen gown, an apron, a mobcap and bonnet for Anika. When he saw the clothing, Great Bear laughed at the breeches and stockings. When he tried them on, the pants were much too short and the boots too small.

Finally, River Otter suggested that Great Bear wear his own leggings and moccasins, along with the shirt, coat and hat, with his long hair tucked out of sight.

Anika found concealing her own hair, now grown into locks well past her shoulders, defied the constraints of the mobcap. In desperation, she took one of the stockings intended for Great Bear, cut off the foot, knotted that end and pulled the open end over her head, pushing all of her hair under the stocking and pulling on the mobcap; the fit was almost unbearably tight. Worse yet, putting on this clothing, after having been accustomed to the relative freedom of her simple tunics and moccasins, brought back the discomforts of the life she had washed away in the lake on that impossibly bright day so long ago.

Tree Stump came to see them off. When Great Bear had consulted him about the trip, the chief had not really asked for his reading of the signs, expecting and fearing that they would not be auspicious. However, the old man seemed not to have been surprised by the news, but welcomed it.

"This is what Anika must do for her spirits. If she asked you to come too, then you should go. But remember; do not sleep with her, even if she seems to agree. It is forbidden until you marry."

"Why is this forbidden to me, when it is common for men and women who intend to marry?"

The powaw sighed in exasperation. "If you cannot take my counsel, then why come and ask my advice? I have told you this is what you must do because you are the *chief!*"

Great Bear felt properly chastened and a little foolish. Of course, he intended to wait until the appropriate time. It was just that he would be with Anika constantly for—he had no idea how long—and he wanted her so badly.

"I realize that I don't always follow your counsel, but, in this important matter, I will take your advice, Tree Stump, I swear it."

The first several miles of the trip through the forest were the most difficult. River Otter and Great Bear pulled the empty wagon around trees and over underbrush, while Anika led the horse, burdened down with cooking utensils, dried grain, the shovels, bags and rope.

When they finally reached a road, they relieved the horse and loaded the wagon. River Otter hitched up the animal and the long ride began. For Great Bear, the experience was both exciting and terrifying. He had never seen a wagon or a road so wide that two or more of these wagons could pass at the same time. In fact, most of the people in his village did not even realize there were such things as horses. It was only through contact with Whites that the Long Island Indians came to use such things. The Unkechaug, even in their early trading days, had never developed a taste for them.

They stopped for the first time at one of the easternmost Shinnecock villages located on their leasehold of over 4,000 acres. River Otter told Great Bear and Anika to remain in the wagon while he went to secure permission for them to be on Shinnecock lands overnight. He returned with a skin of fresh water and some dried pemmican. Anika made a fire and boiled the pemmican along with cornmeal to make a mush, which she served with wild gooseberries she had found growing nearby.

Then they bedded down in the wagon for the night. It was Great Bear who suggested the sleeping arrangements, strategically placing himself as far away from Anika as possible. River Otter slept next to his mother in the front while Great Bear took the rear. It did not help the chief; he spent the first night awake, unaccustomed to the feel of the wagon floor and exquisitely aware of Anika at the other end.

During the following day, to break the tedium of long hours spent just bouncing about on the wagon seat, River Otter recounted, first in English, then in translation for Great Bear's benefit, what had happened when he made his courtship visit to Gentle Fawn.

He'd begun by giving Yellow Bird and Bright Star their presents, a pair of beautifully made spindles and a handful of carded wool for each of them. The girls had never seen such things and wanted to know what they were used for.

"Women use these to spin thread, like this." River Otter had spent about an hour sitting in front of Gentle Fawn's wigwam, showing each girl how to attach an end of wool to the spindle and then set it to spinning on the ground, creating a long thread.

Gentle Fawn found him thus engrossed when she came in from the fields carrying a load of corn and beans in preparation for the evening meal. She did not even attempt to hide her pleasure at seeing him there. When she asked him to join them, he accepted readily, even helping Bright Star with her part of the cooking chores.

He became strangely uneasy, however, when it came time to broach the topic of his visit. "I... would like to ask you to... allow me to come and see you when I return. My mother is... happy here, and so I plan to stay. If you do not find me too ugly, perhaps you could consider me for your husband...."

They were sitting outside; the meal was over and the girls had been sent in to bed. Gentle Fawn had not answered him. River Otter could not even see her reaction, for she had turned away after the first few words. He had no idea that she had completely lost all composure, so deeply had she fallen in love with this impossibly handsome young man. She had assumed he would choose one of the girls just reaching the age of courtship. Then it came to her. Great Bear had arranged this! Of course, her father would try to marry her off to Anika's son and further gain the affections of his mother!

"Are you sure you want a woman with daughters who are almost grown themselves? Have you looked around the village? There are young lasses here who have never known a man. Perhaps one of them would make a better wife than I. I have been alone for so long that I might not be right for any man." Even as she was speaking, Gentle Fawn could feel her heart beating painfully in her side. The village had no unmarried men who were near her in age. The illnesses that had taken all of her brothers, save one, had effectively wiped out most of her male peers. When she first became a widow, the remaining men already had wives, and she would not consider any offers to become a second one. Oh! This son of Anika! Why had he come to tease and torment her now, when she had already resigned herself to being without a husband? Abruptly, she got up as if to go inside.

River Otter sat stunned, but only for a moment. He rose almost at the same time she did, extended a hand toward her, but stopped short of actually touching her. "Clearly, I am clumsier than I thought myself to be," he apologized. "There is no one else in the village who comes close to you in beauty. It was foolish of me to think you would consider someone like me. Forgive my thoughtlessness." He turned as though about to leave.

Gentle Fawn stopped him. "No-no, it is I who am thoughtless and rude. It is just…. Of course you may visit me when you return."

They had parted with only this understanding between them.

River Otter, naturally, had no idea why Gentle Fawn had responded so coolly to his proposal. But Anika understood immediately; the young woman was just trying to protect her heart. Anika had recognized that, although Gentle Fawn had been completely smitten from the first, she was much too proud to accept a marriage that River Otter did not really want. Anika was certain she was only giving him the opportunity to change his mind.

"You must be careful with Gentle Fawn's affections, Willy. She is a good woman and you must not hurt her. If you are not certain you want to marry her, do not make a pretense. It will hurt more than if you just let her alone."

River Otter was silent after this exchange. He truly was not sure about actually wanting to marry anyone.

Great Bear had tried to follow the conversation which had been entirely in English. He gathered that something had happened between River Otter and Gentle Fawn that was not going to lead to a marriage, at least not immediately. And he was not pleased. He spoke up suddenly and rapidly, in hopes that Anika would not be able to follow his words.

"Why did you not let me just *tell* Gentle Fawn to marry you? She is my daughter, and it is my place to select her husband. You are my choice for her! There was no need to go begging at her door! When we return, I will take care of the matter!"

Surprisingly, Anika did understand, at least the tone of his voice. She turned to him and spoke slowly, mostly in Unkechaug, mixing in English where she could not remember the right words.

"Great Bear, Gentle Fawn loves you. She will do what you say. But she also loves Willy—River Otter, too. She has been hurt by one man who always behaves as if he does not love her. Must she now marry another who does not love her either?"

River Otter spoke up in his own defense. "Mother, I never said that I could not come to love Gentle Fawn…."

Anika, without turning around, silenced him with a hand on his arm. She was watching Great Bear's face as he struggled with her words.

As always, whenever she spoke to him directly, he would first experience her voice before he could begin to understand her words. Now, because she was sitting right beside him on the wagon seat, he also had to overcome a surge of desire. But one thing gradually became clear to the chief. For some reason, Anika believed that he, Great Bear, did not care for his daughter!

Anika continued, now warming to her topic while leaning closer to him. "How many nights have you sent Gentle Fawn away from your wigwam? She comes home to cry. I have seen her, and so have Yellow Bird and Bright Star. We were all sad for her. If you love her, why make her cry?"

Great Bear could not think of an answer. Worse yet, he could not justify his behavior, even to himself. In truth, he could never bear to even acknowledge the intense love he felt for Gentle Fawn. But, at that moment, it was turning painfully in his heart, competing with an almost overwhelming need to be alone with Anika, if only for a few minutes.

Suddenly, he ordered River Otter to stop the wagon. The young man did so, and Great Bear got down, disappearing into the woods beside the road. When he returned after some time, he climbed into the rear and sat crosslegged, resting the back of his head against one side. Here, he remained for the rest of that day.

By occasionally applying the whip, River Otter was able to coax the horse into a smart trot that allowed them to cover almost half the total distance within the next three days. On the afternoon of the third day, a group of White men on horseback approached them. The men's horses moved at an easy canter, and they seemed in no particular hurry to get to a destination.

River Otter felt his stomach tighten at the sight of them. He whispered to his mother and Great Bear, "This is probably a local patrol checking on the farms in this area. Let me speak to them, and *please*, no matter what happens, don't get down from the wagon. And say nothing!"

By now, the riders were almost upon them. River Otter pulled hard on the reins, causing the horse and wagon to move to one side of the road away from the men. He stopped, alighted and approached them on foot. One of the men suddenly spurred his horse into a full gallop, heading straight toward the wagon. River Otter stepped into his path, causing the man to pull up sharply.

"Nigger! Where d'y think yer goin'?"

Without addressing anyone in particular, River Otter began a litany of lies and half-truths. "Masters, my name is Stephen. Yonder in the wagon's my mother and stepfather. We all are heading to the ferry landing—going to New York to buy supplies to take home. See, Masters, my free papers."

He produced the British-issued documents, offering them in one outstretched hand. The man who had nearly run him down dismounted, snatched the papers, glanced at them and threw them into the dirt. His companions, having ambled on past him, now shouted for him to mount up and join them—that they didn't have all day to waste on one wagon full of harmless niggers.

When Great Bear saw River Otter's papers scattered in the wind, he tightened like a coiled spring; his right hand moved instinctively to the knife in his belt, its blade resting against his left thigh. Anika felt the movement and quickly placed her hand over his. Great Bear froze; she had never before actually touched him, and it created such internal dissonance that his rage vanished completely.

By then, the man had remounted and raced off to catch up with his companions, who were now almost out of sight. River Otter gathered the papers, smoothed them as best he could and put them away before returning to the wagon. He gave the horse's rump a gentle slap with the reins; his lips curled disdainfully as he explained the encounter, in English, to Anika.

"These patrols are really just militia from the War. They've lost the will to do any honest work but do have a taste for riding about all day and trying to drink their companions under the table every evening." Then he spoke in Unkechaug to mollify the chief. "Great Bear, I am sorry you witnessed my shame. But some of the Whites are very easily provoked and very dangerous. Had that man been alone, he would never have dared to humiliate me. But his friends gave him courage. And you must know these White men are in numbers like the stars in the night sky; that is their greatest strength. They have a special hatred for us Blacks who are not their slaves."

Great Bear nodded in agreement. Even though he had never actually met a White man, all stories about the Ancient Protection included descriptions of the deviousness of White men and the danger posed by allowing any interactions with them.

To save time on the road, River Otter decided to drive all that night. On the following morning, just at daybreak, they finally reached the landing. The ferry that was docked on this day was a flatbed barge, large enough, if not crowded with people, bundles and wheelbarrows, for a horse and wagon. It was still a bit early for the heaviest crowd, so there would be room for the travelers.

As River Otter was maneuvering their way across the rutted clearing on the riverbank, Anika suddenly clutched his arm.

"Look! It's Cicero! If he sees me, he will surely recognize me!"

River Otter got out of the wagon and went around to the rear where he began to rummage through the bundles. At last he found what he had been looking for and called for his mother to get down. He produced a large hood of fabric stretched over a framework of hoops that collapsed when the headgear was not being worn, called a calash. This one was of green silk, old and stained, but when he had seen it, he bought it immediately, instinctively knowing it might come in handy.

"Mother, put this on and pull on the ribbon. It opens like the top to a carriage and will hide your face completely."

Anika put the calash on over the mob cap. The entire effect was quite incongruous; the color and style of it clashed badly with her plain woolen gown and apron. Only fine ladies wore calashes as protection for their often elaborate hairstyles. Still, it served its purpose. Cicero barely glanced at them as the wagon was loaded onto the ferry.

When they reached the Wet Dock, Cicero, with the aid of his crew, moored the ferry and began collecting fares as the few passengers disembarked. He paused over River Otter's fare, a single coin.

Without looking up, he abruptly handed it back. "F' a round-trip, y' pays at th' end."

Before River Otter could reply, Cicero had turned away and was busily preparing to load passengers for his next run.

The trio headed north on Broad Way. The road was wide and level; it bypassed the narrow, congested city streets which were, in most cases, only able to handle carriages and people on foot. The only other vehicle about this early was a night cart loaded with the contents of the city's many chamber pots. The two night-soil carters had been going house to house making their predawn collections, and were now on their way out of town, on the only road wide enough to accommodate the cart and horse, to dump their load in the Collect Pond. The cart turned right onto Fair Street, which allowed the men to avoid having to go through the Negroes Burial Ground to reach their destination. White residents generally tended to avoid that area as much as possible.

When they reached the Commons, River Otter asked Great Bear and Anika to get out of the wagon and help him. Together, they led the horse up to the hilly part of the Burial Ground.

Once there, Anika looked around slowly. Nothing was familiar; almost all of the markers were missing and everything was overgrown with brown, dusty weeds. In this wilderness, she could not remember where the clustered graves of Antobam and her stillborn babies were. For a moment, she felt a rising sense of panic; those precious graves were her reference points.

Then she spotted it, the only young tree growing in the Burial Ground. It had to be the one she had used to mark Osei's grave. "Here! Dig up this tree! He's right beneath it!"

Together, River Otter and Great Bear worked for hours. As the day grew warmer, Great Bear took off the shirt, then the hat. He was about to remove his leggings when River Otter stopped him, explaining that someone might see them and that White men did not approve of nakedness. Finally, they were able to dislodge the entire tree and pull it out by the roots. River Otter was about to toss it aside when Anika stopped him. "No! We have to take the tree back with us. We will plant it near the water."

So both men covered its roots with a large piece of the burlap which they tied in place with ropes. Then they returned to the hole. The coffin was just visible under the rocks and earth that had tumbled back into the grave when the tree was removed.

River Otter and Great Bear dug carefully around the box until it was free enough to be lifted out. It was heavy but completely intact. Anika brought out the rest of the burlap, and the men covered the coffin completely, securing everything with more of the ropes. By the time both men had loaded it and the tree into the wagon, it was late afternoon. River Otter noted the position of the sun and asked Anika how late the ferry stayed in operation.

"Cicero makes his last run at 5:00 o'clock. Are we too late?"

He studied the sky again. "If we leave now and hurry, we may just make it."

River Otter drove the wagon as fast as he could down Broad Way. The thoroughfare was now clogged with many homeward-bound peddlers and their carts. By the time he, Anika and Great Bear reached the Wet Dock, it was a little past the hour. Yet, Cicero still had the barge moored.

Six others had already boarded; a farmer with his barrow laden with goods and supplies, his wife and four children, all apparently close together in age, the oldest no more than six years. They were all crowded around their mother like a litter of piglets rooting under her skirts and attempting to climb all over her. She sat impassively on top of the pile of bundles, nursing the youngest, an infant about two months old. The farmer had apparently lost patience and was shouting to Cicero to "heave to an' move this thing!"

Cicero's response was respectful. "Masta, I certainly does intend t' cast off directly. I sees my las' fare comin' now."

He steadied the boat as River Otter carefully walked the horse onto the ferry.

When the farmer saw that Cicero had held up the run for Black people, he was incensed and said so most profanely. Cicero alternated between agreeing with him and ignoring him until, at length, the man ran out of oaths and went back to sit with his family.

Crossing the river took more than an hour. Cicero had only his mate, Sam, to help him row the barge, and the water was somewhat rough. By the time they reached the Long Island dock, the sun was setting. The farmer and his brood disembarked first, he now shouting at his wife to keep up. River Otter asked Great Bear to take the bridle and lead the horse off the ferry while he paid the fare. Anika remained in the wagon, keeping her head lowered so the calash completely hid her face.

This time, Cicero took the coin when it was offered, but instead of pocketing it, he let it lay in his open palm. Slowly, he extended the hand. "This ain't th' whole fare f' a round trip. I cain't take it."

River Otter whispered urgently. "Please! I have no more!"

The ferryman shifted his weight as the barge rose and fell with the tide. He repeated his refusal, also in a whisper, leaning closer. "I ain' gon' take this. Just tell *her* I thanks Jesus she got away!"

Anika abruptly turned in their direction. She had to go back! She got out of the wagon and boarded the barge, pulling back the ribbon on her bonnet, revealing her face. Then, so quickly that everyone was taken by surprise, she hugged Cicero tightly and kissed his cheek. Just as quickly, she was off the boat and had climbed back onto the wagon seat. Cicero gave a loud shout, snatched off his hat, and began waving it wildly, his nearly toothless mouth spread wide in a grin. Even after River Otter had taken up the reins and driven off, the ferryman still stood waving and testifying his joy.

Great Bear climbed down from the wagon so he could watch everything without having to turn around. He could *feel* Cicero's shock and pleasure at finding himself in Anika's arms. How had she managed to cause this man, a stranger, to care for her so? Even though Great Bear did not really understand the business of the payment, he was absolutely certain that somehow the ferryman had granted them a favor and that he had done it because of Anika!

The trip back was torture for both River Otter and Great Bear. The two men rode together in the front, while Anika remained in the back beside Osei's coffin. With its additional weight, the wagon now bounced and swayed heavily over the deeply rutted road, its wheels frequently getting stuck in the mud churned up by the passage of so many horses and conveyances. Whenever this happened Great Bear would have to get down and push the wagon from behind, while River Otter coaxed the unwilling horse to move, most often by taking its bridle and leading it forward on foot. Because he was completely unfamiliar with horses, Great Bear could do nothing with this one. So, River Otter always had to handle the horse by himself.

Now in the presence of his father's corpse, River Otter finally felt the full weight of his grief and his rage. Like ink spilled on a blotter, the unexpressed passions spread, blackening his mood and rendering him nearly mute. He could not bring himself to speak more than was absolutely necessary for days.

Anika spent both day and night next to the coffin; finally having her husband's body near was a bittersweet release. By day, she leaned against it with bowed head, resting both arms on the burlap-covered lid. At night, she slept next to it, pressed against its side. Within her, there was finally stillness and a sense of becoming connected to him again. He was speaking to her now, very softly—reminding her of what she had promised to do, once they got back to the village. *"Place my coffin in the water so I can find my way home"*

For Great Bear, the pain lay in watching Anika openly pouring out her adoration on a man so long dead. What made it possible for her to even touch the coffin? And why did she, ever so often, smile down on it as though in complete communion with its occupant? His own ancient agony was awakened and he could not sleep. So he stood watch each night, letting River Otter sleep in the back of the wagon.

By the time they had reached the end of the wide road and now faced the forest, both men were thoroughly spent. Anika got down first. "You are both so tired! But please hold on a little longer! Willy and I must carry the coffin down to the water. Great Bear, we need your canoe."

Her voice galvanized them both. River Otter unhitched the horse and handed the reins to Anika; she led the beast, while he and Great Bear hauled the wagon through the woods. When they were finally within sight of the village, Anika tethered the horse to a tree. She and River Otter carefully unloaded the coffin while Great Bear went to fetch his dugout. Once they had all assembled on the shore, he stood watch as they lifted the coffin into the canoe and settled it between them. He had brought down two oars, so both mother and son could row.

"There is a swift current," Great Bear advised them. "It is well out from the shore, but it can catch a canoe and take it far out into the sea. If you do not want the box to come back, place it in this current."

River Otter nodded as he and his mother climbed into the canoe. He began to row with smooth, expert strokes as Anika tried to copy his movements. The dugout was soon almost out of sight of the shoreline. Here the swells rose to heights greater than that of a standing man.

River Otter tested the strength of the current with his oar. "Mother, I think we cannot go further out and still get back safely."

Anika seemed not to be listening. She had unwrapped the burlap and now sat with both hands gently resting on the coffin's lid. "You know how to write your father's true name? I want you to carve it here, so they will know who he is when he gets back home."

For several minutes, River Otter could not remember the first part of his father's name or what Osei had told him about how children were named. Then it came to him—by the days of the week on which they were born! In Akan, the boys' names were Kwadwo for Monday, Kwabena for Tuesday, Kwaku for Wednesday, Yao for Thursday, Kofi for Friday, and Kwame for Saturday. Kwesi was Sunday and Father had said that he too was born on Sunday! River Otter took out his hunting knife and carefully carved the full name:

KWESI OSEI

Together, they eased the coffin over the side, carefully, so as not to tip the canoe. At first, the current took it into a series of swirling circles, rolling it end over end and finally righting it. Anika watched it ride the waves almost as though it were being pulled along.

River Otter sat slumped against the side of the dugout. He could not join her in the vigil; it was all just too much. Now that the journey and the task were over, the spell holding him was broken. Suddenly none of what they had done made any sense to him. How could Mother possibly know that this was what Father had wanted?

"Mother, it's enough! We have to go back now!"

He took up one of the oars and began to row furiously; Anika took the other and silently did the same. She sensed the grief and sadness under his anger; there was no way to make him feel better.

Once they had finally reached the shore and, together, hauled the dugout onto dry land, he turned on her, his voice choked with tears. "Why did he have to do it? Send me away like that? I didn't need to be free if it meant I'd never see him again! He was wrong to do that to me! Wrong! Wrong! It's all wrong!"

Anika simply pulled him into her arms just as she had always done whenever, as a child, he had been hurt or unhappy. At first, he stiffened, but the memory of his mother's comfort was too strong. They both eased themselves onto the ground, he with his face buried in her chest, his arms tightly around her waist. As Anika gently rocked him, River Otter cried until there were no tears left.

Chapter 28

---

*G*reat Bear had watched from the shore until the dugout was no longer in view. Then he went back to the wagon and dragged the tree, along with the shovel, to the cliff overlooking the ocean. This was the best place for it. There was, after all, no way to plant a tree on the shoreline; there were too many rocks. He had actually started to dig the hole when he stopped abruptly, realizing that it was really River Otter's place to plant the tree for his father. He gathered up everything, intending to return to the water's edge.

When he had reached a line of trees that stood just beyond the shore, he saw them, Anika and River Otter. The young man was crying, quite openly, in his mother's arms.

Great Bear stopped in confusion, unsure whether to break in on them. He finally decided, reluctantly, to leave them alone and go back to the village where there were surely duties waiting that now needed his attention. Nevertheless, he paused several times in the forest, stopping just before reaching the first wigwams. Somehow he could not shake free of the feeling that there was something more that needed doing—for Anika. In his heart he simply wanted to know that she would soon be along. And then he saw her, some distance behind him, walking awkwardly in the heavy shoes. Finally, after almost turning an ankle, she pulled off the things and continued in stockinged feet, carrying a shoe in each hand.

He was about to call out when she saw him, dropped the shoes and started running in his direction, running, running with arms opened, hurtling toward him as though she had no intention of stopping! He felt his heart begin to beat like some wild thing caught in his chest. She was upon him almost before he could collect his wits, but he caught her by the wrists and held her away from him. He knew if she touched him at that moment, he would take her, right there on the forest floor!

"Marry me, Anika!"

Just at that moment, Anika could not remember how to say, yes, so she just nodded. He released one of her hands, and, with a nearly vise-like grip on the other, literally dragged her through the village in the direction of Tree Stump's wigwam. In his excitement, he forgot how much longer his stride was, and so she was forced to run to keep from stumbling.

The powaw was seated by his fire, finishing the last of his evening meal. Although he saw them coming through the trees, he continued eating, even as they drew up breathlessly. He let them stand, unacknowledged, until he had cleaned the last bit of stew from the bowl.

"I see Anika can hardly catch her breath. Were you afraid she would change her mind if you walked here instead of running?"

Great Bear accepted the jibe without comment. "How soon can we marry?"

Tree Stump reached for his pipe and filled the bowl with tobacco before answering. "You will both need the sweat lodge. After three days, you may be married. Let Anika go back to her wigwam to change her clothes. Both of you will begin tonight."

When Anika returned to the wigwam, she found River Otter sitting beside the fire pit. Her first thought was to start a fire and make him something to eat. Almost at the same moment, she realized there would be no time for that tonight. And she had to tell him the reason. But she began with a question. "Have you planted your father's tree?"

River Otter nodded silently, his gaze fixed on the dead coals in the pit.

Taking a deep breath, she continued, "Willy, Great Bear has asked me to marry him, and I've said yes."

He idly stirred the cold ashes without looking up. "Do you want to marry him, Mother?"

Her answer was soft but quite firm. "Yes. I think that's why I was brought here—why I came here. Oh Willy! How I wish you could understand what has happened to me! I've been... your father... one day...." Her voice trailed off.

River Otter was staring at her, completely puzzled. It made no sense for her to attempt an explanation. He was not ready to hear it, not yet.

"Tree Stump said Great Bear and I have to spend three days in a a,... I don't know what it is, but it's to get ready, somehow."

He smiled faintly. "A sweat lodge, Mother. It's a steamy, hot place, something like an oven where you become purified by sweating and praying. If you are to begin tonight, you must be ready by nightfall. Go on. I can take care of myself."

He turned his back while she changed out of the traveling clothes and back into her deerskin dress and moccasins. When he was able to turn around again, he noticed how thin she had become; she looked so young, in spite of the fact that there were many gray strands mixed in with the black locks of hair.

She kissed his forehead; then she took his face in both hands. "Remember, Gentle Fawn loves you. Don't court her unless you love her too." And then she was gone.

Once his mother had left, the wigwam suddenly seemed terribly empty. River Otter did not bother to change his clothes. Instead, he wandered over to Gentle Fawn's wigwam. By now, it was getting dark and she was covering the coals of her cooking fire. Yellow Bird and Bright Star had gone inside to get ready for bed.

Standing off to the side, partially hidden by a tree, he watched her movements, a sense of emptiness now growing inside him. For so long, the only woman he had cared about had been his mother. And now he was losing her again, this time of her own volition. Why had he thought it could be otherwise? In no Indian community he had ever visited was there any value in permanent widowhood for a woman or lifelong celibacy for a man. When Anika married Great Bear, the whole village would rejoice.

This meant that he was no longer *obligated* to wed Gentle Fawn, and, tonight, as he stood in the shadows, he was trying to sort through conflicting emotions. As he watched Gentle Fawn, she straightened up, lifted her chin and unconsciously tossed back the heavy mane of hair that swept back from her wide, slightly prominent forehead. Clearly weary, she stretched, raising both arms high overhead and working the kinks out of her back. Women did most of their work bending over or in a crouched position that was hard on the spine and the legs. Nevertheless, Gentle Fawn's back was still ramrod straight, like her father's, and she had his long, muscular legs, but with just enough fat overlaid to create symmetrical curves.

For River Otter, her stretching followed by a wide, unceremonious yawn, triggered a sudden, intense and aching desire. He moved quickly, covering the distance from the trees to her fire pit in only three steps. Catching her by the arm, he turned her around and kissed her. Then he pulled her close in an almost-desperate embrace.

"Let me stay with you tonight!" he whispered, "Please!"

Without replying, Gentle Fawn took one of his hands in both of hers and drew him into the wigwam, dropping the door covering behind them. The girls were sleeping soundly by now, their breathing barely audible. She went to both of them, squatting beside and gently nuzzling each one. Then she picked up a length of stout rope, looped one end in the joint between one of the crossed frames supporting the house and stretched its length taut before tying it off at another joint. She hung two blankets over the suspended rope, creating a private area, behind which she unrolled her bedding.

River Otter watched with relief and growing excitement. Her movements were so sure, so absolutely economical! Unselfconsciously, she removed her dress, revealing a body that was fit and strong from hard work. Then she began to undress *him*. She deftly undid the strange buttons, removing both the breeches and the shirt. He quickly took off the stockings and shoes, then joined her under her blanket.

She smiled at him mischievously. "We will have to be quiet. But I'm afraid that will be hard," she said as she straddled his body and began to caress him all over.

At that moment, River Otter realized he would have to make a confession. "Gentle Fawn, it shames me to say this, but I've never been with a woman. You are so... so beautiful, and I may disappoint you." As he spoke, his heart started racing almost painfully.

"Then, I will be your first and maybe your only woman, if *you* are not the one disappointed!"

As they began, Gentle Fawn covered his clumsiness and inexperience by gently guiding his hips, his hands. It had been more than eight years since she had been touched by someone who desired her, and she had honestly forgotten how sweet that could be. Yet, with this man—with River Otter, he had but to appear at her fire and ask to stay! All that she needed to remember about lovemaking now came back to her in a joyous rush.

At first, River Otter simply followed Gentle Fawn's lead. But once he had entered her, his own passion took over. His heart and body rode what felt like endless spirals of ecstasy rushing toward a sudden climax that, when it came, swept over them both and just as suddenly was over.

In its wake, River Otter was left wrung out with misery. The pain that earlier had drawn him to Gentle Fawn's wigwam now came rushing back, filling his whole being. He had failed to satisfy her; he was sure of it. Why had he even asked her to let him stay? She must realize by now that he had just been using her to keep his own lonely grief at bay.

"I've disappointed you, I know," he whispered. "I'll leave now if you want."

River Otter had rolled off her and was now lying on his back. Instead of answering, Gentle Fawn got on top of him, this time pressing her whole body against his. She wrapped both arms around his neck and rested her cheek against his. River Otter gasped, just once. He realized he was weeping; at the same time he was clutching her so tightly that, had she been less solid, she could easily have been injured. In the midst of his tears, he became acutely aware of her body, of how its heat seemed to penetrate his whole being, igniting a firestorm that raged from his heart, clear down into his loins. He took her again; this time he lasted until he felt an unmistakable undulation deep within her that nearly made him cry out. Here was the prize he had been seeking! Completely spent now, he clung to her until they both fell asleep.

As the pale light of dawn penetrated their hideaway, River Otter awakened. He propped himself on one elbow so that he could watch Gentle Fawn as she slept. She was turned toward him, one hand resting on his thigh. Damp strands of hair clung to her face; ever so gently, he moved each one. He wanted her to awaken, yet at the same time he knew she needed sleep. A painful sweetness filled his chest, threatening to nearly choke off his breath. He could not see himself ever sleeping apart from her again.

Chapter 29

*G*reat Bear was already at Tree Stump's wigwam by the time Anika arrived, breathless and anxious. She was surprised to see that the chief was barefooted and wrapped in a blanket. Tree Stump was backing his way out of his door, his arms full of additional blankets. When he turned and saw that she had finally arrived, he gestured for her to come ahead.

"You are here at last! Great Bear had become worried. Go inside and take off everything. Here. Cover yourself with this."

The powaw handed her one of the blankets and hurried her into his wigwam. Anika was grateful that he promptly went back outside so she would not have to undress in front of him. When she emerged, completely naked except for her belt and wearing the blanket, Tree Stump gestured again, this time for her to follow him; in turn, Great Bear fell in step behind her.

The sweat lodge was some distance away from the village, close to the lake. It was built on a circular foundation of stones and covered with rush mats. In the center of its hollowed out floor, Tree Stump had had a platform of stones placed with a fire laid on top that heated the stones until they glowed red. Two young men, sons of Eagle Eye Woman, served as his assistants in the sweat lodge. It was their job to keep the fire blazing and to continually pour water over the hot stones, thereby creating steam.

On the way there, the powaw explained the ritual for Anika's benefit. Both she and Great Bear were to share the lodge, each sitting opposite the other, while he sang and prayed outside. Neither was to speak or in any way acknowledge the presence of the other. They were to remain in the sweat lodge that night and most of the following day. At the appointed time, he would have them taken out for a bath in the lake. Then they would be given something to drink and Great Bear would be allowed to go home to rest. Tree Stump surprised Anika by insisting that she stay with him instead of returning to her own home. On the next day, the ritual would begin again. Neither was to eat anything for the whole three-day period.

At the end of the first day, River Otter brought Gentle Fawn to Great Bear's wigwam to announce their good news. "We want to marry at the same time that you wed my mother."

Great Bear, still tired from the effects of the heat and fasting, was lying down, so he had invited them inside instead of coming out.

"Gentle Fawn, you have come to your senses and accepted River Otter's proposal, then?" He actually smiled at his daughter.

River Otter spoke up before she could reply. "It is I who am the lucky one. Your daughter does me a great honor by accepting me. In return, I swear to remain with her for the rest of my life!"

"Good! Give me more grandchildren!"

Great Bear closed his eyes, indicating the visit was over and they should leave him alone. In his heart, he was afraid to believe that, at last, everything was beginning to come right for him. Even the small joy that he had taken at his daughter's good fortune in her first marriage had turned to bitterness. Better to remain calm and be prepared for disappointment.

Tree Stump made up a bed for Anika in the corner of his wigwam. After that first day, she was both tired and a little nauseous. He decided it was better to keep watch over her in case a full-blown illness threatened.

"If you become sick, Anika, the whole village will suffer."

Anika did not argue. She was happy not to have to go back to her own wigwam. During her whole time in the sweat lodge, she could swear there had been beings, unseen yet palpable, sitting beside her. In the thick fog of steam, she could not see Great Bear clearly, yet she knew that other beings had been very near him as well. These spirits were different from her voices. They did not speak; they were just *there*—waiting. She had the overwhelming feeling that, although she could sense them, it was Great Bear whom they wanted.

"Tree Stump, who are the… the *people* in the sweat lodge with us?" Anika asked.

Tree Stump looked at her with some surprise. Eagle Eye Woman's sons had to be in and out of the lodge almost constantly, but Anika knew this. Then, a moment later, the powaw understood what she meant.

"It is common to have visions in the sweat lodge. This is what you saw. If they seemed to be spirits, it is of no consequence. Everyone's visions are different."

Anika had the strong feeling he was being deliberately evasive, but she left off asking more questions. Something told her quite clearly these spirits were of great consequence indeed.

That night, while she slept, Tree Stump burned a smudge pot near her head. All night long he sat beside her, fanning the smoldering herbs so she would inhale the essence.

Just after daybreak, Great Bear appeared at the powaw's door, anxious to begin the ceremony. Tree Stump came and stood in the doorway, effectively barring his entry.

"Where is Anika? The sun is up and we should be at the lodge."

"She is still sleeping. I kept her with me last night to make sure she was well enough to continue."

Great Bear felt a stab of fear. Anika *had* to be well enough! He had forced down his raging passions for so long, and now, when he was just about to gain his prize…!

At that moment, Anika appeared over Tree Stump's right shoulder, wrapped in her blanket. She had overheard the powaw's statement just as she was waking up, and a thought had sprung into her head, *she had to be well!* She had jumped up immediately, feeling around the bedding for a blanket. The sudden motion did make her feel a little dizzy, and she needed to close her eyes for a moment. The thought now formed itself into English words, in her own voice, *"Great Bear won't be able to go on if I cannot."* It was so strong that she knew she had to return to the sweat lodge.

"I am fine. We can begin now."

By the time they reached the sweat lodge, the sun was already bright overhead. Eagle Eye Woman's sons had had plenty of time to stoke the fire and thoroughly wet the stones. The interior of the lodge was filled with clouds of steam so thick that, once Anika and Great Bear entered, each became invisible to the other.

Suddenly, Anika felt something brush lightly against her leg and she momentarily panicked, but before she could cry out, a tiny hand covered her mouth. At that same moment, the sense of illness and dis-ease drained out of her, replaced by a calm watchfulness. Yes, there were indeed spirits here! Now she could make them out—a woman and several children, all moving to and fro, sometimes crossing the fire pit, at other times arrayed around the circular walls. And there was one more, a baby who sat on her lap, its face nestled in the hollow of her throat, its body pressed against hers; it had gotten inside the blanket and wedged itself between her breasts. This one was *hers*; it was *Antobam*! She was certain of it! Yet, she could not embrace the being that clung to her; when she tried, her arms closed around air.

Afraid to speak aloud lest she alarm Great Bear, Anika addressed her dead child silently. "My sweet babe! Are you here to keep your Mama company? I've missed you so! Stay with me; please do!"

In response, the tiny sprite wriggled, as though in pleasure. Its movements seemed to attract the attention of one of the other spirits, a small child who drifted over to a spot near Anika's knee. Here, the being became substantial enough for her to make out its features. It was also a baby, a copper-colored little boy, round and dimpled with straight black hair, staring up at her with large, ink-black eyes.

Now the other child-sprites also turned toward her. Swooping in all at once, they encircled mother and ghost-child. Antobam suddenly turned in Anika's lap so that his back was against her chest. His presence seemed to grow larger until he formed a shield between her and the others. Over his shoulder, she saw the woman gesture toward the children, motioning for them to come back to her. Immediately, they all swept away and clustered around her. It seemed the encounter was over, for a moment later all the spirits, including Antobam, vanished.

This time, when Anika and Great Bear emerged from the sweat lodge, Tree Stump had a surprise waiting. The powaw sent Anika to the lake for her bath; he then called the chief aside.

"It will not be necessary for you and Anika to spend tomorrow in the lodge. I have sent word that the marriage will be celebrated this evening. By tonight, Anika will be your wife and you can sleep with her at last!"

Great Bear did not immediately react to this news. Already, his mind was telling him to restrain himself, not to let his heart feel the joy welling up inside. When he spoke at last, it was about River Otter and Gentle Fawn. "They wish to be married at the same time. Is this possible?"

The powaw laughed. "Of course, they can marry today! But their situation is different than yours. It's my understanding that River Otter went to live with your daughter on the same night you asked Anika to marry you."

At the lake, Anika wept as she bathed, although she had no idea whether for joy or sorrow. In the sweat lodge, she had been forcefully reminded that she was now in a world of both the living and the dead. Half-submerged in the cool water, she found herself crying out for answers.

"But why? Why am I the one? How am I supposed to go on, seeing ghosts as I do," she sobbed. "Now that... *my husband* has gone, has my baby come to take his place? Will I still be shown the way?"

When she returned to the lodge, Anika found only Tree Stump waiting. The powaw called her to him. Cupping her face in one weathered hand, he studied her reddened eyes before telling her about the changed plans. "Are you afraid to marry Great Bear?"

"I-I'm not afraid of him. There are *spirits* who want him. I am afraid of *them!*"

Tree Stump sighed deeply. Drawing her arm through his so he could lean on her as they walked, he told her the story of Snow Bird and her sons. He concluded with an admonishment. "You must not show *or feel* fear of these spirits. It is for Great Bear's healing that they have come. You are their doorway into his heart."

The powaw had spoken very simply, using only words she could understand. By the time he had finished, they were in the center of the village. Anika could feel the sting of tears behind her eyes. Poor woman! To lose every one of her sons, and then to die like that! No wonder Great Bear was so badly wounded in spirit. But Tree Stump had one more piece of information which he whispered into her ear just before releasing his hold on her arm.

"Great Bear has never cried for either Snow Bird or his sons. This is a very bad thing—bad for him, and for you!"

Anika had no time to digest this news, for both she and the powaw were now in the midst of a throng of villagers. Word had gotten around, thanks in large part to Eagle Eye Woman's vigorous efforts that *two* important marriages were happening today. There was barely enough time to prepare anything! Women were going to have to bring whatever they had already cooked for the communal wedding feast.

Tree Stump, drawn away by two young men, left Anika standing in the crowd. As she turned around, with no idea what to do next, she felt a gentle tug on her elbow. It was Little Squirrel, her baby strapped to her back.

"Gentle Fawn wants you to come to her wigwam. She will help you get ready."

The girl kept ducking her head as she spoke; most of what she said was addressed to Anika's feet. Normally Little Squirrel tended to be a bit brazen, even with the older women, looking directly into their faces when talking to them. But with Anika, it was different. Ever since the birth of her daughter, Little Squirrel was shy about even approaching her, much less actually saying anything to her.

Inside Gentle Fawn's wigwam, there was minor pandemonium. Both Yellow Bird and Bright Star were competing for attention. Each girl wanted to wear a special necklace of tiny shells that had been made for Gentle Fawn by War-in-Massachusetts when she was still a child.

"Mother! You know that necklace looks better on me! I'm just the right size!"

"But I'm older and I should be the one to wear it!"

Gentle Fawn took the necklace in exasperation. Why on this special day did the girls have to behave so badly! Just as she was about to chastise both children, Anika appeared at the door.

"See, girls, Anika is here! Forget the necklace and help us get ready."

Anika looked from one girl to the other, then at the coveted necklace. "Why don't you each wear it? Yellow Bird can wear it when Gentle Fawn gets married, and Bright Star can wear it for me."

It seemed like a perfect compromise and both girls beamed. Now they could concentrate on the brides. Anika insisted that Gentle Fawn make the choice of clothing for both of them, but she begged the young woman not to suggest Snow Bird's wedding dress. Since they were both widows, it was not necessary to wear anything too elaborate, even though this *was* the village's first family.

Gentle Fawn decided on a dress of soft light brown doe skin trimmed with red and black beads for Anika, and a similar dress, dyed red with white shells for herself. Yellow Bird wanted to give Anika an elaborate hairstyle, but there was too little time. She satisfied herself by interlacing her locks into a mock braid pattern and then tying them at the nape of her neck with a piece of leather lacing to let the rest of the locks hang down her back.

Gentle Fawn simply tied a length of the lacing around her head, leaving her hair loose. She turned to her daughters. "How do we look? Are we fit to be brides?"

Yellow Bird studied the two women solemnly. "I think you are both beautiful."

Then Gentle Fawn turned to Bright Star for her opinion. "Yes. Beautiful."

Anika, too, gazed lovingly at her daughter-in-law-to-be. She thought, *Such a beauty, she is indeed.* And then, *How I wish we could all just stay here and not have to face…* In her mind, Anika was not sure what or who she did not want to face.

With a start, she remembered Great Bear. "Come now! We must go. Our men are waiting!"

Great Bear had been in his wigwam, trying to get it ready for Anika. Were Gentle Fawn not getting married today, as well, he would have had her do it. In desperation, he had sent for River Otter help him. Now, with less than an hour before the weddings, both grooms were engaged in clearing away years of clutter. They worked in silence mostly, except when River Otter needed to ask whether to keep a thing or discard it. The objects they found dirty or broken—stacks of bowls and spoons, several cracked bows and about a dozen arrows, two paddles for the dugout with splits in their handles—all these, they gathered together and placed in a mound behind the wigwam. Everything else they crammed under the long circular bench, so that the center of the room would be completely clear.

By now, it was nearly time for the ceremony and neither man was dressed. Great Bear searched around in several large baskets. At last, he pulled out a cream-colored deer skin shirt made by turning the hide inside-out and softening it until it had the texture of cloth. It had been one of the shirts he had worn during the celebration of his wedding to Snow Bird, but at this moment he did not remember that fact. Silently, River Otter took the shirt and put it on; the fit was almost perfect.

Great Bear's clothing was less of a problem. He would wear the cape and headdress passed on by his father. These he kept carefully put away in a special basket made just for that purpose. The cape was meant to be worn without a shirt. It was of carefully seamed red dyed leather, decorated with feathers, shells and stone beads. The headdress was a conical cap that tied under the chin. It was completely covered with feathers and the same kinds of stone beads that adorned the cape. The effect, when Great Bear had everything on, was so majestic that River Otter wanted to exclaim, having never seen a chief in full ceremonial dress. He restrained himself, however, sensing that to do so would be somehow inappropriate. So they set off in silence with Great Bear leading the way.

The actual wedding ceremonies were brief, much to Anika's surprise. Tree Stump began with a song addressed to the Great Spirit. In it, he asked that each new union be blessed with health and good fortune and that no wicked spirits invade the homes of these new couples.

Then he addressed Great Bear and Anika directly. "Great Bear, this is your wife, Anika. Do you want her?"

"Yes."

"Anika, this is your husband, Great Bear. Do you want him?"

"Yes."

That apparently was it. The powaw turned to River Otter and Gentle Fawn, repeating his questions. Once they had each given the same answer, with a simple wave of one hand, he presented the newlyweds to the assembled villagers who cheered vociferously.

At this point, the celebration began with feasting, followed by singing and dancing. Anika, still somewhat stunned, sat beside Great Bear in a spot that had been specially prepared for them. Gentle Fawn and River Otter had been placed opposite the chief's seat and out of Anika's direct line of vision. Several women brought the first food and drink to both couples and then left them alone.

Just as Anika and Great Bear had finished eating, Tree Stump suddenly appeared before them. He spoke directly to the chief. "You are free to leave now. Your daughter and River Otter have already gone home with your granddaughters."

As they were about to get up, the powaw came close to Anika and placed one hand on her arm as he whispered to her. "Remember, do not be afraid of anything. I will be here when you need me." Then, just as suddenly, he was gone.

Anika always wondered how such an old man could possibly appear and disappear so quickly. When she turned to Great Bear, about to ask this very question, the chief was looking at her fixedly with a naked, hungry stare that was unmistakable in its meaning.

For one panicked moment, her courage deserted her. No man but Osei had ever touched her in a way that gave her pleasure. And although Great Bear's obvious desire both aroused and honored her, she could feel the weight of his need threatening to crush her. Nevertheless, she pushed the fear aside and took one of his hands, fitting her palm firmly into his. Side by side, they walked to his wigwam.

At the doorway, Anika stopped and faced the chief. Something felt strange about the place, and she wanted to experience the wigwam alone first. She asked him to wait outside until she called him.

Inside, a scent swept by her, faintly musky-sweet and slightly rotten, like dead undergrowth. It lingered for only a moment; then it was gone. Slowly, she walked around the room, laying her hands on Great Bear's tools, his assorted baskets and hampers. It was a man's living quarters; everything that in any way would have indicated a woman's presence was absent. She would have to create a real home from scratch.

Great Bear grew anxious, although he remained outside as Anika had asked. By this time, he was experiencing a welter of emotions that completely undermined whatever composure he had left. When, at last, she called him to come in, a fine tremor seized him. His heart began to pulse so powerfully that he could feel it throughout his whole body; even the veins in his neck were pounding.

Anika had undone her locks and spread out the bedding, but she was still fully dressed. He came within an arm's length, took one of her hands and placed it against his chest. Surprisingly, the pressure of her hand against his heart eased its hammering somewhat. He grew calm enough to remove the headdress and cape, carefully returning both to their basket. Now bare headed and bare-chested, he moved closer to Anika and began to undress her very slowly, undoing the lacing that fastened her dress at the shoulders, causing it to drop around her feet.

For a moment, he regarded the leather belt around her waist without touching it. Then, he knelt before her and drew her down with him. Very gently, he began to kiss her, starting at her throat, moving across and between her breasts and down the center of her abdomen, over and around the belt as though it were a natural part of her body. When he could go no further with them both on their knees, he rose, took off his leggings and his breechcloth.

"Anika, lie down."

Completely overwhelmed by his visible passion, Anika did as she was asked. Great Bear's face was almost unrecognizable. The light copper of his skin had flushed to a burnished red and his eyes glowed like twin coals with live embers in their centers. One vein stood in his forehead while another snaked its way along one side of his neck. He continued moving down her body, his lips making a pathway to the area below her navel. Anika entered a dream-like state. She was back in the bath and Osei was gently washing her stomach, her hips, her arms and legs. Just as she was about to surrender to these most exquisite memories, she felt Great Bear nudging her legs apart.

Panicked, she resisted. "No, no, please… not there, not there," she whispered the cry in English. She had let Osei kiss her womanhood but only a few times, because it never seemed clean to her, no matter how much she washed it. "Don't. You won't like it," she spoke more softly, but still insistently, and still in English. Remembering the way Evie used to smell in bed during her menses had always kept Anika from relaxing enough to enjoy the experience.

But tonight Great Bear would not let himself be denied. He heard her protests, but his mind refused to understand the words. Insistently, he opened her legs, baptizing her most private parts with his tongue and lips until she was drenched. Now that she was fully ready, he entered her. At last.

They began to move in a gentle, deliberate rhythm. Great Bear, in his desire to give her as much pleasure as possible, forced himself to slow down his lovemaking so as not to reach a climax too soon. What Tree Stump had said was so true. He had been much too long without a woman. But Anika was more than worth the wait! Everything about her was impossibly delicious! Even the sensations produced when the contents in the pouch on her strange belt rolled against his body excited him so much that he could barely control himself, like a youth in his first encounter! He did not notice the slight breeze that caressed his back as it moved past his head.

Anika, however, not only felt the breeze, she also became aware of the overpowering scent of decaying sweetness that swept in with it. It enveloped her, moving into her nostrils as she breathed and forcing an entrance through her open mouth. She felt a *woman's presence* very close to her, pressing against her face, joining the scent as it passed between her lips and entered her chest. Now she could feel the *woman* flowing through her body, downward, to the secret space where Great Bear moved so rhythmically. And as he did, she could feel the *woman* leaving her body and entering his.

The first thing Snow Bird did was to explore this hot place that she had known only from the outside. In here, she could move through his blood, creating whirling eddies, making it flow faster. She kicked the swirling liquid into waves that crashed against the walls of his veins. When she became tired of watching the swells alone, she called to the children. Each boy entered through the same channel, joining his mother inside his father's loins. Now they all swam upstream as one, stroking and kicking in unison. Their combined movements produced a powerful pulse that followed in their wake.

Great Bear was experiencing the most intense climax in his memory. It began as a fierce pulsing in his loins and spread throughout his belly. But when the pounding filled his chest, it seemed to suck out all the air. For just a moment, he could not draw a breath, and he pushed himself up, hoping to avoid having Anika realize his predicament.

As he raised his head in an attempt to breathe, he saw them for the first time! Suddenly, a rush of air filled his lungs that immediately expelled in a long, terrifying scream! His beloved Snow Bird! Red Cloud! Fish Hawk! Brother Gull and Brother Partridge! Clever One! They were all right there before his very eyes, and he could feel his heart bursting! His dead wife and all of his sons appeared solid now, standing as they had in life. Together, they gathered closely around the bed. The baby, Clever One, had actually reached out his small, pudgy hand and touched his father's cheek. The touch had been palpable, and it had opened a floodgate somewhere inside. When Great Bear started screaming again, he could not stop except to gasp for air.

Inside their wigwam, River Otter first heard the crying in his sleep. Someone had died and a relative was screaming in grief. He was about to allow himself to drift off again when he sat bolt upright! That was neither the weak screaming of an old person nor the cries of a woman! It was a man's voice! His sudden movement awakened Gentle Fawn. Even in the darkness, he could see her eyes widen with fear. In an instant, he was on his feet, running toward Great Bear's wigwam with Gentle Fawn right behind him!

Other villagers, whose wigwams were closer to the chief's had already gathered by the time River Otter reached the clearing in front of Great Bear's door. Tree Stump stood just in front of the fire pit. He had raised the stick that he used to lean on as a means of getting everyone's attention. River Otter was about to rush past the old man.

"My mother!" he shouted, "Something has happened to her! Let me pass!"

The powaw thrust the stick into the young man's chest just forcefully enough to knock him off-balance. River Otter found himself suddenly sitting on the ground.

"Anika is fine! It is Great Bear who is in trouble. He will need to cry for some time. But your mother is there to help him."

The powaw turned to address the crowd, which by now had grown to include everyone in the village who could walk, including Gentle Fawn's daughters. He had to raise his voice to be heard over the screaming.

"All of you who are old enough to remember know the chief never mourned his wife and sons. He is doing that now. We can be grateful that Anika has brought back the spirits of Great Bear's dead family. We may not sleep tonight, but in the morning the worst will be over. You can all go home; I will keep watch here."

Tree Stump, moving stiffly, sat down next to River Otter. The young man called to Gentle Fawn to take Yellow Bird and Bright Star home. "I will stay here with Tree Stump, to make sure your father and my mother are alright."

Anika had been riding the crest of an intensely pleasurable wave of sensations, when she became quite suddenly alert. Great Bear had raised his body up off her and now braced himself on one arm. The other he stretched out toward a spot above her head. She craned her neck in order to see where he was pointing. There, at the head of their bedding, stood Snow Bird and the five sons. And now she realized with horrible clarity that Great Bear could see them as well! The smallest boy, the one who had first approached her in the sweat lodge, toddled forward, reaching for his father. Such a natural gesture for a curious baby! She was touched; her heart went out to this child, so long without his parent.

At the first scream, Anika jumped. It was so loud, so close, so unexpected that she was momentarily unhinged. The baby apparently was also terrified, for he shrank back against his mother. Snow Bird, however, simply gathered the child up in her arms. Then she and her sons began a steady, step-by-step closing in on Great Bear. He screamed again; this time it was his dead wife's full name.

"Soachpo Awassas!"

He followed with the names of every one of his sons. By now, he was gasping between each scream. Tears poured down his face, contorting it into a mask of absolute pain. They fell like a scalding rain, pelting Anika's eyes and running onto her mouth. Even after the names, he continued, this time emitting one long shriek after another. She had to gather her wits and intervene somehow or Great Bear would go on screaming forever.

"Just touch his heart, his throat and his face. He will be able to stop then."

Anika was not sure which of her spirits had spoken, but she was grateful for the directions. As she laid both hands on Great Bear's chest, she could feel the chief's heartbeat slow perceptibly. The same held true when she gently stroked both sides of his neck; the distended veins disappeared almost immediately. Finally she laid one open palm against his cheek and whispered. "Great Bear, don't cry any more. Everyone is satisfied now."

Somehow she knew it was true. Great Bear promptly collapsed, his full weight nearly suffocating her. Although the storm of his grief was over, in its aftermath, the chief was left completely weakened.

The next morning, when Anika awoke, Great Bear was still asleep, his body covering hers in such a way that she could not get up without disturbing him. So she remained where she was, even as the slant of the sunlight coming through the door covering indicated that morning had become afternoon. Desperation finally forced her to slip out in the early evening to use the latrine pit. Just as she was about to relieve herself, she heard his hoarse cry.

"Anika! Anika! Anika!" he kept calling out, his voice becoming louder and more hysterical so that she had to finish in a rush.

As she was hurrying back, Tree Stump suddenly appeared in her path. "I will go in and calm Great Bear. Your daughter has left a pot of food on your fire. Stay out here and eat. Then bring some for your husband."

The powaw went into the wigwam and seated himself close to Great Bear's bed. The chief had awakened and found Anika gone. In his delirium, he thought she had simply vanished. Tree Stump stretched out one hand, touching him lightly on his forehead. Immediately, the shouting ceased.

"Anika is just outside eating. And it is time for you to eat something too. It will help you regain your strength. What has happened to you was to make you remember that which you have tried to forget for so many years. And, Great Bear do not be so afraid Anika will leave you. Already, you have come to depend on the woman too much."

Great Bear tried to focus on Tree Stump's words, but there was this awful dizziness and a roaring in his ears. Finally, he gave up and closed his eyes. Almost immediately, he fell into a sound sleep. The powaw sighed as he rose to leave. The chief had always been slow to take good advice! This healing would be difficult indeed!

During the first two days of his illness, Great Bear did not want to let Anika out of his sight for even a moment. For most of that time, he kept her in bed where he made love to her, endlessly, or so it seemed. What little sleep she could get was repeatedly broken. For whenever she drifted off and perhaps sighed or tried to change position, he would roll over, straddle her hips and kiss her until she came fully awake. Although he tried to be gentle with her, he could not stop himself, even when she was clearly worn out and quite dry. He felt driven, not primarily by need, but out of an overpowering fear that she had somehow become part of his ghostly visitation, and that she too would disappear. His terror at this prospect fueled what felt like a ceaselessly raging desire for her. Her only rest came when, exhausted, he would finally fall asleep.

The slant of the sun as it set behind the tree tops cast a deep, bronze hue over everything. In front of Great Bear's wigwam, all of the boys had finished the evening meal and were gathered around the fire, joking with each other over the day's exploits. Red Cloud was showing off his new game trap, the first one he had made all on his own, without his father's help. Clever One had been running around in circles, displaying this new skill for each of his brothers. Fish Hawk smiled indulgently, ruffling the child's hair as he trotted past. Brother Gull, the older twin by a few minutes, applauded. But Brother Partridge, who seldom had patience for his baby brother, now pointedly ignored the child's antics. Clever One recognized the rebuke; his little face fell and his lower lip quivered. Running to his mother, he crawled onto her lap and began pulling on the front of her dress. Snow Bird immediately loosened the shoulder lacings so he could get to her breast. Snow Bird had not weaned any of her sons until each one completely lost interest in nursing. Clever One looked like he might keep at it the longest. From first rising until he was nearly asleep, he demanded the breast at regular intervals and whenever he needed comfort. Now he curled against her body, one chubby hand resting on her bare skin, the other fingering a cowlick that stuck straight up from his thatch of spiky black hair.

Great Bear stood near a tree, just out of the family's line of sight, watching them as he so often did. He knew the boys would not go inside before he appeared. When he did, they would all clamor for his attention, especially Clever One. The baby just adored his father! As Great Bear was about to move, he discovered that his moccasins had somehow become stuck to the earth. A sudden panic seized him. He attempted to pull his feet out of them, but the roots that held him were growing downward, out of his own body....

The baby was running through a meadow full of sunflowers and dandelions. Great Bear had put his daughter down, intending for her to sit. But she was learning to walk now, and she unfolded her little legs just as her father set her on the ground. Immediately, she took off. Great Bear watched Gentle Fawn take a series of wobbly steps and then fall unceremoniously on her bottom. He laughed as she wailed in frustration, sweeping her up into a hug. He so loved this child! Everything she did gave him the most intense pleasure. Even now, as she squirmed to get free of his arms, he could feel that love moving in his heart, filling his chest. He knelt to release her and she was off again. Only this time, she was older, and now, after running a few steps, she stopped. He thought she might be waiting, for she turned around to face him. And he wanted to go to her so badly, but the distance between them kept stretching farther and farther....

Great Bear opened his eyes on the third day, just at sunrise. He had been dreaming, it seemed, for a very long time, and, for a moment, he lingered in that half-life just before complete wakefulness. Then, the events of the past few days flooded his mind in a rush! Had he gone mad? The whole village must have been panicked by his behavior! Anika?

He turned over to make sure she was really there. She lay on her side with her back to him. Her mass of tangled locks completely covered her face and spread out around her head in magnificent disarray. A frightening surge of emotion went through him. This woman had worked a magic so powerful, so amazing! And she was finally his! He was about to touch her hair when a thought came to him and he got to his feet. Moving quietly, he dressed and prepared to leave. At the doorway, he looked back toward the bed, silently praying that she would be there when he returned.

The burial ground was only a short distance away into the woods just beyond the fields. It held more than a generation of villagers, including Great Bear's parents and all of Snow Bird's immediate family. He had not been to the graves of his wife and sons since her funeral, when Red Cloud was also buried. Today, he needed to be here with them.

It had been agonizing to have their spirits possess him; the memory of all of them surrounding him still hurt. But this morning, there was a sense of release along with the aching. He could remember how each boy looked, how intensely he had loved every one of them. And Snow Bird, his dear wife—she had been the light of his whole life! He had been enraged when she left him!

It was a rage that he had leveled quite deliberately at everyone, living and dead alike!

The graves were clustered within a stand of trees. Every one was marked with something belonging to the person buried there. Each of his sons' graves had a favorite toy or treasured item planted atop the small mound. He stooped to touch each thing, recalling how Snow Bird herself had chosen a rattle, carved by his own hand to adorn Clever One's grave. When Fish Hawk and the twins were buried and Snow Bird was still dangerously ill, he had chosen their markers, a newly strung bow with arrows and a pair of small knives with beautiful bone handles. When he got to Snow Bird's grave, marked with the remnants of her favorite hair ornament, he dropped to his knees. Placing both hands on the mound, he pressed his forehead against it. A few moments later, he got to his feet, brushed the dirt from his leggings and headed back to the village.

Anika did not awaken until well after Great Bear had left. She was at first surprised and then deeply relieved to find herself alone; now she lost no time going outside to use the latrine pit. Once she had finished, she wanted a bath. After three days in bed, she felt the need for a hot one! Whenever she had needed more than a wash in the lake, she would heat water and fill the largest available pot. Then, with soap she made from rendered deer fat and ash, she would scrub herself clean.

Wrapping herself in the blanket that had covered her in bed, Annie went looking for something large enough to hold a quantity of water. Miraculously, she found a real, full-sized barrel behind Great Bear's wigwam. It was large enough for her to stand up in. She pulled the thing around to the fire pit. Gentle Fawn had been tending the fire each day when she brought food for them, and each evening she would leave it banked in preparation for the next day.

Now Anika stirred the coals until they blazed; then she began heating water that she had poured from a large covered pot near the front door into the big iron kettle. She realized she would now have to draw more water for drinking, but at that moment she did not care; the bath was more important to her. She was only able to get the barrel about one quarter full; she had difficulty getting in without tipping the whole thing over and there was no soap. The washing, while more cramped and less satisfying than the lake, did accomplish the task, however. She crawled out feeling clean, finally, though still quite sore between her legs.

Once back inside, Anika remembered that she had no clothing here other than the dress she had gotten married in. She put it back on and was about to leave the wigwam.

"Anika! Where are you going?" Great Bear appeared in the doorway.

She actually jumped; his voice startled her so. She had let herself forget the last three days. For just a moment, she stared at him as though he were a stranger. Then, mercifully, the moment passed before he noticed anything amiss. She opened both arms just in time to receive his embrace. Great Bear held her tightly for so long that she could feel his heart beating against her. The rhythm of it connected to her own heart, and she felt herself melting into him.

His voice seemed to come from somewhere distant. "Anika, I want to visit my daughter. Please stay here until I return."

Those words broke the spell. She pulled away so she could see his face. Why was he asking her not to leave the wigwam? Looking closely, she recognized the fear in his eyes. This would never do! She was not going to let him yield to it and imprison her! "Great Bear, I am going back to my wigwam for my clothes and cooking pots. You have nothing here that a wife needs. I will *not* disappear! Believe me!"

She repeated the last two sentences in English, for emphasis. That seemed to help him come to his senses. Of course, she was right; he had to let her go and trust that she would return.

Chapter 30

*I*n their wigwam, River Otter was having what felt like a near-perfect love affair with Gentle Fawn. His initial admiration and powerful physical attraction had easily blossomed into a strong affection for his new wife that seemed to grow almost daily. Gentle Fawn would never replace Anika in his heart, but she continued to surprise him by anticipating his every unspoken need. In those first days, when he thought only of sharing her sleeping mat and could not bring himself to return to his own wigwam, she had asked no questions. Instead, she and the girls simply brought his few possessions into their home, effectively welcoming him as a family member.

He was deeply touched, especially, that Yellow Bird and Bright Star had helped. Therefore he approached both girls with his marriage proposal before again asking Gentle Fawn. Bright Star's enthusiasm at the idea was so infectious that River Otter never noticed Yellow Bird's silence.

Three days after the weddings, the older sister awakened at dawn, feeling decidedly grumpy. Sitting up, Yellow Bird rubbed the sleep out of her eyes as she tried to remember why she was in such a bad mood. Then she heard it, that *sound*, muffled and indistinct, yet rhythmical. Over the last few nights, whenever she was roused slightly out of a deep sleep, she became aware of it. Not exactly a noise, it was more like a throbbing, as though there were a heart beating somewhere in the room. She had no idea what the sound was, but now she knew it was coming from behind the curtain of blankets that separated Bright Star and her from the place where Gentle Fawn slept with River Otter. Whenever she had been partially awakened, it had made her feel uneasy and unable to fall asleep again. This morning, she was just plain angry!

Flinging off her blankets, Yellow Bird shook her sister awake. "Get up! The sun has risen and I want to get the morning meal ready. You have to help!"

Bright Star opened one eye, regarding her sister with sleepy suspicion. "Mother is up?"

"No! *They're* still asleep! But I don't want to wait for them! Remember yesterday? We didn't eat anything until the middle of the day!"

Yellow Bird delivered this last statement over her shoulder as she was leaving the wigwam. Bright Star got up immediately, rolled her bedding and stowed it under the bench. Then she joined her sister outside. Together, the girls lifted the empty water pot and went to fill it.

It was true Gentle Fawn and River Otter had slept until early afternoon the day before, but not entirely because of newlywed bliss. Ever since their wedding night, they had taken turns keeping a vigil in front of Great Bear's wigwam. Gentle Fawn spent much of her day preparing and bringing food for her father, Anika and Tree Stump, who never left the chief's fire pit. In the evening, after fishing or hunting and preparing the game, River Otter took her place, keeping the powaw company late into the night.

He remained worried about his mother in spite of Tree Stump's assurances that she was well. How could she be, when she had not come out of Great Bear's wigwam for two full days? Gentle Fawn was equally frightened for Anika and for her father. She remembered how often and how suddenly death had stolen too many of her loved ones. When River Otter finally lay down next to her, as exhausted as they both were, he discovered that he could not sleep, and neither could she. So they made love to comfort each other for the rest of the night.

Great Bear was now approaching Gentle Fawn's wigwam just as Yellow Bird and Bright Star were dragging the full water pot to the fire. He stepped behind a tree before they saw him and watched as Yellow Bird fanned the coals, trying to start a flame. Her brow knitted in concentration, she was trying to copy her mother's efficient movements.

Her efforts stirred in him an emotion he did not even recognize. With the same stealth he used to track a deer, he sneaked up on Yellow Bird and, without warning, grabbed her in a bear hug. Before she knew what had happened, Bright Star found herself swooped up also. Both girls screamed, as he lifted them off their feet. Their cries reached Gentle Fawn, still asleep in River Otter's arms, and she came out running, naked except for the blanket from her bedding.

"Mother! Grandfather scared us!" Both girls were shouting in unison.

When he heard this, Great Bear started laughing. Everyone, mother and daughters, stared at him in complete wonder; no one had ever known the chief to laugh before! Great Bear gently set his granddaughters down. "I did not mean to scare you. I just wanted to hug you both and give you kisses!"

Yellow Bird's eyes narrowed suspiciously. This could not be Grandfather, the one who never wanted them around.

"Grandfather, you know you don't like us." She sounded as though she were speaking to her sister.

"But I do like you! I care greatly for both of you! You're my only grand-children!" Great Bear's voice was quite solemn.

The girls exchanged looks questioning his sanity. Yellow Bird had dropped her guard just enough for Great Bear to move in closer. Without warning, he grabbed her again and this time soundly kissed both her cheeks! Then he reached for Bright Star.

"Me too! I want one on both cheeks too!" Not wanting to be outdone, Bright Star had turned an un-kissed cheek to her grandfather.

Yellow Bird surreptitiously pinched her sister. The girl was *always* copying her!

"Yellow Bird pinched me!" Bright Star shouted as loudly as she could.

Great Bear appeared not to have heard her. He released his granddaughters, his eyes fixed on Gentle Fawn. She was still wrapped in the blanket and barefooted, her hair tumbling about her face and shoulders. But he was not seeing the woman; rather, it was his beloved girl-child come to find her father. A familiar painful, twisting ache had begun inside him. Now it moved and swelled in his heart, threatening to overflow it. He tried to speak but could get no further than her name. Instantly, she was in his arms, her face buried in the hollow of his throat. Great Bear held his child so tightly that, if it were possi-ble, he would have enclosed her within himself. His love, so long dammed up, now rushed toward her in a flood that swept up both of them. They each dis-solved into freely flowing tears. And it seemed neither would soon be ready to let go of the other.

By this time, River Otter had pulled on his breechcloth and leggings and had come outside to investigate. He took in the scene as Bright Star came to stand beside him. Silently, he put one arm around her, drawing her close. But when he reached out to do the same with Yellow Bird, she withdrew. For just a moment, he hesitated, weighing whether to let her alone. Then he took firm hold of one shoulder, and pulling her against his other side, he leaned down to kiss the top of her head. "What's wrong? Have I lost favor in your eyes?"

His approach was too seductive for Yellow Bird to resist. Although she did not answer him, she did move closer. Finally, very slowly, she slid an arm around his waist. He responded by gently nuzzling the spot he had kissed.

Yellow Bird, however, far from being comforted, now felt more confused and unhappy than ever. Everything was turned around! Her grandfather had surely lost his mind. Only days ago he was screaming in his wigwam! Now he had come creeping up on his granddaughters, claiming to love them! And her mother! She was, at this very moment, still crying in his arms!

But the first and worst thing of all had been when River Otter told her and Bright Star that he wanted to marry Gentle Fawn. He was supposed to wait for her, Yellow Bird! In two years she would be old enough to marry, and she had hoped—almost expected—that he would choose her. He always had what seemed to be a special smile for her. Moreover, he freely lavished presents, hugs and kisses on her. Yellow Bird had conveniently forgotten that River Otter always gave exactly the same attention to Bright Star. It had never occurred to her that he could be interested in *her mother*.

Eventually, it was Gentle Fawn who recovered enough to release her hold on her father. Great Bear felt her movement and reluctantly loosened his embrace. Even then, he could not yet bear to have her leave him. Taking her face in both hands, he kissed her forehead several times before completely letting her go. Suddenly, she remembered that she had come out without clothes and that the blanket was now on the ground at her feet. More importantly, there was no food ready. "Oh, Father! I slept too long! Please forgive me; nothing is ready!"

"Daughter, it is all right. You are still a new bride and you should have some time with your husband. Let me take the girls to Anika. We will feed them." As he spoke, Great Bear was walking toward River Otter. Both Yellow Bird and Bright Star instinctively shrank from their grandfather when he reached them. But the chief simply took each one's hand and firmly drew them both to his side.

River Otter picked up the fallen blanket and wrapped it around Gentle Fawn. If Great Bear had the girls for the rest of the day, then he and she would be free to spend the whole time together, alone in their wigwam.

Anika found Great Bear and his granddaughters making a fire in front of the wigwam when she returned with the last of her things, two bundles made of a pair of blankets around an iron pot and eating utensils. Yellow Bird was showing Great Bear the correct method for bringing the coals back to life. And he was making a great show out of watching her.

"See, Grandfather. You must knock the white ashes off the live coals underneath. Then you put in only the smallest twigs, one at a time."

They were all crouched around the pit. Bright Star, now completely won over, was leaning on Great Bear's back and peering over his shoulder. She was the first to notice Anika's arrival. "It's Anika! Anika's here! We missed you!" She ran to hug her, as Great Bear stood up, his expression one of absolute joy. Yellow Bird dropped the rest of her twigs and joined her sister in the hugging.

The sight of the girls overwhelmed Anika. That they were here with Great Bear was nothing short of a miracle! Immediately, she thought of Tree Stump. The powaw had been trying to tell her that the chief would be healed through *her*! And it was happening, just as he said!

Chapter 31

QUEBEC (1800)

*T*ekenna did indeed have a plan. Now he understood the importance of both River Otter and Anika to the Unkechaug village. Great Bear was exceedingly fortunate to have in his son-in-law an interpreter who was also a linguist. But it was Anika who was the real prize! The Munsee chief had seen many powaws in a lifetime of celebrations. Whenever peoples from different villages gathered in Ottowa for New Corn, New Moon or Thanksgiving festivals, their many shamen would be present as well. These men were some of the most powerful healers in the entire region. Yet, not one of them was able to summon spirits at will the way Anika had done. Tekenna knew that this woman belonged in his own village! He would allow the Unkechaug to remain here—in exchange, she would accompany his delegation back to Ottowa.

But the Munsee chief also knew there would be great resistance, in general, from the people of this village and from Anika's family, particularly her son and, most especially, her husband. Now that he knew their story, he could see the need to tread most carefully. Only Great Bear could give permission for Anika to leave. And he would never give her up—unless *she* insisted on it. The key for Tekenna was getting Anika to agree to leave with him. He needed to extend the storytelling until he could figure out a strategy.

During the longhouse meeting that evening, the Munsee chief issued a challenge to Great Bear.

"No doubt you wonder when we will render our decision. I confess I have been deliberately delaying because I wanted to know more of your story, especially from your powaw and her spirits. Ask her whether those from whom she ran away ever tried to pursue her. Can her spirits reveal more events that she was not present to see?"

As River Otter was translating Tekenna's words, he turned toward his mother, now seated to the right of the Unkechaug chief. Everyone waited for Great Bear's response.

"Of course, we are glad that our stories have entertained you so far. Anika will tell as much as she can. We do not trouble her spirits for our own entertainment." The chief's voice betrayed none of the rebuke carried by his words. Then he too turned to face his wife. "Anika, are you able to tell the story Tekenna wishes to hear?"

Instead of answering him, Anika got to her feet and again raised both arms. The smoke from the council fire gathered around her and lifted until it spread over the entire ceiling, like a blanket above the gathering. At this point, the women quietly slipped out one by one until all had left. Their places were quickly taken by beings unseen.

NEW YORK - 1792

When their boat had docked in New York harbor that July afternoon in 1785, and Will had not been there to meet them, Phillip immediately suspected there were problems. It was possible that Will had not gotten his message. The acquaintance who promised to have it delivered, a Mr. Blanding, was a lower-level member of Mr. Benjamin Franklin's retinue. Phillip was fairly sure this man could be trusted. But perhaps the man's servant had been unable to locate Will. Somehow, Phillip doubted this was the case. He had put on a brave face before the family, however, insisting that they simply hire a coach and have their belongings sent along after.

"Doubtless, there has been some delay at home or in the office that has kept Will from meeting us."

Evie was occupied with Circe, making sure everyone was accounted for. The family had grown, what with Phillip Junior's new French bride, Sophie's husband, and a son, Alexander, born during their stay abroad. Martha was now seventeen, of marriageable age, and Evan at sixteen was ready to join his father in the business. Everyone was anxious to disembark after more than a month at sea. Evie readily agreed to the hired coach, having paid no attention to anything else Phillip had said. She wanted only to get back to her house and resume a normal life.

The house was shuttered, just as they had left it. Phillip alighted first and paid the coachman. Evie got out quickly, joining her husband. Leaving the rest of the family at the gate, they walked around to the rear of the house. The door to the carriage house stood open, revealing an empty interior. Both the family carriage and the two horses were gone. Together, they climbed the ladder to the top room, which was empty. The bed was rumpled and bloodstained as though its last occupant had sustained wounds of some sort.

With growing horror, the couple hurried back to the front and unlocked the door. Evie rushed inside, her family now forgotten. Where was Annie? Where were Will and Willy? She rushed from room to room; everything was still covered and untouched. She emerged white-faced.

"There's no one here!" she cried, "Phillip, did you not send word we were returning? Did you use a reliable messenger? I know Father's barrister said that he personally spoke to Will when last he was in New York!"

Phillip had been staring at the house across the street where a black face was watching through a downstairs window. He ignored Evie's questions as the face disappeared.

Momentarily, a woman whom he vaguely recognized as the neighbors' maid came out to stand at her family's gate. "Master Hamilton, Sir? Are you looking for your people, Will and Annie?"

"Yes! And their son Willy and their other child! Where are they?"

The woman dropped her head. In that single gesture, Phillip saw the realization of his worst fears. She was about to tell him that something awful had befallen them. He glanced nervously over his shoulder at his family, still clustered at his front gate, and at Evie, now standing in the middle of the street.

"Sir, Will and Annie are both dead."

Phillip heard the harsh intake of breath just behind him. In an instant, Evie had rushed past him and hurled herself at the maid. "You are lying! Where are they!? Where is my Annie!?" Her screams echoed up and down Crown Street.

The poor woman barely escaped by running back inside her front door. Neighbors and servants poured into the street. Evie was now shrieking hysterically. Sophie rushed to her mother's side, attempting to comfort her, but Evie pushed the young woman away and turned on her husband.

"You go find my Annie! Right now! Find her! Find her! Find Will too, And their children!"

As he went to her to try to take her inside Evie slapped his face with all the strength she could muster. At that very moment, something shattered inside of Phillip. Later, he would remember it as the moment he realized how much he truly detested his wife!

It made no difference in their relationship, however, at least outwardly. Phillip did as Evie insisted. He mounted a search of the city, getting the local constabulary to question all of the servants on the street. The whole sad story came out: Will's unfortunate encounter with the thugs and Annie's apparent abduction and murder at the hands of persons unknown. According to those servants, Willy was taken away by the British when they left, and Annie's last baby did not live.

Once armed with the information she'd demanded he get, Phillip forced Evie to accompany him when those same neighbors' servants took him to the Negro Burial Ground so she could also bear witness to Will's and the baby's graves, poorly marked as they were.

The bitterness between them revealed itself in their most intimate moments. Evie had declared herself "in mourning." She told Phillip that they would be sleeping in separate bedrooms for the duration of this period. Angrily, she reminded him that it was his fault Annie had to stay behind. He, for his part, now concluded that Evie was the one at fault. Had she been a more loving wife, he would not have felt the need to seek solace elsewhere. And, more importantly, if she were not so bent on outwitting him, she would have taken Annie with them, and Willy too. They never argued about Will, however. Nothing they could have done would have saved him.

Now, seven years later, Phillip sat at his desk in the warehouse office, wearily going over the latest copy of a shipping inventory. The clerk whom he had hired to copy this manifest had made so many mistakes on the previous drafts that Phillip wondered whether the man could read or write at all. As he poured over the foolscap, using a reading glass, he found himself wishing Will were still alive. Not a day went by that he did not privately miss his manservant. Will would have easily done the work of two or three clerks; Phillip had never been able to replace him.

It was just a little past five o'clock when he finally locked up his office and closed the warehouse. As he stepped into the street, he narrowly missed being clipped by a wagon passing at a good speed. Looking up in annoyance, he barely saw the three occupants. These farmers! They simply did not belong on city streets! With their outsized wagons, they were nothing but a hazard to pedestrians!

Angrily, he stared at the backs in the wagon, now making its way along Beaver Street toward the docks. They belonged to two tall men, one broader across the shoulders than the other, and a woman, seated between them. For some reason, Phillip suddenly became interested in this trio. He followed the path that the wagon had taken, ending at the Wet Dock, where the ferry was moored. By the time he reached the landing, it had left and was a good distance from shore.

He stood watching the river and thinking about Annie for the better part of an hour. Why she had come to mind just now, he could not say. He never let himself think about her at all during his waking hours. In Europe, it had been easier; there were so many new experiences, and Evie was most often on her best behavior. But since their return, Annie had come back to haunt his dreams. Occasionally, he would awaken in tears, unable to reconcile himself to the fact that she had quite simply *vanished*. At last he realized what it was! The woman in the wagon had reminded him of her! Of course, he had only seen her back, and more than fifteen years had intervened. But he was almost certain he would recognize Annie even now! When the barge returned, he would make it his business to question the ferryman!

It was almost eight o'clock when Cicero finally berthed the barge next to a smaller ferry that he used for special runs. As he climbed onto the wharf, he was surprised to see the well-dressed White man apparently waiting for him. He pulled off the soiled hat he always wore and made a small bow before awaiting Master Hamilton's pleasure.

Phillip realized that he would have to speak first, but for the life of him he could not gather his thoughts. The man standing before him was so ugly, with his creased face and loose lips! Phillip expected the ferryman to start drooling at any moment.

Finally, he decided to be direct, at which point he found his voice. "I was on the docks when you cast off this evening, and I noticed your passengers. Do you ferry them regularly?"

Cicero raised his head just enough so he could see the man's face without appearing to be studying him. Then, quite suddenly, he grinned, a wide smile that revealed all of four large yellow teeth.

"Why, yes, Masta, I does. They's my weekly customers. Has they farm not two miles from th' landin'. Th' farmer, he bring in his harvest, 'long wit' his whole family in a wheelbarra'. Anythin' else I kin tell ya, 'bout 'em?"

Phillip shook his head in exasperation. "No-no. Not them, the other people, the ones in the wagon."

Now Cicero's face took on a truly puzzled expression. For a full minute, he stood frowning as though trying to figure out to whom Phillip was referring. At length, he brightened somewhat. "Masta, is ya talkin' 'bout th' Indians?"

It was Phillip's turn to look confused. They were *Indians?* It is true that he had viewed them only from the rear. Without having seen their faces, he could not swear to their race one way or another. He decided to take another tack entirely.

"You Negroes all know one another. Do you remember a man named Will and his wife, Annie?"

Immediately Cicero became sober. His entire face folded into a tragic mask, the lips now turned down at the corners.

"Oh Masta! I knowed 'em both! They was th' best Negroes in New Yawk! Annie, she visited my poor Polly ever' day 'most 'til she died. An' Will, he helped me bury her an' our las' child. I still goes up t' th' Burial Ground t' visit 'em. Will, he was one *faithful* servant, taken care a' his masta's affairs like the gen'lman was right here watchin' 'im. He gettin' his reward in Heav'n, f' sure."

As he spoke, the ferryman actually began to cry. Large tears gathered in both eyes, overflowed and ran down his cheeks. Phillip realized that he was not going to get any more cogent information out of the man. He turned and left Cicero on the pier, leaning against an upright, sobbing loudly.

Phillip returned to a now almost empty house. Both of his married children had left almost immediately upon the family's arrival. Phillip Junior had developed a taste for independence while in France. He and his wife decided to move West in hopes of claiming some of the land now open on the frontier. Sophie and her husband quickly made the decision to join them.

Sophie actually was not nearly as interested in becoming a farm wife as she was anxious to get away from Evie. She had never forgiven her mother's public rejection on that July day. And, although she never spoke about it, she was cold toward Evie ever after. Evie, of course, had completely forgotten about her own behavior, and so she was truly baffled by her daughter's icy distance, especially when she tried to talk Sophie out of going so far away from New York.

Martha had recently married a young politician looking to make his mark on the national scene. He quickly moved his bride to the new capitol of the country, Philadelphia. That left only Evan and Alexander still at home.

When Phillip entered the silent house no servant met him at the front door to relieve him of his hat, coat and gloves. It was just like Evie to have sent the downstairs maid to her quarters instead of having her remain on duty until he got home. Evie always went to her own room directly after supper. She hadn't dined with Phillip since their estrangement.

Only the family butler waited in the dining room where the table was now set for one. Phillip had bought him within a week of their return in an attempt to quickly restaff the house. The man was purchased in haste, an act that Phillip would regret at his leisure. For Tobey, as he was called, was both lame and considerably older than he appeared to be. He was also completely incapable of anything other than glacial movement. By the time he had finished bringing supper from the kitchen, arranging each dish on the sideboard and serving Phillip's plate, most of the food was cold.

Neither Evan nor Alexander was likely to be joining their father either. After business hours, Evan spent as little time in his father's company as possible. Phillip's constant criticism had driven a permanent wedge between them. Alexander, a dreamy somewhat withdrawn child, simply preferred his books and his own imagination to either of his parent's company.

During his solitary supper, Phillip's thoughts returned to his late servant. It saddened him to realize that Evan had never been and probably never would be nearly as adept at the business as Will had been. Part of the reason he always had to recheck everything was because of Evan's laxity. When he was still in his teens, the young man never listened and refused to learn; Phillip actually had to cuff him on more than one occasion! Once Evan reached manhood, however, he would no longer accept being hit; so Phillip took to shouting instead, which all too often produced dangerously heated exchanges between the two. Today, rather than argue with his son yet again, he had sent Evan home early. Now, as he pushed the food around on his plate, he recalled how Will could anticipate his every need. He had missed the man in Europe, but he'd never worried about his affairs as long as he knew they were in Will's hands. Even in the turmoil of their miserable first days back, he had found Will's note about the taxes in his study. When the money turned out to be exactly where the note said it would be, he'd actually burst into tears!

However, when his thoughts turned to Annie, he had a sudden revelation. What if she were not dead? The constables said no body had ever been found, only her bloodied gown and head wrap. She could have been kidnapped, yes, but *she could also have run away*! The more Phillip thought about it, the more convinced he became of the possibility. Will was dead, Willy was gone, and she had no babe to tend. Of course, she ran away! And if she did, it was his right to find her and bring her back! He grew so excited at this new prospect that he shouted an oath and slapped the table with his open hand, causing the dishes to clatter.

Tobey, who had been standing just behind his master's chair, suddenly dropped the wine decanter he'd been holding. Phillip whirled around in his chair to glare at the poor man, now trying to bend his stiffened knees in order to pick up the decanter and mop up the spilled wine. In exasperation, Phillip shouted, "Just leave it and get out!"

Once alone in the dining room, he tried to figure out a plan of action. His first thought was whether to tell Evie about his revelation. On the one hand, she certainly would want to have Annie back in the household. But, on the other, there was the problem of running away itself—a fully punishable crime. Phillip knew that Evie loved Annie too much to allow her any hurt. However, the municipal courts did require that runaways be tried as criminals. Once caught, the woman would have to be punished!

Then Phillip had an absolutely brilliant idea! *He* could intervene on Annie's behalf, get her turned over to *his* custody, and finally lay claim to her fully! In his fevered mind, he had her in his bed before he realized that he had no idea how to find her. And the trail, by now, was completely cold. He decided not to share his thoughts with Evie until after he had spoken to a constable.

All municipal offices were now located in the brand new City Hall on Wall Street. Phillip made this his first stop the very next day. He was able to speak to the head constable once he announced that his business had to do with a possible runaway. The man was solicitous but not very encouraging.

"I am most sorry, Sir, that your maidservant ran away. But, if, as you say, this happened perhaps some seven years ago, I doubt very much that you will find her. We have some luck reclaiming property reported lost within days or weeks of the occurrence. However, the more time that passes, the less successful we are.

"No doubt, the woman was able to cross the river and take up residence somewhere on Long Island. There are several groups,…the Quakers do come to mind. Those people will shelter runaways and do not readily give them up. The local patrols *can* force them to relinquish a slave with the threat of arms, since the Quakers do not, themselves, countenance the carrying of guns, and so will not fight back. There are also various Indian tribes who have taken in Negroes. It is almost impossible to reclaim them from the Indians, however."

Phillip could feel himself growing increasingly impatient. Of what use was the law if a man could not call on it when he needed its help? The man did give him two important leads—the Quakers and the Indians!

"I am a taxpaying citizen and a man of some means! I fully expect that you will launch an investigation by going to both the Quakers and whatever Indian tribes there are on Long Island! You cannot tell me that all hope is lost before you even begin a search!"

The constable sighed. Obviously, this man had no idea what he was proposing. Long Island was over one hundred fifty miles long, from the East River to its end in the Atlantic Ocean, and the City of New York had no jurisdiction over any part it. He would have to divert much needed manpower away from regular municipal duties to accomplish what Phillip was asking. Yet, it would be imprudent for him to refuse; this man could be influential enough to cost him his post!

"Very well, Sir. Please be so good as to provide us with a description of your maidservant. There is a Federal survey currently being conducted by Messrs. Thomas Jefferson and John Adams among the Indians. I will request permission for a City Constable to accompany their party. Also, I will send a pair of constables to ask the local patrols if they can assist in questioning the Quaker community."

Now, that was more like it! Phillip rose, thanked the man and left. As he walked to his offices, his spirits rose. He would send round a written description of Annie that very afternoon! There was no need to tell Evie anything until she was found. And Phillip had no doubt that she would be. He could not have gotten so strong an intuition if she were not still alive somewhere! Yes, he would have her back! He had only to be patient and *persistent.* The day was fine, balmy even, and the sun shone brightly. For the first time since returning home, he found himself actually enjoying the morning.

Chapter 32

LONG ISLAND (1793)

Gentle Fawn had missed her bleeding for three full months before she realized it. She had been completely immersed in her new role as the wife of River Otter, an experience that was exhilarating and at the same time frustrating. The problems all seemed to come from Yellow Bird. The girl had suddenly become stubborn and balky about doing her chores.

Most distressing, however, was Yellow Bird's fractious relationship with her new father. He could do nothing right in her eyes. The more loving attention he paid to her, the more sullen she became. Finally, Gentle Fawn threatened to punish Yellow Bird the very next time she was disrespectful to River Otter. The idea of actually striking her daughter, something that was almost never done to children, made Gentle Fawn so ill that she blamed her morning spells of vomiting on the prospect of meting out the promised punishment.

She told her predicament to Anika as the two were preparing corn for drying. Anika immediately took the ears out of Gentle Fawn's hands. "Sit down. Let me look at you. When did you last pass blood?"

Realization suddenly dawned, and Gentle Fawn covered her mouth in embarrassment. Anika smiled and laid her palms on both of her daughter-in-law's cheeks.

"You are expecting; I am sure of it. I will ask Tree Stump to help me examine you. You do look much heavier."

The two women went immediately to visit the powaw. Tree Stump palpitated Gentle Fawn's belly; then he had Anika do the same. As he directed her movements, he spoke to her.

"Anika. Here, you can feel the womb. Notice its size and shape. She is big for so short a time, and it can mean several things—a very large baby perhaps, or even twins. Snow Bird had twins, so it is not unlikely that Gentle Fawn will as well."

Once the diagnosis was made, the two women returned to Gentle Fawn's original problem, discussing it as they left the powaw's wigwam. Gentle Fawn now feared the situation would be made worse by her pregnancy. If Yellow Bird could not accept River Otter, how would she behave with two new siblings? Gentle Fawn truly needed her older daughter's cooperation.

"Yellow Bird is almost a lass of marriageable age now," Anika began. "Did you not notice how she also watched River Otter when he first came? I think she is jealous of you—and angry with River Otter!"

"Oh, Cwca! How can that be? She is still a child, like her sister! Bright Star loves River Otter! She even calls him, Coas (Father)! Before we married, I thought Yellow Bird loved him too! She is too young to have a woman's feelings for him!"

"Neechuntz (My child), she seems as still a little girl to you, her mother. But she must be about thirteen. She is nearly as tall as you. Did you not say that you got married at fourteen? Your daughter is almost a woman! We need to watch for her first blood. It will come soon, if it is not here already!"

Later that day, Anika approached River Otter with the suggestion that he speak to Yellow Bird. They met in the now unoccupied wigwam first built for them. It was a practice mother and son began soon after their marriages. Whenever they wanted to speak English together, in this place they could do so, away from their respective spouses and combined family.

"Willy, I think you may have given Yellow Bird false hopes when you were so kind to her and her sister. I'm afraid the girl came to fancy you. Now that you've married her mother, she feels hurt. That's why she is so angry with you. But you must talk her out of these bad feelings. I truly don't think she will listen to anyone else."

"Mother, what can I say to her? I had no idea that she fancied me, as you say. To me she was a child. Now I see that she is growing up, but I would still be much too old for her, even now, even were I unmarried and so inclined."

Anika gently touched her son's arm. River Otter took her hand and laid it against his cheek. He still found her presence comforting and he had come to depend on her counsel.

"You are skilled at talking to people. You'll find just the right words to ease Yellow Bird's heart. And when Gentle Fawn gives you her news, you'll be doubly glad you were able to soothe Yellow Bird's anger." With that, Anika kissed her son on the forehead and left.

Yellow Bird was behind their wigwam on her knees, sullenly grinding a measure of corn when River Otter found her. For a moment, he stood before her, watching intently. Then, he squatted directly in front of her, at eye level. Laying both of his hands on hers, he took the pestle out of her right hand while taking her left firmly. The girl raised her eyes slowly and found herself face-to-face with him.

"Stop what you are doing and take a walk with me. No, just leave everything there and come."

Drawing her arm through his, River Otter walked Yellow Bird in the direction of the lake. She did not resist; instead, he thought he saw a flash of excitement in her eyes. He was not sure what he would say to the girl, but he thought it wise to keep her close as he composed his thoughts. One thing that Yellow Bird's anger had done was to cause her to physically distance herself from him.

After about fifteen minutes of silence, he began. "You have every right to be angry with me, Yellow Bird. I did not realize I had hurt you when I married your mother. I did not think about your feelings at all."

Suddenly, she spoke up, her voice high and a bit quavery. "I wanted you to wait for me! Why did you act so kindly to me if you were not going to? I really thought… that you liked me!" At this point, Yellow Bird began to cry.

River Otter put both arms around the poor girl and drew her close. "Yellow Bird, I am too old to be your husband. In a year or so, the young men will come to court you. I have seen a few of them looking at you already, because you are so beautiful. You need a father to choose the best of them for you, and that is one of the reasons I wanted to be in your family. Yes, I love you and Bright Star as much as if you were my own daughters. But that is very different from the way I love your mother. The young man who is allowed to marry you will have to show me that he is brave, trustworthy and able to love you as much as I love Gentle Fawn."

River Otter could feel a subtle yielding in the girl's still rigid body. He kissed the top of her head and gave her an extra squeeze before releasing her. However, he quickly put one arm around her shoulder so she could not move too far away. Their relationship had always needed physical contact, he felt, and never so much as now. Yellow Bird said nothing, but she slid one arm around his waist as they walked back to the village. Finally, just before reaching their wigwam, she whispered, "I will try not to be rude any more. Don't let Mother punish me, if I forget."

"No one but your father can prevent your mother from punishing you. Am I now your father? Will you call me Coas?"

"Yes."

"Then, there shall be no beatings for my daughter—who is almost a woman!"

Finally, between them, the hatchet was buried.

Chapter 33

*I*t took some time for Great Bear to fully believe that Anika was finally his wife. And he made no attempt to hide the fact that she was on his mind almost constantly. During the early morning hours he'd go fishing, or check his oyster traps, tasks that occupied his hands, but would leave his thoughts free to return to his wigwam and their sleeping mat, where he could relive his nights with her. Once the necessary chores were finished, he would use every excuse to find her during the day, sometimes just to stand nearby as she worked alongside the other women until she'd notice him and smile. A small private moment between the two of them. His heart was by now so connected to her that even the sight of her face turning in his direction could alter its rhythm.

Two middle aged men, Tumperun (Seven Men), and Necho-wuchayuh-mocussenus (Ugly Moccasins), along with Eagle Eye Woman, Tree Stump and Great Bear, now comprised the village council. During one of their evening meetings, as the chief sat in the circle around the council fire, he was completely inattentive as usual. Were any of the old men, beside Tree Stump, still alive, who remembered his uxoriousness in his first marriage, there would surely have been snide comparisons with his current attachment to Anika. Tree Stump, however, made no mention of it. Instead, he took it upon himself to introduce the topics that needed the council's attention and to solicit each member's comments.

As it happened, neither Seven Men, nor Ugly Moccasins felt comfortable offering any opinions at all. Both remained silent throughout the whole meeting, content just to smoke and to pass the pipe between them.

Eagle Eye Woman, however, who loved to talk, had quite a bit to say. She could have easily monopolized the discussion, were it not for Tree Stump cutting her off as she was about to repeat all of her points just for emphasis. The powaw then turned to Great Bear for his contribution. After waiting in vain, Tree Stump closed the discussion himself and got to his feet, a signal that the council was finished, at which point the chief, suddenly alert, also rose and left immediately.

As they were walking away from the council fire, Eagle Eye Woman made a whispered aside to Seven Men. "Great Bear never listens at the Council. I wonder why Tree Stump allows him to ignore us in this way."

Tree Stump had moved off some distance, but still heard her remark. "You are only on the Council because of your age and our small numbers. Would you now challenge the authority of the chief or the wisdom of those who named him when you were but a child?"

Eagle Eye Woman said nothing else and decided that, from now on, it was better to keep such thoughts to herself.

Chapter 34

*O*ne night in early fall, Anika was awakened by a gentle pressure against her back. Thinking that Great Bear was signaling a desire to make love, she turned over. Now she could feel the weight on her chest as though someone were lying on top of her. But Great Bear was sound asleep beside her, one arm under his cheek, the other across her waist.

"Mama, come outside. I have something to show you."

Anika was suddenly wide awake. It was Antobam! It had to be! Her baby was now actually speaking to her! Moving carefully, so as not to disturb Great Bear, she eased herself from under the cocoon of blankets. The banked fire provided a little warmth, but the wigwam was still chilly. She pulled on leggings, her dress and moccasins. Then, wrapping a blanket about herself, she slipped around the door covering without raising it so as not to let in the cold night air.

Once they were outside, the spirit child attached himself to Anika with weightless arms tightly clasped around her neck.

"Look, Mama." The sweet, high voice seemed to come at her through the air. *"Look at the fields! The fields are on fire!"*

She ran in the direction of the village's fields. Sure enough, they were bathed in a lurid glow that seemed to rise from the forest line and spread from one end to the other. As she watched, the flames advanced toward her, engulfing row after row of the corn and bean stalks. The whole farm was ablaze!

"Oh no! I must get help! I must sound an alarm!"

Anika found herself spinning around wildly, trying to get her bearings.

"No, Mama. Just watch. Watch... and wait."

Anika made another turn, once more facing the fields. Everything was in complete blackness. No flames, no more reddened sky! The night was cold, still and undisturbed.

Back in their wigwam, Great Bear stirred and reached for Anika. When his groping hand encountered empty blankets, he sat bolt upright. He told himself she had just gone to the latrine pit, but he could feel his heart beating wildly. Unable to wait, he got up, put on his breechcloth, leggings and moccasins. He pulled on his shirt and then ran outside, heading toward the pit. When he did not find her there, he was seized with the most awful panic. This was what he had known would happen someday! She had vanished! Fighting off the edge of hysteria that threatened to have him screaming her name aloud, he made a deliberate circle of the village, to no avail. With his heart now in his throat, he headed toward the fields. And then he saw the blanket-wrapped figure, little more than a blacker shadow against an already jet-black sky.

"Anika!"

She turned toward the shout, only to be caught up in his crushing embrace. Great Bear actually lifted her off her feet.

"Anika! Why did you leave our bed? You... I was... afraid you were gone!" His arms steadily tightened around her, nearly cutting off her breath.

She twisted against his chest until she had worked one shoulder free. Then she pointed toward the silent fields.

"Husband! I had a dream. Actually, I was awake when I saw it, but I must have been dreaming. The fields were all on fire!"

At that moment, Great Bear's heart literally jumped so violently that Anika felt it too. "*You* saw the fields burning?" he repeated in a hoarse whisper. "With your own eyes, you saw the fire?"

She nodded. Suddenly he moaned a low groaning that he kept up the whole while as they headed back to the wigwam. Once they were inside, Great Bear finally released her. He began pacing in a series of tight circles. Anika watched him, painfully aware of his distress but helpless to ease it. What was it about this dream that had frightened him so? For she could see that he was, at bottom, absolutely terrified. Finally, still pacing incessantly, he said, "We must tell the dream to Tree Stump. There must be some way...."

"Some way for what? Husband, what is it that worries you? I dream all the time! I see spirits, too! You know this, so why are you upset tonight?"

"It is not the same!" Great Bear realized he had shouted only after the words were out. He stopped short and pulled Anika to him. Settling himself with her on the floor by the fire pit, he pulled a blanket around them both. "It will be all right. We will see Tree Stump in the morning, and it will be all right."

At first dawn, they went to the powaw's wigwam. Tree Stump no longer rose early unless there was some urgent need. Great Bear had decided, before leaving home and without discussing it with Anika that he had to wake the old man. The powaw was still sleeping soundly under several blankets, now necessary for warmth because of his advanced age.

Great Bear entered quietly, gesturing for Anika to do likewise. They both sat across from the powaw's sleeping mat. Somehow, in spite of their quiet entry, he heard them and awakened.

As soon as he saw the man open his eyes, Great Bear began, his voice unusually harsh, "Anika had the dream. She saw the fields on fire. If she must make the sacrifice, then you choose the next chief! I cannot live without her!"

The powaw sat up slowly, pulling one of his blankets around his shoulders. He fixed Great Bear with a glare more fierce than any Anika had ever seen.

"How do you *dare* to presume that Anika make the sacrifice? Is *she* the powaw? I am the powaw! And I say who makes the sacrifice! You have one role—chief! You must lead the people of our village in their escape. You must give them courage and faith that they can survive this move! That is all you must do, and it is more than enough! No, it is not Anika! The sacrifice is *mine to make!*"

Tree Stump's words literally took the air out of Great Bear's lungs. The man sank into himself as the powaw was speaking. By the time he was done, the chief could only stare at him with red-rimmed eyes. For several minutes both men sat silently.

Great Bear now understood everything. His personal tragedies had all been to prepare him for this role, the greatest any chief could ever hope to play—that of leading his people away from danger into the unknown. He knew that he alone was far from equipped; that was why Anika and her son had come, to be his spine and his counsel when there was no more Tree Stump!

"Go away now. You have much to do and no time. The village must be ready to move tonight! Leave Anika here with me. I have need of her help. Do not look for her until everyone is ready to leave. River Otter knows much about long sea voyages. Talk to him first. Then tell the people what to do. Do not come back here. Farewell."

The powaw turned his face away, indicating that the chief's visit was at an end. Great Bear stood, drawing himself up to his full height. Now completely composed, he left the wigwam, giving Anika the briefest of glances as he passed.

Anika watched the entire spectacle, first in utter confusion, then with growing fear. She was certain that something momentous was about to happen. And, somehow, once again, she was in the center of it. "Please tell me what is happening! Why are you telling Great Bear to get the village ready for a sea voyage?"

The powaw's eyes glittered. In their depths, Anika could see a flash of what she could swear was sheer *joy!*

"Long ago, Manitou gave to the Unkechaug a protection in the form of a prophecy. If the fields around us burned, we were to leave the place where we lived. The Whites, who have eaten up the lands and lives of all the Indians, have never found us. I have always known they would come one day. When you and River Otter reached our village, I knew they could not be far behind. Your dream tells me that they are almost here now and the people must finally leave, this time, by sea."

The powaw tried to rise, but, for the very first time, his legs failed him utterly. Anika, alarmed, crawled toward the old man on hands and knees, intending to help him up. Instead, when she reached him, she threw her arms around the frail shoulders, suddenly crying wildly.

"What else have you not told me? Are you not coming with us? Please do not leave us alone!"

Tree Stump very deliberately gripped her forearms. With a strength that seemed impossible, he forced them down to her sides. Then he rose, this time without appearing to exert any effort whatsoever, so that now Anika was at his feet.

"There is no time for tears! No, I cannot come with you! I must remain behind to guard the dead and protect your journey. We have many preparations to make, Anika. You must now repay our kindness and fulfill your role. Do you understand me?"

Anika nodded yes, unable to say the word aloud. Someone had been whispering into her ear just as Tree Stump finished. The Voice was unfamiliar, but the instructions were crystal clear.

"This man needs one of your totems. Open your pouch and give him the first one you touch."

Heedless of the impropriety of disrobing in front of him, Anika stood up and raised her dress above her waist so she could reach the pouch on her leather belt. It was held closed by a leather drawstring that she had never tried to open. Now she forced the pleats apart, painstakingly sliding them along the thong until she could reach two fingers into the shallow depths. With thumb and forefinger, she withdrew a single smooth black stone about the size and shape of a tiny bird's egg. Wordlessly she offered it to Tree Stump. The powaw said nothing as he took the stone from her outstretched hand. For the space of several heartbeats neither spoke or moved.

Tree Stump was the first to break the spell. He abruptly turned away and began assembling a collection of items: bunches of herbs; two elaborately decorated thunder and lightning sticks, both adorned with bits of copper and quartz; and a beautiful fringed leather bag. To these he added Anika's stone.

"Take these and place them in my cook pot." Tree Stump held out a bunch of herbs.

Anika took them from him, immediately recognizing that they were box-wood. She exclaimed, "But this is a poison!"

The powaw spoke without turning; his voice took on an edge of impatience. "Anika, whatever I tell you to do you must do without question. I cannot explain each step, and you do not need my explanation anyway. Already you know what must happen; otherwise you would not have given me your totem. Do not speak; just listen to the spirits and to me."

He told her to boil the herbs in water until the infusion was strong and pungent, and then to add an equal amount of clear water to the tea. This cooled the pot enough for him to drink the entire amount all at once.

"Now we must move more quickly. Bring the digging tools."

Tree Stump led the way to a corner of the village's burial grounds just beyond the fields. Anika, her arms laden with a heavy hoe and one of the shovels that River Otter had brought back, struggled through rows of vegetables now ready for harvest. What a shame to have to leave behind so much food!

She quickly forced her mind away from thoughts of regret, however, when the powaw gestured to her. He pointed to a spot near a lovely spreading oak whose bottom branches nearly touched the ground.

"Here, you must dig a hole deep enough for sitting in. I know it will be hard for you to do this alone, but you must try. When I return, I will help you."

With that, the old man left her. She watched him slowly making his way back across the fields. Then she fell to digging with all her might after first using the hoe to break up the ground. Surprisingly, the earth gave easily under her shovel, almost as though it were sand. She was able to open a fairly deep pit within an hour. After another hour, the pit was deep enough for her to test by climbing in and getting into a seated position. The fit was still too tight, so she widened the entire hole. By the time it was deep enough to accommodate an upright seated figure, the sun was very near the horizon.

Anika was leaning on the handle of the hoe surveying her handiwork when she saw Tree Stump coming through the fields. She could only gasp in amazement. The old man was absolutely resplendent, wearing a cape decorated with painted symbols and feathers. Part of his sparse hair was caught up into a topknot tied with leather lacing into which he had placed several eagle feathers. Once he was near enough, she could see that he carried the thunder sticks, his bag and a large woven mat carefully rolled up.

"Every powaw must have his own totems ready," Tree Stump said as he handed the roll to her matter-of-factly. "The powaw before me gave me this mat, but I cannot do you that favor. You will have to weave one for yourself as soon as you reach your new home, although I believe you will never need it.

You are a medicine woman, not a thunderer, so you will not have the staff. But your own totems are powerful enough. You will be successful as the next powaw."

Each word seemed to slice through Anika's heart, but she kept silent. Taking both of Tree Stump's hands, she helped him into the pit, lifting him over the edge and lowering him gently into position. Only then could she see that he was becoming paralyzed; his legs folded awkwardly beneath him as he sat. She had to climb in with him in order to cross them properly.

Tree Stump raised his eyes and fixed them on her face as she arranged his limbs. His voice was becoming thick, but his words were clear enough. "Place my things in front of me, and cover me with the mat. Go back to your wigwam; clean yourself up; take what you need and get down to the canoes. Once you leave me, do not turn back."

The Voice spoke in Anika's ear again. *"Give him the next totem."*

She pulled up her dress and reached into the pouch. This time she withdrew something enclosed inside soft leather, suspended on a long metal chain. She carefully draped the chain around Tree Stump's neck. As she did so, she quickly stole one last glimpse at the face she had grown to love. The old man's eyes, now unseeing, were half-closed and his features were set. The paralysis was complete; only a thready pulse in his throat indicated the presence of life. She draped the mat over him and his totems, climbed out of the pit and walked away without a backward glance.

Chapter 35

As soon as he had emerged from the powaw's wigwam, Great Bear had begun a mental litany, an internal recitation of his people's travels, dating from the Ancient Protection to the establishment of the current village. Learning the history verbatim had been part of his initiation, as it had been for his father and grandfather before him. Now he silently recounted each detail, searching for information about what the chief needed to tell his people before a move. All of the village's residents knew the basic story. Retelling it had always been part of every New Moon and Harvest festival, when the people were expected to give thanks to the Great Spirit for allowing this village to survive another year. But only the chief and the powaw knew the entire history.

First, Great Bear decided, he would go to his daughter's wigwam. Although River Otter was not yet thirty and therefore ineligible to sit with the village elders, Tree Stump's instructions were to seek his counsel before speaking to anyone else.

River Otter was outside of his wigwam, giving Bright Star instructions out of Gentle Fawn's hearing. Anika had insisted that she stay off her feet for the last three months in order to prevent the babies being born early. And it had been a difficult time for the whole family since River Otter and both girls were so accustomed to Gentle Fawn taking charge of everything. Nevertheless, he had tried to assume the role of primary parent, settling the inevitable squabbles between the sisters before they could disturb their mother. Although he was proud to have gotten Gentle Fawn pregnant so quickly, he secretly wished, desperately, that she were not having twins. He was quite simply frightened, a looming, stormy foreboding that he hid from his wife and the girls but that haunted his dreams every night.

When he saw Great Bear approaching, he thought the chief had come to visit Gentle Fawn, an almost daily occurrence, or to take the girls with him on some errand. But Great Bear wore a strange expression and barely acknowledged Bright Star's presence.

"I need to speak with you away from my daughter and granddaughters."

River Otter led the way to the empty wigwam. The fear inside him was rising quickly now, and he could hear his heart beating as he sat down facing the chief.

Great Bear presented the momentous news in an even voice.

"Our village must pack up and leave this place by nightfall. The only way left to us is by sea. Since you have traveled these waters before in the White men's boats, we will need your instructions. The village has ten large dugout canoes that can each hold perhaps three or four families, if people take only what they can carry in two hands."

River Otter swallowed hard before speaking. He knew that he needed to choose his words carefully because the chief was clearly adamant about this move. He was in no way sure how best to navigate ten dugouts in such a way as to elude detection by any of the numerous vessels plying the waters between Montauk and Canada.

"We will have two problems, White men and the weather. Until we are clear of Massachusetts, we will need to travel always at night to avoid the White men's fishing boats. Even then, we may well encounter others of their ships. Once we are in the open ocean, we can avoid land until we reach Nova Scotia. Our biggest problem will be the weather. If there is a bad storm, even large schooners are in danger. We will have no chance in dugouts."

Great Bear appeared unfazed. "There will be no storms, nor will we be stopped by any White men's ships. You will serve as my guide in the lead canoe with our family. Whichever way you tell me to row, we will all go that way. Our Protection will keep all who are our enemies away from us."

The young man dropped his head. For a moment he was silent; then he whispered words that he hoped Great Bear would forgive. "Chief, I will do whatever you ask of me. But Gentle Fawn is so close to giving birth that I fear her going into labor on this voyage. Is it wise to go now, so close to her time?"

Great Bear got to his feet before answering. For a long moment, he stood looking down at his son-in-law's bowed head. Next to Anika, Gentle Fawn was the dearest thing to his heart. But the voyage had to begin tonight! Nothing else could matter!

"She will be fine. Get your family ready. I will summon the rest of the village."

Great Bear went next to the wigwams of each council member. Seven Men and Ugly Moccasins, along with their families, joined him in the open area. Eagle Eye Woman sent her two sons to each wigwam to let the whole village know that the chief wished to address them all, without exception. Once everyone had gathered, Great Bear took his place in the center of the circle. He allowed people to murmur and shift about for several minutes before he began. When he started to address the village, for one terrible moment he forgot what he was about to say. Then the words came to him, all at once, as he was speaking them.

"The day that we all knew could not be prevented forever has come." At the first words, a hush fell. "Anika has had the dream of foretelling, and Tree Stump has ordered us to leave tonight. As you know, we must be protected. Tree Stump is now making the sacrifice that will allow us to become invisible to all, save Manitou.

"Families will pack only dry food and supplies that can be carried by each person in two hands, no more. The seagoing canoes can only hold every family if we do not take too many things. You will have to leave behind many dear possessions, as will I. But we will go in safety, and when we reach our new home, you will be able to replace what you lost."

It was the most difficult speech Great Bear had ever given. When he finally finished, people rose silently and dispersed. No one wept. There were no arguments or complaints. Almost immediately, in each wigwam, families began packing quickly.

Only one household had been absent from the gathering. River Otter had to tell Gentle Fawn, Yellow Bird and Bright Star the news of their imminent departure. For the first time in his memory, neither girl put up a bit of fuss. Each began bustling about, assembling packets of dried meats, fish and meal, along with the smallest utensils and necessary tools.

After receiving the news in pensive silence, Gentle Fawn gave everyone quiet encouragement from her pallet. She could see that River Otter was upset. After all, he could not be expected to understand their Ancient Protection and all that it required of the village.

"Husband, do not worry so. If anything happens with me, Anika will be there. And the girls will help you with the rowing. We are going on a journey that was laid out for us long ago. We have no choice but to leave right now!"

At her words, River Otter fought down the rising sense of panic filling his chest. Faith was the one thing in which he had no confidence. He had trusted his father would still be alive when he came back, and that trust had been broken! Why should this sudden voyage be any different? Gentle Fawn, Great Bear, indeed, the whole village was prepared to move on a simple belief that somehow they were protected. Why? Why would they be saved, when his father had not been? Still, he knew he had to hide his deep misgivings, particularly in the face of his family's seemingly unshakeable faith in this divine protection. Besides, Great Bear was depending on him for navigation. He fixed his mind on the tasks at hand. And they were so complex that eventually he forgot about his fears.

At dusk, ten giant dugouts floated in the shallow waters a half mile from the village. Families had begun to assemble with their small bundles. The sorting out of who would be in which canoe was accomplished by heads of households choosing to share a dugout with their nearest neighbors or with related families. Great Bear, waist deep in water, waited beside the first and largest canoe. Eagle Eye Woman, Ten Men and their families would share this boat with the chief's family, albeit, in very cramped quarters, since the whole front half had to be reserved for Gentle Fawn's pallet.

Presently they appeared onshore, Yellow Bird and Bright Star, each carrying four bundles, followed by River Otter carrying Gentle Fawn. Great Bear waded in to meet them. He quickly took Gentle Fawn into his arms, lifting her well above the gentle waves and holding her tightly against his chest. Gentle Fawn, now in her eighth month, was large and quite heavy, but Great Bear hardly noticed; to him, she felt as light as a child. The now-familiar surge of adoration swept over him as he settled her on the pallet of folded blankets then kissed her forehead before covering her with one of his robes.

River Otter lifted each girl over the side and handed each an oar. Then, turning to the chief, he asked, "Where is my mother? Why is she not here with you?"

Great Bear did not answer. Instead, he turned his eyes to the shoreline, scanning the short beach and line of trees. Not once since leaving Tree Stump's wigwam had he let himself think about Anika and what she might be doing. He knew that to do so would have rendered him incapable of completing his own duties. Now, with everything ready, he simply had to wait until she appeared. He hoped that, by his silence, his son-in-law would recognize this was not the time to ask questions.

Once she had left the burial grounds, Anika went directly to Great Bear's wigwam. It was comforting to have a clear set of directives to follow: clean up, pack some food and a few items, leave. She did each thing without thinking about it. By the time she had finished, the sun was down. In the gathering dusk, she hurried out of the village and headed for the beach. She could see the huge dugouts bobbing up and down in a line a short distance from the shore. A torch attached to the prow of the lead canoe, flickered fitfully in the wind.

Great Bear waved to her as she waded out to his dugout. As soon as she got near enough, she was caught up in his arms and swept onboard. Immediately, he began rowing, and as soon as his dugout was underway, each of the others fell in line behind him.

Sometime near the middle of the night, Gentle Fawn began moaning. River Otter had been manning an oar on the opposite side of the dugout, a little behind Great Bear. He heard the low sounds and turned toward her, desperate fear in his eyes.

Without breaking the rhythm of his rowing, he cried out in English, "Mother! She's going into labor! She's going to have the babies tonight! In this canoe!"

Anika answered, also in English. "You mustn't be afraid, son. I can deliver your babies, even here. Gentle Fawn is healthy and strong; her labor will be very short. You'll see."

Anika checked her daughter-in-law's abdomen, feeling for the contractions and the location of each infant's head. Fortunately, both babies were situated head downward, with one almost ready to enter the birth canal.

Except for an occasional groan Gentle Fawn remained silent throughout the examination. When the first powerful urge to push seized her, she fought it. Breathing heavily through her mouth, she waited while Anika checked to see if one of the babies' heads had crowned. Only when Anika nodded did she raise herself to a near sitting position, preparing to push each child out. It was clear that, for this part, she would need help.

Only Great Bear had understood any of what River Otter and Anika were talking about. Much as he ached to help his daughter with the birth, neither he nor River Otter could afford to turn their attention from steering the line of dugouts. As though she had been reading his thoughts, Anika gave voice to them.

"Do not stop rowing, either of you! Yellow Bird and Bright Star are not as strong as any of the other rowers. They can help me with Gentle Fawn. Girls! Come! Each of you, take one arm and help your mother up! Get her into a squatting position!"

Both girls immediately obeyed. They pulled in their oars, leaving Eagle Eye Woman's sons and Ten Men, along with his considerably younger second wife, to the rowing.

Supported in the birthing position by her daughters, Gentle Fawn could begin really bearing down. Although the labor was agonizing, now she refused even to moan, realizing that River Otter would completely lose his concentration if he knew how much she hurt. Holding onto Yellow Bird and Bright Star helped her resolve. By watching her, they were learning that having a baby is difficult but not terrifying.

The first infant, a boy, slipped out, followed by his identical brother. Anika caught each one, cut the cord with the knife given to her by Tree Stump, and laid them side by side on one of the blankets. Then she massaged Gentle Fawn's womb until she was certain that two afterbirths had been expelled. She poured drinking water over each infant before wrapping him in one of the two small blankets that Gentle Fawn had directed her daughters to pack. Just before laying the babies in their mother's arms, she showed River Otter his sons. The young man's eyes swam as he regarded his children. Then, wordlessly, he turned away, not wanting his family to see his tears.

Great Bear never once broke the rhythm of his rowing. But throughout Gentle Fawn's ordeal he was reliving her birth, remembering how courageously her mother had fought to bring her to life. When he heard the first wail, followed by the second, creating a chorus of tiny cries, his heart swelled with pride. Gentle Fawn was, indeed, as brave a woman as Snow Bird had been!

Even as these thoughts crowded his mind, there came with them, an almost visceral need to see Anika's face, to touch her. His position in the bow had made it impossible to turn around, even once. He would have to be satisfied with the sound of her voice. "Anika," he called out. "What did my daughter have?"

Instead of answering him immediately, Anika seated herself with her back resting against his. She leaned against him silently for a few moments. "You have twin grandsons," she said, at last.

She could feel the movement of his breathing, deep and measured, more than adequate to the long hard journey ahead. And she felt the connection between them growing stronger, ever stronger.

Before dawn, the line of canoes had cleared the coast of Rhode Island. Daybreak found them well to the east of Massachusetts, in the open sea.

Chapter 36

NEW YORK (1793)

*T*he constable tapped politely at the front door several times. It was late morning, and he wanted to get this affair over with as quickly as possible. Circe, now elevated to the position of being in charge of the household, was the one who opened the door.

"Please tell your master that I have important news about his, ah, inquiry."

"Master Hamilton is not at home, sir. He has gone to business."

Of course, by this time of day, Mr. Hamilton would be at his place of business. The man got the address and left.

Just as Circe was closing the door behind him, Evie descended the front staircase. Even at fifty, she was still a strikingly pretty woman, albeit a bit too plump. The gold of her hair had not yet faded, and her complexion was still creamy and flawless. What the years had done, however, was to stamp onto her habitual expression a shrewd selfishness. When her face was at rest, the eyes tended to narrow while the lips tightened and curled downward at the corners, as though in disdain of all who happened to be in her presence.

"Who was at the door?"

"A gentleman looking for Master Phillip, Mistress."

"Did he say something about an *inquiry?*"

"Why, yes, Mistress. I believe he did."

Now why would Phillip be making inquiries about which she knew nothing? Evie, ever suspicious, had become more so with their estrangement. Phillip had been unable to extricate her from his business affairs; she was the only other person competent enough to keep his books. But she was certain he was keeping as many personal secrets from her as possible, especially with regard to his sexual exploits. She determined to find out what he had been up to this time.

Phillip was about to go into the warehouse to check on Evan when he saw the constable standing just outside the open door. It was the man who had been put in charge of investigating his case. He quickly stepped out so the man would not come inside looking for him.

As soon as he saw Phillip, the man blurted out his news. "Sir, we've located a runaway, a woman, whom we believe might be your property!"

Phillip's heart leaped. Although his mind had told him not to expect it, he had hoped against hope that Annie could be found.

"She was way out on Long Island," the constable continued. "Apparently, she had been living as the wife of some Indian in one of their villages. The patrols had to fight with those Indians who were trying to keep her from being captured. But, in the end, the boys were able to get her away from them. We have her at Wall Street, behind the Market. If you like, we can bring her to your residence this evening."

Now that Annie was about to be returned, Phillip had to think quickly. He would have to tell Evie, but at the same time she would have to accept his claim to Annie as his property, at least partly. After all, *he* was the one who had initiated the search.

After making arrangements to have Annie brought to the rear of the house after supper, Phillip called out to his son. "I'm leaving for a few hours. Make sure you watch the workers every moment while I'm gone. If I find something has gone awry because you weren't paying attention, there'll be the Devil to pay! And I mean it!"

Evan ignored the threat, as he usually did these days. He had made sure to remain on the other side of the warehouse, well away from his father. It was then easy to pretend that he simply never heard whatever the old man was saying.

Phillip hurried home, his mind working feverishly. By the time he reached his front door, he believed that he had composed just the right speech for Evie. She was standing in the front hall, giving directions to their newest maid. When she saw him enter her eyes widened in surprise.

"Phillip! Why are you home at this hour? Is anything wrong at the warehouse?"

He placed his hat and gloves on a side table and removed his coat before answering her. Then he came close, taking both her hands in his. "Evie, I have amazing news. But you must be sitting down before I give it!"

He drew her into the front parlor, seating her in one of two wing chairs facing each other. Still holding her hands, he took the other.

"Some time ago, I went to the constables' offices to ask for a full investigation of Annie's disappearance. Although they did not want to, I was able to persuade them to initiate a search—just in case she was not dead. And this morning, I got news that they have found her!"

The color had drained out of Evie's face while Phillip was speaking. Her entire expression had softened into joyous wonder; the effect was absolutely breathtaking! For a full moment, he was stunned by her beauty. No one, not her children nor her husband, had ever produced such an obvious overflow of emotion! A twist of jealousy wormed its way into his heart, giving him just the spark of anger he needed to finish his speech.

"As it turns out, Annie ran away, after deliberately attempting, with the bloodstained clothing, to deceive everyone into believing her murdered. Had I not decided to pursue the matter, she might still be living as the wife of some savage in his village on Long Island. Obviously, she had nowhere near the love for you that you still have for her; else she would have waited like a good servant for our return. She must have known how it would grieve you to think that she had been killed!"

Phillip's words were having the desired effect. Evie's color returned. For several minutes, she sat staring at him in silence. Then she got to her feet. He rose with her, still watching her face closely and keeping hold of both her hands.

"A constable is bringing her here tonight. As a runaway, they would ordinarily have flogged her, but I have intervened to prevent it. However, we must face the fact that she is not the same faithful servant you so trustingly left behind. She will need some sort of punishment, and I think I know what would displease her most!"

There, he had intimated it! Evie's eyes narrowed and her face hardened. In another moment, he would know whether he could now have his way with her servant without interference!

"Very well, Phillip. You may… punish her, if you wish. But you must not hurt her or put any marks on her!" With those words, she left the room. Phillip could hear her slowly climbing the stairs.

It seemed that the rest of the day dragged on endlessly. He returned to his business where, fortunately for Evan, nothing untoward had happened. He oversaw the transfer of a tobacco shipment that needed to be on the next schooner bound for England. Then he made his son check the latest inventory. The familiar tasks only served to irritate him today. Inside, he could feel a hum of excitement and a sense of arousal that he had not experienced in a very long time. Six o'clock could not come quickly enough!

Evie went straight to her room after supper; she was much too excited and overwrought to remain in her family's company. Alexander and Evan remained at the table only long enough to finish eating. Then both sons made themselves scarce. While Alexander went to his room to read before retiring, Evan decided to spend the evening at Fraunces' Tavern.

Evan could not remember the servant who had been his nurse before the family moved to France. But he could see that her expected return was of great importance to both of his parents. Since he knew they slept in separate bedrooms, and now that he was grown, he had come to dislike his father rather intensely, he suspected Phillip must have used the woman sexually at one time. And the old lecher was probably planning to do so again! His mother was more of a puzzle. Idly, he wondered what this servant could have meant to her. At twenty-six, Evan was more than ready to be free of both parents; only the fact that he stood to inherit the business kept him at home. So his main desire tonight was to be as far away from this situation as possible.

Just as the mantle clock was striking nine, the same constable who had brought the news now tapped at the front door. Phillip had been waiting anxiously all evening. He had expected the man more than an hour ago, at least! Opening the door, he quickly ushered the constable into the front hall.

"We have your property in the alley behind your house," the man said, somewhat breathlessly. "It might be best for us to bring her into your kitchen."

"Yes, yes! But please hurry. The hour is late and we want to retire!"

Phillip sent the man back out and then called to the maid to fetch her mistress. Evie appeared almost immediately on the upstairs landing. Clutching a lace handkerchief to her lips, she descended the stairs with amazing speed and followed her husband out to the kitchen, her heart racing.

Evie had spent the whole day struggling to sort out the storm of emotions that Annie's return had aroused. Phillip was correct about running away constituting a betrayal. And Evie was resigned to letting him have her servant for a few nights. But she just *knew* that it was not all Annie's fault. Once Will had died, she had become grief-stricken and lonely! That was why she left! And, of course, once she had gone, she could not just come back, not knowing whether her family had returned. Besides, this was *her Annie*, the only person Evie had ever loved so deeply!

The constable met them at the back door. He gestured to a deputy who brought forth a burlap sack tied with rope that completely covered a figure, leaving only the feet, shod in moccasins, visible.

"Oh! Please," Evie cried out, "Do untie her! And take that filthy bag off her!"

The constable turned to his deputy, gesturing for the man to remove the ropes. Then both men pulled up the bottom of the sack. The woman underneath began to struggle, so much so that they had real difficulty getting the thing off. At last, however, she stood before them, filthy and disheveled, wearing a dress and leggings made of some sort of animal hide. Warily, she eyed each person in the room.

Evie's scream startled both the constable and the deputy so much that they dropped the sack and ropes. She screamed again, this time so loudly that

Alexander heard it in his room on the second floor. Even Circe and Tobey heard it up in the garret room they now shared, unbeknownst to either of their masters. Thinking that something awful had happened, everyone came running out to the kitchen. They found Evie on her hands and knees alternately shrieking and sobbing.

Phillip took absolutely no notice of his wife. He stared in utter disbelief, first at the constable and deputy, then at their captive. Then he roared at the top of his lungs "Who is this? This isn't my servant! You have brought the wrong one!"

He continued screaming oaths at the two men while Evie wailed loudly in the background. She stretched out helpless arms to Alexander and Circe. Clutching them both to her bosom, she wept as though her heart had been freshly broken.

In the confusion, no one noticed when the woman eased herself out of the back door and slipped away. She stopped at the end of the alley, only long enough to get her bearings. On this night, the sky was perfectly clear with just a sliver of moon visible. Guided by the position of the stars, she was able to make her way south, taking streets that led toward the waterfront. She knew there was a landing where she had been brought ashore. Once she reached the river, she searched for that landing.

Cicero had been busily securing the barge for the night and, instead of going home, had sat down on the pier to rest when the woman approached him. Recently, he had not been feeling at all well. Almost daily, he experienced frequent pains in his heart and a persistent shortness of breath.

"Suh, kin ya tek me 'cross th' riva'?" The woman whispered softly.

She had sidled up and now crouched at his side. He could barely see her in the darkness, but that did not matter. He remembered the captive, a wooly-haired Black woman wearing Indian clothing. He rose immediately, gesturing for her to follow him. "C'mon, we gon' take th' rowboat. Git down in th' bottom 'n I'm gon' cover ya' up."

It took Cicero over an hour to cross the East River. When he reached Long Island, he avoided the ferry landing, putting ashore close to a wooded area instead.

"Wish't I could help ya' more. Is yuh gon' be alright?"

The woman clasped his hand in hers and held it for a moment. Then she turned toward the forest. "Ah knows how t' fine mah way home." With that she melted into the darkness.

Later that night, as Cicero laid his weary body on his bed, he again had the crushing pain in the center of his chest. This time it was much worse, as though his heart were being squeezed in a vise. Then, almost magically, it disappeared and he was asleep. In his dreams, Polly came to him, took him into her arms and lifted him up to the heavens.

Chapter 37

QUEBEC (1800)

*A*nika's voice trailed off, and stillness fell over the group in the long-house as though the breathing of every man had suddenly been suspended. One and all, they waited for her next words.

"The story is finished," she finally said, quite simply.

Tekenna spoke up, "Well, then! It would seem that I must now have something to say. River Otter, please do my words justice to your chief. I would not want him to misunderstand me."

The Munsee chief's tone immediately put Great Bear on guard. He raised one hand, silencing River Otter's translation of Tekenna's last words.

"Even though you are our guest, and your status as great chief entitles you to speak before me, I would request your indulgence, as host, and would speak first. We Unkechaug are grateful that you have stayed with us for so long and have listened to our tales. As you have heard, our only wish has always been to live in the way that our fathers lived. We took no lives, waged no wars for land; we followed only the instructions given by our Ancient Protection. We hope you will see us as brothers and allow us to stay on your land. But this is a simple request. We will not dishonor you by begging. If we must move on, we will do so."

Tekenna was momentarily flustered. Obviously, the Unkechaug chief had guessed at something—the offer of an unacceptable compromise, perhaps. The Munsee chief decided to try another tack.

"Please convey my thanks to your chief." He again addressed his remarks to River Otter. "I would also beg an indulgence. I would like permission to speak to your powaw—alone. There is a matter of some delicacy that I would like advice about. Even though we do not speak the same language, I feel certain she will understand and be able to advise me."

Now River Otter's senses were humming. He did not think for a moment that the Munsee chief wanted medical advice. Turning to Great Bear, he smoothly altered the translation.

"Tekenna wishes to speak to our powaw, *alone*. Please insist that I be present. Whatever he wishes to say to her, I'm sure we both need to hear."

Great Bear was about to respond when Anika lightly touched his arm. Leaning close, she whispered, "Let me speak with him as he requests. I think I know what he wants, but I need to hear it from him."

He looked at her sharply, a sudden fear rising in him. For a moment, he wrestled with the contradictions in their roles. As her husband, he had the right to refuse Tekenna any meeting with Anika, but, as powaw, she could be alone with whomever she pleased. Underneath it all, however, was his uneasy suspicion that one day she might simply have to leave them all.

"Anika!" he answered, also in a whisper. "How can I let you do this? You heard River Otter! The chief has something else in mind!"

She kept her voice softly even. "I am not afraid of him. And you should not be either! What you have to do is trust me and not give in to old fears."

Great Bear now shifted himself so that he faced Tekenna squarely. Drawing himself up to his full seated height, he addressed the Munsee chief directly. "A matter that is somewhat delicate, as you have said, *should* be discussed privately. Anika will meet with you now, if you want. While I thought River Otter should accompany his mother to translate, the powaw does not wish it so. And I accede to her wishes in these matters." To River Otter he added, "Give the chief my words exactly as I've spoken them."

The gathering broke up immediately. Great Bear left the longhouse first, with Anika and River Otter close behind. Then Tekenna rose and followed them more slowly. Once outside, the Unkechaug chief faced Anika as though about to say something. Abruptly, he stopped himself and walked away in the direction of their wigwam.

River Otter, however, was determined to speak up. "Mother, I know you think that you can control this situation." He was speaking English now. "But you are putting yourself in danger for our sakes. I simply cannot let you do it! This chief is not above kidnapping you as ransom for our right to live on his land! I know these people!"

"Son, I believe you! But now you must believe me! In all these years, have you ever known me to fail if I give my word? It's because I know how to listen! And I always do as I'm told. The protection of this village was placed in my hands, yes. And, thus far, all whom I love have been especially protected. If that means I must put myself in harm's way, then I must. You cannot interfere!"

During this exchange, Tekenna had come up behind them. He stood there, listening to their words, recognizing the English, a language he despised. This was why he wanted Anika away from River Otter. As long as the linguist was around, Tekenna was certain that he would use his ability to thwart any designs on his mother. Why, he was doing so right now! But, fortunately for the Munsee chief, the powaw seemed to be resisting her son. Obviously, she placed the welfare of her village above her or her family's personal wishes.

River Otter spread both palms helplessly before turning toward his own wigwam. With one final desperate glance over his shoulder, he left Anika and Tekenna alone.

The Munsee chief extended a hand, intending for her to follow him. He led the way toward the bluff overlooking the shore where his massive birch-bark canoes had remained berthed for the last two months. Standing close to its edge, he pointed, first to the canoes, then to the river, and finally to her. "You. Come with me!" He spoke loudly, as though volume would translate into meaning. "Your people can stay here!"

Anika took one step toward him and stopped. She raised her head, tilting it to one side as though listening intently. Tekenna confidently waited for her reply, sure that it would be in the affirmative. He now believed she had figured out his plans long before either her husband or her son. This woman was much too powerful to be wasted protecting a single migrant village. He would see to it that every Lenape town in Eastern Canada knew about her. Her presence in his village would assure his own power as well. She would keep even the Whites at bay!

"Step to the man and take his hand."

Just as he was about to touch his own breast to indicate that *he* would now be in charge of her, Anika caught Tekenna's left hand in mid-gesture. Abruptly, the chief gasped as something moved through his palm, along his arm and into his chest. A searing pain accompanied by intense itching caused him to drop to his knees, roaring in agony. "What are you doing to me? Stop! You are hurting me!"

A wind blowing from the east took Tekenna's screams away over the river. The surrounding forest swallowed them utterly. Anika wanted to release him, tried to, but somehow, she could not. Desperately, she looked around for help, but no one heard his cries. Then came the Voice.

"Tell the man to leave you here, or we will kill him!"

"Tekenna, I don't want to hurt you," she said in English. "My Spirits say I have to stay here. I know you don't understand me, but I can't go with you. And, to save your life, you have to leave. Now!"

Suddenly, she was able to release him. And just as suddenly the agony ceased. Tekenna gasped repeatedly for several minutes, staring all the while at Anika as though she had turned onto a deadly viper. When she made a placating gesture toward him, he took to his heels, stumbling, falling even, but racing in his madness to get away from her.

Anika watched him disappear into the woods, heading back toward the village. But she, herself, could not take a single step; she was shaking uncontrollably. For what seemed an eternity, she stood there on the bluff. Finally, a cold wind cutting through her leather dress brought sensation back into her limbs and she was able to force herself to move, haltingly, in the same direction Tekenna had taken. By the time she reached the village, evening had deepened into complete darkness.

Inside their wigwam, Great Bear had already gotten out the bedding and undressed. However, he had found it impossible to lie down as long as Anika was still out there somewhere with Tekenna. Left alone to face his own terrors, he sat up, watching the doorway and waiting for disaster to strike. As soon as she entered, he was on his feet. He caught her by the shoulders and held her fast. She was still breathing hard. "Great Bear," she began.

His heart stopped. She never used his name when they were alone.

"No! Say nothing more!" He realized how loudly he had shouted only after the words were out. "Please," he now whispered, "say no more. Let me have you tonight without words."

Anika started to speak, and then stopped herself. She stood silently as Great Bear began to undress her, very slowly. As he tenderly undid the lacings of her leggings, the sweet, terrible memory of their wedding night flooded her whole being. He believed this was to be their last time together!

"Just let me…," she began.

He covered her mouth with his.

A little before dawn, Great Bear lay in the tangle of their bedding, still awake, still clutching Anika fiercely. She had finally fallen asleep, worn out by his passion. His mind was now working feverishly, making plans for an orderly transfer of leadership from himself to River Otter. When the Munsee took Anika, he would have to follow her, even if it meant going to his own death!

Sunrise found the entire Munsee delegation already packed and standing outside the longhouse. Great Bear heard the commotion and saw them all assembled as soon as he came out of his wigwam. He approached Tekenna questioningly, but the Munsee chief backed away. So he went to River Otter's wigwam to awaken him. Then both men approached Tekenna.

"You are leaving so suddenly! Why? Have we done something to offend you?" Great Bear's question carried real alarm.

"Winter is fast approaching and the river already has ice. I allowed your stories to delay me longer than was safe. That was my fault, not yours." Tekenna's eyes carefully avoided both men as he spoke. "Please do not disturb your women to feed us. We have more than enough for our journey." The

Munsee chief hesitated before continuing. "Your village is welcome to stay here as long as I and my descendents are chiefs. I only ask that you stay on your side of the river. It would appear your *protection* could be dangerous to others."

With that, the Munsee chief waved his wives and daughters ahead, to be followed by his council. He, in turn, brought up the rear.

The procession marched out of the village and down the steep bluff to the shore. The young rowers, who had spent the two months essentially idle, now found themselves ordered to load up and push off immediately. By the time the sun was high, the five enormous canoes were little more than specks in the distance.

Epilogue

The waters of the Gulf of Guinea receive the Atlantic current as it sweeps toward Africa into the Bight of Benin. That same current continues to bathe the coast all the way down to Angola before turning again to the open sea. Here, in these waters, fishermen have drawn their catches from time immemorial. They set out daily in their small boats, sails brilliant in the blazing sun, returning to the shores as sunset burnishes the seas all around them.

On an early morning, several such boats bobbed offshore in the gentle swells. Men, barechested, some with their heads cloth-wrapped, spread their wide nets across the waters and waited for the schools of fish that always came this way. One man, alone on his boat, noticed his net seemed to have caught a large object that had suddenly floated to the surface. Anxious not to tear the net and cause himself the loss of a day's catch, he carefully hauled it in close enough to investigate. Sometimes, valuable cargo from damaged or sunken vessels would wash ashore and be found by some lucky fisherman.

His screams filled the air, reaching the other fishermen who turned their boats in his direction. Trimming their sails, they rowed until they reached their friend who stood screaming and pointing to the coffin now entangled in his nets. The other men hesitated, as afraid to touch the thing as he, since to do so might bring bad luck. At last, one of the men, older than the others, stepped across the bow of his own boat and onto the boat of the man who had made the discovery. Leaning over the side, he noticed the carving on the coffin's lid.

He called to his son who could read. "Ako, come tell us what this says, here!"

Dutifully, the young man joined his father. Together, they pulled the coffin closer, turning it so he could read the inscription. "It's a name, Kwesi Osei."

The father stood up. This was a countryman! He turned to the fisherman who had caught the coffin. "We will have to bring this box ashore! The man inside belonged to one of our villages!"

The other fishermen now reached out with willing hands to raise the coffin. Gently they eased it onto the discoverer's boat and released it from his nets. Under a blood-red sun they all turned their boats toward the land, dipping silent oars into the crimson sea.

CPSIA information can be obtained at www.ICGtesting.com
Printed in the USA
BVOW031835010713

324813BV00001B/15/P

9 781457 515200